By EAB

Black Snow

Published by DREAMSPINNER PRESS
www.dreamspinnerpress.com

Black Snow

EAB

Published by
DREAMSPINNER PRESS

5032 Capital Circle SW, Suite 2, PMB# 279, Tallahassee, FL 32305-7886 USA
www.dreamspinnerpress.com

ISBN: 978-1-63477-719-3
Digital ISBN: 978-1-63477-720-9
Library of Congress Control Number: 2016907093
Published November 2016
v. 1.0

Printed in the United States of America

This paper meets the requirements of
ANSI/NISO Z39.48-1992 (Permanence of Paper).

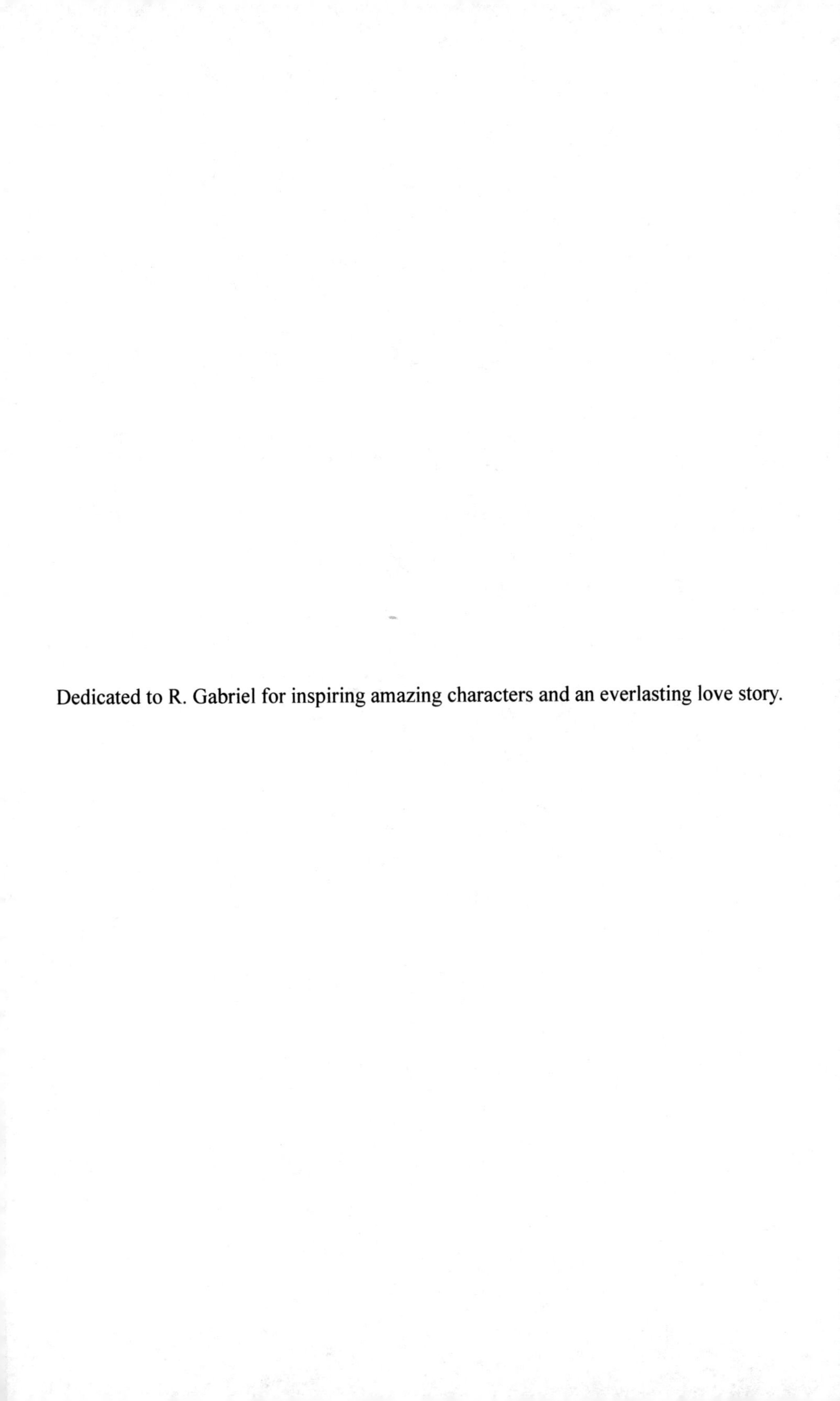

Dedicated to R. Gabriel for inspiring amazing characters and an everlasting love story.

Glossary

Secborn - The secondborn son of a sanctioned union.

Einborn - The firstborn son of a sanctioned union.

Colur gem - A rare colored gem, similar to a diamond in weight and shape, found only in Lirend.

The Divine Three - The original allied countries in the eastern world: Nieraeth, Zhennal, Ranolf. Lirend and Menlor were added to the alliance after the Great War.

The tree of life - According to the gospels, all life began at the ancient tree of Anistra, more commonly known as the tree of life. It was said that men passed on to the afterlife, they returned to its roots.

The law of passage - Under the law of passage, no firstborn son can leave his father's profession without expressly stated leave from the courts of his fief. If a family does not have sons the law of passage applies to their daughters until she is wed, and then marks her husband as the inheritor of the profession.

For example: If someone's father was a politician his firstborn son will be politician too.

Aurelian - A person of noble birth. Usually wealthy Lords and Ladies. Have immense influence in the court.

Professions: Doctors, Fief Lords, Landlords, Family wealth, Scholars

Burges - A working class citizen. Usually moderate/ middle class. High middle to middle income.

Merchants, Teachers, Capital city workers, Public servants, Farm owners, Entertainers

Prolit - Servants. Low class. Little to no income. Most of the Prolits work in jobs of servitude with low wages and room and board accommodations.

Professions: Serfs, Farmers, Beggars

Xenothian - A derogatory name for a refugee from Thenia. Low class, with no rights.

(Thenian terms)

'A'ma el - I love you

Aa'Mele Nuva - Happy birthday

Acai - Please

Ai - Hey! (Exclamatory)

Aida - Papa

Baim - Child

Beith Gheal - A tree indigenous to Thenia. The leaves look silver when they are wet.

Con l'ellar? - Who are we?

Cormin ele aida - Come to your papa.

Diole' - Thank you

Diolenan - Thank you very much.

L'tyva el? - Are you okay? Are you well? How are you?

Mana el man' - If you wish it.

Na - No
Na'saan el - It is good to see you.
Nan - Beloved/ My beloved (Endearment between family, friends, or lovers)
O'ta a min - Give it to me.
Te'na an' - Till then.
Venai - Beautiful
Venur - Welcome home, Hello

Black Snow Settings

Lirend – Located in the eastern world, Lirend lies in the middle of the great kingdoms: Zhennal, Ranolf, Menlor, and Nieraeth. Avenough is the capital of Lirend. The country borders the great sea, which is why most of their import and export is by sea. Wealthiest of the allied nations and second smallest. The most valuable resources from Lirend are their iron and their colur gems. The Aurelians in Lirend hold most of the political power.

Balmur - A precinct located southwest of the Avenough. Open farmlands and landscapes, west from the great sea.

Avenough - Capital city of Lirend.

Aire - Aire is a region north of Avenough, located in Lirend, where the Thenian refugees were sent. Currently it is populated by the first and second generation refugees and the criminals of Avenough. As a result the land is riddled with lawless renegades.

Toe' Caves - The quickest way to the Black Forest is through the Toe' Caves right off of the Nejir River that runs from the forest to the open plains fifty miles wide.

Nejir River- The river runs north to south, from Aire to Sherdoe.

Sherdoe - Open plains, southwest of Aire, ripe for hunting.

The Black Forest - A dense forest north of Avenough. Home to Veti, Ro, and the Ceve guild.

The Square - where Thenians come to sell their wares.

Zhennal - Kingdom north of Lirend. It has the largest army of the Divine Three. The most valuable resources are of Zhennal is their weapons and manpower.

Ranolf - West of Lirend. Although the country is technically the largest it also has the least resources due to its location. It's the farthest country from the great sea. Technically the closest country to Thar, which lies southwest of Ranolf. Ranolf's borders are protected by Zhennal's army. They have open land for agricultural exports.

Nieraeth - A powerhouse of innovation, Nieraeth is the smallest of the Divine Three. Located southwest of Lirend and south of Ranolf. They are known for their medical advancements and schools. They export the bulk of items to Zhennal, through Lirend and Ranolf, in lieu of the country's militia.

Menlor - The seaport country. Moderate militia. Menlor is an island, closest to Lirend. Most valuable resources are their silver and paper. Second wealthiest country after Lirend.

Thar - Located southwest of Lirend and south of Ranolf. Thenia was located in Thar as a sovereign state. Thenians lived in Thar until they refused King Onas' demands for tributes to the army. The fief lords refused the order and the King massacred their villages. Refugees of the Thenian Massacre fled to Lirend where they signed contracts to the crown in protection of their lives. Under the law of passage, their contracts remain.

Sasel - Mutual allied territory for Lirend, Menlor, Ranolf, Nieraeth, and Zhennal. Located directly west of Lirend and east of Ranolf.

PROLOGUE

"LONG AGO, there was a maiden with hair black as ebony and skin as white as the snow, so that they called her Snow White. Her lips were red as the rose," Brier's portly nurse told him, smiling.

"And she sang and danced. And she was very beautiful," Brier added perfunctorily.

"Indeed she was," replied Marietta. "She was kind and comely, and all the kingdom loved her, but the queen of the kingdom was jealous and wanted to get rid of her for good."

"How?"

"She decided to have her killed."

"Oh no!" Brier answered, tone darkening.

"Oh yes!" cried his nurse. "She hired a huntsman to kill her in the wood and bring back her heart, so that she could keep it forever."

Brier slid his legs up and placed his chin on his knees, enraptured in the story about the fair princess whose name was like his own.

"The huntsman did as he was told and took Snow White to the forest. As they entered the forest, they came across a field of flowers. Snow bent down to pick a bouquet of wildflowers, and the huntsman crept behind her and lifted his dagger!"

Brier gasped, horrified. "But he should not kill her!"

"He could not," corrected the nurse, excitement alive in her eyes. "For he had fallen in love with the princess and told her of the evil queen's plan."

"Good gods," Brier exhaled, relieved.

"Snow White ran," Marietta whispered, and Brier hugged his knees more firmly. "She had to run away deeper into the woods to escape the queen's wrath. She found herself alone in the deep, dark wood. 'Get out… out…' the trees whispered all around her, and she was terribly afraid. And rightly so," the nurse added, whipping her head toward Brier almost in warning. "The dark wood is a dangerous place. She tripped and fell into a great crack in the earth. As she fell, a nearby willow's roots seized her and pulled her under."

"Then what happened?" Brier whispered, breath hastening.

"Then she lost hope that anyone would ever find her. She thought that she was doomed to live out her days locked in the roots of the old willow tree. Starving, thirsty, and withering away like an old winter branch. However, this could not be further from her fate. Yes, she was stuck, but a passerby heard her cries in the tree roots. He stopped in his tracks and called his brothers to come investigate. Men that wore beards and were half the size of normal men. Some might call them dwarves. Six more dwarves stopped and listened to the cries coming from the old willow. 'Chop it down!' the eldest brother answered. And so they did, all seven of them. They cut the tree down, and Snow White was saved."

"Hooray!" Brier shouted as he jumped on the pillow top mattress.

"When they took her from the tree, she was dirty and exhausted. The willow had cursed her in its last effort of revenge for cutting it down. She had a scar on her neck in the pattern of a tree leaf, but she was alive, and so they brought her back to their cabin, and they mended her to good health."

"Did she dance and sing again then, Marietta?"

"She did. And how fair she was, thought the dwarves. They spoke of her beauty to other folk who came through the wood. But then, word traveled back to the evil queen. And she was furious! She called for the huntsman, and he confessed that he could not kill Snow White. Enraged, she ordered the guardsmen to kill the huntsman, and, with his dying breath, he confessed his love for the princess."

Brier reached over to grab a pillow off his oversized bed and squeezed. He suddenly had the feeling that the story would take a turn for the worse.

"The queen decided to finish the job the huntsman did not with a poisoned apple. She disguised herself as an ugly elderly woman, and she came to the cabin that Snow White lived in with the dwarves. She showed Snow White the apple she poisoned, bloodred and perilous, but still Snow had the urge to taste it. The princess took a bite of the apple, and when she did, she died."

"How dreadful." Brier shook his head. "Why should the queen hate Snow White so?" he asked, incredulous. "I do not understand."

The nurse chuckled and smiled at him. "Shall I continue?"

"Please do, Marietta. I should like to know the ending," Brier replied with a sad smile.

"Well," the nurse said in a warm voice. "The queen did think that she had finally rid herself of the fair maiden, but alas, there was a crack in her black magic, one that she could not foresee. The magic of the willow was stronger than her own, and it purged the strength of her poison so that Snow White did not die but slept for many years. The prince of the neighboring land did hear of a maiden sleeping soundly in the wood on a bed of wildflowers, in the cabin of seven dwarves."

"And, I suppose, he too was handsome!"

"He was a handsome prince, I should say, though not as handsome as you, Prince Snow." Brier blushed through his wide smile. "He came on his white steed, and he found Snow White sleeping soundly just as the rumors had told. Indeed, she was fair, and the prince decided that he had to have her in death or in life, and so he leaned down and placed a chaste kiss to her rose lips."

"What did happen then I wonder?"

"Then she did wake up, Prince Snow! Her eyelids fluttered open, and she rose from her bed made of daisies and baby's breath! Oh, how happy were the dwarves and the prince. The dark magic that the queen put on Snow White fell upon herself! And she turned into the old and ugly woman she disguised herself as. The queen was so furious that she drove herself mad with rage. And so, Snow White married the prince, and the dwarves sang and danced and were happy. Princess Snow White had many children, and lived ever after." When the story finished, the nurse stood up and helped Brier into the comforter. His eyes were heavy with sleep, but he pursed his lips and sighed.

"Did you not like the story, little prince?"

Brier bit the inside of his lip, struggling. "It is not that, Mar', only that I feel sad for the princess."

"And why should you? Did she not meet a happy end?" the nurse asked as she sat down on the corner of the bed.

"Mayhap," Brier answered, considering. "But how did she come to love the prince who had only loved her for her beauty when the huntsman had loved her for her heart?"

The nurse blinked at the prince's reply. "How indeed."

"And the poor huntsman, who had died, rather than to disgrace himself with the blood of his beloved. 'Tis a sad story indeed, Marietta." Brier pouted. "Although you said it was a happy end."

"Well…." Marietta sighed, bemused. "I did not think of it in that way, little prince." She tucked him in tighter as if swaddling a babe.

"I think that I should marry a huntsman over a prince," Brier decided as he flopped his head into the mountain of pillows, smiling softly.

"And why not a princess?" the nurse questioned, crossing her arms.

"That is because I should like to be kissed by a huntsman," Brier answered matter-of-factly.

CHAPTER 1
OLD SCARS

ROLAND SQUATTED on the flat surface of a smooth rock and waited. The green grass below his feet had sprouted in full luster, and the breeze fluttered the blossoming oak trees. He should have arrived two nights ago, but a rockslide in the caves near the low valleys delayed him. It rained on the whole of his journey, but tonight the air was warm and dry, gravid with summer's heat. The fire he'd started was more for signal than warmth, and he hoped they would see the flickering flames in the deepest part of the Black Forest. Veti, an almost tamed black wolf, rested at his feet, unmoved by Roland's nervous humming. He had not made contact with the men since leaving for Lirend's capital, Avenough, almost a month ago, but whispers traveled in the great black wood, and he'd seen signs of his guild mottled throughout the land like a marked trail.

The Ceve guild existed only in name as far as any citizen in Lirend was concerned. Made up of the scourged citizens from the northwest region of Thenia, their seven members, like all Thenians, were indebted to Lirend's capital and crown. Thenians, who were less charitably called Xenothians by the Aurelians of Lirend, lived in Aire as pawns for Avenough's employ. As it stood, no Thenian could own property in Avenough or legally marry any true-born citizen of Lirend. Any children the Thenians had were considered "equity" of the crown, and the moment they reached their majority, were hastened to sign a contract indebting them as equally as their parents. It was nigh slavery, save for the actual pronouncement.

This was not how Roland and his guild mates had grown up. Thrust from their lush land into the harsh wasteland of Aire, they learned quickly, above all else, to survive. In Aire, one's fortune was his own to make. Not necessarily in money or title, as the former was hard to come by and the latter no longer relevant. No, a man's fortune was in his ability to live and procure some ounce of happiness in this world. Whether that be in carnal pleasure, drink, or keeping what sense of kin one could muster in Aire.

Roland gazed at the fire whose embers began to float into the boundless black sky. This was just the world he lived in. He had no true home.

Around the three-hour mark of waiting, Roland stood and conceded. Perhaps the guild had gotten called out on a last-minute job. He kicked the dirt over the open fire and turned to head toward his cabin when he heard the familiar soft voice.

"*Venur*, Rolande." Roland stopped in his tracks, and a grin spread on his aged face. If anything had been spared in the pillaging of Thenian's culture and the coerced assimilation, their language had been. It was not unusual then for Thenians to carry two names. One, more proper and fitting of the common tongue, and the other that bespoke of their Thenian culture. Therefore, he was Roland or Ro in Avenough, and Rolande with his clan.

Roland lifted up his arm in the pitch dark and waited for the voice's owner to mirror his movement. Forearms bumped in the symbolic *X* of the Ceve guild, and a fair-eyed man gave Roland a tentative grin. Calm and comely, resigned, but not at all prudish in his intimacy. That was Leighis Tamer, a healer and Roland's best friend.

"*Venur*, Leighis." Roland grasped Lei's back in an unbound hug. He smiled and relaxed in the smaller man's embrace. "You're late," he said as he released the healer and looked over the rest of his guild. The men huddled together in a disordered circle and gazed through what little glow came from the single lantern.

"My ass!" Sastania, more commonly known as Sasta, came forward beaming. He held up his arm to make the X. "You were supposed to be here two days ago."

"Forgive me, my friend." Roland touched the younger man's shoulder before crossing wrists. "I got lost going through the caves."

"Lost?" Lei frowned. "Are you hurt?" Lei spent most of his time healing them after blood-heavy missions.

"I'm all right, Lei." Roland nodded.

The shortest member of their company was the quietest. He had wispy brown hair and dark eyes, with a thin mouth and high cheekbones. The man bore a scar from a wound that blinded his left eye in youth. Those who did not know the seer rumored the eye disabled him. Only the guild knew he had the ability to predict the future by reading the stars. "*Venur*, Umhal." Roland inclined his head. Umhal eyed Roland carefully before crossing his arms. Umhal then sat on the outskirts of the group pulling his knees to his chest and staring out into the distance in repose.

"'All right,' or really all right?" Lei raised his brow in suspicion.

"I'm fine." Roland touched Lei's shoulder to ease his friend's worries. "And everything went as planned."

"*You* actually had a plan?" Botcht questioned. Taller than Roland, Botcht had cropped dark hair and a permanent glare. Roland did not cross arms with Botcht, but nodded to acknowledge the man's presence. While he did not particularly care for Botcht, he was once Roland's father's most trusted advisor.

"Let's do get on with it," Caitenia said. Caite yawned beside his sour-faced brother. Similar to Botcht in only the shape of his eyes, Caite wore a long dark ponytail down his back. "We've all got jobs in the morning. Can't be late now, can we?" Caite's rude, albeit prudent, interruption spurred Roland to explain what had transpired in Avenough.

"So the runt is getting booted out of the cushy palace." Caite shrugged as he inspected his dagger for blood over the flame. "Why should we care?"

"Because it is the queen's bid," Roland replied. "She wants us to take him, and she's offering us something we can't refuse."

"Says who?" Caite challenged, gaze tightening to match his challenge.

"Says me." Roland slapped the back of the man's head. "He's our ticket out of here." He settled with one knee raised off the ground. "All we have to do is train him up a bit, and the queen promises us enough money to buy the guild out of our contracts."

"And then we gets to go home?" Durham turned to Sasta. Roland knew that to Dur's touched mind, home meant Thenia. He did not have the heart to tell him the state of their once cherished home. Wrought with war and plague since they'd been driven out. Roland branded the man with a smile instead.

"Or to Menlor!" Sasta offered. "I'd heard they have boats there the size of the great mountain." Dur's eyes widened to twice their size before he wore a dopey smile.

"Aye, or we can just waltz into one of those fancy Aurelian brothels, drink wine, and sleep the day away," mused Caite. Leave it to Caite to think of riches and not freedom, Roland thought reproachfully. If Botcht seemed overly proud, stringent, and uncompromising, Caite appeared precariously aloof. Roland hoped the indifference would fade with age, but the older Caite became, the more detached he grew.

"We can go anywhere." Roland then wondered what he would do if he was suddenly a free man. Free to live wherever his heart desired. Outside of Aire where the atmosphere oozed the darkness and despair of his past. Away from Thenia where living things no longer bloomed. "Whatever we want."

"Or nothing at all…." Botcht mumbled under his breath, but loud enough for Roland to hear him.

"You've something to say, Botcht?" Roland stared directly across the open flame. He did not plan to have a row with his second, but he refused to let the man openly chide him.

"I said, or nothing at all," Botcht repeated. "Only a fool would trust an Aurelian, Rolande."

"You calling me a fool, then?"

All six men stared at Roland as if they could feel his ire swell.

"You said it, not me," Botcht replied. Roland bristled, and Veti lifted his head, black eyes glued to the sturdy man.

"Aye, I said it. And since you're paying so much attention to my words, perhaps you have time to recount the contract we signed to Lirend."

The figurative ax fell on Thenia years ago when their sovereign allies decided the small country had grown too large in number to control or trust. King Onas ordered them to send tribute, one fully grown son per family, to the ruling land of Thar to be assessed, trained, and then sworn to a combined force. If the family had no sons, they were to send one unwed daughter to be married off instead. The lords of Thenia took full offense to the order, stating that they were not aided in their own wars, and thus had no cause or obligation to fight in the tyrannical king's army.

Onas disagreed.

He sent his army to Thenia, flayed villages, upturned homes, crops, and infrastructure. Even now, one could see the damage done in the villages that littered Thenia's mountainous terrain. Caved-in buildings, scalded farmlands, and dredged quarries. Thenians fled from their homeland, bedraggled and forlorn, and resettled in Lirend. Everyone lost someone in the Thenian Massacre.

"I'm not trusting anyone, leastways an Aurelian, but the queen gave more than her word. She's agreed—in writing—to pay us thrice the amount needed to buy ourselves out of our contracts."

All Thenians signed a contract that indebted them to the Aurelians, the aristocracy of Lirend. When called upon, they were used as mere tools. Aurelians picked at the dregs of Lirend's supercilious society. The guild had no chance of ever leaving Aire while their debt still remained.

"And it would be a year wasted tending to a child. We could be gathering more people for the union." While Roland thought the best way was to earn their freedom from servitude, Botcht thought the best way was to take it. Many of the Thenians in Aire felt the same. Incensed by the betrayal of their once sovereign state, Thenia, and tired of living in the squalor of Aire. Botcht wanted to unionize a revolution. Roland just wanted a chance to live without the anchor of his debt. However, they all despised their vast yet binding cage.

"We won't need a union if we're released from our contracts, Botcht. Don't you get it? This kid is the key to our freedom!" Roland implored.

"Or our demise," Botcht retorted. The man narrowed his gaze and Roland felt the dark eyes on him. "Have you forgotten who you are, Rolande? What Ceve stands for?"

"We stand for nothing if we live in shackles, Botcht. The life we once lived in Thenia is over. I no longer adhere to that land's prohibitions."

"Just because you have laid down the shield does not mean you are no longer bound to it. It is your duty."

"If I am bound, it is by my own desire," Roland answered. "Now. I've made my decision."

"To spend your days cleaning up behind an Aurelian mutt?"

"To be free!" Roland spat. "If you wanna spend your life wasting away in this shithole, that's on you! But don't condemn everyone to your miserable fate!"

"You're the last person I want to hear that from, Rolande," Botcht said coldly.

"*Ai*!" Lei's light voice cut in. "Stop it you two! This doesn't solve anything!" Roland huffed out and kicked a rock, making the soil turn to fiery ash, and everyone fell silent.

At length, Caite sat up and let out an exhausted sigh. "The way I see it, we don't have anything to lose." The man stretched his arms and yawned again. "We won't even have to be bothered if the kid stays with Ro."

"Except for his training," Lei pointed out, gently scolding the younger man's nonchalance. "We're holding this boy's future in our hands, as well as our own. It's nothing to take lightly. If we do it, we do it together, and in earnest. We have to be responsible."

"Naturally." Sasta nodded and beamed once more. "And he can't be all bad." Sasta turned to Roland. "How old is he again?"

"Nineteen," Roland grunted. Sasta blinked and widened his eyes.

"So young?"

"He hasn't even reached his majority." Lei sounded slightly worried. The circle grew silent once more before Sasta's cheerful voice broke the tension.

"All the better that he is young!"

"How do you figure?" Lei questioned him.

"Well," Sasta chuckled through his reply. "If he was an old man like Botcht and Ro, we'd really have our hands full." Sasta, Dur, and Caite howled with laughter. Even Lei snorted though he offered Roland a consoling glance.

"All right, all right." Roland cut them all off, but the laughter made the air less stringent. "Are we doing this or aren't we?"

"I vote yes!" Sasta called out. "Definitely!"

Roland turned to Lei.

"I vote yes." Lei nodded. "We owe it ourselves to take the chance."

"Caite?" Caite waved his hand in consent. "Dur?" Roland turned his head toward the giant.

"Aye." Dur nodded once.

Roland turned to Umhal. The man still had not turned their way, but he nodded silently. Then Roland's gaze locked with Botcht's. This time, though, he had the guild to back him up.

"I want to go on record saying I think this is a bad idea," Botcht said. His shoulders hunched as he drew his fingertips together with a pensive expression. Roland understood the man's doubts. Every Thenian in Aire knew Aurelians were not to be trusted. They were cunning liars, apt to destruction, and oblivious to all those they deemed unworthy. Still, this was their hope for redemption, and Roland could not deny the guild that chance. Or himself. "If everyone's in agreement… I won't be the one to dissent."

"So?" Lei probed Botcht and smirked. "Is that a yes, then?" Botcht's pale face grew red under Lei's gaze, and he puffed out his chest.

"Aye."

THE DAY is strange…. Brier thought as he rose from his wooden canopy. The first clue was that his nurse did not come to wake him in the morning. Not that Brier needed a nurse to wake him. He was near grown, but Marietta was a woman of habit, and so she woke him every morning, whether he wanted her to or not. He stared into the garden below his suite and listened to the melancholy song of the rain against the wrought-iron leaves that barred his windows. The palace sat on the summit of a mountainous hill. Brier could stare out and peer over the entire kingdom when he was permitted to do so by Marietta, but in his room there was only the view of the gardens and the towering oak trees. For the palace's part, there was no way in, and there was no way out. The guards accompanied him through halls, down to the gardens, and when he was permitted, outside of the palace. It was the same for many years. Thus, Brier yearned to sit amongst his tulips and roses alone, and recite a quiet song or poem, even in the rain. Marietta told him many times that the flowers loved to hear him sing, though he suspected it was more for her own entertainment. Grasslings only swayed in the breeze and flowers only looked pleasant. They did not listen or speak. In truth, he had no friends.

Never mind that. Brier shook his head. Today there were no flowers or Marietta. Only rain.

He rose from his bed and moved to his washroom, pulling off his white nightgown. As Brier undressed, he recited the morning song Marietta oft did in her booming yet kindly voice.

Whistle whistle....
Calm your bristle....
The day is light and new....
I combed the stars,
And walked afar,
To see a sea calm blue....

Though there was no sunlight this morning and little to whistle about, he sang to the tune his iron music box played, letting the tub fill enough to step in and wash his pale skin.

From the moment he was born, whispers stirred and continued on through his teens. The principal issue, of course, regarded the silver markings, or "scars" as Brier oft called them, on his skin. They swirled in odd spirals on his neck, back, arms, thighs, and calves, making leaf patterns that intertwined on the tail of the stem and continued from a new budding leaf each year since he turned eleven. They'd grown as he grew, and now they covered a modest amount of his pale skin. Still, that the prince was fair was not a matter of opinion, but fact. His skin glowed white as snow, save for the silver scars and speckles on his nose and cheeks. He no longer wore his hair loose down his back like a bairn, but tied his fiery red locks in an intricate threaded braid. Brier was "not a child anymore," and he oft reminded Marietta of this when she tried to persuade him to wear it down by his waist. However, only three years prior, one could catch a young Brier Snow riding his piebald Coloured Cob on the palace grounds without care. Mayhap one might have seen red hair in the breeze with fierce emerald-green eyes that matched the rolling hills, heard unhinged laughter in the great halls, joking about with Marietta and pranking unsuspecting guards, but not now in almost adulthood.

After Brier felt sufficiently clean, he relaxed in the warm water and closed his eyes, listening to the rain patter against the windowpane. The gold faucet did gleam more than usual, and the daylight seemed to glow rather than just to shine, but Brier paid no attention. He counted the books he wanted to finish and inwardly moped that he could not take Frieling out for a ride. It was only when Brier stood to get out that he noticed a candle-like glow upon the marble of his tub. He blinked first at the light coming from his scars, wildly intrigued. It was like fire on his skin, burning internally. Fear replaced his curiosity then, and he frowned.

What in the gods' names...?

Brier hesitantly ran his fingers against his skin, heart racing, as if the marks would burn him. However, his scars felt the same on his fingertips, cool to the touch like gold lace embedded into his skin. Now they glowed luminously, and it discomforted him more than any blood he'd ever drawn.

"Calm your bristle…." he whispered, for he could see now that the glow was harmless, albeit disconcerting. Brier exhaled to steady his thudding heart. The fear eased some when he sang, and then the leaves, like a seasonal foliage, went back to their rightly metallic silver. Brier shook off the uneasiness and dried himself, but made a note to tell Marietta about the change when they met.

Brier dressed in his new gold and green jacket and walked toward the main hall of the palace with a stiff-necked palace guard. The entire palace was open to him, but the queen mostly stayed in the West Hall, so he avoided it at all cost. Marietta usually met him for breakfast in the main dining room, but today she did not wait for him.

Strange indeed.

It was not the first time Brier ate at a dining table alone, but the murky shadows the rain clouds formed on the crème and gray-blue walls did not improve his mood. At least the plate the servants set for him had blueberries. Everyone knew they were his favorite. He spooned a mouthful into his yogurt, mixing them and crushing the juice on the side of his cup. He lifted the spoon toward the cup and then stopped. A smile creased his lips as he considered drinking it straight. Marietta was not here to scold him for not using a spoon this morning. He could be as callow as he liked.

"Your Grace?"

The moment the cup was to his lips the door swung open, startling Brier to his core. He caught the glass from crashing on the table, but the yogurt did not miss his new jacket. He looked up to see the forest green of the guard's jacket and a staunch-faced man holding the dining room door open. The light from the hallway crept in like a church beacon.

"Yes," Brier replied, managing a patient smile. "What is it, Captain Galer?" He placed the cup upright on the plate and wiped the stain from the front of his gold-lined jacket. The servants replaced the napkin and yogurt.

"Pardon the intrusion," he said apologetically. "The queen has asked for your presence today in the Green Hall."

"What time?" Brier asked, lifting only his eyes in Captain Galer's direction.

"As soon as Your Grace is finished with breakfast." Brier contracted his brow and sat up more properly. "You are to tell Marietta to pack your bags and bring a traveling cloak."

"Am I to go outside the palace?" Brier felt a flutter of excitement at the possibility that the queen would let him outside the palace walls, even for a day. The last time he could remember going out was when he had to attend one of the cleric's funerals almost two months ago, and it had been deathly boring.

"I do not know, my prince." But something told Brier that Captain Galer did know, and the man was doing his best not to rouse his suspicion. What Captain Galer did not know was that Brier had already found the day suspicious. The eerie summerlike rain, glowing scars, the stillness of the palace, and Marietta's unexplained absence. "The queen only said that I should accompany you thus."

"*You* accompany me?" Brier peered at the guard waiting on his left. "I do not need the Captain of the Guard to babysit me. I am not a child." He wiped the stain on his jacket once more for good measure. "I will come in my own accord after I finish preparing."

"The queen's instructions were clear, Your Grace."

"And what instructions were those?" Brier arched his brow in question.

"Do not let him out of your sight," Captain Galer answered.

What is all this about, then? His stepmother did sometimes call for him, but never with urgency, and most certainly not with her personal guard.

Unless....

A thought struck him and a chill crept up his spine. Could the queen's sudden interest in him be connected to his scars? They were glowing this morning, and then there was the matter of his majority.

"That is fine, Captain Galer." Brier nodded once, his smile long vanished. He stared down at the cluster of blueberries and tightened his lips. Suddenly he did not feel hungry.

CHAPTER 2
THE SABBATICAL

AFTER BRIER finished his breakfast, he went to look for Marietta. Captain Galer followed him out of the dining hall and then to the kitchens. When they said she was not there, Brier went to the servants' quarters.

"I suppose you have not seen Marietta?" Brier asked as he exited the damp gardens. He faced the guard who did not keep more than two footsteps behind him.

"I have not, Your Grace." The man glanced at the garden's dusky haze and sighed tensely.

Where could Marietta be? Why wasn't she here to keep him calm? By now she would have told Brier that all was well. The queen probably just wanted him for some menial welcoming task. On several occasions she called Brier to put on airs for Aurelians. Mayhap this had to do with coming of age soon? Or the matter of his betrothal?

"Have any ships docked in Avenough, Captain Galer?" The last time he endured such liturgy was his twelfth year when he was told that he would marry the princess of a seaport country called Menlor. A pretty girl, but a girl nonetheless, and in that respect, Brier preferred men. He had a near tantrum until Marietta interjected to remind him of formality. In the end, Adeline Pascal did come to Avenough, but after Brier terrorized the girl till the end of her visit, he heard nothing more of the union.

"No, Your Grace." Brier let out an inward sigh of relief. Captain Galer would not openly lie to him. It seemed there would be no marriage yet. Of course, he was no longer a child. If the queen did beset him with a woman, he would not scream as he did seven years ago. He would do his duty as the Prince of Lirend. Though, admittedly, the prospect of marriage seemed less daunting with Marietta by his side.

When they finally reached the Green Hall, the queen was sitting on his father's throne across from the great oak doors. King Snow had wrought-iron leaves that traveled up from the legs of his throne, vines that snaked around the arms and back, up to the ceiling in an almost endless trail. The room itself appeared more as a greenhouse than a hall, with large open windows and court chairs made from the stumps of the willow trees from the forest toward the west. Thus, it was aptly named Green Hall and was where the former king and queen held most of their court. On sunnier days the light shone through so that the servants did not even need a candle to illuminate the great space. In the days of King Braedon Snow, Brier could remember actual flowers and trees that grew from the open soil, but that was long before, and the growing things inside Green Hall had died since then.

"Your Majesty." Captain Galer bowed lowly. "I brought Prince Snow as you have commanded." The woman did not stand but nodded once to let Captain Galer know she had heard him. Brier approached the throne then and bowed his head slightly.

"Stepmother." He revised quickly: "Queen Evelyn, I could not find Marietta though I did leave word for her under your instructions, that I should have assistance."

"Simple boy. Surely another servant would suffice." The queen answered in the familiar harsh tone. He clenched his jaw. Marietta was his servant, but the queen knew she meant much more than that to him. "Do you know why I have called you here?"

"I do not," Brier answered in monotone.

"Then I dare say, the servants credit your astuteness far more than you deserve." She chuckled darkly. Brier narrowed his green eyes as he fought back the urge to refute her.

"Calm your bristle...." He heard Marietta's nagging voice in his head.

"Mayhap the queen has called me here to insult me thus," Brier muttered. "If this is true, then you needn't have Captain Galer accompany me."

The queen stood, and Brier flinched when she walked toward him. She was a beautiful woman with honey blonde hair and lips like the rose bush in summer. Her body was not like that of a woman in her late season, but of a maiden still freshly plucked. Yes, that the queen was fair Brier could not deny, but her eyes were dark and cold, frozen like the bottom of a well in winter.

"Have you heard of the royal sabbatical?"

"I have only read about such things in books, Your Majesty."

"Books?" She laughed. "Can the scholars not stand your presence enough to teach you?"

"I have learned many things by a scholar. Mostly stately things," Brier answered. "I know three different dialects, and I can recite the great poets. I know the geographies and the extensive histories of our closest allies, Zhennal, Ranolf, Menlor, and Nieraeth. In addition, I can play the harp and the light keys. I am a good rider, and I do have some archery skill... and I can...." He paused before he clutched a small iron box in his pocket.

"Do go on," the queen mocked him in a delighted tone.

"And I can sing." Brier lowered his head then. Singing, he was sure, was not something the queen would deem stately or necessary for a future king.

"Singing like a peasant instead of studying. How fitting." The queen turned away from him, missing the glare Brier gave her. He did study, and he listened to teachers, but sometimes he saw the lapwings' funny courting dance in spring. Once he heard the strangled "peewit-tweet" cry, his lesson was lost. He much preferred to ride Frieling in the open grounds of the palace or lay among the wildflowers in his garden, listening to Marietta's stories of lost loves, great kings, and happily ever after.

"The royal sabbatical, daft boy, is a rite of passage that the Prince of Lirend must undergo before he takes up his station. For most, it is used to allow the future king to have a period of leisure before he takes the throne, but for someone as unskilled as yourself, you will take the time to learn all that the best scholars could not teach you.

You will be an apprentice, and when you come back, when I deem you suitable, you will take the throne."

"Then… I am to go away?" Brier's heart swelled with elation, but he tried hard to hide the excitement in his tone. The queen might decide at the last moment to revoke her decision, seeing it give him some happiness.

"Yes. You will leave for the Mountain Lands tonight."

"What?" Brier's eyes widened.

"So you do know something other than silly songs." The queen pursed her lips in a wicked smile.

"Why should I go to the Mountain Lands?" Fear trickled through his voice. The Mountain Lands held the dark forest Marietta oft spoke of. Only those who were in danger of persecution fled there.

There is a curse on that land.

"There is a village on the peak called Aire. That is where your master lives."

"And why should someone who is to teach me live there? Where there is naught but traitors, outlaws, thieves, and murderers!"

"That is of no consequence to you!" The queen's smile vanished. "This is my order."

"And if I refuse?"

"You will lose your claim to the throne."

"That is not in your power." Brier was sure of that. Technically the queen was only a placeholder until he came of age. Her rule was great but limited to public sectors. Mostly court proceedings and mediation of the people. Brier followed her commands more out of respect than obligation.

"Ah!" The queen latched on to his words. "But it is not my power at work here. Your dear father is the one responsible." She walked to sit on the unrightful throne.

"I do not believe you." Brier raised his chin. "My father loved me. He would never send me away."

"Captain Galer." The queen raised her thin arm and snapped her fingers. "Show Prince Brier the last will of his father." The guard came over hurriedly and handed Brier an aged piece of parchment with official cursive. Upon closer inspection Brier realized he held his father's last will and testament. "Section five," the queen told him.

Brier scanned the paper until he found the part he desired.

Section V—The Sabbatical

"Then, to the matter of my son, Brier Ignacio Snow. He is like his mother Iines, kind in the way of old. He has a calm and gentle spirit that I should wish to keep whole. After his nineteenth year, he should take his sabbatical. In the customary way of Lirend's royalty, a prince might refuse this leave of absence, but if Brier Ignacio so refuses his leave…."

Brier paused.

"He forgoes his claim to the throne, and as such, to any inheritance under Lirend's law of passage."

"I assume you know that much." The queen smirked.

"This says nothing of Aire," Brier uttered calmly, though he was much less confident in his stance.

"I am your guardian, therefore, I choose how long, where, and with whom you take your leave."

Then Brier fell silent. How foolish he'd been to think his stepmother would do him a kindness. Instead, she used the rite of passage to demean him more and cast him away like a wretch. The kingdom would whisper now; how loathsome King Snow's son must be that the queen would send him to live among undesirables.

"Do not despair, Prince Snow. I am merciful, even to those who do not deserve my mercy. If you refuse this sabbatical, you only need renounce your title and claim to the throne. You may still live in the palace, as my ward, and I will provide for you until the end of my days. If you are grateful I will even let you keep your room." The queen let out a cackling laugh. Brier felt sick to his stomach. For not the first time in his life, Brier suffered the sting of her scorn. It was humiliating.

"Oh, but your surprise is truly amusing, Prince Snow."

Brier lifted his head and stared into her black eyes. From the day his father died, his life had been the shadow of the one he had once lived. The queen had done her utmost to strip him of the joy he felt within the palace, leaving him with naught but pain and tired memories. For one moment, he thought that his father's favor could combat the queen's callous rule, but the king passed into the next world long ago. The man could not protect him.

"That you would sentence me like a prisoner at my father's last request does not surprise me," Brier said quietly. "But that you would think me such a coward I would not go to Aire is your own folly."

"What was that?" She raised her brow.

"I will go to Aire." Brier clenched his jaw and ignored the needlelike prickle on his skin.

"Even after my offer to grant a reprieve from your ignoble obligation?"

"Your 'reprieve' is for your own gain. You would keep me here like a trained stallion, and sully my father's name to the people who love him."

"Do not think so highly of yourself. You are a walking abomination!" she spat coldly. "A stain on the tapestry in your father's line."

"Call me what you will. I am no warrior, saint, nor scholar, but I have my honor, and I would not hand that to you so willingly."

"Honor?" The queen laughed again.

"Yes, honor!" Brier straightened his back and stood proudly. "Something you know nothing about."

She tightened her lips. "Who are you to speak to me of honor?"

"I am Brier Snow, only son of Braedon and Iines, Prince of Lirend and future king. You'd do well to remember that." Brier sneered.

Panic flashed in the queen's eyes, but it vanished almost instantly. "Very well, Prince Snow." She drummed her fingertips on the side of the chair. "Captain Galer, see in Roland and have one of the other servants pack Prince Snow's belongings." The man piped up on command and walked toward the entrance hall.

Brier turned his head toward the front. When the doors opened, his breath hitched. A man, standing at least a foot above him, walked in wearing something that looked like elk fur on his cloak and a sable hood that covered his face. His shoulders were broad, hard, and rounded like a wooden shield, but his chest was solid like steel. Brier's pulse quickened as the man's footsteps echoed in the hall toward him.

"Your Majesty." The man's voice reverberated even though he spoke low under his hood.

"This is your pupil for the next year, Prince Brier Snow."

Was he a con or a thief? Brier could not tell. At first glance, he looked like a warrior, tall and dark. Brier hardened his gaze, ready to glare down the imposter master, but blinked when the man took off his hood and turned toward him. He had a coarse black beard, olive-tinged skin, and eyes like Marietta's morning song, like the sea's calm blue. His face was fine and chiseled like polished rock, and the raven of his shoulder-length hair drew the prince's gaze. Brier's enmity fled as he swallowed and bowed his head. The man bowed in return, but Brier noticed the reluctance.

"This is your master, Roland Archer of Aire. He has a cabin in the wood north of here. You will stay with him for one year or until you forgo your claim on the throne."

What can this man teach me?

Likely nothing.

Aire was the land of criminals. What was this man's misdeed? Perhaps a killer, or worse yet, a rapist. The man cut his eye toward Brier when that thought struck him. A wide smirk spread across his lips, and Brier blushed up to his ears, feeling strangely translucent.

"Your horse has already been watered and fed, Brier," the queen told him after the short introduction. "Captain Galer will lead you out of the gates, and then you will be on your own."

Brier jerked his head toward the queen, only now aware that he'd been staring overlong at his master.

"I should say good-bye to Marietta and the others."

"There is no time."

"There is time yet to say good-bye!" Brier protested. "I shall be leaving, and I do not know when or if I shall return!" Voicing his reality made his stomach clench, but he ignored the foreboding truth of his words. "Marietta will surely worry if I do not at least—"

"I said no!" the queen told him, flaring her finely etched nostrils.

"You cannot send me away without letting me say good-bye! Please!" Brier pleaded. "I shouldn't be long, I just want to—"

"Captain Galer."

The guard appeared behind Brier and gripped his arm.

"Release me!" Brier yelled and thrashed his body, but the man only held tighter. The captain twisted Brier's wrist behind his back and pushed him forward. "Get off me!" Brier threw a wild elbow and heard it collide with bone. Captain Galer groaned but collected himself quickly, landing a rough punch to Brier's gut.

"Haah!" The inhale of breath Brier took felt nonexistent. He gasped, holding his stomach as he tried to pull air, but only felt pain. Brier's eyes cinched into slits, but he felt a presence standing over him. Roland leaned next to him and jerked the belt at his waist, lifting him almost off the ground. Brier coughed out through his almost suffocation, desperate for air.

Father.... Mother.... Marietta....

The only people who ever loved him, but he could never say good-bye.

"Come." The man pulled the hood of his dark cloak to cover his face and took hold of Brier once more.

Chapter 3
Long Road Ahead

When Brier woke he was surprised to find himself draped on his horse, Frieling's, neck. He still felt incredibly weak, but there was a warm and solid weight to steady him.

"Are you awake, then?" a baritone voice whispered in his ear. It was then Brier remembered whose solidity he was relying on. He gasped and tried to muster the strength to sit upright on his horse without assistance. Roland gripped Brier's shoulder to pull him back. "It will not do if you fall off your horse at this height," the man said in a cold tone that did not match the concerned words.

"Unhand me. I can sit fine on my horse. I've done so in worse condition," Brier lied.

"Have it your way then."

For Brier, he was used to the sneering tone, and so he did not have any problems telling the man what was what in regards to his condition. He did feel weak, but he would feel worse lying against his master's chest like a woebegone damsel. Roland stopped both of the horses and hopped off Frieling's back to mount his own steed. Brier hardened his brow instead and gathered the strength he had left to ride upright.

They traveled for hours, the sun peering over each green hill they mounted. The grass's hue fluctuated between the summer's emerald green to the fall's desert brown, and the ground cushioned Frieling's hooves, slightly wet from the rains earlier in the day. They were right next to the sea that separated the great lands in the eastern world, Ranolf, Menlor, Zhennal, Nieraeth, and Lirend.

Due to Lirend's proximity to the ocean, the rainy season's changes always brought a heavy fog over the lands. Around dusk the brew of sunlight and condensation created a lazy haze over the terrain that usually made Brier feel peaceful. Today there was no such pleasure. In its place, he felt a heavy cloud of lethargy over his very being. His nurse was gone, and perhaps he would never see her again. His stepmother had taken the throne ever so much more firmly now that he'd been sent away. The people would think he'd been exiled or worse, killed.

The sun now long gone, Brier felt the chill of night air sweep around him. His butt went numb around the hour four mark, and his fingers were beginning to grow stiff as well. It seemed that his master was used to such long traveling, because he did not speak or move more than to guide Frieling over the path laid before them.

"How much longer will we ride?" Brier asked in a limp voice that did not feel like his own. The truth was he was exhausted, and he'd never ridden this long on a horse a day in his life, even at full strength.

"Are you tired?" The man's voice rumbled through him.

Brier considered how to answer his master. He did not want to appear weak, but his body was ready to give out at any moment.

"My horse is not used to such long travels," Brier replied. "Frieling seems a bit slow coming over the pass."

"He's following my lead well enough." The man grunted with a sluggish drawl. It dawned on Brier that perhaps his new master was not from Lirend at all, but of a different region entirely.

Never mind that....

At the moment Brier wanted nothing more than to be off his horse's back.

"I know my horse," Brier assured him, now putting on a more confident air. "It would not do well if he is too exhausted to ride on the whole of our journey." For a while, Roland did not reply. Brier could hear Frieling's hooves crunching the drier parts of the grass and the crickets in the thickets calling as if mourning the end of the summer.

I could just tell him I'm tired. Brier began to consider when Roland still did not stop. However, Brier plucked the thought from his mind. In the first place, he'd already shown Roland too much vulnerability. The queen bested him so easily, and then the way he fainted in the man's arms before they left. Brier could not help the flush of red in his cheeks as he recalled the way the man held him. His first interaction with his master was of him crying and begging to see nothing more than what should be a servant in his house. No. It was too humiliating to show Roland more weakness. Whatever his stepmother told Roland, he would not give her the satisfaction of living up to the deplorable reputation. He would simply have to wait it out.

Brier's stomach growled, and he cleared his throat to cover up the heinous sound. He tried hard to ignore the pang in his gut from missing lunch and he supposed now dinner, but it grew ever more insistent. Where were they going? How long were they going to ride?

Does he plan to starve me to death?

Judging by the size of Roland, Brier estimated the man would easily eat three times his portion of food. He was as tall as Brier's horse and built like a bear not yet come into adulthood. Though he could not see his master's face, he could remember chiseled features and pale blue eyes. A cold shiver ran up his spine, and it was then that he realized that Frieling was slowing down, or rather, being pulled to a stop.

Thank the gods, he thought, closing his eyes, and exhaled. That Brier felt relieved to be stopped in the middle of nowhere with a stranger only indicated his hectic day.

"We'll camp here for the night," Roland said, climbing off his horse with more ease than Brier could muster. Roland held his hand out for Brier to grab hold to, but Brier refused, using Frieling's saddle and the stirrups to support him. Once Brier was finally on the ground, he felt much less steady on his feet than he anticipated. He stumbled over to a large boulder and breathed to settle his temporary vertigo. Frieling wandered over to comfort him, and Brier nuzzled the horse's head, smiling gently.

"You alright, Frie?" Brier asked quietly.

"He'd be a lot stronger if you didn't pamper him so much," Roland said, removing his leather gloves and throwing them to the ground.

Brier sucked his teeth and scowled. "He's strong enough."

"For grandiose walks in Avenough with your guards, and pomegranate juice in the gardens maybe," Roland mocked. "Where I am from, we ride without saddle and through wooded terrain."

"He's a jumping champion for your information," Brier told him rather smugly.

"And yet he's here with you," Roland jeered. "And me." Frieling lifted his head and huffed indignantly.

"After Frieling won Avenough's high jump competition, he lost the national championship. His owner beat him mercilessly and abandoned him in the capital. The incident left him traumatized. Frieling wouldn't come near a man for months," Brier continued, ignoring Roland's banter. "None of the horse trainers could heal Frieling, and he was about to be put down, but I begged Father to spare him." Brier saw the same loneliness in Frieling he felt within himself. He tended to Frieling and kept the horse company. Brier even slept in the stalls to comfort the abused horse. "He's my friend. I didn't care that he was no longer a champion or that people thought him broken." Brier smiled and rubbed the horse's mane affectionately. That Frieling recovered was surprising enough, but the trauma left him skittish and easily shaken. "If I pamper him it is because he deserves it. Everyone decided he didn't matter anymore, but Frieling didn't give up."

Brier looked up and felt his face heat instantly from the intense stare Roland gave him. Was he thinking that he was a fool for taking Frieling in even though he was damaged? Or maybe Roland thought he was silly for considering a horse as a friend. Roland turned away, and Brier was inwardly relieved. Roland's stare unsettled him, and he did not rightly know why.

"Let's eat," Roland told him, grabbing stones and positioning them in a small circle. "I assume you are hungry. It's been hours since we left the palace."

"I am all right enough," Brier replied, watching him set up the camp. Roland surprised Brier when he looked up with a slight smile.

"I see why you like that damn horse so much. He's stubborn like his little prince."

"I am not stubborn!" Brier protested. Though the reply had the opposite effect and only confirmed Roland's words. "And I am not little," Brier added, not realizing his error.

Roland did not answer Brier, but stood up and walked over to his rucksack. He pulled out a smaller bag with something that looked like feathers to Brier and began to gather small twigs and sticks lying in the grass. The patch they were sitting on was green enough, but the hole Roland managed to dig was impressive.

"What are you doing?"

"I'm building a fire, lest we eat nothing but raw potatoes for dinner tonight."

Food. Finally. Brier's famine gave him a momentary clarity, and he nodded once. He stood and began to search for more sticks, finding a large branch. He was about to toss it away when Roland called him to bring it over. "We can use this to stoke the fire when it gets low," Roland said, now clicking two small stones together.

"Firestones?" Brier thought aloud. He had never seen someone use firestones up close, but he'd read about them in several of his textbooks. The friction caused a small spark, which set off a chemical reaction in the stones. Rare for Aurelians to use them, unheard of for commoners.

Who was this man really? Perhaps a scientist who'd gotten into trouble for breaking the ethics laws? Or maybe a sorcerer who'd been exiled for summoning deadly curses. Roland did not look like either of those, but Brier's fertile imagination ran wild nonetheless. When he saw a small spark from the two stones, the feathers began to smoke and grow orange with the beginnings of a flame. In two minutes Roland had a fire going and was adding more sticks to the blaze.

"Those are firestones," Brier informed his master.

"I'm aware." Roland stuffed the bag of feathers into his bag and put the stones back into his pocket, saying nothing more. Brier eyed Roland more carefully as he pulled out something that looked like a jar of old cabbage.

"What's that?" Brier hadn't asked so many questions since he was a youngling. Not that the palace encouraged his inquisitive nature.

"*Rotund*," Roland answered rolling his tongue on the hard *R*. Brier had never heard the word, but knew the language was not his own.

"And what is that?" Brier demanded. "In the common tongue."

"Pig ears," he answered simply.

Pig ears. He'd never considered it, let alone eaten it. He knew that bacon came from pigs, but even that was something he rarely ate at the palace. Aurelians ate mostly vegetables and fruits. On the rare occasion they ate meat, it was mostly poultry or fish, and never more than a thin slice for protein. Pigs were seen as commoner's meat, and so, despite the fact that bacon tasted good, Brier's only experience was with what Marietta gave to him.

Brier didn't like the sound of eating a pig's ear, but did his best not to turn his nose up. That is until Roland actually opened the jar and Brier nearly gagged at the smell. It was like milk gone sour in the kitchens. He held his nose until Roland emptied the contents into a large pan along with a spoon of shortening. It seemed that the man sliced and cleaned the ears before he jarred them. Brier sat on the boulder patiently wondering whether he could stomach the meat. His worries were somewhat soothed when he smelled the familiar aroma of potatoes frying in the pan as well.

Perhaps if he was not on the road to Aire with a criminal, Brier could find excitement in trying something new. As it stood he only dreaded the taste and experience. Roland handed him the wooden plate, and Brier grimaced. He picked up the ear and inspected the would-be delicacy, sniffing it, rubbing his fingertips against the hard curled edge of the stick. He had to admit the ears at least smelled better fried.

"Do you intend to eat and get your strength up? Or will I have to carry you tomorrow as well?" Roland asked with his mouth full of food. The allusion to Brier's earlier frailty gave Brier just the motive he needed to take a bite of the ear and actually chew.

Well.... Brier took another bite and another. It wasn't bacon, but it certainly wasn't bad. The saltiness overwhelmed any adversity to the grainy texture he had. By the end of the meal, Brier could even admit that the potatoes were some of the best he'd tasted, though certainly not out loud. He watched as Roland stood up and began to clean the now cool pan.

"Will you teach me to build a fire with firestones?" Brier asked sleepily. He did not want to show how much he'd enjoyed the meal, but his fullness had a way of improving his mood.

"Yes. I'll teach you to use dry wood as well. Perhaps tomorrow after you've had a good night's rest."

"I've never seen someone use firestones before," Brier said with some caution. He knew Roland's purpose was to teach him, but he still felt wary around his master. "It was quite... interesting to see."

"I don't know how interesting scraping rocks together is." Roland shrugged Brier's enthusiasm off his broad shoulders.

"'Tis not the rock, but the chemistry behind them," Brier contradicted the man though he did not fully know why.

"I wouldn't know since I didn't make them. That's Umhal's specialty."

"Um-hal?" Brier's brow quirked.

"Aye. He's part of the Ceve guild."

"The Ceve guild?"

"Yes, my comrades that will assist me in your training." Brier did not like the idea of associating with even more renegades, but he supposed his opinion, like always, did not matter. "We can teach you everything you'll need to know—if you take heed. But first we have quite a way to travel, little prince. Aire is over two thousand miles north of here, and I won't coddle you the whole of the journey." Brier gave him a dubious stare, and Roland smiled knowingly. "Or did you think I would go easy on you because you are the future king of Lirend?"

No. Brier hadn't thought that. In fact, he'd thought that his stepmother would find the cruelest man she could to teach him. However, crass as the man might behave, his authenticity caught Brier off guard.

"I am a man you know," Brier answered coldly. "I do not want pity or special treatment."

"Right," Roland replied stalely. "Just remember, there are no shortcuts in Aire, little prince."

"It's Brier," Brier said, tightening his jaw.

"Excuse me?"

"My name... is Brier." He huffed. "And what should I call you? Master?" The man stood up and grabbed two blankets out of the bags he carried.

"No." Roland replied, turning away in his comforter. "Ro will be fine."

The temperature was high enough with the fire that they did not need to set up the tent that evening. When Brier finally settled, he felt warm and full, but the unknown future gave him an ominous feeling he could not shake. If he were at home, he'd take a warm bath to wash away the day's stresses. He'd ask Marietta to wash and braid his hair and tell her all about the strange man with wintery blue eyes who spoke with an accent like he'd never heard before. He'd ask her why he felt so strange when he stared at Roland overlong, and also how to avoid those feelings. He'd ask her about his scars that had glowed earlier. Right now Brier wanted nothing more than to be at home in his four-poster, canopy, king-size bed, but it seemed like so long ago that he was sitting at his window watching the rain pelt against the glass.

CHAPTER 4
SECRETS & VOWS

FOR THE first time in several weeks, Roland felt relieved when he opened his eyes. They were a half day from his cabin in Aire, and summer had stalled through the whole of their journey. The ground was still soft without the permafrost that usually covered the mountains this high, and the winds only picked up in the evenings when the sun had died. Looking up he could see the tumultuous clouds coming in from the west. It took them a week to cross over the trodden valleys of Ilk, another week through Sherdoe, and then toward the acicular cliffs. They would pass through the Toe' Caves and then have a three-day walk through the Black Forest. The straight path led through the coniferous trees where his home was, far from the eyes of any thieves.

Roland removed his cloak and breathed in the mountain air. Unlike the salt-heavy winds in Avenough, he could smell the fresh water from the blue ponds that littered the flat terrain and hear the pheasants calling as they flew from the Ilk Lands. Lirend was right on the ocean's border, but Aire was farther north, a little over three weeks ride on saddle back, deep into the mountains. Roland's cabin hid nestled in the Black Forest where it was nigh impossible to find a person that did not want to be found. More than a good fit for a man like Roland.

The prince, Brier, was not yet awake and that also suited Roland. Over the past weeks, the boy's countless questions and niggling arrogance only made Roland weary. He was used to being alone, save for the guild's commissions.

The first week Roland showed Brier how to make fire with the stones since it was much easier than the dry wood technique. He'd lit the stone simply enough, but he had trouble learning the dry wood technique. Brier's hands were tar-black and nearly bleeding trying to get the spark to catch and kindle. For two weeks they traveled through rough terrain. Still the prince didn't give up until Roland saw the embers of smoke and smelled the kindling feathers burning. If the rains didn't wash him out, Roland was sure Brier would have sat up all night trying to light the log aflame. Arrogant—no, that wasn't the right word to describe the young prince. It was more sheltered ignorance than boastful pride. It seemed that Brier had something to prove, but Roland was not sure what that something was yet.

"Should I boil water for your coffee, Master Roland?"

Roland hadn't noticed the boy sitting next to him, deep as he was in thought. He caught the flaming hair in his peripheral, but inspected the fire to distract his gaze.

"Will you stop calling me that?" Roland grunted. "The fire is still going. Add a few fresh sticks to burn." He still had not told the boy much about his home in Aire, and that was mostly because he had not expected Brier to last this long. It was more than just his reaction to pig ears. Roland could tell the boy had never gone farther than Avenough, so he assumed the prince would cry and beg to go back the moment they reached the Nejir River. But he did not.

"I would like to try and build a new one using the dry wood," the boy said, gathering the wood and beginning to dig.

"We don't have all day for you to waste." Roland picked up a large branch and began to add more wood to the existing flame. "If you want to help, go wrap the blankets and make sure your horse is fed." The boy stared at him with a strange sense of rebellion. He was small in stature, Roland noticed, but surpassed general comeliness. Even for an Aurelian.

"Fine." Brier walked over to tend to his horse instead. Stubborn he'd called the boy, though determined was probably more fitting. Roland smirked to himself and began to prepare their breakfast.

The quickest way to Aire was through an opening through the Toe' Caves right off of the Nejir River. That river ran through the open plains of Sherdoe, fifty miles wide. In the fall Roland usually hunted there, but in the winter and spring, he stayed at home taking odd jobs in the closest village and selling firewood for food and burning oil. The temperature in Aire reached below freezing in the winter. The inhabitants did not venture outside of their homes in the winter months unless they had to, and only for short periods of time. The summer and fall were spent selling and gathering supplies to outlast the cold.

Roland stood outside the cave and inspected the triangular opening carefully. Even if they managed to squeeze through, there was no way a horse would fit.

"Does your horse know the way back to Avenough?" Roland turned to the boy.

"Why do you ask?" Brier asked, holding the horse's reins tighter.

"The horses have to be released. They can't fit through the caves."

"Then why would you lead us this way?" Brier narrowed his gaze.

"*I* always travel this way. Why would I alter my route for you and your pony?"

"Right then…." Roland could see the trepidation forming in Brier's green eyes. "Then we'll just have to find another way," the prince replied in a forced calm.

"*This* is the best way," Roland countered crossing his arms to his chest. "The cliffs are fast, but too dangerous. Going around the mountains would take another two or three weeks at least, and the season is changing. It could take longer if we're caught in a storm." He walked up to the black-and-white horse with his boots crunching the jagged rocks. Frieling immediately huffed and butted his head to drive him away. Roland stepped back from the beast with his eye twitching. "He'll be much safer back at the palace with your moth—"

"I'm not sending him away." Brier cut off Roland's speech. He mounted his horse and held the reins as if he planned on moving with or without Roland by his side. "We'll take the cliffs."

"My ass. It's a two-hundred-foot drop. I'm not risking my life for a horse!"

"He's not just a horse," the boy said, looking scandalized by Roland's accusation. "If you don't want to accompany us, then suit yourself. I will lead him."

"Into the sea? You don't even know where you're going!"

"We will manage."

Roland narrowed his eyes, and Brier mimicked him. There was no way Roland was going over the cliffs with an obstinate horse and a know-nothing brat like this one. Not only would the boy die, but he'd take Roland to a watery grave with him. Anger rose in his chest, but he did not know how to fix the source. If he went through the caves alone, the boy would easily get lost on his way to the cliffs, or killed, or worse, captured! What would the queen say if Brier was kidnaped and taken for ransom under Roland's watch? He could say farewell to their freedom.

"You two are a pain in my ass!" Roland cursed and grabbed the reins of the horse, pulling Frieling back away from the cave. Roland's own horse grazed at her own pace, unfazed by her freedom. He knew she would find her way back to Black Forest eventually.

"Naturally," Brier answered with a smug grin. The boy kicked the side of Frieling to get him to move away from the narrow cave entrance with Roland walking alongside them.

"And make sure that damn beast is ready. We've little room to work with on the cliffs and we can't rest or stop until we make it completely through. It's not going to be easy."

"As long as we have you there to guide us, we will definitely make it through," Brier declared.

Roland stopped walking, and Brier pulled the reins to give Frieling a short stop. His heart thudded and yet he was not doing anything strenuous. The subtle compliment just caught him off guard. Roland stared at the prince, frowning and trying hard not to lose his resolve at the innocence staring back at him. "Perhaps you've settled yourself into a false sense of security with me. That is not wise," Roland said calmly. Enough people had already died depending on him to protect them. "Up until now you've been safe, but I will be completely honest with you. I can't ensure your safety on the cliffs." Brier considered him. For a moment Roland thought he may have convinced him to abandon his foolish plan, but then Roland watched the crease of the prince's mouth twist into a grimace.

"Even if we make it through the caves safely, it won't matter if I have no one left. The queen has taken everything from me. I won't let her take Frieling too." Roland felt something squeeze in his chest at Brier's words. It was both sad and frighteningly akin to the words he'd spoken so many years ago.

"Just make sure you're focused." Perhaps Roland assumed too much about the prince, but he did not expect proclamations from an Aurelian. "If you're dead it won't matter what she takes," Roland muttered as he turned away.

It took them nigh on three hours just to climb the steep slope leading to the perilous cliffs that bordered the open sea. If they made it over, the cliffs led them right to the edge of the Black Forest. From the top of the precipice, the fall appeared like a quick and painless death, but Roland knew better. If they fell the men would tumble for minutes down the puncturing earth, likely fracturing their skulls in several places, and finally meet their end in a watery grave. The best case scenario was to die before the impact, but there was no silver lining.

A STORM made its debut at dusk, right when they reached the midpoint of the cliffs. Since going back would be just as dangerous, they moved forward, and the night steadily crept over them.

Thankfully Brier's horse had taken to the edges rather gracefully as they made their way toward the final leg of their hike, but as the storm gained momentum, the wind whipped against the cliffs, freezing their skin and making the rocks shift under their worn boots. Just when Roland thought the conditions could not get worse, he felt the droplets of rain on his forehead and cheek.

"How much farther?" Brier's voice was lost in the breeze. Roland heard the faint cry before he saw the horse backtracking in a frenzy.

"Don't move, Brier!" Roland yelled to deter Brier from following Frieling, but the boy had already raised his arms, trying to calm the horse down. The crazed neighs reverberated against the rush of the wind and water, and the gust seemed hell-bent on blowing them over.

"Hand me the reins!" Roland yelled. Roland extended his arm and pushed through to reach them. Brier opened his mouth to reply but closed it immediately when the wind swept him back.

"Brier!" The prince's head slammed against the base of the mountain. Then another gust snapped at Brier's cloak, catching him off-balance.

Brier cried out in surprise as he fell, but he caught the edge of the cliff quickly, fingers grasping hard at the pebbles. The prince lowered himself precariously onto a narrow ledge right below the main path. The rain was pouring now, making it difficult to breathe and nigh impossible to hear Brier scream. Roland watched in terror as the horse continued to thrash about. "Save him!"

"Not until I save you first!" Roland roared back.

"He's just scared! He'll fall if you don't get him now!" Roland darted his eyes between the two of them, heart pounding against the howl of the wind and rain. One more gust and it would pull Brier's small frame clean off the rocks. Brier gritted his teeth and secured himself more on the edge. "Save him! I can hold on!" Roland swallowed the fear that stilled him. He cursed under his breath and angled himself against the cliff, inching closer to the Coloured Cob.

"Come on…." Roland grunted and scraped his boots against the gravel. When he was close enough, he rose carefully and narrowed in to grip the horse's reins and reel him in with brute strength. Then the horse pawed at the ground, and Roland hesitated before he took another step forward. Frieling was breathing heavily, amber eyes piercing against Roland's blue.

"Frieling." The horse's ears perked. The rain was still falling, but the blasting wind died down enough to hear Brier's steady voice. "You have to move forward or you'll die." Roland continued to hold the leather straps dangling from the horse's bit.

"Please…. Frieling…." Brier tried to pull himself up, but he could only reach the path's edge before sliding back down onto the ledge. Brier steadied himself on a sapling with his feet tenuously on the rocks. The horse huffed out but refused to move farther.

"Good. Go ahead and abandon him after he saved you!" Roland yelled at the horse, glaring. The horse neighed angrily, jumping up before stomping his front legs into the soggy dirt and moving up several feet toward the flat terrain. Roland clenched his jaw together as the rain continued to seep through his cloak and boots. "Show him what a waste you are! Prove everyone right about you!" Again Frieling moved feet forward, trying to run the man off the cliff, but getting closer and closer to safety. "Stand there and die, you damn beast! And after you do, I'll take your precious little prince!" Frieling butted his head toward him to drive him off, and Roland seized the opportunity to pull him all the way up and forward to the flat terrain, grabbing the rope that was on his saddle. The horse bucked, but Roland dodged the horse's hooves. Then he coaxed Frieling enough into the clear to yank the horse onto the sturdy ground. Roland ran back over to where Brier had levered himself onto the ledge and was holding tightly.

"You all right down there, little prince?" Roland called, grinning despite the struggle with Brier's horse. He was dripping wet and tired, but he could see Brier was safe.

"I'm all right," Brier yelled, looking up at him, terror evident on his face. "Is Frieling okay?"

"Right as rain!" Roland answered. He threw the rope down for Brier to hold on to. "Grab hold!" he yelled, trying to move quickly before the winds picked back up. The rain was still whipping against them both, but at least the winds had died considerably. "I'm going to pull you up!" He watched as Brier reached up from the safety of his ledge and held on to the rope. Once Roland saw Brier had the rope securely, he began to pull Brier up. He hadn't realized what a distance the prince had fallen until he heaved him up, slowly and meticulously so he would not shred the rope. He pulled until the boy was close enough to grab hold of his hand, and Roland reached out to grab Brier.

Crack!

In the same instant he took hold of Brier's hand, a loud crack of lightning resounded, disintegrating the rock ledge. Brier screamed like a pig being gutted, and Roland felt his fingers slipping. He lunged forward and slapped both of his hands around Brier's wrist firmly. The rope dropped into the abyss.

"Brier!" Roland yelled so loudly the vein in his neck pulsated. He squeezed him tighter, using his weight to hold him up. Brier scrambled, trying to use his feet to leverage his body against the cliff, but the rocks crumbled under his slippery boots.

"R-Ro...." Brier breathed out as he struggled to keep a hold on the cliff and Roland's hand. Brier's fingers dug in hard, but the rain kept causing them to slide. "I can't hold it!" Brier cried out. Roland narrowed his eyes and gritted his teeth. He could only think of the night he'd lost everything.

Ronan....

Heat like fire pushed at his back as if to incinerate him from the very memory.

"Don't fucking let go!" Roland yelled through the wind with Brier staring up at him.

"Please!" he begged with his face twisted in horror. "Don't let me fall!" Roland could not tell where the rain started and the tears stopped.

Curse the gods! Roland didn't hesitate. He grunted and breathed in deep before he let out a guttural scream.

The lightning illuminated the night sky like a flickering candle. Roland used every ounce of strength he had to drag Brier up, feeling the pain in his stomach from straining to lift him and the boy's dangling weight. Brier grabbed hold and clutched him for dear life.

When they finally reached the edge, Brier collapsed against Roland, holding on to him with shaking arms. Roland felt his own heart racing crazily, terrified of what could have been. Of what might have been if he'd hesitated only for a moment. "You're okay," Roland whispered though he knew Brier could not hear him through the falling rain and thunder. "Just hold on to me."

THEY WERE both sopping wet from the storm. Roland was able to set up camp under a large oak tree leading toward the Black Forest and assembled the tent to keep them warm and dry from the drizzle. It was made of deer hide with a leather coating to protect against the rain and insulate in the colder months. There was enough space to start a fire inside, but neither of them had the dynamism to manage it. Instead, Roland lit a small oil lamp to give them some light in the pitch-black tent. He did not know how long the storm would keep up, but Brier was soaked to his first layer.

"You should take off your wet clothes," Roland told Brier as he began to strip away his own wet garb. The last thing he wanted was for Brier to fall ill after such a close call, though the concern Roland felt was unexpected. As a younger man, he'd learned an important lesson of life. That everyone died eventually, whether from old age, plague, or an arrow to the heart.

Foes... friends... family... lovers....

They were all dangling on an inescapable cliff, holding on just a little longer. Death was always imminent.

Roland watched Brier take off his heavy traveling cloak and then a tattered jacket with missing gold buttons and faint, green embroidered designs on the breast. Then he stopped and looked up at Roland with wide eyes and faintly red cheeks.

"Are you all right?" Roland asked, frowning at how uncomfortable Brier suddenly seemed. The boy shook his head and held his worn tunic more closely. It seemed the trauma of Brier's near death had emerged. "You are safe now, you know," Roland whispered. "I promise you, Brier."

"I know I am safe...." Brier muttered.

"Then take off that wet shirt." Roland moved to grab the blankets. "Wrap these blankets around you to keep warm."

Brier shook his head. He turned away still gripping at the tunic uncomfortably. "I will be all right."

"You won't be all right if you're dead from a rain fever." Roland tossed the blanket in Brier's lap and scowled. He sounded like Lei with his worrying. Why was he making such a fuss?

The prince peered down, fingers entwined into the wool fabric. "Just…." Brier sighed heavily before averting his gaze. "Turn away from me for a moment."

"Turn away?" Roland asked incredulously. Brier's jaw hardened and Roland crossed his arms against his broad chest. "Why do you shield yourself? Are you hurt somewhere?" Roland demanded.

"It's nothing like that!" Brier cried out. He breathed steadily and shook his head. "Just—trust me, okay?" They stared at each other for several seconds before Brier gritted his teeth and said, "I'm not taking it off until you do." Roland huffed as he stomped to the other side of the tent.

What in the hell….

He could hear Brier shuffling to take off his wet shirt. Roland thought to peek while he undressed—just to make sure he wasn't hiding any injuries, of course. However, he quickly dismissed the idea as both childish and overly dishonest even for him. Perhaps Aurelians had some silly rule about modesty to uphold. Not that it should matter for a man to see another man. If Brier was a woman, Roland could understand the prudence somewhat, but certainly he should not be embarrassed around Roland. Or rather… why would he be embarrassed around him? What was he hiding? By the time Roland had turned back, Brier had the blanket thrown around him.

Roland eyed him suspiciously. Brier pulled the cover closer to hide his pale shoulders completely. "Will you please stop staring?" Brier's face grew redder as he fumbled a square dark box in his hands.

"You know…." Roland grabbed a loaf of the stored bread and tore it in half. "Gratitude is nothing to sniff at."

"Shall I smile and curtsy, Lord Roland?"

Roland chuckled wryly at the honorific. "I don't need your fake titles or smiles, but a thank-you would suffice." He handed Brier the piece of bread. There was a brief pause before the prince extended his hand in apology.

"Thank you for the bread." Brier took a timid bite. "And thank you… for saving me. I owe you my life."

"I didn't do it so that you would owe me," Roland answered immediately. "It is my job to protect you. I vowed to train you."

"Of course, but I owe you just the same."

Roland sighed and leaned back on the palms of his hands.

An Aurelian feels indebted to me?

"I was foolish enough to think I could do it on my own. Were it not for you, I'd be dead."

"Were it not for the gods, we'd all be dead," Roland recited in a singsong voice. "I always say, we save our tears for the outcome and not the possibility."

"Ha-ha—" Brier held his hand up to his mouth to hide his smile. "By gods, I never thought I'd say this, but you sound like my nurse, Roland."

"Is that so?"

"Yes. She's always saying things like that."

"Perhaps she is kin. Is she over six foot with a perfect beard?"

"I think not." Brier laughed out loud this time, shaking his head. "She's four-eleven with a large bosom. Rather wide around the middle. Eats more than you. Drinks ale at breakfast."

"Sounds like a classy lady."

"The classiest." Brier chuckled again and took a large bite of the bread. "Oh, but don't cross her. She's got a wallop like a horse kick. Trust me, I've been at the end of it a few times."

"A few times?" Roland eyed Brier dubiously.

"All right, plenty of times." He rolled his eyes.

"Good on her." Roland nodded in approval. Brier narrowed his eyes before laughing again. "Wallops build character. And character is the only thing that is constant in this world."

"But surely there are plenty of people who change for the better, or in my stepmother's case, the worse."

Roland yawned and lay fully on the ground. He stared at Brier, listening to the rain plunk against the patent leather exterior.

"Stations change, but people do not." No matter what he did or where he went, he would always be who he was. No amount of good deeds would wipe out his past.

"Marietta always says fate is the only thing that is constant in this world, but…." Brier's smile faltered, and Roland felt a pang in his gut.

"You don't believe her?" Roland asked.

Brier eyed a piece of half-eaten bread. "Aren't you tired of hearing me ramble, Roland?" He smirked. "'Tis not your duty to listen to the bygones and woes of a homesick prince."

"Am I to be bound to you by duty alone?" Brier's eyes jerked upward and Roland tilted his head, waiting.

"Sometimes I think there is no such thing as fate or else…." Brier bit his lip. "Or else why would fate lead me here?"

Why indeed? Roland thought, gazing at the timid boy.

"I do not know which way to go. Every step I take feels misguided. How should I know what path to take when it is lost in the fog? Even the path before me is riddled with pitfalls. Verily, it would be easier just to give up and go home."

"Wherefore this sudden loss of confidence?" Roland knit his brow. "It is not like you."

"'Tis not a loss of confidence, but a realization, Roland. Mayhap… mayhap I am not fit to be a king." Brier watched him with questioning eyes. Even though Brier did not say it aloud, Roland understood. The prince was afraid: of the unfamiliar path with no one to guide him; a longing in the prince's heart that was once sated with love; the insecurity of never being good enough. Roland understood it because he felt it every day of his life.

"Everyone thinks I will fail. Who is to say I will not?"

"Whose authority is it to say that you will?" Roland challenged.

"No one's, I suppose."

"Wrong. Only you have that power." Brier blinked, baffled into silence by Roland's serious tone. "Every decision you make in your life is your own. Most certainly it is easier to go back home, but easy does not mean it is the right thing to do. I wanted to go through the caves because they were easier, and you wanted to go through the cliffs."

"And look where that led us," Brier scoffed.

"It led us here. In this tent. Safe. Warm. Whole. You wanted Frieling to come with us, and he did. You made your decision, and you saw it through. Who cares if you stumble through the journey? The only thing that matters is that you make it to the end."

"And…." Brier faced him. "Do you think I will make it to the end?"

The prince looked so exposed then, with his rain-slicked red hair and his lean body peeking through the blanket meant to shield him. Roland raised his hands and covered Brier's cheeks. "I don't know the answer to that," Roland replied honestly. "Though I must say, I have never met someone quite as stubborn as you, little prince." Brier's mouth twisted upward, and Roland grinned, satisfied at the effect of his words. A real smile. If Roland had his way, Brier would always laugh and smile. Roland moved his thumbs gently across the fire-like blush spreading through his cheeks. Like petals in early spring, Roland was surprised at how soft Brier's skin was on his fingertips. Then he leaned in and stared at the boy's pink lips. Thinking how much he'd like to see for himself just how supple they were. Thinking how different he and the prince were, and why fate, as Brier had called it, brought them together. Roland swallowed. At that moment, a trickle of heat slid down his body and settled in his groin.

"Roland…." Brier whispered, smile long vanished. Brier did not pull away, but there was panic and uncertainty in his eyes.

What are you doing?

Roland removed his hands from Brier's flushed cheeks when reason tugged at the back of his head.

"Finish your bread and rest," Roland told Brier quietly. He rolled over to dim the oil lamp in their tent.

And what the hell was that?

He lay down on the blanket with his heart pounding. He knew exactly what that was, and he hadn't felt it in years.

Desire.

Brier finished the last piece of bread, wrapped up in the wool blanket, twisted away from the oil lamp, and did not say another word. Roland waited until he heard the gentle rhythm of Brier's breath before he turned and watched the prince sleep. Roland exhaled deeply to cool his head, wishing he had a strong ale instead.

CHAPTER 5
AIRE

THE NEXT morning did not look much better than yestereve. Brier mounted his horse and drank in the black clouds setting behind the dense trees. The Black Forest. It was the first time Brier had ever seen it since he'd never ventured this far north, but the gravity of its beauty pulled him in like a heavy current. What little sun they had peeked through the open crevices of the tall larch trees. Unlike Brier's gardens filled with chirping birds, buzzing insects, and the occasional mew of a stray cat, the Black Forest was silent, like the trees took a collective inhale of breath. Unnerving as it was, Brier still could not look away. This was his home for the next year. He was really leaving his world in Avenough behind. The reality was harsh and sobering.

The fog that covered the entrance to the forest instantly dissipated when he and Frieling treaded into the trees' coverage; Brier felt as though he stepped under the water, and the muffled sound gave him a feeling of claustrophobia.

"Why is it so quiet here?" Brier asked, an invisible weight pressing down on him.

"It is not quiet, little prince. That is only the forest's illusion." Brier felt a chill climb up his back.

"Why would the forest want to deceive us?"

"There are people who believe that this forest has a magical casting over it," Roland mused. "The creatures here are often solitary and rarely seen by the noninhabitants. Some of the Southerners come to Aire under the impression they will find something." Roland stopped walking and turned his head slowly to the east. Brier followed his gaze to the now risen sun.

"And do they?"

"Shh. Listen." Roland held his arm up suddenly. Brier held his breath. He strained his ears to ascertain what the other had heard, but he could only recognize his quickened heartbeat. Roland took two steps. The leather stomping the dried leaves made a rustling instead of the crunching Brier expected.

"Wha—what is it—"

"Shh." Roland hushed him again, but this time Brier felt slightly annoyed. He had a right mind to dismount Frieling and see for himself what Roland was listening for, but then he no longer needed to.

"Awooooooo!"

A piercing howl made Brier's ears ring. He looked up with a pained expression when he realized Roland had made the sound.

"Care to explain to me what you are doing!" Brier's alarmed voice echoed.

"Saying hello to a friend," Roland answered, smiling.

Brier searched his surroundings. Even if a person concealed themselves, they would not be able to hide so well. Unless they were invisible. Brier whipped his head to the direction Roland had called. "There is no one here… save for me. And Frieling."

"I assure you, 'twas not at you, and definitely not at your prancing pony."

Brier scoffed before he kicked the sides of Frieling to move him forward. The horse walked a total of three steps before he stopped, and Brier could feel him tense. In the next instant, he heard heavy paws pummeling the ground at a rapid pace. At first he thought Frieling stomped into the dirt, but then he saw black fur whip past him like a shadow. One second later and Roland was on his back being mauled by an enormous wolf. Frieling raised up on his hind legs, caught between agitation and fear.

"*Ai*!" Roland screamed out. Brier's eyes widened, and he tried to hold Frieling steady enough to help his master. The horse continued to thrash. At this rate Roland would be dead in seconds.

"Veti! You mongrel!"

Except…. Roland wasn't screaming out in pain. Brier finally calmed Frieling enough to see the wolf licking the man's face affectionately.

Roland laughed. "Let me breathe, idiot!" he yelled, pushing the creature off of him with some difficulty. The wolf finally let up, and Roland righted himself once more.

"You know this creature?" Brier asked, failing to keep his voice steady.

Roland gave Brier a roguish grin before he rubbed the black wolf's head. "He's been following us for a while." Frieling shook his mane, disgruntled, and Brier rubbed the top of the horse's head to soothe him. "Did I frighten you?"

"I should say so! By gods I thought you were—I thought that creature had—" Brier could not form proper words through his exasperation and fear. If the wolf snatched Roland away from him, then where would he be? But before Brier could answer his own question, he realized Roland was laughing and whole. The relief Brier felt infuriated him even more.

"I suppose you have never read the tale of the boy who cried wolf," Brier snapped as they began to move.

"I have. Although, calling someone my age a boy is more than a stretch."

"You could have truly been in danger, and then where would you be?"

"Dead I suppose," Roland answered, shrugging. He patted the wolf's head with such familiarity one would think they were master and pet.

"You can shrug your life away so easily?" Brier asked, dubious.

Roland turned toward him deliberately and stopped walking. "All men die someday. Verily, by all accounts I should have died years ago. When it is my time, I will go without a fuss."

Brier frowned at his instructor's nonchalance and pursed his lips. "If it is all the same, then I would rather you not die with me by your side."

"Do you hear that, Veti? Our future king was worried." Roland folded his arms across his chest. "Does this mean you've taken a liking to me after all, little prince?"

Brier flushed up to his ears, and he held Frieling's reins tighter. "If you want to throw your life away, that's fine, but your trick made Frieling almost buck me off. I don't plan to die in this forest on account of your games."

"Is that a yes, then?"

Brier lifted his head defiantly before he strode in front. Roland was his master. Whether he liked the man or not held no bearing on his future. If he said yes, he felt as though he'd reveal more than just a predilection for Roland's company, and saying no seemed like bad form, especially since Roland had saved his life. Silence was best, Brier decided, and he directed Frieling forward without another word. They walked for hours through the forest with the great black wolf for company. Brier had to admit he felt safer in the overgrown dog's company, but he was still miffed. He tried to convince himself it was because of the trick, but Brier knew it was not true. After all, that was the nature of their relationship. He'd grown accustomed to Roland's caustic personality and constant attempts to bait Brier. In fact, even he tried his hand, poking fun at Roland's sluggish gait when he was not on horseback and teasing Roland about the time he spent primping his black beard. Perhaps tension over a mere jest was unfounded, but the true reason for Brier's discomfort was no joke.

Last night....

Last night they'd lain with the rain pattering against the enclosed, dark tent. Roland's heavy hands made him feel secure when he could not shake the chills and anxiety. But then something strange happened. His master leaned in, and Brier felt the warmth of Roland's breath on his upper lip, a sensation that made his entirety melt. He lost himself in blue eyes that seemed cavernous. Something stirred, like a feather that tickled his gut. "Roland...." Brier had called the man's name aloud because he could not think of anything else to say when his chest felt tight enough to combust. He just wanted Roland's hands off him or on him more. Brier could not really decide even now. Roland released him and Brier felt the air rising in his lungs, but a sense of longing rose with it. The worst thing was that Brier did not know what he was yearning for.

It was dusk when Brier saw the first signs of a path, and a small cabin came into view shortly afterward. To Brier it looked like the shed that the stableboy kept the spare saddles in, but he could see the shape of a house more distinctly as they came closer, and a goodly portion of the home was hidden by shrubbery and overgrown vines. The cabin would be difficult to find if one did not know the exact location since the greenery made the home blend in to the cluster of trees. The paint had shaved off on the corners, replaced by worn wood and the weathered stone of the foundation. All in all, Brier could not remember living in such modest quarters, and yet, the home had a warmth he could not deny.

It was perfect. All Brier could do was grin. So happy was he to see the place that they'd journeyed so long to reach. Roland did not speak, but Brier thought he noticed more speed in the man's footsteps as he walked.

After they'd put Frieling away in the barn adjacent to the cottage, Brier followed Roland and Veti into the house. From the outside, the cabin looked worn and dank, but when Roland lit the candle, Brier's eyes lit with it. As he suspected, the inside was a lot larger than what the outside projected. The entryway was wide enough to fit two men Roland's size. The ceilings were as high as a small temple, arched into a perfect half circle and carved intricately with patterns of lacewing and vines. The floors were wooden and thick like aged pine trees, stained and placed skillfully into neat rows. Brier went to the kitchen and touched the large dining table that sat in the middle of the room. The surface was so smooth on his fingertips, he thought that it must be marble but upon further inspection discovered it was polished stone. He made his way to the living room next and found new things to stimulate his curiosity. He lounged on the large sofa near the hearth and stretched out into the feathered cushions. Roland's couch was softer than Brier's bed at the palace, but before he could rest, his eye caught something that shimmered in the rough candlelight.

Brier stood up fully and walked over to stand in front of a mirror. The frame to encase the glass had the design of a silver snake, the mouth starting at the top and the long tail winding around the entirety. He stared into the mirror for a long while, losing himself in the leafy hue of his own eyes. Were they always so green, he wondered, feeling suddenly light-headed. However, when Brier focused his eyes, he could not see his own reflection at all, but the reflection of his stepmother staring back at him. Black eyes bore into his green. Unveiled malice etched over what appeared to be her laughing face. Terror flooded through him, and he inhaled and held his breath. How could she have followed him this far? Here, where he thought he was safe from her villainy. Brier shook his head. Surely the mirror was designed to trick the onlooker, mayhap a liquid mirage or a trick of the light. This was Roland's house after all. Brier reached up to expose the mirror for the gag it most certainly was, but the glass was solid to the touch. "How is this possible?"

"How is what possible?"

Brier nearly shrieked when he saw Roland's image staring down at him.

"Are you so fascinated with a mirror? Surely you have them at the palace."

"Yes, but…." Brier started to explain that he did not only see his reflection in the mirror, but then he realized how foolish that would have sounded to Roland. Especially since it seemed his exhaustion was causing him to hallucinate. For now, when Brier looked he could see himself clearly: red hair unkempt, boots muddied and worn, dirtier than he'd ever been in his nineteen years. "Never mind," he whispered and resumed his spot on the couch.

"I know it is nothing like the palace, but it will grow on you," Roland told him, lighting a fire. Brier leaned his head back and let out a deep yawn. The fire heated the small space almost instantly, so unlike the palace where they needed multiple fireplaces and steam pots for one room. No palace guards lurking around every corner to watch him here. So different were the stone pillars and marble floors of the great halls, the stumps where trees once lived, and the wrought-iron gates and barred windows to keep Brier in. Not so here. From wooden sculptures of sparrows, warm paintings of a valley in full bloom, and the black wolf splayed and asleep on a large hearth rug, the clock standing by the mantle ticking with a pendulum swinging, and the fur throw hanging on the back of the couch for comfort and added warmth. Roland was right. The cabin was nothing like the palace.

Brier traced his fingertips against the lithographed wood on the arm of the sofa. In the corner sat a piano with a chair large enough to fit Roland. Furnishings of every size littered the parlor, sanded and stained.

"This is stunning." The wall held a gigantic shield with a branded *X*. Carved into the alderwood was the gods' tree of life.

"The tree of life," Roland answered quietly. "It was my father's."

But of course, Brier recognized the shield immediately. According to the gospels, all life began at the ancient tree of Anistra. It was said that when men passed on to the afterlife, they returned to its roots. Everyone, peasant or royal, child or elder, sick or well, knew the story of the tree of life, and those pious enough would visit Sasel, allied territory north of Lirend where the tree supposedly sat, to worship and praise.

"Did he make all of this?" He turned to Roland, bemused.

"Most of it," Roland answered as he took off his heavy cloak and gestured for Brier to do the same. "Some of the pieces are my own."

"A bit skilled for a huntsman," Brier noted.

"My father was a carpenter. He taught wood carving, so he taught it to me and my brother as well."

Brier blinked and stared at Roland curiously. "Are you a Secborn?"

"I am an Einborn."

"Then how did you come to be a huntsman?"

Roland cut his eye toward Brier as he hung up their coats. "Where I am from, we did not adhere to Lirend's abominable law of passage." Under the law of passage, no firstborn son could leave his father's profession without expressly stated leave from the courts of his fief. Therefore, if one's father was a politician, his firstborn son was a politician too. Brier's father was the great and loved King Braedon Snow.

"Abominable?" Brier looked stricken. "Surely you jest."

"The law of passage has made it nearly impossible for the peasants in Lirend to rise from their stations."

"My line enacted that law," Brier replied pointedly.

"Aye, and as the future king, you should know the repercussions of such classism."

Lirend was right on the border of the ocean, a sovereign state in its own right, made up of ten small fiefs, including Avenough. The country itself was not at all big, but rich from hundreds of years of cultivating its natural resources: iron, gold, and colorful diamonds indigenous only to Lirend called colur gems. In the days before the dictated law, many children left their parents to pursue an interest in the colur gem mines and free-trade market. The result was that their parents and the business died out. Not so important were the blacksmiths and the bakers, but the farmers had no one to take over when they grew too old to plow the land. When the farming population dwindled down to less than 20 percent, Théoden Snow enacted a law to put an end to the fleeing youth.

"If a son does not do his 'duty,' he faces more than treason; his line is branded as ruinous. It is common knowledge in Lirend that children inherit the consequences of their parents' actions. Many would rather die than beset their children with such a burden."

"'Tis not a matter of classicism, but survival," Brier refuted, offended by Roland's claim. "What would we do if the peasants abandoned their post? Avenough cannot afford to let people just do as they wish on whim. There must be order." Brier did not put on airs of his experience in ruling, but the importance of order and loyalty from his citizens had been thrust upon him since birth.

"Perhaps if you treated them as more than servants, they would cherish their stations and stay. As it stands the working class generate the coin, but see none of the return."

Brier considered the man's words. He knew little of the in-depth tax brackets and the intricate ways by which the crown generated coin. He'd lived in luxury the entirety of his life but never questioned the lives of his citizens beyond his lessons in economy. However, if there was strife in the lower class, Brier could blame no one but the citizens who voted their representatives to the court.

"If there is such suffering as you say, Master Roland, then the people should take your claim to their fief lords and representatives."

"That they should be imprisoned for treason?"

"That they may speak on behalf of their own interest." That was the purpose of a representative regime. In order to avoid revolts and unrest in the country, the fief lords and appointed citizens were responsible for their own people.

"Forgive me, Prince Snow, but spare me your rhetoric. You expect a nobleman to challenge the law of passage?"

"Most certainly, on behalf of their working class. Is that not the purpose of representation?"

"Your naivety would be sweet were it not so crass," Roland scoffed. Brier bristled at his insult. "Most nobles do not care, and the other half are discouraged by the political retribution. Speak to other nobles on the behalf of peasants? How can they when their reputations depend on it? The ones who enter by vote are little more than puppets for the fiefs they serve." Roland sighed and sat beside him on the couch. "Verily, little prince, I am no Aurelian. I do not live in Avenough. I cannot speak about the Prolit and Burges save for what I've seen when I am granted permission to enter Avenough for jobs. But anyone who is not blind can see your low class suffers."

"I am not blind." Brier shifted uncomfortably.

"Then you must see the error in your ways."

"Mayhap...." Hate as he'd like to admit it, he'd never thought of the political implications to challenging fief lords. "But this is all for nothing since I can do nothing to change it," Brier muttered.

"If not you, then who? Are you not the future king?" Roland asked, accusation ripe in his tone.

"Queen Evelyn despises me, and the Aurelians barely know me, save for what she has told them about me." His forced absence in court did more to ruin his standing than any rumors could.

"Then get the people on your side."

"How? I have little experience, and I haven't even reached my majority," Brier sighed out. "Why should they listen to me?"

"The people will listen to who unlocks the door. Not those who claim to hold the key."

Brier stared at the man, confused. He always hated when Marietta would speak in riddles. "What do you mean?"

"I mean it is impossible to be perfect, Brier. You won't do a good job if you're too focused on proving yourself to others. You are the king, not Queen Evelyn. You were born to rule by your blood." Brier fell into a despondent silence. More and more he questioned that very fact, but whether it was true or not did not rightly matter. At length, he thought of something else the huntsman had disclosed and decided to probe the man more about that instead.

"These men you said will help with my training...," Brier whispered.

"Aye. The Ceve guild."

"Yes, Ceve. What is that?"

"When we came from Thenia, we had no means of protection in Aire. The Ceve guild banded and avowed their allegiance to me."

"But what does the Ceve guild do?"

"We fulfill... unsavory Aurelian contracts."

"Unsavory?" Brier blinked. "You mean criminal activity?"

"If necessary." Brier blinked again before he widened his eyes. "I swore to protect our people by whatever means necessary. When Thenians first came to Lirend, we signed a contract that indebted us to you Aurelians, but we knew nothing of your law of passage." Roland's jaw tightened. "We've regretted it ever since."

"Why don't you just leave if you hate it here so much?" Brier pursed his lips.

"We've tried. Several times. We even aided The Divine Three in the hopes they would win during the great wars. Of course that was before Lirend joined the alliance."

"Then you've gone against Lirend before in combat?"

Roland stared at him blankly. "In the past we've had altercations with the crown, but it's been years since blood was shed on either side. We don't have the manpower to sustain ourselves."

"Naturally. Lirend's armies have grown since the great wars. Most Aurelians don't even serve in the military anymore."

"That is because Aurelians use *my* people's labor in payment for land that we don't want. Land that we sustain, and yet, are unable to leave freely."

"Mayhap." Brier considered Roland's words. "But where would you go if you left Aire?"

"Anywhere but here. Alone where I can die in peace."

"Are you so eager to die, Master Roland?" Brier raised his brow.

"I do what I must to survive," he answered simply.

"And these men of the guild.... You trust them?"

"With my life." Roland grinned as he stood from the couch. "Now have you quenched your thirst for knowledge this eve?"

"Mm... may I ask you something else?"

"Go ahead, little prince."

"You said they avowed themselves to you and no other, but why is that, Master? You are a huntsman here in Aire, but what job did you do in Thenia?" Roland stared at him with a mix of confusion and awe. Brier did not know what spurred that kind of reaction, but he wished immediately he had not asked the huntsman about his past. "Sorry, Master Roland. I did not mean to pry overmuch."

"No. It's fine," Roland replied, though Brier could sense his hesitancy. "Someday I will tell you, little prince. But for now that is enough talk of politics. I suspect you are hungry and exhausted." Roland patted his head once and walked toward the kitchen once more.

Roland cooked a pot of stew from the leftover rabbit he'd caught earlier in the day. Veti was surprisingly docile indoors, and he lay under Roland's chair as the two men ate in silence. It'd been weeks since Brier sat at a table, and he felt rather out of sorts. Marietta's strict tableside manner contrasted with Roland's lack of decorum. So while Brier spooned the stew slowly, trying hard not to spill on his already dirtied jacket, Roland ate quickly and used his bread to mop the remainder of the soup in his bowl.

After they ate, Roland showed him to the bathroom where Brier was surprised to find a tub. It was similar to his palace suite's in size, though without running water, and certainly less embellishment. Roland filled the tub up with water, with fire stones heating the tub from below. Brier waited until it was warm enough to enter. Then he closed his eyes and sank to his chin.

"Thank the gods for this." It'd been almost a month since he'd taken a proper bath. Some part of him still could not believe this would be his home for the next year, and what would Roland teach him? Mayhap how to carve such beautiful furnishings or how to cook a stew so delectable it could make Roland's mouth water. Or maybe he'd teach Brier how to use that crossbow he kept or the sword he observed Roland oft polish. All Brier knew was that he'd be with Roland. The thought made the tickling sensation in his gut return. The scars on his skin glowed gold, but this time Brier did not panic.

Calm your bristle.... Brier sang to himself. The sweet melody coaxed him to calm and Brier stood out of the tub.

Why was he so happy in Roland's presence anyway? There was nothing untoward between them, but every time Brier stared into his eyes, a strong desire to avoid Roland Archer rose within him.

Knock knock.

Brier jumped behind the door just in time to avoid Roland stepping into the restroom and holding a towel.

"Are you here?"

Brier shut his eyes, cursing under his breath. "Yes… I'm here behind the door." The scars on his skin returned to their normal silver, and he was grateful for that. He would not be able to hide if they glowed. Roland turned to look at him, and Brier held the door tighter. "Is there something you need, Roland?"

"I was just… bringing you a towel."

"Oh. Thank you. Please just leave it by the tub."

"Is everything all right—"

"Fine."

Roland looked as though he was going to pull the door, and Brier squeezed the knob tighter.

Gods.... Brier swore he could hear his heart thudding.

"Are you sure you're all right?"

Brier listened, abashed from the man's concerned tone, but he still could not show himself. Roland was the first nonservant who did not shun him for his appearance, but Brier was sure his scars would repulse him. Past experiences had taught him that. "All is well. I assure you."

"All right. I've made up the couch for you."

"I'll be out soon." Brier heard Roland's feet creaking the wood, but then Roland stopped once more.

"One more thing… I'm sorry for not telling you about Veti. The truth is I did not expect him to bolt out like that." Brier's eyes shot open. He was so tired when they arrived, and so apprehensive now, that he'd completely forgotten about their earlier rift. "'Twas not my intention to trick you, Brier." The man calling him by his actual name compounded his sincerity.

"Thank you…." When Brier was sure Roland was gone, he shut the door and leaned his forehead against it. Anything had to be better than this, recoiling with humiliation and hiding like a shy maiden. In the silence, he could hear how hard his heart was beating. He wiped his face and realized his palms were damp. Mayhap Aire really was a place of dark magic or mayhap he'd sat in the tub too long. All he knew was that his body felt hot with shame and something else he could not yet describe. "What spell is on me?" Brier whispered, swallowing hard.

"IS HE still sleeping all righ'?"

"Don't know. What time is it?"

"Almost noon, I hope he's all right."

"I'd say he's got the right idea."

"He's all right. Give him some room."

"What do you expect from an Aurelian?"

WHEN BRIER woke he felt something wet and rough on his cheek. He remembered his younger days, sleeping in the green pastures, among the flowers and the bees buzzing. The sun setting on his face, burning his pale skin, spotty freckles, and flame red hair. Frieling would come when the sun would set too low and lick his face. Brier would smile, lift up his scrawny arms from the greenage, and stroke his silky mane. He extended his hand in real time, but instead of silky blond hair, he felt a rough collar and thick fur.

"Veti!" Brier heard Roland's gruff voice, and his eyes shot open to Veti's black. The wolf licked his face once more for good measure and pattered away as seven sets of eyes took the wolf's place. He shot up off of the couch, wide-eyed and cautious. Of the seven, he recognized one, and yet, most of the men were smiling at him expectantly.

"Good morning." Roland handed Brier a towel. "Sorry about that. Veti gets a little lively in the morning." He did not speak, but clenched his jaw and held the fur blanket more firmly.

"He said good morning," an older man with gray-black hair and dark eyes grumbled. He folded his arms and glared at him as though Brier's silence was a personal affront.

"Can't ya talk?" a huge man asked. Brier's mouth fell open at his size, but he quickly closed it when he heard another scolding voice.

"Of course he can talk, you idiot," a younger man said. He was a few years older than Brier with a long brunet ponytail down his back.

"All right, you two." Brier darted his gaze to a silvery blond who bowed toward him. Of all of the men, including Roland, his face was the kindest and gentlest. "Sorry we scared you, Your Grace." The man dipped his head. "It has been a moment since these lugs have been in the company of an Aurelian, leastways a prince."

"That…." Brier's voice squeaked when he tried to find it. "That is all right. You need not bow to me." Brier shook his head and tried to regain his composure. He inclined his head and lowered the blanket. "I apologize for my own rudeness." He found strength in his legs and stood from the couch in front of the seven men, trying hard to look confident. "My name is Prince Brier Snow of Lirend," he proclaimed. "Please tell me your names, if you don't mind."

"Certainly not, Your Grace," the blond replied still smiling warmly. "My name is Lei, but *acai*, please call me Leighis." He pointed to the huge mountain closest to his right and continued. "This is Dur." The giant nodded. "And to his left is Caite."

"*Venur*." Caite smirked.

"To the right of me is Umhal." The mouselike man did not move or speak, but stared at Brier with one deep, hoary eye. "This is—"

"I'm Sasta." A smaller male hugged him. Brier's eyes widened once more, and he turned to Leighis for help.

"It's all right. Sasta is just a bit excited that you're finally here. We've been waiting for over a month, you see." Brier nodded as he swallowed that piece of information. No one had ever waited for him in his life.

"Of course you know your escort, Ro." Roland's half smile made Brier's heart race lightly, but he nodded anyway. "And this charming fellow"—Leighis touched the older man's thick chest lightly—"is Botcht." The man did not smile, nod, or wave. He glared at Brier with pinched eyes, as though he hated the very sight of him, and Brier quickly averted his gaze.

"It is a pleasure." Brier tried to smile. "Had Master Roland told me there would be guests, I would have woken earlier."

"Master?" Leighis quirked his head to Roland, whose face reddened.

"I told him not to call me that." Roland shrugged and walked toward the kitchen. Brier could smell something sweet cooking.

"Sure you did." Brier felt Caite's arm around his shoulder. "You're nineteen, right?" he asked with a wide grin.

"Yes." Brier nodded rather shakily. Caite walked toward the kitchen, and Brier followed his guide. "I'll be twenty in the spring."

"The Aurelian prince." Caite dissected him thoroughly. "I'd heard whispers that the prince of Lirend was a sickly creature." Brier's chest tightened. It seemed the rumors of the curse on his skin had somewhat reached Aire.

"As you can see I am not sickly." Brier stared into Caite's autumn-cool hazel eyes. He noticed they were the same almond shape of Botcht's, though of a different color. And mayhap less cold?

"*Na*. You're so young and pretty, how did they ever let you go?" Caite smirked, and Brier tensed.

No. Caite's eyes were not less cold, only more distant.

"Don't tease him, Caite!" Sasta whined and yanked the man's ponytail. "You're not much older." Brier used the distraction to shrug away. "I'm twenty-six," Sasta declared. "Caite is twenty-two. And you've a horse, don't you?"

"Yes…." Brier tried to compose himself.

"What's his name?"

"Frieling." Brier could not help but smile at the man's enthusiasm. "He's a Coloured Cob." Sasta whistled and looked over at Caite, impressed.

"What's so great about that?" Caite slumped in a chair at the table.

"Only the Aurelians are allowed them. They're only bred in Lirend's capital."

"So they're worthless." Botcht ambled in and took a seat at the table. Brier frowned before turning to answer Sasta.

"He's a seasoned horse, but he's very friendly." Roland scoffed as he turned around with a large bowl of oatmeal. "To those who deserve it," Brier amended in Frieling's defense. Dur ducked, coming to join them in the kitchen. Brier then found himself in the middle of the tightly packed cookery. Heat sogged the room, and the table set the previous night was for only two. Now seven men clamored into whatever vacant seats they could find. Brier thought first of the dogs that bordered the palace's galley for meats and discarded delicacies.

Roland ladled the grain into eight empty bowls and each man swiped his own. After eating mostly meat for the past month, the sweet oatmeal tasted heavenly. Brier could smell the honey and cinnamon from the steam wafting, and his stomach gave an appreciative growl.

"Coloured Cob." Dur spoke with a mouthful of porridge. "Never seen one of those o'fore."

"Neither have I." Sasta nodded and spooned his breakfast.

"I'll let you ride him if you'd like." Brier scraped the spoon on the inside of the bowl when he realized he'd finished it. Before he could ask, Roland grabbed his bowl and ladled him a second serving. Brier peered up ready to say thanks when Dur interrupted him.

"Really?" Dur grinned.

"Not you, idiot. You'll break the damn horse," Caite told him. Brier watched the giant's grin falter, and he reached over to touch the man's wrist.

"I think it will be fine, Dur." Caite's eyes slid toward him, and Brier smirked. Leighis snorted at their childlike interaction.

"No one's riding anything until you lumps help me with the firewood," Roland cut in.

"But—Rolande!" Sasta whined.

"No buts. Got twenty orders while I was away."

"And probably missed twenty more," Botcht added. Brier watched Roland tense before he agreed.

"Exactly. All the more reason for us to get a move on it."

"Aye," Caite huffed out. "But when do we get to train the Aurelian?" Brier began clearing the bowls off the table.

"When the Aurelian is ready." Roland used the hand pump to fill the sink. Brier grabbed a copper rag and began to clean the dishes. A strange sense of longing overwhelmed him. The Aurelian. It was much better than creature or abomination, but Brier hadn't realized he'd gotten used to Roland calling him little prince. Brier peered up to a rift in the wood where a window might be. He could see no sunlight, only the cloak of fog and the mere beginnings of daybreak.

CHAPTER 6
THE CIRCLE SQUARE

THOUGH ROLAND told Caite Brier should train when he was ready, several weeks passed, and Brier had not touched the hilt of a sword, bow, nor arrow. Instead, his master gave him menial tasks. Washing clothes, gathering water, tending to the landscape, and the most wretched task, chopping firewood like Dur, Sasta, and Caite, the youngest of the guild. Brier's arms tired quickly, and by the end of it, he looked like he'd taken the ax to himself instead of the hearty logs. More than once Brier swung the ax wildly and without care, and his impatience often times rendered the wood uneven, and thereby useless.

Chop!

"Stand up straight!"

Chop!

Today he chopped under the tutelage, or rather scrutiny, of Botcht Everdane. Worst tempered of the seven in the Ceve guild.

Chop!

"You're putting too much weight on the swing!" Botcht came over to correct Brier's stance for the third time that day. He could hold it well enough, but when he swung he lost the grip and teetered forward.

"I'm trying to hold it!" Brier spat back, but the ax was too heavy for Brier's thin arms.

"Try harder!" Botcht bellowed. Brier had the urge to throw the ax at him.

"*L' tyva el*?" A throaty voice broke through their squabbling. Brier clung to it like a child lost in Avenough's square. "Everything all right?"

"No," Brier answered. "I'm trying as best as I can, but I can't chop the wood perfect enough for Botcht!"

"The palace has made him flimsy in form and airheaded in concentration. If you want to pamper him go right ahead, Rolande. I'm not about to repeat myself more than once!" Botcht stomped away through the dirt, and Brier tightened his jaw. The worst part was that he knew the man's words held truth.

"Why does he have to be such a—such a—"

"Such a horse's ass?" Roland asked.

"Yes!" Brier affirmed, though he did not repeat the imprecation.

"Come on, then." Roland nudged his chin suggestively. "Let's see what you've got." Brier sagged the ax in his arms and sliced down with preemptive dismay.

Chop!

The wood splintered into several pieces. He cursed under his breath, and Roland gripped the handle of the ax from him securely.

"Hmm… I see." Roland gazed at him with less malice than Botcht, but equal consideration. "Perhaps you need a break from your toiling," Roland offered. He rounded on his master at once with nods and an appreciative smile. They had not left the cabin since he'd arrived, save for the trips to the river, and he despised the ax more than Botcht.

"Yes, yes, please anything!"

Roland made a motion to the cart that Sasta and Caite readied. "The boys are going out to sell the firewood in the Square. It's only a quarter hour ride. Would you like to join them on the path?"

"Oh yes!" Brier nearly burst at the thought of a day away from chopping wood. "Just let me wash and get changed."

FOR ALL his stubbornness, Brier had to admit the ax had bested him once more. He hated the confounded thing, and hated Botcht for the man's unrelenting cold stare. Where Botcht was concerned, he failed in everything. Roland tried to ease him along, but Brier could tell his patience wore thin from his lack of skill in the domestic capacity. For Brier, he did not understand why his master continued to employ him in the jobs to begin with. Verily, he was more suited to sell, as his master had today suggested. And when was Roland planning to actually train him? When was Roland going to bestow "everything he knew" on him? And what was the extent of that knowledge?

When they rode out to the village square, Brier bounced in his seat. They passed straight through the Black Forest, which led them to an actual trail fit for riding. Brier suspected this road merged onto a path that led to a safer route to Avenough, but instead of traveling around the mountains, Roland preferred to journey straight over them.

They reached the merchant square in short time, or what Brier could only ordain in name a circle. Unlike the square in Avenough, where hundreds of stores encircled a most magnificent fountain, Aire's hub only had about twenty stores, and they all sold merchant ware; fabric, flowers, slate wood, weapons, mirrors, and trinkets. Brier came upon a beauteous woman who had wildflowers for sale. He smiled at her when she curtsied low and offered him a flower with a sly wink. Then he wished he'd packed some coin to buy them all.

The circle had a few stone paths, but mostly clayed dirt to walk on. The stores themselves resembled the stands back in Avenough. Instead of building actual fronts, which they could only use a few months out of the year due to Aire's ghastly temperatures, they used their carts to haul their wares instead. That is save for one, a large stone building along the open space, sat apart like abandoned property. Indeed, the only thing that set Aire's square beside Avenough's was the populace, so overrun with customers that Brier could barely breathe in the stuffiness.

Sasta, Caite, and he unloaded the cart hastily as the customers lined up to buy firewood. They used Lirend's coin, but Brier suspected things cost less here than they did in Avenough. More importantly, the money in Aire did not mean the same as money in Avenough. In Avenough one might shave off a few coins from something if the merchant was in a haggling mood, but here in Aire, bartering was the trade. How much could one give, without actually giving, for a week's supply of firewood? Brier quickly found out, as person upon person came to the cart trading for one thing or another. At first Brier felt put off by the heated exchanges Sasta and Caite barreled into, but eventually Brier found the amusement in them. By lunch they'd sold half their stock, and Brier's pride heightened if only a smidgen.

When they'd just sat down to rest, Brier saw a man coming over to their cart. He assured Caite and Sasta before he went to greet the patron.

"Good afternoon." Brier tried not to sound too proper. The man did not look as base as the rest of the Xenothians, but nowhere did he come close to matching the pomp of Avenough's Aurelians.

"Good afternoon," the man said and eyed him curiously. Brier tried to discern the man's needs as Sasta had taught him by watching the man's line of vision on their wares. Unfortunately he had not looked at the firewood once but kept fixed eyes on Brier.

"May I help you?" Brier decided to ask. Though he always felt discomfited when people stared overlong, a condition of his upbringing, he did not want the sale to go to waste.

"Yes, indeed you may." The patron grinned. "I would like to buy all of your remaining firewood." Brier blinked before he grinned, delighted.

"Of course, of course." He calculated the amount quickly. There were thirty-five pieces left. At 5G each that was 175G. "I can have my comrades load it up for you if you'd like."

"Aye yes." The man continued to stare. "But I wonder, what cover fee *Nan* is." Brier frowned at the unfamiliar last word, but more at the patron's question.

"I've just told you, it is 175G." Brier faltered. "If it is too much, we can always lessen the amount of wood."

"*Na*, no amount is too much for good wood." Brier might have imagined it, but the man's words spoke of more than just wood to burn for the hearth. He eyed Sasta, who was still eating his lunch, chatting merrily with a bored-looking Caite.

"Do you want the wood or not?" Brier asked, now losing his sales charm. He began to worry the man had simply played with him, sensing his foreignness to the job, and had no intentions to buy wood at all.

"Let's go back to my cart. It'll be cheaper than a room," the man offered.

Brier paled first at the man's words, but then flushed when he realized what the man meant. Of course, he knew the basics of sexual intercourse from Marietta, but he'd never more than stoked his own pleasure. Since Brier spent most of his time indoors, he did not have the privilege of spending his lust in brothels. And even if he were free to, he wouldn't. In the first place, he did not prefer women in any capacity other than friendship, and in the second place, he loathed the thought of bedding a stranger. Furthermore, he wondered about sexual liaisons in Aire. Was it so common for men to couple with one another that they dare ask for it right on the street?

Brier flushed again then at his own foolishness. How could he detest something he'd never experienced? He'd never even had his first kiss.

"I'm sorry, but I am not interested," Brier hastily told him. "I don't know what gave you that idea."

"You flounced around well enough." The man let out a boorish laugh, and Brier colored even further. Flouncing the man had called it. Brier only conducted himself in a manner fitting of a prince, not some lowborn Xenothian arse.

"I'm sorry if you took my general way as flirtatious, but I assure you, that was not my intention. I'm selling firewood. Nothing more."

"Come on, I know Rolande has you up to it." The sound of his master's name almost burned through him.

"Roland?" Brier inquired. "What's this have to do with Master Roland?"

"Oh? Master Roland is it he likes to be called?" The men flashed Brier a bawdy grin. "Well, I can be a *Master* too, you know." The man grabbed Brier's bicep and pulled him close. "Don't worry. You'll feel good too, I promise." Brier struggled to unhand himself from the larger male's grasp, but his squirming did nothing to free him. He wanted to call out, but the thought of screaming for help in a square full of Xenothians mortified him.

"Let go of me, you filthy scab." Brier wrestled through the man's taut grip.

"Not until I've gotten my money's worth."

"I already told you, I'm not for sale!" Brier groaned but he could feel himself being dragged off from the cart. He looked over to call for Caite and Sasta, but they'd vanished from his sight.

"Let me go! Hel—"

"Shut up! Stop making such a fuss!" The man held his mouth. Brier watched as the citizens looked at them in alarm. Some of the men looked troubled, but hesitant to actually stop the exchange. There were no laws in Aire save for one unspoken: survive.

Brier gritted his teeth when he realized no one would come to help him. He resolved himself to struggle as much as possible, though, and bucked and kicked through the strenuous hold.

"Ngh!" Brier place a well-aimed kick to the man's shin, and he felt the hold loosen.

"You little—" A hard slap across his face made Brier's ears ring, and he fell to the ground with a thud. He coughed when he tasted blood in his mouth. Tears crept into his eyes from the sheer force at which he'd been struck. "You capital trash! Don't you ever lay your hands on me again!" The man raised his hand, and Brier flinched, but this time he need not have.

"What the fuck are you doing, Ganel?" Umhal's raspy voice spat.

"Umhal!" the man barked. "Since when did Rolande employ such hardheaded shits? This little trull is playing hard to get!"

"Your pardon, Ganel. In the first place he is not a trull, but an Aurelian. Rolande's student," Umhal whispered.

Ganel paled when Umhal called his master's name. Brier took some comfort in the man's obvious discomfort. "But then, why does he offer himself to me like a whore?" He felt Umhal's cold stare.

"I did not!" Brier found strength through his humiliation and stood with his chest puffed. "I merely tried to sell him firewood!" He pointed at the man. "He was the one who tried to proposition me!"

"Because I thought he was using that as a cover!" Ganel argued. "By the gods, didn't Rolande tell him what else goes on in this market?" Brier suddenly inhaled at the man's words.

"Rolande often times does not think. Sending a boy like this one to the market is akin to selling fresh meat," Umhal replied.

It all made sense now. The carts with women selling wares like weapons and the like. Of course, some men probably did buy weapons, but Brier saw too many go into the one building that stood alone in Aire's merchant square. Unmarked. Full. And likely full of whores. Brier almost hurled at the thought.

Umhal released Ganel's arm but Brier wished he hadn't. Now he tensed once more, vulnerable with Ganel free to touch him. Umhal turned his blind eye toward Brier. Brier immediately averted his gaze.

"Look, I'm sorry about all this." The man bowed in what Brier assumed was deference to Umhal. He scampered off before Umhal acknowledged him, cowering toward the center of the Square.

"What's going on?" Sasta asked when he came back to the cart. "Haah!" The man held his mouth, ran over to Brier, and touched his bruised cheek. "What's—what's happened to you!"

"He ran into Ganel," Umhal, answered still eyeing Brier. Brier tried not to show Sasta his face, but the man nearly toppled him over when he'd run toward him.

"Ganel?" Sasta frowned. "By the gods, you don't mean he-he thought Brier was a—"

"A whore," Umhal said in a monotone.

"How are we so sure he isn't?" Caite snorted.

"I'm not!" Brier roared.

"Regardless, you two should have kept your eyes on him."

"We only went to the bathroom," Sasta replied, suddenly forlorn. "I didn't realize. I'm—I'm sorry—"

"It's not our fault! He told us he was okay!"

"Nevertheless Rolande will not be pleased. He trusted you to watch him. Caitenia," Umhal uttered, tone icy.

Caite flicked an irate eye to Brier before he lowered his head and whispered, "Aye. He did. I apologize for my negligence."

"Save your apologies for Rolande."

"It's not their fault!" Brier's voice rose over Umhal's in defense. "Had Roland told me what this place was, I would never have come!"

"He saw no need to divulge information not relevant to the task at hand. An error he oftentimes commits." Brier gazed into the man's unseeing eye and despite the fair weather, a shiver ran up his spine. "Still I admit my surprise. I did not think the prince of Lirend would be so easily conquered." Rather than showing disdain, Umhal's mouth curled into an amused smile. "Let's go back," the man whispered and seemed to glide away. Caite and Sasta loaded the remainder of the wood, and they headed back to Roland's cabin in the Black Forest.

IF BRIER thought Umhal had come down hard on Sasta and Caite, Roland outdid the precedent. The man swelled before he screamed a slew of profanities in Thenian. He called Caite an idiot and chastised Sasta for incompetence. Brier had never seen his master so angry or commanding.

"Don't ever let him out of your sight again!"

"Forgive me, Rolande," Sasta whispered when Roland had finished his rant. He lowered his head, clearly ashamed at his own failure.

"I apologize, Rolande," Caite gritted through his teeth. Brier avoided Caite's mutinous gaze. It was his fault Roland berated them, and Brier could only watch with pity. Yet again he showed he was no match for anyone. Not even a lowly patron.

Brier sighed out. His cheek burned from Ganel's slap, but his heart practically ached with his own worthlessness. Now he really did feel the sting of a hard day's work.

After Caite and Sasta left the cabin, shoulders slack and faces full of melancholy, Roland stood and Brier watched him gather his things for bed. They'd eaten in almost silence. Then afterward Roland gave his underlings a monumental tongue-lashing. Brier did not know which one felt worse. The fact that Roland did not think him capable of protecting himself, or the reality that he could not.

Brier laid his cheek on the cool table base and sighed out. Would Sasta hate him now? Or Caite, who never truly took to him? He was sure Botcht would have quite a few words about his own inability to protect himself against naught but a whore seeker.

"Do not worry overmuch." Brier felt gentle hands in his hair. He closed his eyes and wished they did not calm his spirit so effortlessly.

"It is not that I worry for myself. I only feel bad for Sasta and Caite. They should not take what should be my own lashing."

"I told them to watch you. If Umhal hadn't kept his eye on you, you might have gotten hurt. They failed in their task."

"Because I didn't call for their help earlier," Brier admitted.

"The Square is littered with men like Ganel, who search for companionship. Caite and Sasta know this and yet they did not make you a priority. I trusted them with your care. That is why they are being punished."

"You were worried about me?" Brier suddenly asked. The man did not speak but Brier could feel Roland's gaze. "Ganel…." Brier continued to fill the dead space. "He thought you put me up to sell."

"I would never."

"Do you sell others?" Brier questioned. Roland paused before he answered.

"We sell firewood in the Square. Ganel might be remembering the days when we were young. I visited the brothels quite often. Sometimes our tastes would overlap."

"But not anymore?"

"*Na*, little prince," Roland assured him. "Not for a very long time." Brier exhaled anxiety he did not even realize he'd held. Why did it matter to him what

Roland did? Or who the man coupled with? If he wanted to lay with whores, it was his own prerogative.

"Mm…." But that was a lie. He did not want Roland to lay with anyone… but him.

"I think it's time for bed." Roland's hand slid away from Brier's head.

"Just a little longer?" Brier held his master's hand firmly. "I don't want to be alone right now."

"Tell me." Roland's husky voice permeated the air. "Why didn't you call to Caite and Sasta for help?"

"Because…." Umhal had seen it in the stars. Ganel had conquered him. "It made me feel helpless. Ganel had his hands on me, and I wanted to fight back, but I didn't know how. I wanted to defend myself, but I couldn't." Brier shook his head. "I just felt… useless."

"You are not useless, Brier. You are the prince of Lirend. True, you lack some skills necessary, but there is a light that shines in you that you have not yet discovered."

"And you've discovered it?" Again Roland did not speak. Brier lifted his head off the table to entreat his master. "Will you teach me to fight?" he asked, gazing up at Roland from his knees. Roland held Brier's arms and stood him upright.

"I told you when we rode from Avenough. I will teach you all you need to know." Roland walked away, and Brier watched him, somehow stoked from the seriousness of Roland's voice. He might have been a jokester when it came to meaningless things, but in teaching him, Roland had focus.

"Open your hands," Roland told him. Brier gawked at his master, but did so ungrudgingly. "Now close your eyes." This request took a bit more on Brier's part. He began to suspect that Roland had decided to play a trick on him after all, but when his face still looked sincere, Brier did not fight him. "This is what you need to fight." The huntsman placed something heavy in his hand. Brier thought for a moment it might be a sword. Titillation crept up into his belly. However, when he opened his eyes, he saw only the ax he despised.

"This damn ax?" Brier asked, incredulous. "How about a sword to fend off the likes of Ganel?"

"There are no shortcuts in Aire, little prince. This is what will help you most."

"How?" he asked Roland through gritted teeth. His frustration at being made a fool of in the Square began to seep out now that Roland had reminded him of his other failure that day. "I cannot even hold it!"

"Because you must build your strength first." Roland wrapped Brier's hands around the base of the axe. "Then skill." Brier inhaled when he felt Roland's hand around his own. Roland stepped behind him and held up the ax with ease. He tried to hide the flush of his cheeks, but Brier could not hide the firmness in his breeches when Roland aligned his hips. "I will teach you how, one strike at a time."

Dear gods…. Brier prayed to help him calm. At length, Roland pulled away and Brier exhaled.

"Tomorrow we'll start from the beginning."

Brier bit his lip and nodded.

Chop! Chop! Chop!

The pale pinks, oranges, and blues commingled into a misty dusk. The mountains appeared miles onward, but Brier knew they were buried in the Black Forest with trees and strewn branches circumjacent. Brier's labored breaths merged with the hacking of Roland's heavy ax. Each time he lifted it, he felt the vibration of the metal against tree, bone, and flesh. The splinters no longer bothered his calloused hands.

Veti padded over to scrape his paw on the back of his torn jodhpurs, but Brier was so focused he hardly noticed he'd reached his last piece of firewood for the day.

"Quitting time already?" Brier rubbed the wolf's shaggy mane. He tossed the last piece of cubed wood into a dense hill by Roland's shed. He'd cut more today than he had yesterday, and considerably more than three months ago when Roland showed him how to wield an ax. His arms no longer ached the next day when he cut the firewood. He could lift two casks of water from the river a mile onward, and he'd more than perfected his fire-making technique.

The red hair stuck to his flushed cheeks as if pasted on. His face burned slightly from bitter cold, but he knew the warmth of the fire would thaw him almost instantly. Roland was inside making dinner for them, and he would scold Brier if he came in too late.

Brier's days were now spent with the guild hiking up the craggy rock mountains and fishing in the river before his afternoon training. Each day of the week, he practiced a skill with another member of the guild. For the physical side, Botcht taught him the longsword while Caite taught him how to use knives and daggers. Dur focused on his endurance and combat. He lifted rocks, logs, and sparred with the giant once a week. Leighis's training mostly consisted of gathering medicinal herbs and showing Brier how to tend to combat wounds. After that, Umhal would take him to his lab and teach him how to create salves and concoctions used for fighting infections. This training suited Brier the best. Nonetheless, Brier enjoyed all his lessons with the members of Ceve. They'd become an almost family to him. With Sasta, Dur, and Caite as his brothers, Leighis and Botcht as his strict parents. Umhal as his uncle and Roland....

"Hungry?" Roland asked Brier as he stepped inside. He could smell the simmering lamb on the burner and the boiling potatoes on the fire next to it.

"Starving." He took off a fox fur cloak Roland had mended to fit him and sat on his couch to remove his heavy boots. Roland reinforced the leather on the heel and toe to give him more traction. They were heavier, but made him sturdier when they climbed the rocks. Roland also made him a small bookshelf for the books Brier managed to borrow from Leighis, and a dresser drawer to keep his clothes. Then he built him a bed to sleep in, citing that the couch had grown lumpy since Brier began to sleep on it. For Brier, it seemed there was nothing Roland could not build or mend.

"Dinner's almost ready."

"I'll go wash, then." Brier had also successfully kept the scars hidden from his proxy, taking care to bathe early mornings or late in the evenings when Roland went to bed. He did feel a tinge of dishonesty when he woke before the sunrise in order to clean himself, but on several occasions, the scars glowed noticeably. At those moments any guilt he had about keeping himself hidden vanished. Explaining the eyesores on his skin was one thing, but if they glowed, Roland might think him blighted.

"Haah!" Brier came out of the washroom and stopped as if Roland hammered him into the floor. His master had removed the shirt he wore when Brier first entered the house. His arms flexed as he lifted the heavy basin and sat it on the counter. Brier could not help but stare at the—what felt like sudden—change of garb. He felt a spark of heat flare his cheeks and stepped quickly past Roland into the pantry where they kept the bread.

"Are you still cold?" Roland asked Brier, ladling the potatoes into bowls.

Brier pressed his lips together, grabbing a half loaf before sitting down across from his mentor. "No.... Why do you ask?"

"Your face is red."

Brier lifted his hands to his face to hide his cheeks, staring into the slate-blue eyes. "I'm a little chilly... I suppose," he mumbled as the steam from the pot of roasted lamb clouded his vision.

"You only go red when you're cold, out of breath, or excited." Roland shaved off a piece of light meat and plated it for him. Did Roland study his reactions so closely or was he just so transparent? He'd seen the man's naked chest at least once every day, but the vision still made him flush. It was more than foolish.

Brier focused on his meal instead, sipping the broth from the potatoes and chewing the seasoned lamb.

"Speaking of cold, in a week's time we'll go to the open plains before the frost sets in."

"Are you saying it gets colder than this?" Brier asked incredulously.

"Much colder." Roland soaked his bread in the broth. "We'll go out on the hunt for meat to store for the worst of it. Once winter sets fully, there won't be anything."

"Surely there's a rabbit or deer?"

"Nothing. Not even rabbits come through this way."

Brier nodded, understanding the situation. The trip needed to be successful or the guild wouldn't have enough food to last them through the freeze. Brier never needed to worry about his basic needs. Food, clothing, water, shelter, were all provided in the palace. In Aire, if Brier wanted to be warm, he had to build the fire. If he wanted to make Roland's early morning coffee, and his afternoon tea, he needed to fetch the water. If he wanted to take Frieling out for a stroll, he needed to make sure he'd completed all his chores and training. Roland was strict and oftentimes uncompromising. Brier even helped to make the clothes on his back. Perhaps he should have missed his life in Avenough, but it was difficult to when he'd found so much purpose with the guild. Back home no one needed him or wanted him. He was a blemish in everyone's eyes, save for Marietta. However, here in Aire he'd found a friend in the guild and especially his rugged master.

Brier continued to sip his broth. He noticed the huntsman hadn't spoken of the others regarding this trip to Sherdoe. "Will it just be...." Brier thought how to ask Roland without causing him to misconstrue the question. "Will the others join us?"

"*Na*," Roland answered in Thenian, a habit he often did when they were alone. Brier could understand some of the language with ease, as dialects had always been his best skill in school.

"Lei and Botcht have a contract to take care of. Umhal needs to prepare stones and medicines for the winter. Caite, Sasta, and Dur will stay here to mind the cabin and sell our remaining store of firewood." Brier's heart raced when the realization crept over him. He would be alone, hunting with his master. He tried to stifle the excitement he felt, but he knew it was for nothing. Roland had become the main source of his happiness, and while Brier enjoyed the guild's company, alone time with his master could not compare.

"I've never been hunting before," Brier confessed. He wanted to banish any preconceived ideas his master might have had about his hunting skills.

"I figured as much. A prince of Lirend doesn't need to know how to catch his own food."

"He does if he wants to survive in Aire."

"You're right about that." Roland nodded, impressed at his reply. "You live well or you die hard. There are no—"

"*Shortcuts in Aire, little prince.*" Brier imitated the man's booming voice.

"Ha-ha! I see my lessons are working." He stood and grabbed the empty plates.

"Your lessons?" Brier scoffed and began to wrap the leftovers. For Roland's part, he had not trained him in anything. Leighis told him Roland's specialty was the bow and arrow, but Brier never saw the huntsman use his bow, save for stray birds near the cabin. "You just repeat the same thing over and over again. 'Work hard or die.' Even the gods give us more options than that, Roland."

"There's only one option in life." Roland turned toward him.

"Which is?" Brier quirked his eyebrow.

"To live until your very unfortunate, very gruesome, and very untimely death."

"Dear gods! Why does everything need to be so morbid with you?"

"Because that is life, Brier." Roland dried his massive hands and reached out to pat Brier's head. Brier tensed at the contact, but mellowed when he felt the familiar calm Roland's touch brought him.

"And what about love?" Brier piped. No matter what Roland said, life consisted of more than just avoiding death. He'd read about lively adventures and forgotten treasures and passionate affairs. He felt Roland's hand move uneasily from his crown. When he peered up, blue eyes were on him.

"What about love?" Roland asked accusingly.

"If you're living just to survive, just to exist one more day, surely there's no time for friendships or family or—" Brier paused and averted his gaze. "Or lovers...."

"No time. And no point." Roland's boots echoed on the wood as he stepped away and settled into a humongous hearthside armchair. Brier trailed the man's footsteps tentatively.

"Marietta says there is always a point to love." He kneeled down and began to untie Roland's boots. He did not know when this routine became normal to him. Conversation between them was always aimless and easy. Even when they disagreed,

Roland never begrudged him for it, and Brier had long grown accustomed to Roland's brazen exterior.

"On this one your nursemaid and I will have to disagree. You're a prince. Royal marriages are often arranged for a purpose other than love." Roland leaned his head back, smiled, and closed his eyes; he would not be long for sleep now. Brier could tell by the lazy way he lifted his foot and the small quiver of his Adam's apple as he spoke, and the man's husky voice, which made Brier's stomach knot. "But who knows. Maybe you'll love her."

"I doubt that. Women do not interest me." Brier pulled off the second boot. He debated whether or not to tell Roland about Adeline. They were not engaged, but something told Brier if he was forced to marry, it would be a blonde from across the sea.

"Mm." Roland yawned. "That is because you are still young, little prince. When you get older you'll find a woman who makes your heart race. She'll make you feel like you belong together, like nothing else in the world matters but the two of you. You'll feel like you're floating and falling at the same time."

Floating and falling? Brier stared into the man's content face. The way Roland spoke, it was as if he'd experienced such a sensation before.

"Nothing makes sense, and yet you feel a calm only she can trigger. It'll make you question everything—from your morals to the things you hold dear. All at once you understand what love really means, and then after that...." Roland exhaled sleepily.

Brier sprawled at Roland's feet, in a trance, enraptured by his mentor's words. "After that?"

"After that you learn what loss means." Brier swallowed the lump that formed in his throat. Just now... just now what had he expected Roland to say?

"Just focus on your training for now, Brier. Don't get caught up in abstract things like love. You'll only get hurt."

Brier lowered his head and let out a shaky laugh to stifle the disappointment. Despite the man's shell of misanthropy, Brier could tell there was benevolence. It was the little things mostly. He covered Frieling with a blanket when the stalls grew too cold and gave the elderly woman five miles up the road free firewood to warm her house. The way he smiled with Leighis and laughed with the guild. Roland shaved Brier's wooden training sword to make it easier to wield and bought him a carving knife to teach him how to whittle the fantastical designs on his furnishings. Roland would even make his favorite foods when Brier felt drained after a strenuous day of training or especially homesick.

Veti came to lick Roland's fingertips clean of lamb residue, and Brier giggled. Mayhap the most telling sign of his master's kindness was how Roland came by Veti, an orphan cub after his mother was killed. He took the wolf in and raised him. Despite the frequent complaints of having to care for the creature, Brier knew Roland loved him. Why did the man pretend not to care?

Brier exhaled deeply and laid his head against Roland's legs as the man slept. The fire cracked on the logs he'd chopped, and he lost himself in the burning wood, wondering how to turn off the feeling growing inside him. Brier had the opposite problem of his mentor. Rather than caring, Brier found pretending not to care the most difficult. He did not want to offend the man who'd given him so much, and he was sure Roland would meet his adoration with revulsion or condemnation. Brier could not bear either. Certainly he'd been snubbed and rejected before, but the thought of Roland shunning him brought him close to tears. No. He could and would not share his blossoming feelings. Not now or ever.

CHAPTER 7
BEITH GHEAL

BRIER WOKE before dawn on the day of their hunting trip. He stretched out in the tub, taking care to relish the warmth of the steel tub, not knowing how long till he could fully bathe again. Roland had said two months, but if they did not catch enough game to last them, they would have to extend their trip through the beginnings of winter. His life here trumped anything he'd had in Lirend. Here, away from the cold stare of his stepmother and the hardened gazes of the courtiers.

"Brier." He lifted his head to the gentle knock at the lavatory door.

"Yes?"

"When you're done, come to the shed." Brier could not help his smile. He loved to hear the graininess of Roland's voice before he'd had his coffee. "I've something to give you."

"All right." He nodded and then spoke, realizing Roland could not see him behind the door. They'd be outside for most of the day and sleeping in a tent at night. It did not rain much in Aire, but Roland warned him the ground in the Sherdoe Valley was hard and brittle from the iced soil. He'd read about travelers in the north embracing to regulate their body temperatures. Brier would not mind if Roland wrapped his burly arms around him to warm up. Mayhap the man would press his back against Brier's to hold him steady against the howling wind? Brier closed his eyes and thought then of the winter months. He and Roland would be together for the worst of the winter. Alone. The thought spurred Brier to smile at first, before he remembered how good Roland felt pressed up against him, and he breathed deep.

Shirtless... naked even....

Roland's form sent shivers up his spine and made the blood rush directly to his pink-tinged member. He often thought about Roland in this way. How firm the man would hold him as he stroked himself to hardness. Roland's rough hands skating down his back and over his shimmering silver scars. A kiss to his neck, and shoulder, and lips. The tongue Brier watched when Roland spoke, thrust against his own. Fingertips down his chest, over his stomach, and then between his legs.

Sweet gods....

Brier flushed at his own hardness, poking through the lukewarm water.

That would not happen. More than likely they would have their own sleep sacks like the trip from Avenough to Aire. He dreaded restless sleep curled up against the freeze. There would be no Veti to keep him warm either. The wolf had disappeared some days ago, something that did not faze Roland in the least.

Brier stroked himself until he found relief and satiation. His master would never touch him thus. Roland and he would sleep, and nothing more.

"Ro?" He stepped into the dank shed and narrowed his gaze at the shadowy figure. The sun was fully risen, but Roland insulated the house, the stables, and the shed. Brier could barely recognize him through the hanging saddles and hooks.

"I'm here, hold on." He came through the leather hides and skins holding an angular piece of wood. At first Brier thought it was a new piece of furniture his mentor was working on. Roland knew Brier loved to help, even if it was just to sand or paint the wood, but when Roland stepped into the light fully, Brier could see clearly what his master held.

"A bow?" Brier blinked and reached out his hand cautiously to touch the pointed nock. The wood felt smooth on his fingertips. More than that, the belly of the bow had carvings that eerily matched the leaves that peppered his skin. Heat enflamed Brier's ears and cheeks. Had Roland somehow seen his scars? When Brier always made sure he hid them?

"These markings," Brier whispered.

"You… don't like them?" His mentor's brows stitched worriedly, and Brier quickly shook his head.

"No—it's—"

What am I thinking?

Of course the man had not seen his scars. Here was the proof of that in his hand. Roland would never give him a gift if he knew about the dark marks on his pale skin.

"It's wonderful. I love it." He put his finger on the grip of the bow. "This woodwork, it's beautiful," he assured his master. He had never received anything this refined in his life, save for the clothes his stepmother ordered him for royal parties. However, those were fitted, tailored, and bought. No thought needed, only coin. Those clothes did not have the care of finely etched carvings or the polished oak on his fingertips. "But why did you choose this pattern?"

"Do you not like it?" Roland repeated.

"I just told you, that's not it…." Brier mumbled. His hold tightened on the bow's wood. Roland stared at him as if discerning his thoughts, but since Brier decided not to focus on the slate-blue eyes, the man eventually averted his gaze.

"In truth it is because of you that I chose the leaf pattern." Roland smiled as he stepped out of the shed and Brier followed eagerly.

"But why leaves?" A loud thud resounded as Roland loaded up the rest of their things onto the cart led by an impatient Frieling. Brier could hear the guild chatting animatedly as they waited to bid Roland farewell.

"Hmm…." Roland picked up several saddles he'd made for neighboring homes and loaded them into the cart as well. He stopped to turn toward Brier with sweat dots on the top of the permanent wrinkle in his brow. "Where I come from we have a tree called *beith gheal*." Brier's face twisted at the foreign tongue. "Back home we had rows of those trees. We'd ride out before the sun rose over the morning dew and stand in the perfect spot, just above the valley, to watch the leaves shine like silver. It was like a sea of shimmering treasure." Brier had never heard his mentor speak so wistfully. It was as if he was telling him a dream or a fairy tale. Unreal.

"Then?"

Then do I remind him of that beautiful scene? Beith gheal, beautiful, but filled with a listless undertone.

"Well," Roland finished as Brier trailed. "You're the prince of Lirend, lord of colur gems and rare metals." Roland shrugged and walked to the front of the carriage. "For me, it just fit."

Brier nodded slowly. He did not even know what answer he expected. For Roland it just "fit," but for Brier it made him painfully uneasy. When he was with this man, his soul felt stripped bare. Brier railed his fingertips against the woodworked leaves once more and willed himself to calm. There was nothing for it. Even if he racked his brain the entire ride out to Sherdoe, there was no absolution. Roland did not make him a token of affection, but something practical to use. Something to teach Brier to kill with. A weapon to fulfill their binding task. More than anything, Brier wanted to learn everything he could in what was beginning to feel like their short time together. Working was the only thing that helped to avoid his painful crush. Brier bit his lip apprehensively as he cut his gaze to his master. All the while Roland sat beside him without a hint of unquiet.

WHEN THEY reached the part of terrain where the trees were less dense, Roland began to slow their cart. The roads in Aire were choppy and difficult to navigate for an untrained eye, but Roland had lived here for many years, and Brier came to know that Roland had a natural head for direction. They stopped just below a deep valley, which led to the open part of the meadow, and was adjacent to the largest source of free-flowing freshwater north of Avenough. The Nejir River ran from a huge depot in the northern mountains of Aire's ice caps, and down the entire terrain. The shorter days meant less sunlight for growing things, but most of the indigenous life in Aire was accustomed to the winter climate. This was the time of year when the hibernating mammals would store food for their long hiatus. They would venture into the meadow to eat the longer grasses that could not grow under the towering pine trees of the forest. In order to sustain themselves through the entirety of the winter season, they needed to store fat and food, perfect conditions for hunting large game.

"If we're lucky, we'll catch at least one young stag."

"Are the younger ones easier to catch, then?" Brier helped Roland unload the large tent under the cover of a large timber.

"Technically speaking." Roland set out the poles and began to tie the heavy tarp covering. "None of them are easy to catch, but the younger ones are more inexperienced. For many of them, it will be their first autumn alone."

"Why do they travel alone?" Brier asked, grabbing the thick pad of wool mesh to cover the floor of their tent. The hide would protect them from the worst of the cold, and they had a leather tarp to repel any rain.

“It’s mating season.” The image of a buff and eager stag settled into Brier’s mind. He fumbled with the copper teakettle and sighed. The prospect of coupling with a female was natural he supposed, yet he had no desire to do so. Mayhap if it was Roland, he would feel more inclined to couple? How would it feel to have his mentor like the stag, buff and eager to mount him? As if to encourage him, Brier felt his member twitch involuntarily at that particular thought. Brier’s cheeks flared instantly as he disappeared into their tent.

After they fully erected the tent, Roland finally began grabbing supplies out of the cart to store. Their cache had weapons, skinning tools, cutlery, bowls, basins, and pots for cooking. It was not easy work unloading two months’ worth of food and all the necessary wares. When they finished Brier let out an audible sigh and collapsed into the feather down futon on the ground. He lay on his stomach to mute the hungry grumbling of his gut and to avoid his back, riddled in sweat. He’d have to walk to the river some yards from here in order to fetch water for a basin wash.

And when do I plan to do that? he thought, chastising his own lethargy. He fumbled the iron music box in his hands and opened the lid to hear the low melody.

Whistle whistle....
Calm your bristle....
The day is light and new....
I combed the stars,
And walked afar,
To see a sea calm blue....

THE SUN had begun to set, but he was too exhausted to care. Eventually he’d have to get up, but the ride and unpacking wore him, and Brier ached for a hot bath in Roland’s faraway cabin.

“Don’t sleep until you’ve eaten something.” Roland’s deep voice startled Brier out of his repose. Roland grabbed a loaf of bread and some leftover smoked meat. He topped it off with some apples he’d ground and mixed into a jarred sauce. Brier chewed noisily, sliding his finger across the plate to taste the juice from the apples.

“What would Marietta say to see you eat in such a way?”

“Hmm? That would depend,” Brier answered, leaning back casually on his elbows. “If she was in a good mood she’d just give me a cross eye and remind me who I am.”

“And if she was in a bad mood?”

“In a bad mood she’d tell me it is uncouth for a prince to eat like a field hand, and that if my father were still alive it would make him sick with worry.”

“A bit melodramatic, but fair.” Roland finished his bread loaf.

“And if she was drunk....” Brier grinned. “She’d pop my hand with a wooden spoon and holler ‘Aye lad, lick that plate again and I’ll smack yer arse. Yer not too old to go o’er me knee!’”

“Aye, per peasant and Thenian.” Roland broke into roaring laughter, and Brier let out a nervous chuckle. He’d never imitated his nursemaid in front of anyone before, though it was something he was apt to do when she'd upset him overmuch. "Botcht told me you understood him and Caite speaking Thenian the other day."

"Not really...." Brier avoided his master's gaze. Would Roland scold him like Botcht had done during their training? "I know a few words, but Botcht says it's not proper for me to speak Thenian."

"Why not? Since you obviously have a knack for language," Roland replied. "Perhaps not in front of Botcht. He's a tight ass when it comes to things like that."

"I've noticed." Brier frowned. "He treats everyone like underlings, Master. Save for you and Leighis."

"That is because the only one he respects is me, and the only one he cares about is Leighis."

"And Caite?" Brier questioned. "They are kin, yes?"

Roland gazed at him searchingly. "Did Caite tell you that?"

Brier blinked when he realized he'd said something wrong. "*Na*.... They just... they look similar. I just assumed." Brier flinched from the hardened stare.

"His brother," Roland told him.

"Brother?" Brier yelped.

"Aye," Roland answered somberly.

"But Caite does not call him brother, and they don't act as kin."

"Because they don't share the same father," Roland replied firmly. "Their mother was a Thenian prostitute who was sent to Menlor at the request of an Aurelian merchant. She met Caite's father at that time. He promised her he would marry her and give her and Botcht legal citizenship, but when he found out she was with child, he abandoned her."

"Disgusting," Brier spat.

"More than that, some see it as a stain on his bloodline that his mother had taken up with an Aurelian."

"But she had no choice!" Brier argued.

"To lay with him no, but to love him...." Roland shook his head. "As far as Botcht is concerned it's a travesty."

"And what of Caite? Does he know about his father?"

"Aye, he knows he is half Aurelian." The huntsman nodded. "Their mother died when Caite was only a child. By all rights Botcht could have searched for Caite's father and possibly gained citizenship in Lirend under the law of passage, but Botcht refused and shrilled at the suggestion."

"I do not understand." Brier shook his head. "If there is love, what does bloodline matter?"

"Blood means everything when you have nothing, Brier," the huntsman answered. Brier's mind buzzed with several more questions, but he decided not to push his luck.

"Anyway, feel free to speak to me in Thenian whenever you wish. It will be nice to hear it with a capital tongue." Brier snorted and Roland grinned.

"*Diole'*." Brier responded when his master gave him permission. He hummed as he ate and repeated the words of Marietta's morning song.

I combed the stars,

And walked afar,
To see a sea calm blue....

Roland chuckled lightly, and Brier peered up as he chewed a piece of bread.

"What is it?" Brier blinked.

"That song...." Roland smirked. "You sing it often."

"My nursemaid sang it to me often as a child." Brier fumbled in his coat and pulled out the iron music box to show his master.

"What is that?"

"It is a music box." Brier smiled and set his plate beside him, eager to teach his master something for once. He turned the key in the back of the dark box. Then he opened the lid and released the redheaded figurine once more, listening to the dreamy melody.

"Where did you get this?" Roland asked him when the song finally ended.

"My father, well, technically it was a gift to my mother, from my father... before she died."

"And he gave it to you before he died?"

"Aye. As a keepsake of hers." He'd never shown anyone his mother's music box, save for Marietta. "She died when I was a baby I heard. Of a fatal illness."

"I'm sorry," Roland whispered. "My mother died when I was around your age. I know how hard that is."

"I don't remember much about her." Brier tried to shrug off the now doleful atmosphere. "But Marietta says that I am a great deal like her. Fiery in spirit and red in color."

"Then she must have been very beautiful and resilient." The man handed him back the box, and Brier chuckled.

"You think so?"

"I do." Roland smiled genially. "In all honesty I worried about how you would adjust to this kind of life, but you've fared well, little prince." Brier blinked several times before his lips curved into an impish smile.

"Careful, that sounded like a compliment, Master Roland."

"Am I not allowed to compliment His Grace?" Roland tilted his head quizzically, and Brier's smile turned into a pensive stare. Roland never used titles between them unless the talk turned to politics or regarding the details of his sabbatical. Usually for Roland to obnoxiously remind him of the purpose for their venture together. "Your stepmother tried to constrict you. She thought she could hold you in her grasp, impede your path with her cunning, but you've formed your own way."

"I only follow where you lead me," Brier replied and shook his head.

"Yet you only met me less than half a year ago, and you've kept your head just the same," Roland uttered pointedly. "Most flowers can only grow with enough light, good soil, and proper care, but there are some that bloom regardless of the attention they receive. You continue to persevere through whatever hardship she tries to make for you."

"You compare your crown prince to a flower?" Brier twisted his lips. "I am no woman, Roland." Despite the man's praise, Brier could not help but point out the egregious metaphor.

"You are utterly and respectfully almost a fully grown man," the huntsman readily agreed, mimicking Brier's formal tone.

"Well, then? Should I be flattered at your collation?"

Roland pondered Brier's question for several moments before answering. "When a man calls a woman a flower, it is not to compare the curve of a petal to her womanness, but to compare its distinctive beauty to her own. Is it such a crime then to call another man beautiful?" Roland leaned in and wiped a smudge of applesauce off Brier's chin. "If so then I will pay my fine."

"You've nothing to offer me but your arrogance," Brier whispered. He could smell Roland's heavy musk from working through the day. Brier pursed his lips to stop them from trembling. Roland leaned closer.

"Then if I were to say you are the fairest man I've ever met, would that suffice?"

Familiar heat warmed Brier's cheeks, and he avoided Roland's gaze. It was not a matter of satisfaction, but he did not like the thought of Roland pretending to see him in such a way. It would only make him more confused than he already was. "I think I've had enough compliments from you today."

"Is that so?" Roland flashed him a roguish smile. Brier wrinkled his nose before he stood to go and fetch the water for their after-dinner wash. "But…," Roland replied when Brier reached the unsealed flap in their tent. "You certainly seemed pleased enough." Brier turned and gave the man a deathly scowl to which Roland merely smiled and rested his chin on his weathered knuckle.

"NOW SET your feet," Roland told him as he adjusted his legs apart and his feet awkwardly paralleled. Roland turned his head centimeters to the left, right, and upward, so that he stood correctly in order to shoot. Brier felt more like a mannequin than a pupil, but he tensed his jaw and tried to take it in stride. "Relax. You'll never shoot straight with that much tension in your shoulders."

Brier bit back a huffy reply. This was his thirty-first training day. Every time he picked up his bow he felt like throwing it hours later. Or perhaps strangling his mentor in his sleep with the weapon, whichever one was less trouble for him. Roland's teaching style clashed with everything Brier's previous instructors taught him. Normally he had no trouble taking directions, but he found it difficult to throw away all his schooling and go the way of his mentor. He narrowed his eyes and lifted the bow up straight.

Look straight. Fix your form. Strengthen your chest. Stand tall.

The dictatorship-style teaching ran a loop in his head. He released the arrow prematurely and it landed in the dirt near the padded X Roland set up for his practicing. They set up right on the peak of a low hill. The outskirts had miniature trees lined around, but Sherdoe's mainland consisted of endless hills and curves. The open meadows and high grasses made the location prime for hunting and Roland plucked off game like chess pawns, his arrow hitting the mark every time. Brier did not think he could grow more enchanted with his master, but watching Roland hunt roused his admiration.

"You're still thinking too much."

"Of course I'm thinking! I'm trying to make sure I remember everything you told me to do."

"You should know it by now. We've been going over it for a month," Roland replied calmly.

"And a great deal it's done me! By the gods! I could at least hit the bull's-eye before!" He lifted up his bow and really considered throwing it this time, but the leaf design caught his eye, and he could not bring himself to toss it away. "Here." He handed the bow back to Roland and lowered his head to yield defeat. "I'm dreadful at the bow."

Roland stepped in front of Brier, frowning. "You're not dreadful at the bow. You just need practice."

"As you said, it's been a month. I'm just not getting it."

"I also said you're thinking too much." Roland raised his hands, and Brier felt the now familiar rough palms on his cheeks. Roland forced Brier to enter his gaze, and the slate-blue eyes sent a shiver up the prince's spine that had nothing to do with wind. "You have to clear your mind. Feel only the bow. Let it be an extension of you, Brier." It was always a sentiment when Roland called him by his name. It meant Roland was either being serious or genuine. In this case, both were applicable. "Close your eyes," Roland told him. Brier opened his mouth to speak, but Roland placed a finger on his lips. "I know you're used to doing things your way, Brier, but I need you to trust me."

Trust him? It was not such a demanding request. After all, this man was the only one who'd ever given him a chance to prove himself. He never assumed too much or too little. He never put unrealistic expectations on him and certainly not when learning new skills. Most importantly, his master never gave up on him. If Brier failed with Roland, it was his own doing.

"All right." Brier closed his eyes and drew his bow. The moment he did he wished he hadn't. Roland stood behind him with his chiseled chest pressed up against the angular points of Brier's back. Roland's body curved toward Brier in order to fix his form and held Brier's waist firmly to set him properly. He could feel Roland's fingers trailing up his side until finally they reached to cuff under Brier's arm, and Brier shivered.

By the gods... It was torture having the man touch him so freely. The problem between his legs, which he'd tried to ignore the past several weeks, twitched to life at the scent of his master so close to him. Brier just prayed the man would not have to shift his pelvis to align his form. If he did Roland would certainly find an unwelcome surprise.

"Where is your arrow going to hit?" Roland demanded.

"Probably the ground."

"If you can't see your arrow hitting the mark, you definitely won't. What are you thinking about? Right now?" Roland whispered in his ear. A surging heat trickled through Brier, and his throat tightened at the husky tone. In his mind, instead of Roland teaching him the art of archery, the man was teaching him the art of lovemaking. Roland took his time showing him which form to take him best, and how best to please him. Brier had read about sex between a man and a woman several times in some of the books Marietta had given him, and of course, he was instructed in the biological workings of a woman and a man when he turned fourteen to avoid any royal "accidents." However, this was something different. When Roland was near Brier, his whole body lit up like a raging wildfire in late summer.

"I…." The words died on Brier's lips as he swallowed a forming lump in his throat. "I'm not sure… my head is full of a lot of things."

"Let go of all of that." Roland continued to caress Brier with his voice, and he clenched his eyes tight, trying to escape his contrived decadence. He had no idea how to vanquish the thoughts that plagued him, but standing a bow's hair away from his mentor, with Roland's powerful hand on his back to steady him, certainly did not help. "Only feel the bow. Listen to your arrow whispering on the wind, little prince. Close your eyes and focus." The *S* on the man's lips lingered against the nape of his neck, and Brier unclenched his jaw and shuddered. Roland of Aire was going to be the death of him. "You have the technique. It is only the focus and confidence that you lack." Brier could only think of one thing, and that was pleasing his mentor. Mayhap the reason he felt so hopeless was due to the disappointed tone Roland used when Brier missed the mark. He did not want to fail him again, so he'd stopped giving it his full effort. "Your arrow is going to hit the mark."

Focus… focus…. Brier felt Roland's hand release from his back, and he opened his eyes. Even though he was not in his line of sight, Brier could feel Roland's aura pinning him to the spot. Roland had a hold over him. Brier exhaled a deep, shaky breath and felt his arrow release.

Chapter 8
The First Kill

"You're actually getting quite good." Roland nodded in approval. He pulled one of Brier's arrows and took his bow to draw it back. "Use your upper strength to hit with more power." He released the arrow straight through the marked wooden staff. "Precision is only one half of hunting with a bow. Power is the other half. You will only need one arrow to bring down a deer when you shoot to kill." He squeezed Brier's firm bicep. "Lifting wood has done you well, little prince." Roland met Brier's bashful grin and felt something akin to pride surging through him. The prince had grown so much in such a short time.

"Thanks to you," Brier said as he shouldered his bow carefully. He grabbed his arrow and stored it tip first into the quiver. "I don't know what I'd do without you." Roland gave Brier what he hoped was a gentle smile. Now that they'd grown more comfortable in each other's company, Brier often regarded him with gratitude, but Roland dismissed the acknowledgment. It was his job to teach Brier everything he could. The prince's thanks was neither required nor necessary.

"I've done nothing. It's all your hard work, but thank you." Roland still appreciated the sentiment. "Come on, I think we should go out before a storm comes." In the days they'd spent in the Sherdoe Valley, Roland had jarred the meat of twelve deer, ten foxes, two lynx, rabbits to last them southward, and skinned coats. They scored enough food for themselves, the guild, and the neighboring folk to sell or trade for fuel and candle wax. Some were too old to hunt for themselves and others were too unskilled. The merchantry in Aire was both beneficial and essential for survival. Contrary to what most in Lirend believed, the number of upstanding citizens far outweighed the number of criminals in Aire. The bulk of the reason for their deplorable reputation had to do with the few renegades who stirred up trouble for the refugees. Stringent traveling policies made it nigh impossible for residents of Aire to move freely between the north and south. The soldiers patrolled the surrounding borders to keep tenants occupying the depreciated land sequestered through winter. They needed the generational northerners to farm, graze, and hunt the land to keep the indigenous wildlife at bay, but the queen used her influence to shun the existing Thenian population.

They stalked a spot bordering the wood before Roland pulled Brier down with him into a thick patch of trees. They'd done well this trip, and they still had weeks left before the worst of the winter settled. Roland suspected Brier would be glad when they could depart for his cabin north of Sherdoe. In his years living in the cabin, Roland learned to embrace Aire's formidable freeze. But the bitter air did not agree with the fair-skinned youth, and he oft complained of lack of warm baths and soft beds.

Roland stared upward as sky and cloud commingled.

Storm.... Roland thought, reminiscing of the last time he and Brier felt the lash of lightning and thunder. Storms were unavoidable in this terrain, but Roland hoped they could beat the worst of it. Then Roland heard a rustling like wind through the brush. A wide mass of black strolled through the opens, and Brier's breath hitched. He held his hand to the boy's mouth as the bear strutted through the terrain.

"What was that?"

"A black bear," Roland whispered. "Looks like he's heading south." Thankfully away from their camp. They lay in brush with Brier's breath still stagnant.

"Ro—" Brier whispered harshly and gripped his bow arm. Roland's eyes lit up. Enormous tawny antlers peeked out from the forest trees. Brier gaped at the elegant creature. They'd sighted their first stag since they rode to Sherdoe over a month ago.

"Do you think you can make it?" Roland whispered out the side of his mouth. Brier whipped his head toward Roland, looking horrified.

"*Na. Na.*" Brier shook his head. "I'm not ready yet."

"Well, now's the time to get ready." Roland pulled an arrow out of Brier's quiver. He honestly did not intend to have Brier try for a hit today, and on such a fine stag no less, but the rain would last for at least two days. If Brier failed, he'd have time to lick his wounds and recover in their tent. Now seemed as good a time as any to test his skill.

Roland breathed deep as they stood quietly. "Aim for the chest. It should take him down in one go." The stag stopped and stared across the valley, ears twitching to listen for even an iota of sound. Brier squirmed before he set his bow and gave Roland a final dubious look before he lifted his arms. "Don't forget to breathe," he mouthed to Brier, directing him to aim steadily. He watched as Brier let out a silent breath and used his finger to sight his mark perfectly. Brier had finally learned to let go and trust his instincts. A swallow of pride warmed in Roland's gut. As much as he wanted to deny it, he'd grown attached to his princely pupil.

Whomp.

The steel broadhead sliced through the deer's flesh. Brier gasped when the beast ran into the wood with the arrow sticking from its side.

"It ran!" Brier faced Roland frantically. "I hit it but it ran!"

"I can see that, Brier." Roland stood up fully and grabbed Brier's bow. "Don't worry, it won't get far." He ran down a hump of land with staggered steps and continued into the forest to find the wounded creature. Brier tried to trail Roland quietly, but he could hear the prince's heavy, untrained feet crunching the dried leaves and pinecones.

"Do we have to kill him?" Brier muttered, stepping over a fallen branch. They'd walked at least a mile inward, and the deer was nowhere in sight. "Can't we just—let him go?"

"Your arrow hit him just below the neck. If we leave him, he'll bleed out or suffocate." Not only that, Roland wanted that stag. "Isn't it better to take him out of his misery?"

Brier nodded with his face red from the cold. "I don't want him to suffer."

They stood quiet in the semidarkness listening for the uneven footsteps or a telling whine. Clouds of smoke from deep breaths filled the air. Roland heard a thud and stepped quickly through the close trees. When he stopped he saw the deer straining for breath on the forest floor. He did not hesitate, raising his bow and piercing the beast directly. His back legs twitched once, and then the animal went completely still. He turned his gaze to Brier, who stared at the buck with wide eyes. This was the prince's first kill. "Are you all right?" Roland touched Brier's wrist, noticing his hands shaking.

Brier blinked back with a glossy gaze and shook his head, smiling. "I'm all right," he croaked out and kneeled down to the fallen deer. Brier smoothed his hand down over the warm fur and closed the buck's eyes. "I wonder…," he whispered, stroking the stag's coat. "I wonder if this is how humans look when they die." Roland reached out and patted Brier's head gently.

"Humans and this beast are not so different." When people died they went still like a log floating on a steady river. Eyes closed. Pulse languid. Soul liberated. The light that made them "alive" vanquished with wind. Roland kneeled down and pulled the arrows out of the deer's neck. "We all die someday. This was just his time."

"That's what they said when my father died too. 'It was his time.'" Roland flinched at the mention of King Braedon Snow. Save for politically, the prince rarely spoke of his father. "Who gets to decide when people are supposed to die? Do the gods just—" Brier appeared flustered. "Just take their mark and shoot whomever they wish?"

Roland's brow creased at the question. He did not know the answer, and he never wanted to know. It was not their place to question the order of life, but simply to live it. "I don't know, Brier." He stared into the green eyes and sighed. "Some things just can't be explained." Roland did not know why Brier was left alone in this world or why the gods decided to abandon those who needed them the most. All he knew was that everyone had an expiration date. He gazed at Brier steadily. Even the future king of Lirend.

Roland squinted upward. The rain droplets on his forehead cautioned him to the blackened sky. They'd spent so much time in the forest trying to find the beast he did not notice the sharpening mizzle. "We've gotta go," Roland told him squeezing his shoulder. "There's a storm coming."

"But…." Brier looked to the deer. "We can't just leave him here." Roland gazed at the back of Brier's head.

"He's gone, Brier. He's not going to come back no matter how long we sit here," Roland told him more harshly than he'd intended.

Brier stood up to his full height. "Whoever said death was beautiful was a liar." Roland's mouth twitched at the boy's callous tone. He stepped over to Roland's side and wiped his hands of blood. "What do you want to do with him?"

"Grab his antlers. We'll cover him till morning."

Roland made quick work of field dressing the stag and covering the creature. The frigid air would preserve it till dawn. By the time they reached the camp, they were both soaked to the skin and shivering from the cold. Roland was happy to get into the tent to change his clothing, but Brier waited until there was a break in the storm to scurry outside to remove his clothes. Roland did not fight him. At some point it became normal for Brier to hide his naked skin.

Roland ate in silence, listening to the rain pelt the side of the tent and the thunder rumbling in the distance. The worst of the storm had not rolled in, but by the time they settled for bed, the thunder blared and the lightning flickered through the small chinks of their tent. Brier had not spoken one word since leaving the deer in the wood. Perhaps he'd been too insensitive. Roland's intention was not to discourage his pupil, but to make reality clear. Dead and gone was just that. No matter how much you wished for faded love… the gods would not grant that request.

ROLAND STOOD in a field of blazing fire. The hills that once glimmered with silver now burned in blood and smoke. He held his sword with a dripping hand and looked down at the faces of his slain clan.

"Brother…." Roland reached out to touch Rysel's cold cheek. He turned to his left and saw his cousin Lark with an arrow through his head. The blood still oozed slowly from the heinous wound. He stood and continued to walk through the burning village, ignoring the screams in the distance. He stopped when he came upon the woman lying in the blanket of snow, frozen in her pure white lace negligee. A peaceful smile on her lips, a red stain on her belly, she lay unmoving.

"Helenas, my angel…." Roland whispered. He kneeled and laid his hand to her pale face. Roland winced. Cold skin. He bristled from the heat of the fire engulfing his home. "Helenas…." He knew that she was dead but he wanted to call her name anyway. It'd been so long since he could. "I'm sorry I could not protect you." Roland held her tightly in his arms and gripped her frail back. "I'm sorry. Forgive me…." Roland held her limp body against his chest.

"Acai…. Ronan…."

Roland heard Brier's voice, faint in his sleep. He peered through the darkness and blinked.

"Please, Roland, don't let me fall!" Thunder shocked the earth, but Roland did not fully stir until he felt Brier's heat on his back. "Don't let go!" He screamed out. Roland's eyes widened when the boy clutched his arm.

"Hey, hey." Roland turned and held Brier's cheek to steady him. "What's wrong?" The lightning flickered teasingly outside of their pitched tent. The rain spattered against the tarp like winter hail.

"I'm sorry." Fear laced Brier's panted breath. His gaze slid away though his fingers still gripped at Roland. "That cliff. I dreamed I was hanging from that cliff! And I was getting ready to fall!"

"Shhh… it was just a nightmare." Roland reached out and pulled Brier toward his chest. Thunder cracked nearby, and Brier pressed in closer. "We're safe in here."

"I feel like a coward." Brier scrubbed the fresh tears from his eyes. Roland wrapped his arms around Brier's entire back to assure him.

"It's okay to be a coward with me…." Roland held Brier tighter to ease his shaking. He could hear Brier inhale softly as he was pulled close. "I'll watch over you." He would protect his prince from any storm or turbulence. "Just sleep, little prince." Roland stared down as Brier rested on his chest. He reached up, filtering his hands through the red mane of straight hair to soothe him. Brier sighed out and closed his eyes.

"I can't sleep with noise like this."

"Mmn…." Roland felt Brier's heart beating against his chest. "I enjoy storms. The falling rain is peaceful, and the lightning gives you glimpses of the darkness around you. I can see where it would be somewhat troubling after what you've been through."

"I don't feel troubled," Brier whispered sheepishly. "I feel…." Roland's hand paused on the top of Brier's head when he felt something hard press against him. He tried to slide his leg away, but Brier sank his fingernails into the fabric of his pants. "I feel strange…." Roland felt Brier's gentle breath on his shoulder.

"A storm can make you feel things you don't want to feel, especially if you're scared." As he finished his sentence, the lightning flashed and he could see Brier staring at him. He raised his hand to the boy's face and touched his flushed cheek. "But sometimes the storm lets you feel things you want to feel." His voice was low and husky. Brier's erection pressed against Roland's thigh, and his heart sped dangerously.

"And what things would that be?" Brier whispered.

"Confusion… worry…."

Lust... need....

Roland's body stiffened in the prince's grip, and Brier's leg slid up over his own. "Brier." He moved his hand from Brier's face and stared down between them. In this position their shafts would align perfectly. "You should sleep…." Brier leaned in over him and shifted his eyes as if debating what to do. Roland stilled his hands and heart using his last bit of control not to pull Brier down into a kiss. He never stopped wanting to taste Brier's lips, and lack of sexual release for the past few weeks made for poor self-control.

"I told you…." Brier leaned into him and kissed Roland's lips gently, chaste and yet filled with all the heat of the moment. "I can't sleep."

Roland's body stiffened at the feel of Brier's lean figure practically straddling him. "Little prince." He ran his thumb against Brier's bottom lip. "Why would you do such a thing?"

Brier sighed before recoiling from Roland's question. "Why would I not?"

Roland did not reply. His reasoning was as crude as his current thoughts.

Brier drew back and rested his hand on Roland's chest. "Did you not like it?"

Roland's throat tightened before he answered. "It does not matter if I liked it. You are a child who knows nothing of the way the world works." And a kiss such as that spoke of more than just friendship. Did the prince even consider the implications of his actions?

"I am no child, Roland." Brier glared at him with unflinching green eyes.

"You are but a child compared to me, little prince." Roland had already reached his thirty-eighth year, and Brier, at nineteen, had not even reached his majority.

"I am old enough to know this feeling." Brier leaned in and kissed him deeper still. Roland's tongue slid out instinctively, and Brier melted against him. "Nghn…." Brier's fingertips tickled up his stomach, and Roland's body tensed as he audibly shuddered.

"W-wait...." Roland stammered. Brier kneaded his abs and traced the contours of his muscular obliques. It'd been too long since he felt another person's heat.

His fingers.... Roland closed his eyes in a keen surrender.

Feel so good....

However, a nagging voice inside of Roland replayed the promise from months ago. He was going to help the prince. He was going to give him the tools he needed to succeed. Bedding a man during a storm—no—bedding a child when he obviously felt vulnerable....

"Brier...." He broke the kiss, lifting Brier above his naked chest.

"It's all right... I want this." Brier leaned in once more, but this time Roland avoided the prince's soft lips.

"Don't. I will not have you this night."

"Is it because I'm a man?"

Roland shook his head, sighing out. His impending erection answered that question. "Male or not, I would not take you. You are my pupil."

"I will not always be your pupil, Rolande." Roland's member twitched at the sultry quality Brier's voice took when he spoke his name in Thenian. It must have surprised Brier as well because he lowered his gaze and bit his lip.

"You are just pent up. If you need time to—"

"Rolande." Brier held his face and spoke clearly. "I've tried to ignore it, but this feeling...." Brier trailed off. "What I feel for you... will not just go away."

Roland's body burned when Brier touched him, but his heart ached, torn between lust and the chains of his past, between his desire and his duty to the future king. He pressed his lips together before swallowing and speaking in his deep bass. "If you only understood what you ask of me you would not ask it."

"But—"

"And furthermore." Roland hardened his tone. "Furthermore whatever you feel for me... I do not feel for you. This would have been a way to release and nothing more."

"Then...." Brier squeezed Roland's erection. He gripped Brier's wrist and glared.

"Future king of Lirend, Prince Brier Snow. Do not disgrace yourself more than this."

Roland's use of Brier's title struck first and then permeated. Brier narrowed his gaze. He swallowed the sear of Roland's words and yanked out of his grasp.

"Brier...." Roland whispered softly. He did not want to hurt Brier, but it was easier to scorn the prince than face the truth. "What you feel for me is admiration. And if you knew the real me, you would not even feel that." Brier covered his face with the heavy quilt but did not answer. Roland's heart hammered against the cage in his chest, the sound unbearable compared to the calm eye of the storm. For once Roland closed his heavy lids and prayed that his own words were not true.

CHAPTER 9
UNTAMED BEAST

BRIER CURLED up against the draft of air that filtered through the opening of their tent. A chill crept up his spine from his toes, but he refused to open his eyes.

Last night....

Last night he'd humiliated himself more than even his stepmother could manage. One moment he was lying content in his mentor's arms, and the next their lips sealed. Roland lured him in and Brier swooned like a lovesick drunkard. The thought of giving himself to Roland terrified yet thrilled him.

Still the man refused him. Roland interrupted their almost tryst, and Brier had shamed himself further and grabbed the thick flesh between Roland's legs. How had he become so desperate? He wanted Roland to touch him and kiss him and ignite the spark of heat that rose within him. Roland denied him even that.

"Little prince?" Brier stiffened at the soft tone with which Roland called him. "Are you asleep?"

"*Na.*" Brier could try to feign sleep, but it was well past daybreak, and Roland was not the type to excuse lethargy. He half rolled to his side and gazed at his master fully dressed. Roland folded his arms.

"Heh—I thought you were dead, but I see now that you're just sulking."

"I am not sulking." Brier scowled. Roland did not answer, but smirked as he stepped away. Brier's eyes followed him over to the place where they stored the food, but he turned when Roland rummaged overlong. He heard plates clanking, and then his mentor stepped over to where he lay. Brier did not need to face Roland; he could feel the man's rigid aura pressing down on his back.

"Are you hungry?"

"*Na.*" Of course it was a lie, but he could not suppress the urge to curl up in the feathered blankets and avoid Roland.

"All right, then." The man sighed. He pushed a wooden plate in front of Brier and patted the top of his head. Brier's pulse hastened at the quiet affection. "When you're ready." Roland stood and headed toward the exit without another word. Brier stared at the plate with cheese, bread, and a bittersweet preserve akin to honey. Brier told Roland how much he fancied the copper-toned jelly and wanted to believe he had served it specially to perk his mood.

No.... That kind of thinking had led to last night's events. The harshness of Roland's words still made his heart sting. He had a mind just to lie in bed all day, but his stomach let out a vengeful growl. Starving himself would not help. Even if he refused to eat, it would not change his predicament. Roland still stomped through their tent as if last night had not even happened. Unaffected. Oblivious.

As always, Brier thought, seething and chewing the cheese. If Roland could pretend nothing had happened between them, Brier certainly could.

Roland had gone without him to settle the score with their forest stag. When Roland returned his hands were wiped clean, but Brier could see the stained blood under his fingernails from skinning the beast.

"I grabbed water from the river," Brier mumbled as he stuffed the dirty clothes that needed laundering in a sack. He made sure he was dressed and washed this time when Roland returned. "I also started the laundry and cooked." He tried to occupy his mind during the day so that he would not dwell on last night, but whenever Brier remembered Roland's dismissive tone and the look of disgust on his face, his mood plummeted.

"Thanks." Roland grabbed the cooling water in the corner of the tent and a fresh rag to wash. Dinner consisted of a leftover roast Roland had skewered three days prior and a nest of pheasant eggs Brier raided near the river.

"You took down a hell of a stag yesterday," Roland offered for dinner conversation. "And I had to drag his ass all the way from the wood while you slept the day away." Brier's nostrils flared at Roland's teasing banter. "Wouldn't be surprised if something picked up my scent."

"You don't smell any worse than usual." Roland merely laughed at Brier's comeback and stuffed his face with more food. Brier kept his gaze locked on his plate the entirety of the meal, but when he reached out to grab a boiled egg, his fingertips brushed against his master's.

"Sorry." Brier pulled back as though he'd touched a branding iron and stood up, visibly ruffled. He skirted off toward the dish tub and placed his uneaten food in a sack they used for bait. What the hell was wrong with him? Surely he could get through one meal without turning into a blushing idiot.

"Prince Snow."

Brier turned toward Roland and tried to keep his voice calm. "Yes?"

"We need to talk." The worst words to hear, or rather, the worst in this predicament. Brier could not imagine what Roland would say. He'd said more than enough last night.

"Come sit."

"Why?" Brier quirked his brow. Roland shot him an impatient glare, and then Brier thought better of refusing his master. He wandered over to Roland and sat adjacent with crossed legs. What if Roland sent him away? What if Roland never wanted to see him again? Brier gazed at his mentor, both silent and anxious. He had no intention of discussing their night of almost passion, but at this rate the stark atmosphere would ruin the rest of the trip.

"Bri—"

"You hate me, right?" Before Roland finished his name, a wave of apprehension crumbled Brier's resolve.

"Sorry, but no." Roland's hand outstretched to pat Brier's red mane. "Actually I was going to say I want us to continue with the closeness we've had of late."

"Even though I kissed you…." Brier peered up cautiously. His heart thudded as though made of steel. "And touched you." Roland's hand paused on his head as the man cleared his throat.

"That was my fault. I should have stopped you before things went that far."

"I didn't want you to stop me! I wanted you to bed me!" Brier spat out. He slapped his hand over his mouth at the admission and stared downcast.

By the gods…. If he continued in this way, even his friendship would be unwelcome.

"I'm sorry. I know it's disgraceful for two men to couple," Brier mumbled.

"I shouldn't have said that last night. In my country, there is nothing wrong with two men having sex." Roland pulled Brier's hand away from his mouth and lifted his chin. Brier felt the man's fingertips on his flushed face and his body burned. "And with the life I've lived, I've no right to speak to you about disgrace. I don't deserve to be in your presence, let alone given the honor of being your teacher."

"Honor?" Brier scoffed. "'Tis no honor to be treated as an ignorant child by the man you love!" Roland's eyes widened, but Brier did not retreat this time. He had to present himself with resolute terms if he ever expected Roland to take him seriously. "You view me as a youngling, and mayhap that is my own doing. I admit I am sheltered. I don't claim to know you, or the life you've lived, but don't presume you know everything about me, Rolande. Starting with who I am and what I want." He spoke calmly but with a concrete declaration. Roland gazed at him with a pensive expression.

"All right then… who are you?"

"I am Prince Brier Snow, future king of Lirend."

"Exactly. *My* future king," Roland whispered as he licked his lips. "What fate do you think there is for a huntsman and a prince?" Brier felt the man's heavy gaze, and he resisted the urge to lean in and kiss his master.

"I don't know." Brier shook his head and breathed out his desire. "All I know is that I want you, Roland. And that will not change." He peered up at his mentor's hard eyes, cold and unyielding, like a sea storm blue. Roland's mouth tightened into a strict line, before his expression warmed into an apprehensive smile.

"When you take the throne, your stubbornness will be legendary, little prince." Roland ruffled Brier's hair. "But don't punish me with your silence. I cannot bear it should I not see your smile."

Brier exhaled, defeated. No matter what he said, Roland always treated him like a child. "What will you do when I am gone I wonder?" he retorted. He expected a quick reply, but Roland twisted the ends of Brier's hair around his finger like red yarn.

"I'll try hard to forget you," Roland answered in a somber tone. "And fail miserably." Roland chuckled softly, and Brier felt his heart squeeze. As always Roland's words eluded Brier, and he could not tell whether his master yearned to hold on or forget.

"READY?" ROLAND asked Brier, loading the last of their belongings on the cart. Brier stared down at the place where their tent had parched the earth. Two months had passed much too quickly, and now they were six months into his sabbatical. Once they returned to Aire they'd have a break before the winter together, and then he'd be heading back to his palace prison. Since the night of "almost," Roland had made his position clear within their relationship. The touches grew less intimate, and he stressed the need for distance, especially when they slept. Roland even took to leaving the tent when Brier needed to wash and change. Brier knew he should thank the gods that he no longer needed to worry about exposing his scars, but his prayers for extended time remained unanswered.

Brier frowned as something hopped in his peripheral. He knelt down and watched as the arid grass swayed and a camouflaged frog hopped in front of him. Brier smiled despite his present melancholy. Aside from the color, the frog reminded him of his garden at the palace. The only place where he could escape the constraints of iron and his stepmother's watchful eye.

"Better get out of here," Brier whispered, cupping the frog in his hands. "He'll eat anything that kicks." He held the frog against the side of his cloak and walked toward the back of the cart. "I want to fetch Frieling some fresh water before we go," Brier told his mentor.

"I've just fed and watered him," Roland replied, hitching up the harness. He could feel Roland's conspicuous gaze.

"Can't be too careful." He grabbed an empty bucket, tossed the frog inside, and hurried to the water's edge.

"There you go." He released the sepia-colored hopper onto a rock near the river's edge and watched him lie croaking. "Shoo." He waved his hand. The frog plopped into the water and Brier smiled, satisfied with his good deed. He turned to walk back toward the cart, but froze in his step.

Brier gasped and covered his mouth.

The black bear stood visible within a step, dark fur rippling. Brier whimpered audibly and the beast raised its head with fangs that flashed in the rising sun. It stepped closer, and Brier trembled, paralyzed from fear. He swallowed the growing lump in his throat.

A fierce growl vibrated through the rush of river water, and Brier dropped the tin bucket with a loud clang. The bear watched the bucket float away while Brier panicked. He didn't know whether to run or stay still, but he could not see any outcome other than death. He clenched his eyes and let out a shaky breath. It was just as Roland had said.

To live until your very unfortunate, very gruesome, and very untimely death.

"*Ai*!" Brier's eyes shot open when he heard his master's deep voice. "Hey! Hey! Over here, you big varmint!" Brier watched as the bear whipped his head toward the voice. He used Roland's distraction to skid across the shallow river's edge.

"Come on!" Roland waved his hands as Brier tried to make it out of the water. He wobbled from the threat of the beast so close to him. "Here!"

Brier trudged through the current with his heart pounding, but his heavy garb made it difficult to walk.

"Brier!"

Brier gasped when his back landed hard on the riverbank and his mind went blank. The mass of the bear crushed the air from his lungs, but he kicked frantically, writhing for his life.

The bear roared, and Brier winced and turned from the rancid breath against his neck and face. He spotted the pail stuck between two rocks, and he groped for the submerged handle. *Clang!* He crushed the pail against the bear's heavy jaw before it reared. The bear raised up, and Brier slid back up the muddy river's edge.

"Brier!" The ends of his wet hair whipped his face as he turned toward Roland's voice. Then the bear rose up once more, fangs bared.

"Stay back!" Brier yelled wildly. The beast paused. Brier watched the bear's eyes narrow before it drove down and snapped at him. He threw his arm up in defense before acute pain paralyzed him. The feel of punctured flesh, the blood that'd spattered his tongue, the bear's musty fur. Brier watched the jaws clamp down.

"Ahhh!" Brier let out a howling scream. He flailed more desperately and wailed as the razor-like claws raked through his clothing.

"Come to me!" Brier watched as a head-sized boulder knocked into the side of the bear's irate face. "To me!" Roland yelled louder and danced around to get the bear's relentless attention. The bear released Brier's arm and about-faced in slow motion and challenged his master in a full rage. Brier scrambled to crawl back toward land with harsh gasps for breath. He fought to keep his vision through the insufferable pain.

Roland growled and leveled his body to full height. The man had a spear steady in his hand as he circled the bear, barking and growling in a dominant standoff. He used the spear like a skilled talon, picking and jabbing at the exposed flesh to incense the beast. Brier watched in horror as Roland roared and the bear lashed out. It lunged at Roland with full force but missed him completely. Roland hurdle-jumped over the creature's back and stabbed the bear's heels as he landed. Before the beast could turn to face its attacker, it fell onto its front legs and roared in distress.

"Ro!" Brier yelled at the bear's outstretched paw. The beast swiped the back of Roland's calf as if to clip him, and Roland fell on his back facing the beast head on. "No!" But the bear lurched, and Brier heard the familiar crunch of bone.

No-no-no! Brier sobbed and wheezed incoherently, but there was no movement. Only silence.

"Rolande…." Brier's voice grew faint as the pain crippled him to the spot. He could only see the bear's fur ripple from the place where he lay helpless.

"Mghn…." Brier heard a low grunt before he saw his master roll free from the beast's weight.

"Ro," Brier panted out as Roland limped toward him. Brier choked on the gurgle of his own spit and blood. Roland knelt down and held the wound to stop the oozing from his dead arm.

"Brier!" He yelled with his crimson face covered in sweat. Roland stared down at him, but Brier did not see anger… or the sea's calm blue.

"Rolande." He saw the slightest trace of tears welling up in Roland's eyes. "I'm sorry…."

"Don't apologize! And don't you dare die!" Brier felt Roland's deathly cold touch on his cheek, and he inhaled deeply. "Do you hear me?" The voice sounded muffled to Brier, as if he lay not on solid ground but underneath water. "Don't die, little prince."

"…can't die…." Brier sputtered out his last words before exhaustion and blood loss took him. "Not before…." His world went dark, and his words trailed to nothing.

CHAPTER 10
RECOVERY

BRIER LAY on the bed of sheep coats and heavy furs to warm his gray skin. Lei held the boy's head and watched him with an expression Roland could not easily read. When his best friend did not speak for several moments, Roland could not take the suspense, and he finally asked, "Is he all right, Lei?" He'd journeyed through Sherdoe with godlike speed, making the journey in two days, as opposed to the full three. Frieling had done his part to get down the hills and through the unbidden paths gracefully, but Brier lost much blood when the bear attacked him, and despite Roland's applied salves and care, the prince had nearly faded.

Lei waited at the door when they neared the cabin with Umhal at his side. The seer had seen plight on Brier's star, and though he did not know what ailment befell the prince, Umhal informed Lei at once.

Now after several days of an unresponsive Brier, Roland could not take more of the silence. He needed answers.

"He has a fever," Lei replied softly. "I've tried every way I know to break it, save for tossing him into the ice."

"Can't we do that?"

"Not without risking hypothermia. He's lost too much blood, Rolande." Roland nodded and swallowed the stiff knot in his throat.

"Will he...?" Roland whispered. He could not utter the word die. Even the thought made him nauseous. Lei eyed him carefully before he stood and held his shoulder.

"He's stable, Rolande. Despite his fever, he shows no sign of infection. His wounds are healing, and his heart beats steadily." Lei paused before he added, "This isn't like Helenas."

Despite that, Roland could not peer down at Brier without seeing the face of his deceased wife. Helenas, in all her beauty, had died because he could not protect her, and now, if Brier died, it would also be Roland's fault.

"I should have watched him better!" Roland suddenly yelled. "I should have made sure he did not wander off!"

"You could not have stopped the bear from attacking you both, Rolande! From what you've told me it was the bear's insistence on Brier that allowed you to best him." Roland gritted his teeth and slumped into the chair beside Brier's bed. He held his hands on the top of his head and covered his eyes.

"Rolande...," Brier breathed and Roland's eyes widened. Lei hurried over to the boy and felt his pulse. "*Rolan... de....*"

"Shhh...." Lei brushed the red hair from Brier's face. "Rolande is here." Lei pulled Roland's hand to touch Brier's warm but pale face. "So that he feels your presence," Lei explained as he drew a vial of blood from Brier. Roland stared at his sleeping face, wishing he could see the green of his eyes.

"There is one more thing," Lei told Roland when he prepared to head home to grab more supplies.

"What is it?" Roland asked, startled by Lei's serious tone.

"I don't know how to say this, but there are marks on Brier's skin."

"Scars from the bear?"

"*Na.*" Lei shook his head. "They take the shape of leaves, usually silver. They glowed gold when we first tended to him." Roland was not allowed in his own room when Lei and Umhal worked tirelessly to bring Brier back from the brink.

"What is it? A blight?"

"I don't know, Rolande. I thought perhaps they might be causing the fever, but I don't think that's the case." Then Roland thought of the night so many nights ago, when Brier shivered in the tent on their journey from Avenough. He did his utmost to hide his skin from view. He bathed before Roland woke and never showed himself shirtless. The marks had existed long before the bear.

"All right Leighis. *Diole'.*" He grabbed the man in a tight embrace. "I will watch over him."

ROLAND GRABBED the rag out of the basin and watched as the water dripped. The fire was low, but he could see the still embers holding on to the last of the light. Roland sat at the prince's side like a permanent fixture, barely moving since his return.

Roland lifted up in the chair and leaned over to dab Brier's face with the misted towel. Roland dragged the cloth along his forehead and neck, and watched a dribble of liquid slide down the side of Brier's face and onto his jagged collarbone.

Brier's crusted lips were parted slightly, but his face looked ghostly white in the darkness. The heavy lids hid the most brilliant emerald-green eyes Roland had ever come upon.

His fingertips danced over the low dip of Brier's chest now visible to him. He traced the circular patterns in his skin, like carvings in woodwork, silver, enchanting, beautiful. At first glance he mistook the markings for scars from the beast, but he cleaned Brier's body methodically each day, and the leaf patterns did not heal or fade. Lei said they looked like some kind of spell or curse. Then it all made sense to him why he would hide himself. If Brier thought him averse to the markings on his skin, of course he would conceal them.

"Mm...." Roland heard Brier's low whimper followed by a deep breath. He swallowed. Brier's smooth skin tickled Roland's calloused hands, and he unwrapped the bandages that covered the boy's arm. Bloody stitches and scabs replaced the maimed flesh from three days prior.

Roland dabbed the wound with witch hazel and water, and Brier responded with a guttural moan. "Sorry." He held Brier's arm steady and sighed. "I know this stings."

"Rol—" Brier's voice cracked. His leg moved under the heavy fur quilt, and he tried to speak again. "Rolande."

"I'm here," Roland answered. He touched the top of Brier's damp forehead to soothe him. "Just stay still, all right?"

"What happened?" Brier wheezed out in a voice that did not sound like his own. "Are you all right?"

"Fine, fine." Roland reached down and smoothed the hair away from Brier's forehead. "I only had a scratch on my calf." He spoke in order to distract him as he bound the arm. When Roland finished he used the rag to wipe the sweat from his neck and chest. "You, on the other hand, have been in and out for days with a dangerous fever."

Brier's eyes shot open, and he reached to grab Roland's wrist with his undamaged arm. He tried to sit up, but Roland held Brier's chest. "Don't move, all right?" Brier did not listen. He strained with one arm to pull the fur covering.

"My scars," Brier whispered, his voice trembling. "You've seen them."

"Is that what you call them?" They did not look like scars to Roland. The way the ropes of lace were etched as though they'd adorned his pale skin for quite some time.

"You shouldn't have…," Brier whined. The prince pressed his lips together, clenched his eyes, and his breath hastened. "I didn't want you to see them."

"I saw more than that actually, since I've been bathing and tending to you with Leighis for the past three days." Brier did not reply, but his face glowed red. Roland dropped the rag into the basin and sighed. "Do not worry overmuch, little prince," he told Brier to encourage him. "I did nothing untoward."

"I didn't think you would," he mumbled. No. Roland had done his best to earn and keep the prince's trust, and he had every intention to continue his course. A weak-hearted moment in Sherdoe threatened to ruin his resolution, but thankfully that never came to pass. Now Brier's insecurity remained regarding marks on his skin. "Scars" the prince called them, though Roland could not see the disfigurement.

"You should rest more." Roland stood to fetch his pupil something to eat. He'd spoon-fed Brier water to keep him hydrated, but the prince hadn't eaten an actual meal in three days.

Roland stood over the open fire stovetop and stirred the lamb stew, a dish to help Brier's wound heal. Then he added garlic to help fight infection in Brier's wounds and sage as an antiseptic. By the time he'd finished, Brier drifted back to sleep. Roland sat the tray down and touched his damp forehead. Since he'd woken up fully, the fever had gone down some, but not completely. Brier's skin still paled deathly white, and his usual pink lips had a tinge of gray. The blood loss took his strength, but the perilous journey back to Aire was what nearly killed him. On the whole, Roland prayed to the gods to keep him alive.

Roland stared down at Brier's bruised shoulder peeking through. If not for his youth, Brier would have died already.

"Rolande…." A soft mutter. Out of duty or desire he did not know, but for the past three nights he'd listened to his name muttered on the prince's lips.

"I'm here, Brier." He touched Brier's flushed cheek. "Do you think you can eat? I brought you something." Brier reached up and held his hand. "It's a lamb stew. A little heavy but I think it'll do you go—" He paused when Brier squeezed his hand.

"I forgot to thank you earlier for saving me. Forgive me."

"It's nothing." Roland's heart sped. He cleared his throat and shook his head to dispel his awkward silence.

"'Tis not nothing." Brier did not let go of his hand. "You saved me in the river and stayed at my deathbed—"

"You're not dying, little prince."

"But I could have," Brier replied. "Were it not for you, I'd be dead." Roland tightened his lip before he turned toward the stew.

"Enough." He held his hand under the spoon to catch the broth. "Will you eat? It's been days." Brier's lip twitched, but he nodded once before opening his mouth. He chewed slowly before Roland scooped another mouthful.

"I can eat myself, you know," Brier said, but did not appear bothered by Roland's coddling.

"I know you can." He spoon-fed Brier another healthy bite. "But it's easier if I do it."

"With me sleeping in your bed and you feeding me thus…." Brier grinned sheepishly. "I'll get spoiled."

Roland chuckled. "That might be okay." He used a napkin to wipe the corner of Brier's mouth. "Just until your arm heals." Brier peered upward with glazed emerald eyes. Roland averted his gaze to the steaming bowl of stew and blew on the spoon.

"Yeah…." Brier leaned up to take another bite. "Just until it heals."

"BUT I can get into the bath myself," Brier argued when they reached the tub. Roland had finally agreed to let Brier outside after weeks of bed rest, but leaving him alone in the tub seemed unwise.

"Your arm is still bound, and you barely have the strength to walk. Lei said I should help you."

"I'm not walking. I'm sitting."

"And what happens if you faint while you're in the tub?" he pressed the prince. "It's not like I haven't seen you naked. Why are you acting like an innocent maiden?" Brier's face flushed at any mention of the fact that Roland had seen him bare more than once. It was a reality his pupil wanted to avoid.

"Fine, if you insist on staying. I'm not going to be the only one naked," Brier declared, pursing his lips.

"Excuse me?"

"You heard me. If you want to sit in the bathroom with me, then you'll have to strip too!"

Roland stared at Brier in disbelief before he rippled into a fit of laughter.

"You are such a child." He shook his head and stripped his first and second layer, revealing his chest. Compared to Brier, whose body had not fully recovered, Roland appeared mountainous. When they reached the tub, he helped Brier remove his robe. He did his best not to stare at the smooth milky skin, but Brier took overlong binding his flaming hair one-handed. Roland caught Brier's eye as he settled into the tub, and the boy's gaze immediately drifted.

"Guess I'll take off my pants too." Roland stood to pull the drawstring at his waist.

"Never mind." Brier held up his hand. "Don't." Roland did not know if the heat in the prince's face was from a setting fever or discomfort.

"I thought you wanted me to join you?"

"I did. But I can't bear to have you naked so near me. Shirtless is enough."

"I admit I am not as fit as I used to be when I was your age, but…." Roland watched Brier's head jerk upward. "Surely you can stand the sight of me." He winked.

"I can't stand it, actually." Brier averted his hot gaze. "I'd forgotten in Sherdoe, but your bare chest makes me…."

"Makes you what?" Roland snorted.

"It arouses me, all right?" Brier clenched his jaw, presumably mortified at his confession. Roland pressed his lips together to still his own expression. He would not tease Brier about this.

"All right." Roland put on his light tunic once more and rolled the frayed sleeves. He knew that Brier had found him "arousing" the night they shared during the storm, but he chose to ignore the temptation. It would not end well for either of them. He lathered the cloth and began to wipe away the sweat and bedridden odor. Brier was far from filthy since Roland made sure to wash him daily, but a sponge bath could not compare to a thorough soak in a warm basin. The marks on his skin nearly glowed when Brier fully submerged his pale skin. When he touched the prince's shoulder, Brier shivered and covered the silver leaf.

"Why do you hide them?" Roland slid his hand away and washed the inside of the prince's arm instead.

"Because they're hideous," Brier whispered. He curled over when Roland washed his spine.

"I don't think so. They remind me of an ancient ritual they once held in my village during the spring."

Brier did not answer right away, but eventually he removed his hand and turned toward Roland. "They wore leaves on their skin?"

"The women would paint themselves with leaf patterns and pray to the goddess of fertility. Budding *beith gheal* leaves are a sign of spring, the beginning of new life."

"Or in my case, an abomination," Brier scoffed. Roland picked up a smaller basin and dipped it into the water to wash the soap off Brier's skin. "I've worn these marks since birth. When I was younger, I tried to claw them off with my fingernails even, but that only ended in bloody cuts and lashings from Marietta. They are… nothing more than an eyesore."

"The women in my village did not see it that way." He unbound Brier's hair and began to rake through thick locks of red. "Perhaps you should change your perspective."

Roland massaged Brier's scalp as he doused his hair in warm water. Brier leaned back as he closed his eyes, exposing a perky pink nipple out of the now grayish water.

"I am no woman, Master." Brier yawned sleepily.

"I know that." He continued to wash Brier's hair in silence, ogling the boy's form. His cuts and bruises were healing well. The scratches had begun to scab over, and the blue marks from the bear's pounding were nearly black.

"My father once told me I was special because of these marks. He told me they were a gift from the gods. 'One day you'll understand this blessing,'" Brier whispered nostalgically.

Roland stared at Brier's innocent face. A sharp nose to match his high cheekbones. Combined with the lengthy red hair and pale skin, Brier easily surpassed generic beauty. The prince did not open his emerald eyes for Roland's pleasure.

"Instead they have only caused me pain and misery."

Roland cleared his throat and replied, "Sometimes things that are beautiful are also painful."

"Like?"

"Like… love."

Brier paused before answering. "I suppose so."

Love.

The answer came to him so suddenly he hadn't had time to revise it for Brier's ears. And yet, Roland convinced himself that he no longer wanted or needed love.

"Rolande." Brier called his name. He loved the sound of Thenian in Brier's accent, rolling off Brier's tongue.

"Hmm?"

"Do you have any scars?"

"I do." Roland grinned as he continued to wash Brier's hair, glad for the change in conversation. "On the inside of my leg."

"What from?" Brier wiped a piece of curled hair from his forehead.

"I was stabbed."

"By an enemy?"

"By my brother."

"Your brother?" Roland chuckled at Brier's puckered forehead.

"Aye. He and I once sparred with daggers when we were round your age, I suspect.

"By the gods, what for?" Brier asked with his frown still prominent.

"He'd broken my only leather saddle at the time, and I was livid. I fought like I was a man of the King's Guard, and he fought like an overzealous warrior. Rysel was always quicker than me, though. Struck me in the leg with one blow. Blood everywhere. My mother nearly skinned us both with the sandpaper."

The boy laughed out. "The King's Guard, eh? But I suppose you're not too far off…." The prince smirked, impressed. "And your brother? Did he ever become a warrior?"

"Aye, he did." Roland's smile faltered. "Before he was killed."

"I'm sorry." As their eyes met, Roland could see genuine sadness. "I'm sure he was very brave."

"Yes." He nodded. "Rysel was the bravest and the wisest."

"How did he…?" Roland's chest tightened as he clenched his fist.

"I killed him," Roland whispered.

"You—" Brier's deep frown made Roland stand. "You killed your younger brother?" The jade eyes Roland loved now narrowed in speculation.

"My actions did," Roland clarified. "After he died, I took the lives of the people who wronged me and my village. Their lives were nothing compared to my anger and pain. I lost everything, so I killed them all."

Brier did not reply, but Roland could see the prince's beautiful mind trying to absorb all his sordid confession. "Tell me." He laid his weathered fingertips on Brier's cheek and challenged the prince's frightful gaze.

"Does it frighten you? To know that I have killed with these hands?"

"Why?" Brier whispered. "Why did you kill them?"

"A reason to kill?" Perhaps at some point he might have had a reason, but Roland had slayed the same men in his dreams countless times as the acrid smoke burned his lungs and the fire made him perspire through his torn jerkin.

"Only a blind man raises arms out of anger, coin, or revenge. And they pay for such crimes, in ways I hope you never know, little prince."

Now he knew he killed those men for pure pleasure. For vengeance in the name of his village. To remember her last words in the hazed memory. Roland stood and stepped back from the oversized steel basin.

Ronan….

Her sweet voice whispered.

Acai….

He turned and walked toward the door. "I have to go." The thought of his own wretchedness made his stomach lurch.

"Roland!" Brier's voice echoed in the bathroom, and Roland squeezed the bronze handle. The water sloshed as Brier stood in the tub, water dripping from the lurid skin. "I'm certain…." Roland could hear the hesitance cracking Brier's voice. "I'm certain that if you killed them, you had your reasons. Your bravery saved me, and Frieling for that matter. You are not the type of man who would kill for nothing."

"You don't know what type of man I am." Roland grunted. "I've told you, I'm not what you think."

"And I've told you nor am I!" Brier spat back. Roland could hear Brier's panted breath, and he willed himself not to pivot toward the prince's flushed face. "Are you so afraid to face me as the real you, Rolande?"

"How dare you tell me to show you the real me, when you hid yourself from me since the beginning!" The steam-heavy air tensed, but he refused to face Brier. Roland gritted his teeth when the boy spoke softly.

"It doesn't matter what you've done in your past." Brier's voice shook. Roland swallowed the guilty aftertaste of his words. "You lived through it, whatever it was. Isn't that enough?"

"*Na.*" Roland shook his head.

"Why not? Why do you burden yourself with guilt?" Brier accused.

"Because." He opened the door fully and left his pupil alone. "I don't deserve to be forgiven."

ROLAND STARED at the red and orange flames in the wood, smoking stale tobacco and drinking aged shine. He pulled the cover he'd brought closer around his shoulders and back. The first snow had fallen, and the cold began to soak through his marrow, but he could not go back yet. Veti had disappeared, which left him alone with Brier, crown prince of Lirend.

"The real you...."

Roland spat on the ground. He was not even sure who that was anymore. Free from the tyranny in Thenia, but forced to live as an exile in Lirend. Alone in the darkness, but given an unobtainable light in Prince Brier Snow. Had the gods blessed or forsaken him? His life was in a constant state of exigency. So many times he'd convinced himself that he was happy to live the remainder of his existence alone... until he met Brier. Roland did not want to let anyone in, but especially not this boy who made his heart ache with fragile innocence and sorrowful loneliness, so similar to his own. Simply living, as Brier had said so many times, was all he could manage to do.

Roland paused. He heard the crunch of snow and he gripped his spear before he saw pale skin and spotted red cheeks.

"Are you okay?" Brier's teeth chattered as he walked toward him, nursing the wounded arm.

"I'm fine." Roland jumped up and took off the blanket he wore to cover Brier. "What are you doing out here? You'll catch your death!"

"You didn't come back...." Brier leaned in and held Roland's cloak. "You just—" The harsh breaths clouded his face. "Disappeared after saying that." Brier sniffed. "I thought you'd leave me alone and I didn't—I mean, I can't—"

"Idiot." Roland wrapped his arms around Brier's back and pulled him in close. "How could I leave you like this?" He was freezing, they both were, but somehow it did not matter.

"You've seen my scars." Brier spoke softly. "I didn't trust you with the worst part of me, and that was because I was afraid you'd shun me. I was afraid that... you would treat me like a wretch."

"I would never."

"I know you wouldn't. It was the possibility that made me unsure."

Roland kissed the top of the boy's head and Brier shuddered. "Little prince, there is so much I wish I could tell you," Roland whispered. Brier stepped in closer.

"Then tell me," Brier pleaded. "*Acai.*" He wanted to, but their impending separation made him silent. Brier did not understand yet, but Roland knew. Eventually Brier would return to Lirend and leave Roland alone once more.

CHAPTER 11
YENSIRA

BRIER WOKE the next morning with a stiff arm. Roland's weight pressed him into the bed, so he elevated his left arm on a mound of pillows to avoid crushing the still tender bones. As a result, his right arm fell asleep halfway through their restless sleep. Brier couldn't care less. Last night Roland held him as if he belonged to the huntsman. Roland clutched his back and though the air frostbit his fingertips, Brier shivered from the man's touch.

Now Roland slept soundly, his angular features at complete rest and stillness, despite the dreams that often plagued his sleep. Brier caught only a glimpse last night of Roland's recondite past. After hearing that his master killed not one, but many, Brier was not sure if he wanted to hear anymore. And yet, try as he might, he could not love Roland any less. He could not discard his heart's desire.

Brier slid out of the bed, dressed in his cloak, and headed for the stables to walk Frieling for the morning. The weather had chilled since their return from Sherdoe, but the winter had not officially settled. Brier paced along the cobblestone, grabbed a fitted saddle, and headed for the stables. When he heard a low whine call from Roland's workshop, he gripped the saddle in his hands.

"Nghh!"

Brier stopped dead and his eyes bulged. He turned toward the noise and waited to see if he would hear it again.

"*Ahh*! *Harder*! *Acai*!"

Now Brier skipped past the stables and crept over to the barn, where he heard the desperate begging and sucking breaths.

"Leighis, you're too loud," a dark voice whispered in Thenian.

"*Acai*…." The man mewled something Brier could not understand. "Hurry and put it back in." Brier swallowed the tension in his throat and hardened at the sound of Leighis's pants. He wanted to move closer, but the door barely had a crack. Brier peeked inside and saw Leighis splayed out on his master's worktable.

Whump.

The saddle dropped as Brier stared, nonplussed.

"Patience, Leighis," Botcht murmured huskily as he pushed Leighis back toward the wood grain. The man's fingers worked at pulling down Leighis's pants to his ankles, exposing more of the chalk white skin. There was a hunger to Botcht's gaze Brier had never seen, and he captured Leighis's lips into a kiss. He forced his hips up into a pummeling thrust, causing Leighis to scream out.

"Aye... deeper...." Leighis matched the push down with a grind upward, and twisted his legs in the air.

"You are mighty eager to be filled...." Botcht ground his hips and Leighis's cheeks slapped against the swordsman. He kissed Leighis deep with staccato licks to the inside of his cheek, coaxing Leighis's tongue to entwine with his own.

Sweet gods.... Brier gaped without words to vindicate him.

Botcht thrust his hips and slammed the man nigh through the sturdy wood.

"Does it turn you on, Leinan? The thought of being caught like this?"

"Aye, Botcht!" Lei screamed and held Botcht's arms for strength. Each time Leighis tried to regain himself, Botcht trampled him down with a violent thrust. Leighis's skin flushed and his legs tightened around Botcht's waist. The healer pulled hard at the tassels on the swordsman's jacket, burying Botch's shaft to the hilt. Brier tried to turn his gaze away from the intimate display, but his eyes rooted him to the spot, and his boots stayed.

Botcht continued to hump Leighis senseless, panting as he repositioned the man's legs almost over his head.

Brier bit his lip and shivered. Were all Thenians so rough with their lovemaking? He wondered how it would feel if Roland took him.

Leighis dragged his nails into Botcht's neck, and the man leaned in to kiss him breathless. "Ngh!" Botcht grunted, and Brier frowned at the man's sudden tension in his thrust.

"Coming... don't stop... don't stop...." Leighis begged as he pulled Botcht in closer. Botcht stiffened as he emptied himself deep inside of Leighis's ass.

"Pervert," Leighis huffed.

"Me? Who was it that could not wait? Making us hump in a barn like couple of horny pubes!" Botcht protested.

"I suppose we should have waited until *Yensira*," Leighis snorted.

Botcht scowled. "Don't mock the gods, Lei. If you displease them they will never bless you with a wife of your own."

"If I've displeased the gods, so be it." Brier heard their lips smack. "There is only one man I want in my life."

They both went still then, but with heavy breath. Sweat stuck to Botcht's graying hair around the nape of his jacket. Brier realized how foolish he appeared, espying the intimate scene. He took two steps backward before he followed the trail toward the stalls and tended his impatient horse, Frieling.

"IT'S A little big."

"I'd say that's an understatement."

"Don't worry, I'll adjust it."

Brier stood with his good arm out before Leighis mended the hem of Sasta's dress robe with a long needle and thread.

"Will it be ready in time?" Brier whispered.

"Aye, don't worry. You'll definitely make it to *Yensira*," the man replied with a knowing smirk. Brier gazed at the top of the blond's silvery hair and considered him. *Yensira* marked the end of the year for Thenians, just as the winter gained momentum.

"Does everyone dress up for a mere festival?" Brier wondered.

"*Yensira* is no mere festival, Brinan."

"Nan." Brier frowned. He'd heard the word several times. "What does it mean, Leighis?"

"Nan is a way we Thenians show one another affection, for family, friends, and lovers. *Yensira* is the Thenians' celebration of love, family, and culture. We dress in our best to show our thanks to the gods. It is also a time many couples marry."

"Because of the festival?"

"*Na*." Leighis shook his head. "Because it is said that those who couple on *Yensira* will be together for the rest of their lives. They also wish for the gods to bless them with children."

For the rest of their lives?

"Those who couple...." Brier tightened his lip and wondered how best to ask Leighis about that particular part of *Yensira*. "In an intimate way?"

"Aye." The man peered up at him. "You know the way Botcht and I did yesterday." Brier's face grew three shades redder. "You saw us, didn't you?" The man smiled and Brier cringed.

"I—I didn't mean to—I mean I heard something and I came to see—"

"'Tis all right." Leighis shook his head, laughing. "You are a young man. It is normal to be curious about those kinds of things."

"How did you know I was there?"

"You left your horse's saddle right by the door of the barn. I assume you took your time watching."

Brier lowered his gaze, mortified Leighis caught him peeping. "Forgive me. It was wrong of me to watch you."

"It is all right, Brinan. Really." Leighis stood and clapped his shoulder, but Brier squirmed at the reassuring touch.

"You couple with Botcht in that way... and you enjoy it?"

"I love it," Leighis answered with a smirk. Brier's expression remained dubious.

"And he enjoys it that way as well?"

"Botcht enjoys a stag rutting from time to time."

"By the gods!" Brier's brain fizzled at the man's crudeness. He did not want to imagine Botcht playing anyone's doe.

"You say that now, but one day you might want to mount someone too, Brinan." Brier blinked and flushed anew. Roland as his doe? Even the thought abashed him.

"Why do you look so appalled? Did what you saw disgust you?"

"*Na*!" Brier shook his head. "It's just I...." Brier bit his lip. "Is it all right to couple with a man? In that way?"

"Making love is a natural thing. The gender matters not when there is love involved."

"And when there is no love?" Brier thought then of the conversation he'd had with Roland in Sherdoe. The huntsman had specified that if they ever did couple as

Leighis and Botcht had, it would be for mere pleasure. Not love. "Is it all right to couple with a man who does not feel for you?"

Leighis eyed him warily, and Brier had the impression the man knew exactly of who he spoke. He sighed out and led Brier to the couch in Roland's cramped parlor.

"Is this about Rolande?" Leighis asked him simply. Brier hesitated. He knew Roland and Leighis were close, but he'd also grown close to the healer in the time he'd spent in Aire.

"Aye." Brier nodded. "We kissed only once but I… I can't stop thinking about him."

"Have you told him this?"

"Yes—well. I told him in Sherdoe that I wanted him to bed me." Leighis let out a snort and Brier frowned. "Did I do something wrong?"

"*Na*." Leighis shook his head. "If that was your desire then you did nothing wrong by professing it."

"Well, Ro did not think so," Brier whispered. "He refused me and told me not to disgrace myself."

"He what?"

"But he apologized for saying that later!" Brier hastily added when Leighis bellowed from rage. The man let out an indignant huff and crossed his arms. "He thinks of me as naught but a child, Leighis. I don't know how I can get him to see me as a man."

"It will be difficult. You are his pupil and many years his junior," Leighis conceded.

"Aye, but I do not care about that. I love him. I think about him every moment of every day. I wonder what he thinks, how he feels, how best to make him happy."

"But does Rolande feel the same way?"

There Brier could not answer in surety. There the question remained. "Roland shields his heart from me," Brier admitted. "He says I do not know the real him." Brier shook his head. "I know that there are still things in his past that I do not know about, but I want to know. I pray to the gods he will trust me. I pray that he will let me in. Even if I am only a child."

"You are not a child." Leighis gazed at him consolingly. "Rolande was only a year older than you when he married and—"

"Married?" Brier's heart stopped. Leighis's fair eyes widened before he clapped his hand over his mouth.

"Pretend I didn't say that." Leighis shook his head and flushed red.

"Master Roland was married?" Brier's chest tightened.

"Aye, Brinan." Leighis nodded. "To a woman named Helenas." The thought of Roland belonging to someone, to anyone but him… the thought made his heart ache.

"What happened to her?" Brier croaked.

"She died—" Leighis paused. "A very long time ago." Brier pressed his lips together and shook his head.

"I… didn't know."

"How could you?" Leighis asked. "Rolande is very private about these things. It is not in his nature to trust others. Even now, on *Yensira*, he mopes alone at a tree on the west bank. He has led a hard life, Brier."

"I want to ease his burden, not add to it." Brier knew Roland lived with darkness. He'd heard Roland's cries when he slept and seen the shadow that crossed the huntsman's face every so often. And yet, Roland's past did not matter to Brier.

"I love Rolande, Leighis. He is the only man for me," Brier said clearly.

"I hope you know that loving him will not be as simple as a tumble in bed." Brier hoped not, because he wanted so much more than a night of coupling with the man he loved. "Nevertheless, it appears he has misled you on one thing."

"Oh?" Brier's brows raised.

"You asked me about a man who does not feel for you, but Rolande is not the type to kiss someone he does not at least have feelings for." Brier's heart raced at Leighis's encouraging words.

"*Diole'*, Leighis."

"Think nothing of it." Leighis shook his head. He clapped Brier's hand into his own. "Now there is one more issue we need to discuss, Brier." Brier tilted his head. "If you do plan to have Rolande 'bed' you, there are a few things you need to know."

Leighis went into a full rant then. He explained to Brier the differences between a man's body and woman's. There were ways one needed to clean and different salves and oils to use for lubrication. In addition, Brier needed to prepare himself for a considerable amount of pain.

"Rolande is no lightweight." Brier sat rose red. He'd never heard anyone speak so graphically about sexual intercourse, and he did not expect Leighis to speak candidly about his own intimacy. Brier perked only when Leighis mentioned Roland's size and prowess in bed. Another pang of jealousy racked his chest when the possibility Leighis knew Roland intimately struck him.

"You've… you and Rolande?"

"Me and Rolande?" Leighis gazed at him, perplexed.

"Have you and Rolande coupled before?"

Leighis's untamed laughter made Brier jump. "By the gods, no!" Leighis shook his head.

"Then how is it you know about the size of his… and his skill in bed?"

"Because we grew up together," Leighis answered the first question. "And it's not as if he told me himself, but women do talk." Leighis chuckled again. "I have only known one man intimately, and Rolande has known none."

"None?" Brier repeated.

"None. As far as I know. He'd already married before he'd ventured that far left." Brier bit his lip. "But that does not mean he is not open to possibility," Leighis added as if to bolster his prospects. "The most important thing to remember, Brier, is to never give yourself wholly to a man who does not love you, and never take a man you do not love."

"But how will I know if he loves me, Leighis?" He did not think Roland would ever utter those words to him.

"You will know, Brinan." Leighis kissed his forehead and Brier sighed.

"One more question?"

"Go ahead."

"Do you call Botcht *nan*?" Despite the conversation's candid nature, only that question made Leighis's face red.

"*Na*," Leighis lowered his head. "It wouldn't be proper."

"But Botcht called *you Leinan*?"

"It was a slip of his tongue, I'm sure." Leighis grimaced as he stood.

Love, sex, affection; Brier still didn't understand the difference. Was it all right to call Roland nan if they coupled? How many had called Roland "nan" before?

"Now, shall we finish preparing for the festival?"

"Aye, *diole'*, for talking to me." Brier reached out and gripped Leighis into a hug.

"Think nothing of it." Leighis squeezed him. "Just do not mention this to Botcht." Brier chuckled softly before he stood so that Leighis could finish hemming the sleeve of the robe.

ROLAND SAT in the campfire circle with the guild, save for Lei, dressed in thick cloaks and leather boots. Their dress jackets would not shield them from the blistering cold, even with the bonfires and lit wedges around the festival grounds. Roland perched on the slab of wood unaffected, while the others lifted their gloved hands against the flames. At length, Botcht's grainy voice broke the silence.

"Is it impossible for an Aurelian to be on time?"

"Brier is not the only one who's not on time," Caite said. Botcht scowled at his brother, and the man yawned.

"Lei and Brier had to hem the robe I let him borrow," Sasta informed them. "Brier is small for his age."

"Aye," Caite answered dryly. "He is a runt after all."

"He'll grow, Caitenia. He's only nineteen," Sasta replied curtly. Roland cut his eye to Caite, and the boy smirked. "How is he doing, Rolande? Does his arm still ail him?"

"Only a slight," Roland answered. "Mostly when he's first waking up."

"Well good." Sasta smiled, but Botcht eyed him carefully. "I'm glad he's doing better."

"Yeah, he's fine." Roland remembered the way he'd held Brier in his arms yestereve and his heart began to race. "He's… more than fine." Roland grinned sheepishly.

"More than fine?" Botcht raised his brow in suspicion. "What do you mean, more than fine?"

"I mean…." Roland shook his head. If he had to say, the prince was exquisite, but he could not admit that out loud.

"Fine like aged wine?" Sasta piped.

"Not hardly," Roland deadpanned.

"Fine like fire dust?" Dur tilted his head.

"*Na*."

"Well what did you mean by more than fine?" Sasta repeated.

"Nothing, I—"

"On a scale from Sasta with a puppy and Dur with a crossbow, where does the lad fall?" Caite added.

"Just forget what I said, okay? He's fine. Just regular fine." The guild finally dropped it, but Roland could still feel Umhal's spying gaze. Whether it was due to the man's ability to predict the stars Roland did not know, but the seer had a knack for sifting through people's thoughts.

Roland heard boots through the crunchy layer of snow. He turned toward the shapes forming and his mouth fell open at the sight of Brier and Lei.

"*Venur*," Lei uttered before he strode to Botcht's side when they reached the campfire.

Then the guild sat stock-still. One, because of Brier's almost ethereal glow, and two, because the dress robes outdid anything they'd ever seen during *Yensira*… outdid anything Roland had ever seen.

Brier's ensemble had a winter theme. The under-robe fabric was a moiré pattern, like frozen lake water. They painted tone-on-tone leaves and silver cording at the sleeve and garment hem. The translucent silk overrobe was hand-dyed between white and pale blue with silver leaves, almost identical to those on Brier's arms and neck. The overrobe bell sleeves were gathered up with blue leaf-shaped buttons. For his embellishment, a pewter leaf brooch on his bear fur coat and silver silk sash belt with rope cords.

Roland almost jumped when Brier stepped toward him.

"*Venur*, Rolande." Brier inclined his head, his right arm still bound over his chest.

"*V-venur*…." He tripped over his own tongue and then grew silent. So titillated was Roland that he simply stared in awe.

"Come now, Rolande." Lei's light voice rang out. "Close your mouth before a *sapwig* flies in." Roland promptly tightened his lips and flushed up to his ears.

"Let's go before it gets too crowded," Caite said, sounding bored. "I don't want to sift through a crowd of idiots just to get a good spot."

"Is that the same robe?" Roland heard Sasta whisper to Lei as they traipsed through the thin layer of snow. Lei, Botcht, and Sasta held the front line, Dur, Umhal and Caite in the middle, while Brier and Roland took up the end. He kept a close eye on Brier, flicking his head every so often to make sure he could manage with healing wounds.

"Are you feeling all right?" Brier suddenly asked him. He turned toward Brier and knit his dark brow.

"I'm fine. Why do you ask?"

"You're just quiet," Brier mumbled.

"Forgive me, I'm a bit surprised," Roland answered quietly so that the others could not hear. "You do look exquisite."

"*Diole'*." Brier grinned and Roland's heart fluttered. "But honestly, this was Leighis's doing. He's quite the tailor."

"Aye, he is." Roland swallowed the tension in his throat. "But I meant you." He paused on the edge of the dip in the terrain. "You are stunning, Brinan." They continued to walk until they neared the edge of the festival, and Brier gazed at him with wide eyes. He could not take his words back now, and he wouldn't even if he could.

"Brinan!" Roland heard Sasta squeal with excitement. Sasta bolstered over to Brier and grabbed the prince's arm. "Come on! I want to show you the lanterns!" Sasta dragged Brier down the bricked pathway, and Roland watched the tail of his robe before he disappeared from view.

The festival had three posts to mass the attendees from the cold. The first post had the musicians and the dance floor, which held a hearty gang of Thenians who stomped the wood dance floor with leather boots and twirled their partners with calloused hands.

The second platform held the food tables. Enough to feed the hundreds of hungry Thenians with *rotund*, roasted potatoes, fried trout, pulled deer meat, sautéed turnips, crispy fried brussels sprouts, and an array of greens, boiled and seasoned to salted taste, and cream-filled tarts for dessert. Men, women, and children alike filled their plates, scraped them clean, and circled back for more.

Finally, the last encampment held the open lantern field. The Thenians from across Aire made use of their prolific talent to build lanterns. At the chime of midnight, they would release the light spheres into the air as offering to the gods and the hope their wishes would come true.

Roland kept a distance from Brier, but still felt the urge to claim him, a feeling Roland tried to ignore. The prince spent most of his time with Lei and Sasta, but even entertained Caite for a few moments at dinner. When they headed to the dance floor, Sasta tried teaching Brier the Thenian folk dances. When he'd learned the basics adequately, Sasta took the lead and helped Brier to the dance floor over the hopping drums. The fiddles accompanied the mandolins, flutes, and wind pipes.

"Be my partner, Brinan!" Sasta called over the music. "Remember the step. One, two, three." He tapped his foot. "And then turn back around." He grabbed Brier's arm and pulled him to the center where the groups kept the pace with rhythmic claps. The men formed a large circle, tapping, twisting, and turning, while the women formed a smaller inside circle. The prince gave Roland a hesitant glance before the next song started and Brier followed Botcht's sturdy form when he danced. Roland only kept his gaze on Brier. He made mistakes during the dance, but grinned fully. White smoke puffed when he laughed, and when Sasta claimed him in two partner dances, Brier led the slightly taller boy in chorus of two steps.

"Are you just going to watch him all night?" Lei's light voice sprang up over the music, and Roland narrowed his gaze.

"He is my pupil. Should I not make sure he's all right?"

"Only your pupil?"

"Should there be something more?"

"I wonder," Lei mumbled. "Since you've been waiting for him to come over here."

"I am—" Roland started to say not, but then he noted Lei's perceptive gaze. "Am I that obvious?"

"*Na*." The man shook his head. "Anyone else would think you've just taken a page out of Botcht's gloomy book." Lei chuckled. "But even he has abandoned his melancholy for one night." Lei nudged his chin to Botcht who smiled and held a large goblet of wine. "I know Brier is hoping for you to ask him to dance."

Roland glanced toward the red-faced youth and caught his gaze for only a moment before he disappeared into a crowd of Thenians.

"There is nothing for it, Lei." Roland shook his head. "He's almost twenty years my junior."

"Clearly that does not affect your desire for him."

"My desire?" Roland tried to sound surprised.

"Aye," Lei replied. "We all saw the way you ogled him. I've seen that look in Botcht's eye too many times. You wanted to have him there." Roland cursed under his breath but Lei only laughed.

"He has not even reached his majority."

"And? You laid half the girls at school before you met Helenas, Ronan."

Helenas....

"Lei," Roland whispered. "Please don't call me that.... It reminds me of her."

"You want to forget her so badly?"

"*Na.* I just...." The memory of Helenas made his chest tighten. She was Roland's everything, and yet he'd lost her. He was her protector, and he'd failed.

"Do not discard the people who bring light into your eyes, Rolande."

"He is the prince of Lirend, lest you forget."

"Lest *you* forget, he is as much an outcast in Lirend as we are," Lei countered.

"That will not always be the case," Roland warned the man for his optimism. "One day he will take the throne. The court will bow to him and show him deference whether they want to or not," Roland added when he saw Lei open his mouth to speak.

"One day," Lei answered. "Not this eve, Ronan."

Lei stood and patted Roland's shoulder. Roland watched Lei's blue robe shuffle through the snow, silvery blond hair unbound at his waist. "Oh, and one more thing," Lei said before he too disappeared into the crowd. "I told Brier about Helenas."

ROLAND STOOD outside of the tents and gazed up at the twinkling sky. He leaned on the weight of a large oak tree and slanted his hips upward to dig his heels into the snow.

He'd grown up in Thenia among the *beith gheal* and the sequoias. His first *Yensira* consisted of squabbles with his brother. They fought with wooden swords over who'd made the best lantern while their mother hushed them through the royal temple chants and prayers. Afterward Rysel begged their father to carry him on his shoulders, sword long forgotten, and Roland, wide-eyed, watched the paper sail with glowing lights.

In youth he'd ride out with Rysel down the dirt paths toward the section that housed the fancy trulls with red lips and wide hips. They'd ride back before their now-widowed mother found out. They reached the village's festivities, just in time for *Yensira*, hoping to catch the lanterns before they were released.

Then on his wedding night with Helenas. They'd waited for this day to marry under the same stars and moon so many nights ago. Rysel and Lei at his side. They were all too drunk to dance, but they danced into the night. He held Helenas tight against his chest when the lanterns flew, and he prayed to never part from her. In his dreams

Helenas waited for him in the burning village. Waiting for him to die. To sleep amongst the fire and wildflowers.

"Is it all right if I join you?" Roland heard the prince's voice, and he stood tall.

"Aye." He watched as Brier nursed his arm and walked down the shallow slope. Roland held out his hand so Brier would not slip. "Be careful, Brinan." The boy tensed when Roland called him affectionately and peered upward. Brier slunk against the tree and leaned his head against the base. "Where is your Red Knight, Sasta?" Roland teased and Brier snorted.

"More than likely he's climbed to the highest perch he can find to watch the lanterns."

"You did not want to join him?" Roland asked as he crouched next to him.

"*Na.* As much as I hate to admit it, my arm is not fully healed. Sasta has a bit too much energy, even for me."

"Ha-ha, he can be a bit spirited when he gets excited."

"Verily. And Dur is not much better, but at least he contents himself with Umhal. Sasta needs more attention than I can expend at the moment."

"What of Leighis, Botcht, and Caite?"

"Caite disappeared quite a while ago. Leighis seems to think he visited the Square for a different kind of celebration. As for he and Botcht, they are quite delighted with themselves at the moment." Brier wore a knowing smile and Roland wondered just how much Brier knew of Botcht and Lei's relationship.

"So…." Roland jeered. "You sought me out?" Brier flushed slightly before he averted his gaze.

"Leighis told me you spend *Yensira* moping under this tree." The prince gazed toward the ice-capped mountains and starry sky. Roland could hear the Thenians' humming chant. "I can understand why. The view is very beautiful."

"Not moping… mourning."

"Mourning…." Brier froze. Roland wondered if Brier would question him about Helenas, but he held his tongue.

"Aye, mourning, little prince. For dreams long dead." Roland sighed out. "The trees lose their green, the daylight sleeps, and the birds fly south. The land is dying."

Brier peered upward toward the stars before he spoke. "The land isn't really dying, though," Brier marked. "Only sleeping… waiting for the spring to begin again."

They heard the whistle of a firecracker before it popped and shimmered in the air.

"They're going to release the lanterns," he informed Brier. "Come." He stood and helped the prince farther down the bank where the river started.

Then they both watched the sky until Roland saw the first lantern float above them. Brier gasped and gripped his arm. Warm gold splattered the purple darkness.

"There are so many stars."

"Umhal says that each person born has a star in the sky," Roland said. "And when you die, your star fades into nothing. Like the stars, the lanterns only light up the night sky for a short time." He stared at the flush in Brier's cheek. "But look how splendidly they shine."

"It's—" Brier turned to face him. Roland gazed at the cluster of freckles on Brier's nose and cheeks. "How do you say beautiful in Thenian?" Brier's smile faltered when Roland reached up to touch his cheek.

"*Venai*," Roland whispered.

"*Venai*," Brier repeated breathless. "*Yensira il venai.*" Roland leaned in and placed a soft kiss on Brier's lips.

"*El naa venai*, Brinan."

"You are… beautiful."

Brier translated slowly before Roland kissed him once more. This time he lifted the boy's chin and slid his tongue against the bottom of Brier's trembling lip. "You called me '*Nan*' again."

"Aye." Roland did not pull away. "Does it bother you?"

"*Na.*" Brier jerked his head. "It makes me feel—" Roland kissed the prince again, and this time Brier clutched the bottom of his jacket. Tongues licked slow and deliberate, breath frigid and smoking when they pulled away grudgingly. The loud pop and bang from the resumed fireworks excited Roland more. Brier's nose felt cold and wet, sweating in his heated embrace. Brier huffed when they parted. Roland let him catch his breath before he held Brier's face.

"I wished on the lanterns for this."

"For me to kiss you?"

"For you to hold me thus." Roland felt Brier nuzzle his chest as they watched the sparks fizzle in the air.

"Are you cold?" Roland held the prince tighter.

"*Na.*" Brier closed his eyes. "I feel warm."

CHAPTER 12
EQUAL HEARTS

THEY LAY together in Roland's wool-lined bed with a fox fur spread. It took them a while to warm up from the freezing air, but they snuggled with the raging fire and insulated walls to protect them. At first their lips touched faintly and he pulled Brier in closer, but soon his control began to unravel, and he pressed their lips together more firmly. Brier's body stiffened, but Roland slid his tongue inside of the prince's mouth, holding his back. Roland thought the freeze would chill this heat, but spending nights with Brier in his bed only exasperated his lust.

"Rolande."

"Hmm?"

"I love you…."

Roland kissed Brier's lips to taste his sweet tongue.

"Mmnh…." He let out a breathless moan and Roland's member hardened in response. A wave of heat washed over him, and he rolled Brier to his back. Brier's tongue twined around his, and their bodies melded like slow-dripping wax.

"Rolande—" Brier tried to call his name, but Roland silenced him with a kiss that was more need than skill. Brier yanked the hem of his shirt, and Roland found that he wanted it off. He lifted up to strip his chest bare, and Brier's good hand moved up to his pecs reflexively.

"You said you like my chest?" Roland whispered as he undid the string that held Brier's pants. Brier's face glowed hot red, but he nodded through his discomfort, sliding his fingers through the prickly stubble. "Touch me here." Roland leaned down to suck the boy's soft fingers before he guided Brier's fingertips to his hard nipples. Brier visibly shivered with permission to touch Roland freely. Roland's shoulders were thick and muscular. Age had made his body less defined, but he was still very much physical. Faint lines on Roland's abs lead to the smooth hair on his stomach leading to his throbbing member. He pushed up Brier's tunic revealing the scratches the bear had left, but when Roland slid down Brier's pants, he could the see the tip of his pink-headed shaft hard and dripping.

"Wait!" Brier gripped his hand and Roland smirked.

"What is it?"

Brier opened his mouth to speak, but Roland ravaged the prince with a kiss. Slender legs wrapped around Roland's waist, and he watched Brier roll his hips upward with need.

"I want…." Brier trailed, turning his bright red face away. It dawned on Roland then that Brier had probably never asked anyone else to touch him.

"Tell me. So I know exactly." Roland held Brier's working arm down on the bed and kissed his chin. "You want my hand…." Roland slid his hand down Brier's chest and stomach, rubbing the wet tip of his member. "Here?"

"Mnhhnn!" Brier whimpered struggling against Roland's grip. "Aye—touch me… with your… with your hand…." Roland took Brier's length in his hand and began to stroke him in a steady rhythm, kissing his neck and using his tongue and lips to suck the boy's flushed skin more fervently.

"Rolande." Roland shuddered when he felt Brier's panted breaths on his neck and shoulder. Something in him told him to stop, but the heat of Brier's groin and sound of his name on Brier's sweet lips drove him nigh insane. He undid his own pants with one hand and exposed himself for the first time to his wide-eyed pupil. Roland did not think Brier's face could grow redder, but upon seeing his manhood, the prince's body tensed.

"It's all right." He released Brier's arm and pulled his hand toward his sizable length. "Don't worry, I'm not expecting anything," Roland assured as he kissed Brier's ear lobe. "Just touch the tip with your palm, all right?" Brier nodded in a rushed acquiesce, and Roland continued to work on Brier's desperate-for-more member. The precum eased the slick of his hand against Brier's heavy crown. Roland pressed the side between his thumb and index finger, hitting pressure points to stimulate him more. Brier nearly shook as the pace of the stroking grew faster. Simultaneously, Roland felt a throb of pleasure ignite in his groin. The prince's hold on Roland's shaft grew more bold and aggressive.

"That feels good. Keep going," Roland huffed.

"Ah—please—I can't hold it in, Ro." Brier's own shaft brimmed on the edge in the mess of precum he'd already released. His breath grew rapid and shallow, his legs squeezing and grinding against Roland's thighs. "*Acai*," Brier panted, holding Roland's thick shaft hostage.

Roland stared down at him and thrust his hips upward in Brier's hand earnestly. Brier did not know what he was asking for, and Roland did not know if he was capable of giving it to him. He'd never had sex with a man before, and Brier had not even lain with a woman yet.

"Don't hold it in," Roland groaned out, holding Brier's hot and tensed shaft. "Come on, I've got you." In the next moment Roland felt Brier's soft fingers slide up his bare back.

"Rolande!" Brier clung to him and dragged him into a biting kiss. "Mmngghhh!" Roland felt the warmth of hot cum on his fingertips, spurting from Brier's throbbing member.

"Mmh…. Mmh…." Brier's seed sprayed him like warm water and Roland's shaft erupted with a thick load of cum on Brier's stomach and chest. Brier whined as he came, but Roland cursed.

"Hgnn!" Roland huffed. He'd lost his edge when he felt Brier panting and still clinging to him. It'd been quite some time since he relieved himself, and he had not lain with anyone since his wife passed. Roland used his shirt to wipe Brier's stomach of seed, apologizing, but he seemed unbothered by the mess. Brier pulled him in for another heated kiss, and Roland pushed the prince's chest lightly.

"Have you not had enough?" He smirked, leaning in to give Brier a chaste peck.

"Not hardly." Brier slid his fingers from Roland's stomach to his chest. "I want to feel you."

"In what way?"

"In the way that men couple," Brier answered reflexively. Roland's eyebrows shot upward at the timed retort, but Brier only smirked.

"What do you know of men coupling?"

"I know enough." Brier smiled mischievously.

"You've lain with a man before?" Roland frowned.

Brier wrapped his good arm around Roland's neck and leaned in to kiss him. "I told you, you don't know everything about me, Rolande." From Brier's behavior earlier Roland assumed he was a virgin, but the way Brier's tongue pressed up against his own now… perhaps the prince just needed to warm up.

"Brier…." Roland's deep voice permeated between their huffing. "You are very tempting." He pulled away from the kiss only inches so that he could feel the breath from Brier's mouth on his lips. "But I don't want this night to be something you regret."

"Why would I regret this night?" Brier breathed out before capturing Roland's lips into another tender kiss. "*Acai*, Rolande, don't push me away."

Sex would only complicate their time together and make it harder for him to ignore the way he felt for Brier. Roland shook his head. "Won't I be just another forgotten man and memory when you take your place as king?" And in that moment Roland realized he did not want to be only a man whom Brier had a heated night with. Roland felt Brier's grip loosen.

"Have I truly given you that impression of me? Or is it you who would want to forget?" Brier asked coolly. The boy slid from under him. "If you don't want to continue, then tell me instead of placing blame on me."

Roland held Brier's face and half glared. "I could not forget if I tried, and trust me, I have tried from the moment I met you. Whether or not I want to, I feel something for you, I do. But I am no fool. I do not pretend nor pacify myself with the false hopes and dreams that you have."

Brier yanked his face from Roland's grasp and glared. "I meant it when I said I love you, Rolande. Why can't you believe me?"

"It's not that I don't believe you." Roland shook his head. He saw the tears brimming in Brier's eyes and his heart ached. "You are… very young, Brier—" The prince scoffed and turned his body away completely. "I know you do not want to hear that but it is the truth. You mean these words now, in this bed, with me lying next to you. It would be a dream to forget our stations and love each other. A lie and fantasy."

Brier lifted up on a single arm and rose off the bed clumsily. "I think it's best we sleep separately tonight. I'll go to the parlor."

"Brier." Roland grabbed his wrist. "I don't want you to leave."

"Then why do you conceal your heart from me?"

"Because I… don't want to lose you."

"Do you truly believe I could just stop caring for you, Rolande?" Roland did not reply, but his grip loosened on the prince's arm.

"You don't know this world like I do." Roland's voice hardened. "You've lived behind iron walls your entire life and shielded yourself from the world I live in. I'm not an Aurelian, Brier—hell—I'm not even a citizen of Lirend! I can't pretend I'm something I'm not! I can't—" Roland cursed under his breath. "What would you have me do, Brier? Bed you? Pretend this doesn't matter?"

"Our stations don't matter."

"But they *do* matter!"

"Not to me!" Brier spat. Roland watched the prince shiver under the thin layer of silk from his robe. "You ask what I would have you do? I would have you love me as I love you," Brier whispered, voice choked with the tears. Roland reached out to touch Brier, but the prince pulled away. "I would have you see me as more than just a child to indulge." He stood tall. Roland watched as he headed for the bedroom door.

"What can a man like me give to a future king?" Roland uttered quietly, and Brier paused.

"Nothing if you can't give me your trust." Roland heard Brier sniff his shed tears and the door shut with a solid thud.

WHEN ROLAND woke he had the weight of guilt on his shoulders. Brier left his bed last night, and true to his word, the prince slept in the parlor. Something Brier had not done since the bear attack.

"Good morning, Master Roland." Brier stood in front of the stove with a kettle and two mugs. "I made breakfast. I hope you're hungry." Brier smiled and sat two plates down on the table. "Leighis came by here earlier. He said to tell you not to forget about the meeting tonight." Brier brushed a piece of red hair from his face before he poured steaming water. Roland eyed him cautiously, wondering where the sudden change in mood had come from. He expected the boy to sulk the day away after their row, but Brier appeared unaffected by last night.

"I won't forget." Roland sat down at the table and picked up the mug of coffee.

"Will the guild meet through winter?" Brier asked, plating their food.

"*Na*, this will be the last before winter. I think a storm is brewing, I want to search for Veti before it comes." His black wolf had not returned since they left for Sherdoe and despite Roland's outward passiveness, he grew more worried each day. "The winds have changed. If it's a blizzard, we'll be trapped in here for some time until the snow melts."

"I see." Roland thought he caught a flash of apprehension before Brier smiled. "Then it's best I prepare myself for a long winter." Brier sipped his tea.

They ate in mostly silence, save for the knock of wooden spoon against wooden plate. Brier did not look up once, but Roland could feel something off between them.

"Last night…." Roland started but Brier's chair screeched on the hardwood as he stood.

"We don't need to talk about it." Brier smiled and shook his head. "I now understand our status. You don't need to explain."

"And what status is that?" Roland demanded.

"You are my master, and I am nothing more than your student," he said simply.

"And you are content with that?"

"Does it matter if I am content or not?" Brier's thin brow rose, and Roland considered the prince's words. It did matter. Roland did not want Brier to hate him for something he could not control.

"It matters," Roland whispered as he stood. "I care for you, Brinan. It's just I—"

"It's just you don't trust me," Brier told him. He moved to the sink to scrape his plate. Roland stood and walked over to Brier's side.

"It's not a matter of trust, Brier, but—"

"But you have to show caution when bedding an Aurelian?"

"I am cautious because I know what happens when you're not cautious in this world."

"So what do you want from me?" Brier snapped. "You want me to pretend there is nothing between us but friendship, I'll do that. You want me to warm your bed? I'll do that too. But you can't expect me to pretend I feel nothing for you, Rolande!" Roland flushed as Brier called his given name. Last night when they'd touched, Brier called his name right through his shuddering orgasm.

"I…." He fought to form words against the onslaught of last night's memory. "I don't want anything from you, Brier. I've never wanted a man in this way. I never expected to—to feel…." Roland tensed his jaw and Brier stared, unyielding.

"To feel what?" Brier whispered.

"To feel desire for you," Roland answered truthfully. "I just want to protect you."

"You still treat me like a child." Brier shook his head.

"Because you are young enough to be my son."

"But I am not your son," Brier said clearly. The prince held Roland's face in a tight grip. "I am in love with you, Rolande." Brier leaned in and kissed him gently. Even the light brush of skin made Roland tense. "I know you want to protect me, but you can't control my heart."

The prince stepped away and went to the parlor. Roland watched Brier grab his cloak and put on his boots. "Where are you going?" he asked, still flushed from Brier's kiss.

"To search for Veti." He fitted the gloves over his hands. "Come on, old man."

THEY HELD the last meeting for the Ceve guild in a location deep in the Black Forest. Roland had to walk near an hour to get there, and it took him fifteen minutes to find the precise spot. Umhal had already arrived, with Leighis, Caite, and Botcht arriving shortly afterward. Finally Sasta and Dur arrived with their news from Avenough.

"Unrest," Umhal whispered. "All throughout Lirend's capital, but especially in the south."

"They've increased the security on the border," Sasta informed them. "I'd heard from two down in the Square but I only confirmed with reliable sources."

"Why here, though?" Roland frowned. "There hasn't been any unrest in Aire for nigh a decade. They've no cause to detain us."

"Perhaps they realize we're gaining in numbers," Botcht proposed. "If we joined the forces in Avenough, they would have difficulty containing both borders. They want to confine us before we rise up against them." Roland fought the urge to roll his eyes.

"No one's rising up against anyone," Roland huffed. "We've come too far just to topple the tower over again." Roland turned to Umhal. "I want you to keep an eye on their activities."

"In the conventional way?" Umhal's voice always sounded like a hoarse whisper.

"*Na.*" Roland shook his head. "The first storm will set any day now. I don't want you to get stranded." The man only nodded before Botcht's grumbling voice cut in.

"How long are we going to let the Aurelians dictate our every move, Rolande? The citizens are taking a stand. Isn't it time we put an end to our own tyranny?"

"And risk our necks? For what, Botcht?" Roland demanded. "What cause do we have to fight when they have not harmed anyone?"

"Yet," Caite uttered coldly.

"Aye, yet," Roland fumed. "And they won't if we don't provoke them."

"Heh—" Botcht scoffed. "When did you become so blind? You of all people know they don't play fair!" Roland tensed his jaw.

"I know the devastation Aurelians cause," Roland answered as the painful memories tightened his chest. "And it is precisely for that reason I will not send men to war for foolish pride."

"Foolish?"

"Aye, foolish!" Roland yelled. Botcht narrowed his dark gaze and Roland met him head on.

"You sleep with the prince of Lirend in your bed and you dare to call me foolish?"

The words slapped him so hard Roland's face burned. He averted his gaze before he answered, "Brier has naught to do with this."

"*Na.* I think he has everything to do with this. Isn't that why you shut down our post in the Square?"

"The Ceve guild does not need money from outside jobs. The wood we've sold and the money from the queen has put us in more than good standing."

"And yet that never mattered to you before!" Botcht narrowed his gaze. "Why did you shut down our post in the Square? Because Brier was accosted?"

"Come now, Botcht," Lei's warm voice offered. "Rolande has wanted to shut that post down long before Brier came."

"But he didn't!" Botcht raged at Lei's defense. "Not until *that boy* got here!"

"That *boy* is our ticket out of here!"

"Or maybe just *your* ticket to Avenough." Roland jerked toward Caite. The boy smirked and leaned in toward the wavering flames. "Why should we wait around for Avenough to exterminate us, while you fuck Aurelian trash?"

"Rolande!" Lei's startled voice called as Roland bounded for Caite.

He jumped quicker than Roland could react and gripped Roland's arm behind his back. He held the back of Roland's neck and shoved his chest into the dirt.

"Release me," Roland hissed.

"You're losing your edge, old man." He could feel the point of Caite's dagger pressed against his Adam's apple. Roland jerked his arms and Caite chuckled darkly. "Heh—don't be a fool, Rolande. They will say anything to dry fuck you." He dragged the edge of the dagger under Roland's bearded chin. Caite ground against his hips and Roland shuddered. "Did he promise to take you back to Avenough with him? He won't, you know."

"I know he won't," Roland sneered back with the dagger still positioned at his throat. He knew Brier would never take him to Avenough as more than a servant or prisoner. "I am no fool."

"Enough of this!" Botcht's rough voice called as his silver sword gleamed. "*Caitenia*, let him go!"

Caite leaned in and his lips grazed Roland's ear. "*Te'na an'*," Caite whispered and Roland pulled an elbow free. He knocked the point of his arm into Caite's face and placed a well-aimed kick backward. He heard the dagger drop first before Caite clapped his hands to his bleeding face.

"Caitenia." Lei rushed over to help the bleeding boy, but Caite shoved him aside. He stormed out of the circle and stomped through the wood with Lei following.

"You should teach your brother some respect before he gets himself killed!" Roland's neck stung from the sharp blade.

"As ill-tamed as Caite's words are, he speaks the truth, Rolande. You are infatuated with that boy. So much so that you're losing sight of what matters!"

"The only thing that matters is our freedom!" Roland sneered.

"And his affection?" Botcht questioned. "You care for him, do you not?" Roland swallowed the truth of Botcht's words and diverted his gaze. Of course he cared for Brier, but….

"When it is time to let him go, I will."

"Will you?" Botcht accused. "You don't seem so sure who you are anymore, Rolande, and neither am I." Roland hardened his jaw. Botcht sheathed his sword before he headed off to find Lei and Caite.

"Come on, Dur," Sasta whispered. "Let's go back." They shuffled through the snow and out of sight. Roland stood silent in the blistering cold, and Umhal gazed at him nonplussed.

Chapter 13
Gold, Wood, and Iron

BRIER WOKE to the sound of a light melody from the keys and plinking from the first rain of the winter. He pulled the blanket from his chin and stood on the cool hardwood with fire still roaring adjacent. Roland must have lit a fire after sneaking out of bed. The thought brought an impish smile to Brier's lips before he slipped on the leather slippers Roland had made him. He slid on Roland's heavy elk fur cloak to avoid the cabin's morning chill and cracked the door open to find his master.

The sound grew louder as he stepped into the atrium, and Brier watched Roland play the light keys in silence. It was a song about a flower who'd bloomed too early and died in the winter's frost. Roland seemed to know it well. He pounded the keys at the chorus when the wind howled and quieted as the snow began to fall. When the flower's last petal fell, Roland played the sharp notes. Slow, soft, sorrowful. He paused when finished and Brier hesitated before speaking.

"You play beautifully." Roland turned toward him and Brier smiled.

"Thank you." Roland returned his gaze. "How long have you been there?"

"Only just." He sat down beside Roland before wiggling his fingers over the keys. It'd been ages since he played, almost a year since he'd left the palace. "Who taught you that song?"

"My wife."

Brier took a deep inhale of breath, unsure of what to say.

"It is alright, Brinan." Roland patted his head. "Leighis already told me he told you about Helenas."

Brier nodded and lowered his gaze. "How did you meet her?"

"Helenas?" Roland asked him. Brier nodded despite the knot forming in his gut. He wanted to know, but also didn't. The contradiction made him restless.

"Our fathers knew each other, actually," Roland explained. "My father was a lord of a place called Hilrook. My wife's father ran a village called Agnon."

"So you were a lord in Thenia?" Brier blinked at the realization.

"Aye. But not in the same way as in Lirend. In Thenia, 'lord' is just a fancy way of saying leader. My village was made up of mostly what you would consider Prolit."

"Still…." Brier understood now why the guild treated Roland with so much respect. "You were a lord in your own right."

"You sound like Botcht." Roland chuckled mirthlessly. "My father was a carpenter. Her father was a shepherd. We married on *Yensira*, on the year's first snow."

"Leighis told me… that she died." Brier could hear the thud in his chest. "Is that true?"

Roland avoided his gaze before he answered, "Yes," softly.

"What happened—" Brier paused. "Will you tell me please, Rolande? What happened to Helenas?"

Roland turned toward him slowly and sighed before he shook his head. "Do you really want to know?"

Brier nodded but did not speak. He wanted to know everything about this man.

"I remember that night like yestereve. We were expecting our first child, and though she was tired a lot now that it was closer to the date, I was overjoyed, for the child was to be my first. On the day of the Thenian Massacre, I'd thought to pick her a bouquet of wildflowers. She loved flowers, Brinan. And singing and dancing and laughing. And she was beautiful too; her hair was like gold. And more cunning a woman than I have ever known…." Brier's lips tightened at the reverence in Roland's tone.

"On the night of her death I smelled the fire and then I saw the smoke, thick clouds like black mushrooms. I could hear women screaming and men yelling to the warriors. The valley our village sat in was wide and low. When I ran uphill I saw nothing but pillows of smoke, but when I looked down I saw carnage. Our village had been sacked. Soldiers with their swords raised against my people. I came behind the first man and used my bare hands to crush his skull. I used his sword to kill dozens of his own men, maybe hundreds—I do not know and I don't want to know."

Brier swallowed as he watched the huntsman's face harden.

"My hands were bloodied. I fought so hard I could not even hold a sword upright. The earth burned, hungry for my blood, but I searched for my Helenas. Everywhere. Amongst dead bodies, men, women, and even children. Their faces looked in terror towards me, as if pleading for me to save them, but I'd already failed them all. I searched for my Helenas. I wanted her to somehow be alive. I needed her at least out of everyone to live."

Roland's voice choked, and Brier felt warmth under his lids.

"I came upon our house, ablaze with fire, and I raced towards the flames with the last strength I had, lugging the sword behind me. *Helenas!* I yelled through the inferno. The blood smeared through the house as though a dead body had been dragged. By then I probably knew the truth, but I did not want to admit it. *Helenas!* I screamed for her louder, hoping she would call to me, but I knew she wouldn't, Brinan. There was no way she could…." His breath shook. "I thought she was dead. I did not move. I could only stare at her. Because—" The man croaked. "Because of all the men I killed that night, Helenas was the first dead person I saw. My wife. Facedown in a pool of her own blood. Maybe it would have been better if I'd left then. But then her fingers twitched."

Gods…. Brier shook his head.

"The blood dripped from her pale lips. She turned to me then on the ground with crying eyes, and I knelt beside her and touched the wound on her stomach, but I did not need to. She was dying and our child was dead. *My beloved…* She called to me, but her voice was like the wind's whisper. Her smile was still beautiful even with pale lips.

Shhh... don't speak, Helenas. I kissed her with tears in my eyes, and I picked her frail body up to carry her out. *Ronan.* I think if she wouldn't have spoken to me, I would have stayed by her side in the fire. But I could not let her body burn. I could not let her beauty fade into ash. When I walked outside, the sky was orange with dawn. She smiled at me again when I laid her on the hard earth, and I wept like a child. *Don't go.* I begged her because I needed her to stay with me. *It's my fault. Acai.* To the gods, to anyone, I begged them." *Acai, don't take her.* Roland lowered his head.

"She died at dawn. I used her blood-drenched gown to cover her breast."

"Did they…?" Brier trailed.

"Rape her?" Roland's strained voice finished his question. "Even now… I don't know… and I don't want to know."

"I'm sorry, Rolande. To do that… to a woman… to an innocent person." Brier could not stand the thought of it. "Those men who killed Helenas were cowards." Brier shook his head with tears in his eyes. "All of them cowards, Rolande."

"*Na*…." Roland shook his head. "It was my fault. My hubris, my conceit when the King of Thar tried to bargain with Rysel and I. Rysel tried to convince me, but my hatred for Aurelians made me blind."

"And your brother…. Rysel…."

"They slayed my brother, my wife, and killed my child with her, and I came too late. Too late to die and too late still to save anyone. My entire life was gone in one night. So I killed them. I killed them all."

"No one would fault you for avenging your village and wife."

"I slayed those men because I wanted to, Brier. I thirsted for their blood more than air in my lungs," Roland whispered. "My revenge came later. I killed the ruler Onas, stabbed him in the heart in his sleep, and I thought even to kill his wife and child who'd seen me do it."

Roland's expression grew darker with every word. Brier lifted his hands and wiped the tears that built in the corners of Roland's eyes. Brier cried too, but did not wipe his own tears. "I was not strong enough to give her true justice and I was not brave enough to take my own life. So I just held her in my arms and wept."

"I understand you, Rolande. You miss your wife like I miss my father." Brier held Roland's face with an unusually firm grasp. "Constantly. Longingly. The loss hurts so bad it makes your body ache to think of them… and you think of them every day. Right?" He searched Roland's teary eyes.

"Every day, little prince… but more now because you make me remember how it felt to be loved."

"LET US sing something not so dismal," Brier said.

"It is in my nature to be dismal," Roland chuckled.

"Mayhap, but you have your moments of reprieve," Brier teased. He watched Roland rub his chin in seeming thought.

"Okay." The huntsman nodded. "Okay, how about this one."

Calam an brin,
Tae da lih an na,

Ei bom tae,
An ven afir,
Ot min a' ase alm ma.

Roland sang in his low voice, a song less melancholy than the first, but still wistful in meaning. As far as Brier could translate.

"That song… is very lovely," Brier said as Roland reached out to touch the tip of his braid. "What does it mean?"

"'Tis a love proposal, I suppose. Helenas sang it often," Roland mused. "The man in the song says, *'An ven afir. Ot min a' ase alm ma.'* Literally it translates to: 'And when you're alone, of me think seas blue.'"

"Think of seas blue?"

"Colors have meanings in Thenian. He tells her to think of the blue sea. He means to calm her."

A sea's calm blue….

"I see." Truthfully, Brier could not understand how any man could feel calm in love. The tension between he and Roland almost drove him mad these past months locked in a cabin.

"I think we may be able to scout the area today. Some of the snow has finally melted." Brier could hear the rushing water from the unfrozen river. The winter freeze started two months ago and had not let up. Brier had never stayed inside for so long, but there was nowhere to go in six feet of snow. What little sun reached the cabin dispersed between the colossal trees and never melted more than the first layer of snow. Before the temperatures reached below freezing, Roland shoveled the path to the enclosed barn where they kept the wood and Frieling, making sure the horse had proper covering and food. Roland procured batches of hay and they had more than enough food, wood, and water to last them.

"Mayhap Veti will finally come back," Brier answered.

"*Na*, I do not think so, little prince. Veti is not like Frieling. He is a wild animal. I'm surprised he stayed as long as he did."

"But this is his home." Brier frowned. Roland shook his head.

"His home is in the Black Forest." Roland's rigid fingers streaked through his red hair. "Just like your home is in Avenough."

Brier exhaled and laid his chin against the yellow birchwood, enjoying Roland's gentle massage. In two months' time his sabbatical would be up. He would be back in the barren halls and cold chambers. Away from the guild, from Aire, from Roland. Winter had come and gone too quickly.

"Mm…. That feels good," Brier whispered as he leaned into the huntsman's grasp. He felt his breath grow still, and he contemplated sleeping against the man's limbering hand.

"Are you going to sleep?"

"The fire is warm and your fingers feel good." Brier yawned.

"You sleep your days away like a pampered cat." The familiar heat rose in his cheeks when Roland beamed at him. "I think you have cabin fever."

"Mayhap... I certainly feel hot these days," Brier whispered. They had not touched each other since *Yensira*, but at least Brier had made his feelings clear. Brier wanted to hold his master, touch him, kiss him.

And Roland?

Roland raised his hand off Brier's head before he slid off the piano stool.

Cold as ever, Brier noted as he shuffled toward the couch to lie down there instead.

"Do you miss the palace?" Roland stretched his back and arms.

"In a way," Brier answered. He stared at Roland's stomach as the man continued to stretch. Roland had hair on the pecs of his chest, down his stomach, and to the base of his sizable member. Just thinking of it made Brier flush, but he pursed his lips to hide his unwarranted bashfulness.

"In what way?" Roland asked.

"I miss certain parts of it. My bathtub," he said pointedly. "Marietta of course, and my father's study."

"You go there often?"

"Mm.... mostly to read, but one time when I was younger he decorated the entire room with frond and petals. It was just he and I. He sang to me on my birthday. It's strange, the memories of my father are so scattered and long ago. Sometimes I don't even remember his face, but I remember that day so vividly."

"That is a good memory to have, I think."

Brier nodded and sighed out. "There are too few of those in my life."

"What will you do when you return to Avenough, I wonder?" Now Roland asked Brier the question he'd wondered since Roland had lain with him. Admittedly, it was not in the way he most desired, but when Roland touched him something inside of his body ached to be filled.

"I don't know." Brier hid his red cheeks with the fur couch duvet. "My coronation will be this spring once I've of come of age. I'll be twenty in—" Brier blinked. He let out a light chuckle before he covered his mouth.

"What is it?" Roland probed him with a grin.

"I should be twenty within the day." Brier let out a raucous laugh. Roland continued to stare at him perplexed. "I'm sorry, but it seems I've forgotten my own birthday."

"Ha-ha!" Roland joined him in the joke and shook his head.

"How—" Brier's cheeks ached from laughter. "How can I miss the palace when you make me forget the day?"

"How indeed." Brier gazed quietly. As always Brier lost himself in Roland's raspy voice. How he longed to stay by this man's side. What he would give to belong to Rolande of Thenia.

"So it's your birthday?" Roland leaned his head back against the couch contemplating. Brier did not interrupt him. He enjoyed listening to Roland's steady breath against the crackling logs by the hearthside. "Well, then, I suppose we should celebrate."

Brier blinked before he shook his head. "There's no need to go through trouble. It's not all that important really. I'm used to people forgetting my birthday, Rolande."

No one mentioned it, save for Marietta, and even then they held intimate parties with just the two of them.

"But surely you'd like something." Brier paused at Roland's words. There was something. Something that only Roland could give him. "Come now." Roland frowned. "It's not every day a man reaches his majority." Roland reached over and patted his head lightly. "And a prince no less. How about we have our own little celebration. Just the two of us." Brier looked up at the hand that caressed him and smiled. For the first time since he came to Aire, Roland had called him a man, and not a boy. If reaching his majority had any sway over Roland's ultimate view of their relationship, Brier could not refuse his master.

THE NEXT morning Brier woke to the scent of fresh fried eggs and a slab of honey ham that'd been cooked out on the open fire. He could smell the lard sizzling in the fryer, along with a heavenly scent of fresh baking bread. He rose quickly from Roland's bed and began to dress for his official birthday. Today he was twenty. Ten months ago he'd undertaken his sabbatical with a man he knew nothing about, save for his hooded face and baritone voice. In two months more Brier would return to Lirend.

And then what?

The question remained a constant in his mind. He did not know what then. Certainly his stepmother would have expectations of him, or more accurately, criticisms. However, now that he'd reached his majority, and met his father's conditions, Brier would have full rein over King Braedon's throne.

"Good morning, Brier." Brier turned toward a burly man with dark hair and eyes like a peaceful tide.

"Good morning, Roland." Roland set down the tray arranged with his favorite foods. He'd smelled the bread and ham cooking, but Roland added a glaze of honey over the crisp breakfast rolls and gave him the last reserve of blueberries from the cooling box.

"Where did you find these!" Brier exclaimed. He'd scoured the terrain during the late summer but did not find any growing.

"You told me they were a favorite of yours, so I traded some wood for them a while back." Roland handed him a fork. "I'll add some to your cake as well."

"There's cake too?"

"Most certainly. What is a birthday without cake?" Roland asked him, moving back toward the kitchen.

"Well let me finish this, and I'll help you—"

"*Na*!" Roland's voice rose. Brier stared at him curiously before raising one brow. "It's your birthday. Sit and enjoy a day off." Brier frowned slightly, before he felt the tense energy emanating from Roland. His master was up to something, but he would not probe Roland about his plans.

"All right." Brier smiled and nodded. "I'll leave you to it, then."

By the end of the day Brier had worked himself up to a nervous wreck thinking of the night's possibilities. He'd washed thoroughly and stretched as much as he could, despite his embarrassment. Brier wanted to ask the man about his plans, but Roland's secretiveness continued. He spent most of the day locked in the shed pounding and tinkering.

When the sun set and the dusk began to settle, Brier could no longer suffer through his restlessness. He wrenched open Roland's bedroom door and stepped out into the darkened parlor.

"Ro?" There was no fire and not even a candle lit. His first impression was that Roland had gone out on an errand run, but Brier thought he would at least inform him. Brier pressed his lips together and felt a growing knot of apprehension in his stomach. Had Roland given up and decided to venture into the wood instead? Roland often took night excursions to "clear his mind" supposedly. Had his birthday become a burden? Mayhap he'd expected too much?

He searched for a match in the black room hoping to see more thoroughly. However, when he stood upright, the kitchen began to glow and that notion was lost. Brier's eyes widened to candles that popped and fizzled atop a round and puffed cake.

"Happy birthday, little prince." Roland's white teeth shone against the glimmer of candlelight. Roland outstretched his hand and Brier saw a small wooden box in his palm. Brier threaded his fingers over the faint carvings. He opened the box curiously and his face was passive until he heard the song that played. A figurine with red hair down his back and a bow in his hand spun as if floating in thin air.

"Is this me?"

"Aye." Roland nodded.

It was so like the box he'd shown Roland many months before in Sherdoe. Save for the material. His mother's box was made of iron; this one was made of wood.

"I opened up your mother's box to see how to replicate it. I hope you don't mind."

Mind? Brier opened his mouth but no sound came.

"It took me all day to figure out the right tune."

Just then Brier recognized the song playing as the one Roland sang yesterday:

'Tis a love proposal I suppose.

"This is...." Words escaped him. "You are...." He replaced his last phrase with a bone-crunching hug. Roland laughed nervously and held him close. Brier basked in the warmth and sturdiness of his embrace. He reached up to touch Roland's cheek affectionately, but pulled back at the smoothness on his hand.

"You like it?"

Brier gaped openly at the sight of his master's shaven face. He'd never seen Roland without his beard before. He had the urge to lick or bite his master's freshly shaven skin, but he cleared his throat. "I love it." He touched Roland's chin and beamed.

"I meant the music box." Roland smirked.

"Oh." A flush of red crept up to Brier's ears. "Yes, it's amazing. Thank you." Roland placed the box on the table and pushed the small cake toward him. White icing covered the cake, but Roland sprinkled blueberries atop like he'd promised.

"Now, make a wish, and blow out the candle," Roland instructed. Brier stared at his angular face and let out an apprehensive chuckle. There was only one thing he wanted in this world. He leaned down and blew out the candles, which put them in darkness. Brier did not speak, and neither did Roland, but Roland's deep breaths pulsated through him.

"*Aa'Mele Nuva*, Brinan."

Then their lips met. A warm sensation spread through him as he felt the familiar kindling of excitement. Roland's tongue slid in against his own, and he clung to the shirt for leverage against the kiss.

"Rolande." Was he imagining this moment? He did not want to speak for fear of ruining the dream.

"Is it all right?"

It was more than all right. Brier pulled Roland into another heavy kiss. This time Roland pushed him down into the ridge of the table and Brier slid his fingers through his mentor's black shoulder-length hair. His breath turned into pants, and then his pants evolved into whining moans.

"Ngh.... Rolande...." He slid his hands between Roland's thighs to confirm the girth he'd felt so many nights ago. This time he was not going to allow Roland to avoid him. If he was going to give himself to anyone, it had to be Roland.

"To the bed, take me." He breathed low but spoke steady. Roland dragged him across the table and lifted him up into a powerful hold. Brier felt the man's hands cuff underneath his thighs and backside as Roland carried him to his bedroom. He clung to Roland's neck and back, resuming the kiss they'd started in the kitchen. Brier flicked his tongue to Roland's guided rhythm and smoothed his hands over the huntsman's chest.

When they reached the bed, cake long forgotten, Roland pulled off his own tunic and jerkin. The sight of his master's chest sent a thrill up Brier's spine, and he leaned in to stroke Roland's dark chest hair and chiseled pecs with supple fingers.

"Mghnn...." The huntsman's low grunt made him heady. He leaned in to lick Roland's neck and chest sensually.

"I want you." Brier slid his hand to Roland's engorged member pressed against the seat of his trousers. Roland's heavy hand wrapped around his wrist, and Brier peered up to stare into his slate-blue gaze.

"Are you certain?" Roland's hold loosened slightly. "I don't want to hurt you."

Brier slid off Roland's lap and stood in front of him. He wanted Roland to see him, fully. Not as a son, not as a boy to chaperone, but as a man to guide. Brier removed his shirt and exposed his fair chest and shoulders. Faint leaves that trailed into spirals stood out on his skin. He untied the braid in his hair and tousled his fingers through. Then he loosened his britches to expose himself fully hard to Roland.

"I want you." Brier blushed despite his resolution, but his expression radiated calm. Roland's intense eyes made his skin burn with longing. Brier bore himself willingly and without reservation. Even though Roland had seen him bare, Brier had never felt so incredibly naked.

"I am certain." Brier stepped forward and settled into Roland's lap. A shiver danced up his spine as Roland's rough fingers slid down his back and against the crease leading to his entrance. "Have me, Rolande." Roland licked Brier's neck and whispered into his ear.

"I think I must…." Brier bit his lower lip before his hand was slid around Roland's unclothed length. "Since I'm already like this." His breath hitched as Roland thrust up into his hand. Brier tightened his fingers and pumped downward as he moved his body to straddle Roland completely. He swayed his hips and rubbed, skin to skin, in delicious friction. Brier muffled his moans with Roland's undulant tongue.

"Ngh…." Roland mouthed Brier hungrily. "Who taught you to rouse men in this way I wonder?"

"No one has taught me thus," Brier whispered heatedly against his master's lips. "Save for your guidance." Brier pushed Roland's shoulder into the bed and arched his back. "And your sword." Brier flushed at his own daring words.

"Aye, but you are no innocent."

"Says who?" Brier frowned.

"Says you." Roland smirked, kissing Brier's wrist. "When we last lay together."

"I said that I know the way men couple." Brier dragged the man's fingers to his lips to lick Roland's fingertips. "The palace cook has a lover." He fibbed to conceal Leighis's identity. "I've come upon them from time to time."

"Ha-ha." Brier watched Roland's chuckle rumble through his chest. Then he felt Roland's heavy hands spread his bottom, and his breath hitched once more. "A prince who peeps on his servants' lovemaking." Brier exhaled as Roland moved on top of him and his fingers slid across broad shoulders, heart skittering. "How crude."

"Rolande…." Brier clenched his eyes as the rough pad of Roland's thumb slid over the tight ring of muscle between his legs. Any trepidation disappeared when even a small touch could send a wave of need throughout his body.

"When we are through with this night, do not hate me, little prince," Roland warned him.

"I could never hate you." Brier moaned before Roland leaned in for another breathtaking kiss. Roland's thick shaft rubbed against his cleft, stretching and teasing, but not penetrating. His own member throbbed against his master's muscular thigh as Roland sucked and licked Brier's tingling tongue. Brier caressed every inch of Roland that he could reach. He memorized the dip of Roland's spine and the curve of his waist.

Will I ever feel him this way again?

Roland ground against him, and Brier tensed. He swallowed as Roland paused momentarily, but tensed when he felt something slick press into him. "Nghn." Brier instinctively clenched and shifted, but Roland's fingers continued to ease inside of him. Leighis told him initial penetration would hurt, but heat ignited his groin. "Rol—" He tried to say his master's name, but his body burst with a lascivious ache between his legs.

"Brinan." Roland held his face firmly. "Look at me," Roland commanded. Brier fought to keep his gaze from swimming in the dim firelight. "If it hurts don't push yourself, okay?"

"Okay," Brier whispered. His heart felt bruised, it thudded so hard. If it hurt, he did not care. He would bear anything to please this man. Roland's fingers slid out, but with the next breath Brier's body nearly spasmed. "Ah-haah!" He gasped when the sharp bones of Roland's pelvis connected against his meaty thighs. Brier gripped Roland's shoulders, nails scraping thick skin, paralyzed from the pain.

“Is it—” The man paused in his thrust before he pushed all the way and Brier whimpered. “—all right?” Brier nodded even as startled tears beaded at the corners of his eyes. It hurt more than anything, and yet with each dull thrust, vibrant heat trickled up his spine. Roland’s pelvis pressed against him, and the sensation continued to build with the rolling of the man’s hips.

“You’re so tight,” Roland mumbled, breathless.

“I told you I took no other.”

Brier bore down against the slide of flesh, and his toes curled when Roland’s thick member brushed against a spot that made him cringe from pleasure.

Dear gods.... He was going to faint, or worse, say something dreadfully daft.

“Brinan....” Roland whispered in Brier’s ear and his skin tingled. “Are you okay?”

“Aye—Rolande....” Brier wheezed out a shaky breath and nodded. He tried to speak, but all words were lost to him as Roland rode him, grating that luscious spot with almost every thrust.

“Don’t stop.” Brier’s vision blurred with tears, but he could see lace scars ignite his skin. The golden shimmer that once frightened Brier now urged him to fruition.

“*Acai*.” His ache to be filled turned into need. “Touch me.” Rough yet familiar fingers slid down Brier’s chest and turned into a tight grip around his leaking shaft.

“Rolande!” Roland’s hand worked between them and stroked him in rhythm to the huntsman’s powerful thrusts.

“Ro—I can’t hold it!” Brier warned, but Roland’s pace quickened. Brier cried out his master’s name to the gods and anyone who would listen. His fingers clawed into the huntsman’s back, and creeping titillation gave way to shuddering pleasure. Brier snapped up and tightened as he released clear seed between them. His face dripped with concupiscent sweat. His scars shimmered gold like a clarion dawn.

“Hgnn....” Brier trembled from the bursting spasms deep within him. His legs felt loose, or as it were, nonexistent. A still euphoria washed over him, deaf to Roland’s enervated pants.

“Forgive me.” Only the sound of his master’s raspy voice and the feel of kisses on his damp neck and shoulder could lure Brier back to consciousness. “I did not mean to spill inside of you.”

A wide grin spread up to Brier’s ears as he slid his hand up Roland’s welted back. “Do I look upset?” He kissed the corner of Roland’s mouth almost innocently. “This is everything I’ve ever wanted.” To be here in this man’s arms, coupled and full.

“There is still much to gain.” Roland leaned in to kiss his forehead. “You will understand that when you take the throne.”

“But not without you by my side.”

Roland sighed. “You cannot rule with me by your side, Brier.”

“Then I choose... not to rule.” Roland did not reply, but eased out in a steady slide. “Ah—” Brier winced and squeezed his shoulder. The sword that stabbed him left an empty void.

“Are you very sore?” Roland asked, cupping Brier’s cleft and sac. Roland spread the salve he used as lubricant to soothe the ache between Brier’s cheeks. The healing salve had already begun to numb the ache.

"I'm tired, but not sore." He would have to clean himself, but right now his legs felt too numb to move.

Roland lifted up, but Brier squeezed his arm to hold him. "Will you lay with me?"

"Aye. Of course." He nuzzled into Roland's chest. Heavy like oak, but rough and dark like engraved mahogany. Give up his father's iron for wood? There was no question in Brier's mind.

"Rolande," Brier breathed.

"Hmm?" Roland slipped into limbo.

"*A'ma el.*" Brier confessed his love, not with expectancy, but will-less honesty.

"Aye." Roland's deep voice cut through him. "I know, little prince."

CHAPTER 14
A PRINCE'S WISH

ROLAND DID not want to wake the next morning. He'd fallen asleep exhausted and slick with sweat, but for the first time since his wife died, he slept without nightmares. His vision clouded when he stared through the skylight in his bedroom. No rain this morning. Only sunshine.

"Mmhm…." Brier whimpered. The prince rolled over and nuzzled against him. Roland reached to touch Brier's supple lips and smooth his disheveled hair. Brier had undone his braid and stripped bare for Roland to see last night.

Last night….

The memory still burned hot in his mind. Roland stood up to avoid the tension on his side of the bed. Brier had not fully woken, and he did not know how the prince would recover from their night of passion.

"Good morning." Roland stared down at Brier who blinked up at him with tired emerald eyes.

"Good morning, Brier." Roland reached out to touch Brier's forehead. "How do you feel?" Brier strained to rise off the bed, but smiled despite obvious pain.

Roland shook his head. "You should rest." Although he'd told Brier to tell him if he was too rough, a part of him knew the prince wouldn't. He had no practice in coupling with men, so his only instruction was Brier's twisted face, moaning voice, and shaking breaths. While he managed to hold out for a goodly while, he'd lost his head during the final moments and released deep within Brier.

"I'm fine." Brier gritted his teeth. "'Tis only a dull ache." Brier stood up, still naked, and bent over to grab his undergarments from yestereve.

Roland cleared his throat and averted his gaze. "Where are you going?"

"I want to go to the river and restock our reserve. Besides, it's been ages since I rode Frieling, and I'm sure he misses the outdoors overmuch."

"Don't push yourself today. It would be bad if you get hurt right as the weather breaks," Roland warned.

"Aye." Brier nodded and leaned in to kiss his clean-shaven cheek. "I won't, Rolande."

The way he calls my name….

Roland blushed as Brier bit his bottom lip with a mischievous smile. Roland could not tell whether Brier knew the effect he had. "Are you all right?"

"Fine. Why do you ask?"

"Your face is red." Brier chuckled. The boy held his cheeks where the beard would normally cover. Roland felt his ears burning. If he had to say, Brier definitely knew his effect.

"I'm fine." He cleared his throat. "I'll go make us breakfast."

HIS PLACE is in Avenough.

Despite Brier's confessions last night, Roland had no intention of keeping Brier in this wasteland.

His place is in Avenough.

Roland opened up the wooden music box and listened to the low melody.

No amount of love will change that.

"Rolande!" He snapped the box shut and looked up at the prince. Brier stormed in with his boots coated in corn snow. "Master, you've got to look outside!"

"What? Why? What's happened?"

"Just come on." Roland frowned as Brier panted. He grabbed his coat just as Brier wrenched the door open, gripped his bicep, and pulled him along. The prince stumbled a bit on the sheet of ice outside the cabin door but balanced when they reached the snowy ridge. They ran to the top, with Brier practically dragging him upward, bouncing with excitement.

"All right, all right." Roland wheezed when they reached the summit. "What is it?" His breath smoked in the open air. Brier reached out to point downward into the valley.

"It's Veti!" He laughed out. "Look! Look!" Roland blinked and watched a black wolf lead the pack of seven.

"That could be any wolf," Roland replied, though he stepped closer to get a better view. He had not seen the beast in over six months. "There's no certainty it's—"

"Awooooo!" Brier's voice broke out into a deep howl. Roland's eyes widened. He jerked his hand over Brier's mouth.

"Are you insane?" he grunted in a whisper. "Those are wild wolves. They'll have us for breakfast if you don't—"

"*Awooooo*!" Roland fell silent, but the wolf's howl grew more powerful.

Roland released Brier's mouth and used his hands to create a tunnel over his mouth.

"Awwwooooo!" The bellowing howl shook his lungs.

"It's him!" Brier shouted and bounced. "It's him, master!" Roland panted and watched as the black wolf ran toward him. He collapsed on the ground as the furry beast collided with him.

"Veti." He rubbed through the thick coat. Veti licked his face and pawed at his chest. "Where have you been, you mutt?" He rubbed the wolf's collar, and Veti nuzzled his neck affectionately.

"I told you." Brier sniffed, wiping his eyes. He kneeled down and rubbed Veti's head gently. "And he's got a family now! Look, Rolande!" Roland grinned as Brier wept happy tears for him and his overgrown pup's reunion. "I told you he'd come back!"

"You did." He lifted up in the snow and touched Brier's chin. "*Diole'*." Roland leaned in and kissed the boy's supple lips. Brier's damp face flushed from the cold. Roland slid his tongue against the prince's, and he held Brier's red mane in a delicate grip. Brier met his tongue's thrust, and huffed when Roland sucked Brier's bottom lip hungrily.

Veti whined when they finally broke, and licked Brier's face to gain his attention. "All right, Veti." He continued to rub the wolf's back gently. Roland stared at Brier's wet eyes, his own heart racing.

He has to go.

The sun cascaded over the snow, yellow skies with a pink burst of color.

He has to go back.

Regardless of what he wanted, Brier's place was in Avenough.

"Rolande?" He blinked when he heard Brier's voice. "Are you ready to go back?" He stood with Veti at his side, licking his fingertips.

"Aye," Roland answered quietly. "Let's go home."

THEY SAT at the table sipping their tea and listening to the water on the stove bubble. Roland stared at the prince as he rebraided his flaming hair, but cut his gaze when Brier made eye contact.

"Is everything all right?" Brier frowned as the braid flicked against his back.

"Fine," Roland lied and disappeared behind the large mug. He couldn't tell Brier his thoughts right now. It would only confuse Brier… and him, for that matter. Regardless of how he felt, there were lines put in place for a reason. Brier would remain an Aurelian royal, and he would remain a Thenian. An outcast. A killer.

"Liar." Brier pursed his lips. "You've been deep in thought for the last hour. If there's something… if I've done something or—"

"You've done nothing wrong, little prince." Roland shook his head, feeling guilty. Roland did not want to make Brier uncomfortable, but his own ambivalence made him restless. "I fear it is I that has failed as your mentor."

Brier placed the teacup down on the saucer with a gentle clink and spoke softly. "How can you say that when you've given me everything? You who have taught me more in one year than in my entire lifetime."

"Brier—"

"When I am king, I plan to change things for the people of Lirend. Aurelians have hoarded their power and wealth long enough."

"Brier—"

"Even the Xeno—" Brier paused. "Even the Thenians who live in Aire. They shouldn't be subjugated to criminals just because they live here. If there are not enough prisons to hold criminals in Avenough, then mayhap we need to figure out *why* there are so many criminals."

"Brier." Roland held Brier's mouth. The boy stared at him with emerald eyes, and his heart raced. "Will you listen to me?" Brier nodded and Roland tightened his lip.

"I'm not who you think I am," Roland started quietly. For the past months it was Brier who'd given him everything: kindness, intimacy, strength. This boy, or man rather, relentless in love. "There's something… I need to tell you."

Knock. Knock.

The tap on the cabin door startled him.

"I'll get it." Brier caught the dangerous glare in his eyes and stood from the table.

Roland followed him to the kitchen and waited to name his guest.

"Brier Ignacio Snow, Aurelian Lord and leader of the great land of Lirend. Son of the late King Braedon Ennis Snow and Queen Iines Fallon Snow."

Roland stood when he heard the guard's salutation. The guard lifted his head and stood at attention with a glimmering sword shining at his waist. A dumpier man, with a heavy fur cloak and a bald head split through two men. He beamed at the sight of Brier and bowed his head in deference.

"Lord Tamil?" Brier blinked twice before turning toward Roland as if to confirm the lord's presence. He turned to Lord Tamil without acknowledging the guard's elegant locution. "What brings you so far north?"

"Hello, Your Grace. I've come with a message from your Queen Regent, Evelyn Gormlaith Snow."

"And what business does the queen have with me?" Brier asked, his tone even and sure. "Is it so urgent she would send you in the middle of winter to Aire?" Roland watched as Brier straightened his back.

"Yes, Your Grace," Lord Tamil answered. He pressed his lips together in obvious distaste of Brier's poise. "The court has decided unanimously that you are to take up the throne."

Roland stepped away from the door and walked toward the table where they'd breakfasted.

"Lirend's people grow restless with Queen Evelyn now that you are of age."

"I've only just…." Brier's voice shook now with uncertainty. "I have only just reached my majority."

"And His Grace is needed in Lirend."

"You did not need me a year ago when she sent me away," Brier replied coolly. "The queen sent me here for one year, and it has only been ten months. Wherefore the sudden urgency?"

"Had we but known of the queen's decision to send you away, we would have intervened before you left." He smiled gently and stepped closer to the prince. "Brier, your place is not here. You belong with your people. Back in Avenough."

"I'm sure this has nothing to do with the rumor I'd heard before winter?" Roland interjected.

"And what rumor would that be?" Lord Tamil raised one of his black brows. The man's face was round, but he had unkind, almond eyes and a bald head with prominent ears.

"That the people grow restless without a true king to rule them," Roland disclosed. Umhal had told him about the unrest in Lirend. Although they had no stake in the kingdom's monarchy, if a civil war broke, Thenians might benefit from the discord. "That your kingdom is in jeopardy of the people revolting."

Lord Tamil let out a patronizing chuckle and shook his head. "Where did you hear such a farce?"

"Whispers on the wind." Roland grimaced.

"When the food supply is low and the winters are harsh, it is convenient to blame the ones in charge. Unfortunately we have no control over the seasons. Better the people pray to the gods for benevolence than threaten Lirend's queen with unrest. It would do you well to ignore uninformed rabble, Lord Roland." There was a warning in Lord Tamil's springy voice.

Roland stiffened. "I am no Lord," he answered coldly.

"Indeed. You are not." The man returned his glare. Roland did not concede. For a man like Lord Tamil to come this far for Brier, something more devious was at hand.

"If it is only the people's will, it can wait for my return," the prince finally cut in. "I have no intention of leaving before my time is up with Roland. There are still things to learn here."

"Whatever there is to learn here, surely you can learn it in Avenough?" Lord Tamil replied gently to Brier.

"Mayhap...." Roland could feel Brier losing his nerve. "But Rol—"

"Will be properly compensated for his service." Lord Tamil inclined his head toward Roland and held out a sealed envelope. "Queen Evelyn has informed me of the arrangement."

Roland took the envelope and opened it slowly. The black ink nearly seeped through the page. The thick paper felt heavy in Roland's shaking hands as he read the contents.

Greetings Lord Roland Archer,

I assume you remember our first meeting so long ago.

Roland swallowed the growing knot in his throat. He remembered their first meeting vividly.

The palace. It was more spectacular on the inside than he'd imagined, but also colder. Roland stepped into the hall alone and timid. High arches were known in Lirend's architecture, but this room also had a circular dome that gave the room a feel of a temple. Roland heard his boots echo on the white marble floors. Pearl and gold gates opened, and a woman with blonde hair and razor-sharp eyes glided into the hall. There Roland stood in the center of the large empty room with King Braedon's emblazoned silver leaf. Perhaps it was a room of worship, but Roland had always heard Aurelians prayed in temples.

"Speak, huntsman." Her voice, vibrant yet threatening, echoed through the chamber.

Roland abjectly bowed to his knees. "My name is Roland Archer, son of Renlor. I was told you needed my assistance, Your Majesty." The woman picked up a goblet of what Roland assumed was wine, but he did not raise his head to know exactly.

"Rise." The chair she sat in had a long and curled back, the arms of the chair in iron rose. "I assume you know why I've called you here."

"Forgive my ignorance, but I do not." He inclined his head apologetically and balanced his hand on the end of his massive crossbow. "However, whatever use Your Majesty has for me, I am at your service." He'd learned long ago about the deference paid to the Royal House of Snow. Regardless of their treachery, his father had schooled him in the proper way to address those with whom they owed a debt.

"I have a job for you." The woman's mouth curled into a depthless smile. Roland did not know what amusement she got from using a once lord as a hireling, but he did not let his pride outwit him. He needed this job. The Ceve guild needed whatever this job could afford them.

"Aye, Your Majesty."

"You are aware of the king's son?" She raised her brow.

"Prince Snow?" Roland had heard of the boy. After the late king was put to rest, he'd been kept away from the general public. Roland had heard many rumors about the prince. Some said that he was very ill and that he had to have care constantly. Some said that a curse was laid upon the prince at his birth. He'd even heard that looking into the prince's eyes would cause a person to go insane. In all of the rumors there were whispers of the man's great beauty.

"I want you to take Prince Snow. Show him the way of the sword and the bow. Build his strength so that he may one day hold the king's heavy crown upon his head."

Roland was silent at the request. How was he supposed to teach a boy how to be a man? More importantly, why him? Roland frowned and the queen clenched her jaw.

"Does what I say displease you, hunter?"

"No, Your Majesty." He shook his head quickly. "Only that I wonder why you have accosted me, milady. Of all the hunters in this land, I think that there is one more suited to handle His Grace. I am a mere mountain dweller. I do not know the qualities needed to rear an Aurelian king."

"And you think that the queen does not know this fact?" Her mouth slid into a smile. She was beautiful, Roland supposed, but a dark aura oozed from her regal form, which made Roland more distressed than allured. "Another man might have been better skilled than Roland of Aire. But you are no ordinary huntsman." She smirked and narrowed her eyes. "Isn't that right.... Rolande."

Roland could feel Brier's eyes on him and his body burned with shame. He had no right to claim he loved the prince when his own secrets threatened to ruin Brier's only chance at happiness. Roland finished the letter and crushed it in his hands.

"Rolande?" The prince tilted his head. "What does it say?" Brier's voice cracked, heavy with uncertainty.

"It says… you must go with him," Roland croaked out. He felt his heart breaking as the words continued to spill from his mouth. "It says that you will take your place, in Avenough, as the rightful king." Where Brier should be. Away from the danger of Aire. Brier continued to stare at him, but Roland kept his face impassive. If he showed even the slightest emotion in his countenance, Brier would see the opposition stirring in his heart.

"Do you want me to go?" Brier stood in front of Roland.

"It does not matter what I want." Roland shook his head, still averting his gaze. He was only one man, an undesirable. Once a lord, now a lowly wretch. "The queen will take no excuses. These men have come a long way to get you, Prince Snow." Roland used the prince's title hoping to define his decision, but Brier only pushed harder.

"Only as long we have traveled to get here." Roland could hear the anger cooling the prince's tone. Brier turned to Lord Tamil and lifted his chin. "I presume I have the right to say whether or not I leave with you."

"Of course you do," Lord Tamil crooned as he inclined his head. "Though, there is someone else who would have you come home." Roland only cut his eye to the guard clad in the royal blue jacket. He wore a heavy cloak made of fine velvet for the harsh winds in Aire, and a heavy scarf, green and draped decoratively around his neck. When he came back, Roland heard the footsteps of not one, but two.

"Brier…." A woman's voice made Roland finally lift his head. He saw a plump woman with a stern face, but with kind, nurturing brown eyes.

"Mari-Marietta?" Brier nearly screeched when he saw the woman holding a heavy shawl and scarf around her head. Roland noticed she too was dressed well. His unshaved face, cramped cabin, and handmade clothes did not fit the scene of obvious royalty. "Dear gods!" Brier's crunching hug nearly toppled the woman over. "How? When? By the gods I—I've missed you!"

Marietta let out a laugh and rubbed the back of the prince's head to soothe his stuttering. "Lord Tamil told me that they were coming for you and asked whether I would like to join the convoy."

"Goodness." Brier's face blushed, alight with joy. "I thought—" He shook his head and caught his breath. "Mar', when I could not say good-bye to you, I thought the worst." Roland could not imagine what Brier must have thought not able to properly say farewell to the woman he viewed much like a mother. For Roland life was simple; he was alone with no one left to worry for in this world.

"That's all done now. Yes?" She kissed the top of Brier's forehead, leaving the pale skin flushed. "We're going back now, together. That's all that matters." Her face lit with an open smile, but she faltered when Brier's mouth grew tight.

"I'm sorry but—" Brier swallowed. Roland tried to look away, but the immovable emerald gaze held him in place. He could read the prince's eyes indubitably. Brier had no intention of leaving this cabin and it did not matter who or what called him home. "I would like to stay with Master Roland."

"*Acai*—" Roland clenched his jaw. The pained expression on Brier's face made Roland nearly sick with guilt. "Your place is with your people, Prince Snow."

"Roland, I… I told you my wish." Brier moved completely away from Marietta.

"Heh—your wish?" Roland scoffed away Brier's words as childish ramblings.

"Yes." Brier's gaze did not falter although his face reddened. "Last night… in your bed." The room grew silent. It was not so strange for a master and his pupil to share the same bed, but Brier's tone held unsavory allusions none of the visitors could ignore.

Roland's heart began to race.

Last night.

He'd held Brier tight in his embrace, drowning in the sweet taste of his tongue and trembling from the heat of his body. The beautiful marks that danced on Brier's pale skin and the sound of the prince's ecstasy.

"Aye." Roland wanted to lean in to kiss Brier, to ease the prince's obvious discomfort at his own disclosure. To claim his prince, and in turn be claimed. However, Roland knew in the end they would only have sorrow and regret. Roland nodded and turned his face away. "Last night was a mistake," he answered roughly.

"No. You don't mean that, you—" Brier shook his head. "You're just saying that because you are afraid, but in my heart there is no doubt." Roland felt Brier's soft hands on his face and his gaze steadied against Brier's. His body stiffened at the teary eyes peering up at him. Unlike Roland there was no apprehension in Brier's eyes, only sadness at Roland's perceived betrayal. "Forget our stations. Look into your heart and tell me what you feel, Ronan."

Roland's eyes widened in shock. Hearing that name from Brier's lips broke Roland where he stood. He held Brier's wrist from his face and gripped tightly.

"Who told you to call me that? Leighis?"

"*N-na.*" Brier choked. "Y-you moaned it in your sleep—"

"What is it that you want from me?" Rage ensnared him. "Do you intend to guilt me into complying to your whims?" His voice darkened as black as sludge, and he shoved the prince's arm. The guard held his sword, but Lord Tamil stayed the sentry. "I told you many nights ago, this is what our fate would be!"

"Fate?" The agony in Brier's quivering voice made Roland's chest tighten. All at once his anger dissipated, and he stood facing his desperate lover. "How can you call this fate, Rolande?" Roland could not refute Brier. The excuse was for nothing but his inadequacy. And fragmented love. "Is this your fate?" Brier demanded through his sobs. "To hurt me thus?"

For a moment, Roland could not breathe. His body went rigid like an arrow-struck stag. He'd never wanted to hurt Brier, and yet, he knew he could not love him. Roland's tired eyes lowered. He stepped away from Brier and moved over to the corner as he turned his back. "I'm sorry, Your Grace," Roland whispered. The sorrow in his heart threatened to consume him. The silence felt like it lasted forever. Roland knew there were others in the room, but it felt like he and Brier stood alone in time. Just he and his beautiful, yet unattainable, prince.

"You're right." Brier's voice grew cold, then distant. "You are sorry." The prince walked away and whispered something into Marietta's ear, not speaking aloud for Roland to hear. Roland knew the damage was done. His words had cut Brier deeper than any sword or bear claw ever could.

"I am sorry things turned out this way." Lord Tamil gave his condolences, but Roland could hear the indifference in the man's apology.

"Do you need time to gather your things, Brier?" Marietta's voice actually did sound somber. Perhaps she knew the breaking of her would-be child's heart. Perhaps she only mirrored Brier's mournful visage.

"No, Marietta." Brier's monotone rang out one last time before his form turned into memory. "There is nothing here that I need."

Chapter 15
Reckoning

Roland closed the door behind him as he heard the hooves fade with distance. He leaned his head back against the door with his eyes closed.

It's enough.

Roland stumbled over to the table and lowered his head. The tears stung his eyelids, and he pounded the table with his fist, and the wooden box tilted to its side.

It's enough. The tune filled the vastness of the kitchen, and he watched as the figurine danced on the endless loop.

"Rolande," Lei's light voice called before a violent shake. "Get up."

"Hgn?" he groaned out with his head throbbing. He hadn't moved from the kitchen table in days.

"Curse the gods." Lei tried to sit him up. "It's freezing in here." Without the warmth of the fire, the cabin's wood grew stale and cold. Lei placed a blanket around his shoulders and lit a hearth fire. Roland opened his eyes slowly and gazed at the fire through the empty bottle of moonshine.

"You stink, Rolande," Lei scolded him. "Have you just been drinking your days away?"

"What does it matter if I have?" Roland answered groggily. He slid back from the table with a grunt and stumbled over to the cabinet for another bottle. Lei grabbed the bottle out of his hand before he could uncap the top and poured the liquor into the sink.

"What'd you go and do that for?" Roland slumped down into his chair by the fire. He could remember Brier at his feet. The boy singing his song while he petted Veti's black coat.

How pitiful I am, he thought, smiling sadly. That the memory filled him up with sadness and happiness in the same chord.

"You need to eat, Rolande." Lei searched the pantry for food. "You're too old to sit boozing the entire damn day. Do you want to kill yourself?"

"Mayhap, that would be better than this."

"You are a true fool if you believe that!" Lei opened the front door and the freezing air whooshed through his cabin. Roland pulled the blanket closer around him and watched as Lei stomped through the snow. At length, he wondered if Lei abandoned him, but then he heard leather boots through the atrium.

The healer dropped two heavy buckets of water and lit a fire on the stovetop. He slammed a wooden cup onto the table and filled it.

"Drink."

Roland peered up at Lei with bloodred eyes. "Why?"

"Drink, you idiot, before I wallop you!" Roland glared before he took the cup of water. He sipped it at first, but then guzzled.

"Haah—" He breathed out and pulled the cup from his mouth. He didn't realize how thirsty he was until the icy water slid down his throat. "More," he grunted, and Lei dipped the cup into the tin. He drank the second cup more slowly.

"You've got to pull it together, Rolande." Lei watched him warily. "There are soldiers filtering through Aire. They've completely shut down the Square. Botcht is furious."

"And what do I have to do with that?" Roland asked tiredly.

"You've a duty to your people and the guild—"

"I've no duty to anyone but myself." Roland stood up and sat the cup on the table. "I'm a free man now. I can do what I want."

"Free?" Lei scoffed as Roland searched the cabinets for more liquor. "Hiding in your cabin? Running away from your brothers? Ignoring your fate?"

Roland slammed the cabinet shut and Lei jumped.

"What do you want from me?" he asked coldly. "We are all free to do as we wish. Sasta and Dur have decided to go to Menlor, Lei. Duty to my brothers? What brothers? The guild is gone. Done and finished. I've done my duty!"

"And what of Brier?" Lei narrowed his gaze. "How long will you pretend to feel nothing for him?" Roland stared at pale eyes before he tensed his jaw.

"Whatever I feel…," Roland whispered. "It matters not. He's gone back where he belongs. And I'm back where I belong."

"Back to a life of emptiness." Lei shook his head. "For the both of you."

"I don't deserve more than this."

"Why?" Lei frowned.

"Because… Lei…."

"Because of what happened in Thenia?"

"*Na*." Roland shook his head. "He knows about that."

"Because he is an Aurelian? Why does it matter so much to you, Rolande?"

"Because… more than that… I…."

"Because you what?"

"Because… I was hired to kill him, Lei."

"What?" Lei's reply came out breathless.

"You heard me."

"How? You said that the queen hired you."

"The queen contracted me to train him, but someone intercepted me on my way from the palace, Lei. Someone who wanted Brier dead." The words made his heart sting. "For our contracts—to make sure that we would have our freedom I—"

"Agreed to kill a stranger?" The man's tone berated him more than the words. "How could you do such a thing?"

"To ensure we would have our freedom!"

"For the cost of Brier's life?" Lei asked.

"How many lives have we lost at Lirend's whims? How many women sent to bend over as their whores, our men to fight in their wars, our children made to sign their fucking lives away?"

"So you will match their cowardice? Their trickery? Their dishonor?" Lei accused him. "I would have never agreed to train Brier if I would have known about this!"

"Which is why you didn't know…." Roland shook his head. "Which is why no one knows." Roland stumbled over to the table and laid his head on the cool wood. "It was just a backup plan. In case the queen decided to back out of our deal. I thought I could do it, but the instant I saw him… the first time I held him in my arms… when I kissed him…." Roland's voice trailed. He turned toward Lei, who still gazed at him disgusted. He'd kept the secret this long, but now it was too late to hold on to it.

"It doesn't matter anymore," Roland croaked out. "Brier's gone. He's safe away from me."

"And you?" Lei whispered. "What will you do now, Rolande?" He honestly did not know. Helenas was gone. Brier was gone. All he had left were the memories.

Lei's boots stomped lightly on the wood before Roland felt the man's palm on his neck. "I think you should consider leaving with Dur and Sasta."

"There is nothing for me in Menlor."

"And there's something for you here?" Lei countered. "Brier is in Avenough. As you said, he's safe. If you stay here, you'll just torment yourself with regret."

"I do regret it…." Roland's eyes welled with tears. "Deceiving him, lying to the guild. I regret it. I'm sorry."

"Foolish as it was, you made your choice, Rolande." Lei sighed and patted Roland's head to let him know all was forgiven.

"I am foolish," Roland admitted. "I was a fool for taking the job, and I'm fool for letting him go…. Now there is nothing left for me."

"Go to Menlor," Lei repeated. "Start a new life, Rolande. Forget about the past and find a different path."

"And what if there is no path for me?" Roland squeezed the hand that held his head.

"It is a risk you must take," Lei whispered. His fingers still stroked Roland's matted hair. "You will never figure out the gods' plan, Rolande. We can only let fate decide."

Roland closed his eyes and wept silent tears. He pined for something he'd once had. Something he'd lost. Something he'd found. And he'd lost it again.

BRIER STARED at the top of the domed ceiling and counted the colur gems in the decorative iron leaf. After sleeping by a burly huntsman for so long, he felt miniscule in the four-poster bed. This room was bigger than the cabin's parlor and kitchen combined. He had a custom-made mahogany armoire with a chaise lounge at the foot of his bed.

The bookshelves they'd added gave the room an atmosphere of a study, and light blue curtains veiled the windows and veranda adjacent. His furnishings were fit for a king, his room fit for an Aurelian, and yet Brier had never felt so alone or empty. The tears burned his tired eyes, but he could not stop them.

"Prince Snow…." A gentle knock made him turn toward his bedroom door. Iron leaves and gold encased his father's once bedroom. The moment he entered the palace, Lord Tamil informed him that his things had been moved to the king's suite. In a month's time, the coronation would take place. In a month's time, he would present himself to the people of Lirend as their king.

"Brier. I'm coming in." He did not have the strength or will to refute her. His heart felt heavy and his body felt numb. The engraved door swung open, and Brier listened as Marietta shuffled in. She set down a teacup and kettle before moving over to the basin on his bedside. "I told Finnas to fetch your breakfast." She filled the tin bowl with water and dropped a cloth for washing. "Have ya gotten outta this bed once today?"

"No," Brier mumbled.

"Then I suppose you plan on wasting another day in here." Marietta ripped the curtains open and the light spilled into the dank room. Brier winced from the day.

"Please leave me, Marietta." Brier groaned and turned his head away from the sunlight. "I don't want to be seen."

"I understand that much." Marietta moved back to the basin. "But you've got to come out of this room. You've been holed up here for a week, Prince Snow."

"Has it only been a week?" It felt like a year since he'd returned to the palace. It felt like a century since he'd left Roland.

"Yes, it's been a week. Lord Renli has sent you several invitations for breakfast, and Lord Tamil needs your assistance with the coronation ball." She grabbed his robe and began to strip him. He did not want to see anyone. He did not want to breathe. He did not want to live without Roland by his side.

"Have Finnas help Lord Tamil with the preparations. As for Lord Renli, tell him I'm sick."

"You can tell 'im yourself if you're fit to tell me."

Brier pursed his lips together. "What good does it do me to have advisors if I must personally see to every invitation?"

"And a good deal it's done ya to ignore everyone." Brier did not fight her as she began to wipe down his arms and chest.

"They're getting darker," the woman said warily. "Have they glowed at all since you've been back?" Brier held his pillow and shook his head. For once he paid no attention to his silver scars.

"Lord Renli would never invite me anywhere before. Why should things change now that I am to be king?" Brier's face flushed as she turned him to his side and wiped his naked back and behind. When he lay flat once more, he turned toward his nursemaid with a scowl.

"Because you've got different responsibilities now, Brier. It's your job to make sure you're hospitable. Even to the likes of Lord Renli."

"Everyone was content to discard me before I came back to Avenough. They only want my company now because I will take the throne."

"Of course they only want your company because you are going to be king. In less than a month's time, you're going to be the law of this land, Prince Snow."

"I don't need them to pretend to care about my well-being," Brier said bitterly. Before he left for Aire everyone treated him like a permanent stain, but the upcoming coronation brought the bootlickers out in full. "Being ignored suits me just fine."

"How long are ya gonna act like a spoiled child?" Marietta glared at him. Brier tightened his jaw at the snub, but the anger quickly turned to despair. Mayhap he was a spoiled child and that was why Roland let him go. Mayhap he'd let himself get carried away in his own illusion of love. He stared up at the ceiling and felt his chest tightening. The silence broke when Finnas came into the bedroom with a breakfast tray of fruit and thin-sliced bread. Gone was the smell of smoked pork and crisp fried bacon for breakfast.

"Did you need anything else, Your Grace?" Finnas cautiously asked. Although Marietta hired the man for personal assistance, Brier had not spoken one word to his new retainer since his arrival in Avenough.

"That will be all, Finnas, thank you," he whispered. He waited for the door to close before he lifted up and rubbed the bags under his teary eyes.

"Forgive me, Marietta. I—" Before he could finish, Marietta held him in a warm embrace. He clung to the back of her shirt and shed more desperate tears. "I don't know what to do. I feel so helpless, Mar'."

"Shhh…." The woman held him tighter. "It's all right, my child." She rubbed his back in light circles and just allowed Brier to weep. "You're feeling the sting of the love bug, my dear."

"'Tis more like a tick." Brier sniffed and pulled away. Marietta reached over to grab a bit of toast. "It's draining me."

"Yes, but ya cannot waste away pining over a mere huntsman."

"Ronan is not a mere huntsman, Marietta!" Brier shook his head, aghast. "I love him. I cannot live without him."

"Ya can and ya will!" She slapped the toast into his hand. "You are Brier Snow, future king of Lirend. Your value does not lie in whether or not Roland Archer believes you are worthy."

But Brier did not feel worthy. Roland had thrown him away, and as always his path was hidden.

"Now eat. You're as thin as a beggar." Brier nibbled the toast begrudgingly. He stared down at the bread and swallowed. Food had not tasted the same for some time now. Nothing felt the same.

"I didn't… think it would hurt this much to be away from him, Marietta."

"And it'll hurt a lot longer than this." She broke off a piece of cantaloupe and handed Brier the plate. "Focus on the coronation and give it time. This too shall pass, my prince."

"Even this hole in my heart?" The woman stared at him with unveiled pity in her eyes. She did not need to answer him because he already knew the truth. He would never forget Rolande, no matter how much time had passed.

BRIER SET aside his anguish momentarily and followed Marietta's advice to busy himself with the coronation preparations. The event proved a good distraction, and Lord Tamil took a firm interest in Brier. The man made it his priority to familiarize him with the inner workings of the palace, and promised Brier that after the ball he would help him with the courtiers. As for the invitations from Aurelians, Brier respectfully declined. He had no time to entertain men and their wives. No time or patience.

"And as this day draws to its close, I know that my abiding memory of it will be, not only the solemnity and beauty of the ceremony, but the inspiration of your loyalty and affection. I thank you all from a full heart. May the gods bless you all." He peered down for the reaction of the guards who stood in front of him. One of them let out a deep yawn and Brier scowled. His constant supervision would be the first thing he changed when he was king. Brier heard a light clap from the shadows of the hall, and he lifted his gaze from the altar where he stood. Fear crept up his spine as he heard the slow click of heels on the white marble floors.

"A very good speech, Prince Snow." Queen Evelyn's voice rang out into the hall, and Brier stood to his full height.

"It is a good omen that Her Majesty approves." He stared at his stepmother coldly.

"Indeed. I had heard that you were sick when returning from your trip from Aire. How are you feeling now?" Did she hear about his row with the huntsman? Mayhap the guard or Lord Tamil informed her of the affair. Her dark eyes and smirking red lips enraged him, but he could not let her rouse him the day before his coronation.

"I feel fine. Thank you." Brier inclined his head.

"I am glad to see that you have made a full recovery in time for the ball. It would be a pity to let *personal ailments* affect your blessed reign." This time Brier was sure she alluded to Roland. There was no ailment more painful than his broken heart.

"Is there something you need, Your Majesty?" He smiled through the ache in his chest.

"I only came to wish you luck." The queen smirked and bowed her head.

"Thank you for taking the time." Brier continued to smile. "I imagine it must be a busy time for you as well, preparing your speech of resignation." Her lips turned into a thin line, and Brier returned her menacing glare. Despite all his suffering, Evelyn sending him to Aire was her worst transgression.

"Prince Snow." Lord Tamil's voice rang out into the hall and he bowed. "Queen Evelyn."

"What is it, Lord Tamil?" she snapped at the plump advisor.

"Prince Snow is needed in the royal chamber for his final fitting." Brier cut his gaze to the queen, who refined her face. He could still tell she was seething, but there was not much she could say in front of a respected member of the court like Lord Tamil.

"Thank you." Brier stepped away from the altar and followed Lord Tamil out of the hall. He did not look back, even as he heard the queen's yell echo through the heavy ballroom doors.

Chapter 16
A Stately Affair

"THEREFORE I am sure that this, my coronation, is not just the symbol of power and splendor, but a declaration of our hopes for the future, and for the years I may, by the gods' grace and mercy, be given to reign and serve you as your king."

The royal ballroom shone like he'd never seen, gold and green glittering from the domed ceiling and floors. The moonlight from the open glass walls filtered in. The effect made the room look like a twinkling constellation, or a shooting star.

Brier sat on his father's throne and peered out into the sea of people. Nobles, high-ranking military, and lords and ladies from all over the kingdom had come to celebrate his reign. Women in bright-colored dresses, embroidered with silk and fine sequins to mimic the decor. Men with their finest jackets, riddled with gold buttons, silver studs, and their house colors draped garishly around their waists. The men strode through the room like mating peacocks, and the women swooned and showered them all with attention. It might have been amusing if he were not dressed in the same drag. His pure white jacket outshone all others, and his gleaming crown, littered with colur gems, glared off the glass walls and monumental chandeliers. He was glad when Lord Tamil told him he could rise from the iron-leaf throne and mingle with his twittering guests.

Brier watched the lords and ladies sway across the ballroom in unison. The smooth and slow melody was so unlike the bouncing jig he danced in Aire, but the ladies' dresses flowed beautifully, and he found himself chuckling as he imagined them hopping in such elegant wear. Most of the couples came to him individually to offer their regards and well-wishes, but some of the unwed women came with their fathers, and even some of the men introduced themselves in a showy manner. Brier did not know whether his taste for men had spread, and he honestly did not care. When he did not take a wife, his predilection would become clear, and damn anyone who objected. Even the thought of lying with women made him uncomfortable. As the rightful king, he would at least grant himself that pardon.

"I should think that a king, on his coronation, and at a ball such as this, should at least manage a smile." Brier turned toward the low whisper in his ear and he held the nape of his neck. The crooning voice made the fine hairs stand on end.

The king glanced over at the man who stood before him. A blond with soft curls atop his head that matched his saccharine accent. He wore an orange jacket with silver buttons. Tassels hung at his waist, with a long decorative sword to mark his station. This man was a prince. The coat matched perfectly with an orange, white, and red sash across his chest, signifying his royal standing. Brier had to even his breath before he spoke, but he managed a tempered reply.

"It has been a long day." Brier bowed his head in acknowledgment. "But I thank Your Grace for gracing my coronation with his presence."

"The pleasure is all mine, King Brier." The man lifted Brier's wrist and kissed his knuckles in deference. Brier watched the prince silently. His blue eyes lit against the colur gem in his ring. His black boots shone like glass.

Brier pulled away his hand feeling sheepish and stuttered his next words. "Forgive my ignorance, but I do not think we have met."

"Do not apologize, Your Majesty," the prince said, still bowing. "It is I who should apologize for not making a king's acquaintance before his coronation ball. Please forgive my bad taste. Had I known of Lirend's handsome prince, I would have made my mam send me west with my dear sister, and made my presence known long before today." The prince chuckled and raised his blond head. "But then again, I would not have had the opportunity to speak to you thus, so I should say, it has all worked out. For both our favors, I'm sure." A gentle blush rose to Brier's cheeks, more from discomfort than pleasure at the man's showy nature. Brier had never met a man who spoke so confidently, dressed so well, and looked so, well... charming.

"Perhaps that is true." Brier did his best to match the prince's charisma. "But you still have not given me your name."

The prince let out a hearty chuckle and shook his head. "And I still manage to elude myself to His Majesty." He held up his right hand and placed it on his heart, while placing his left hand behind his back in a rigid formal bow. "Prince Quintin Pascal, son of Bastian Pascal of Menlor."

Menlor. Brier's eyes grew wide.

"Might you be kin of Adeline Pascal?"

"I am her youngest brother," the prince answered proudly, and Brier could not help the chuckle that escaped him at Quintin's confession. Memories of him begging Marietta not to make him marry the "sheep-haired princess," as Brier had once called Adeline Pascal, came flooding back to him.

Quintin raised his brow at Brier's sudden laughter. "Am I to take it she made such an impression on her trip here years ago?"

"That is not the case at all." Brier shook his head, winded. "Please do send my apologies to your dear sister. When she visited here many years ago, I may have been unkind to her."

"That someone as sweet as you were unkind? I do not believe it."

Brier finally controlled his laughter and gave Quintin a half smile. "An indiscretion of youth, I'm afraid."

"Then I am sure she'll be more than happy to forgive His Majesty."

"And what makes you so sure?" Brier found that he enjoyed the prince's twanged accent and nostalgic memories.

"Because her brother will vouch for you." He gave a slight shrug. "For the right price." The prince smirked and Brier pursed his lips.

"And what price would that be?"

Quintin stepped forward and held out his hand. "Only a dance."

Brier's eyes flickered to the hand held out to him and he felt a wave of apprehension. He hadn't predicted Quintin's price would be so candid, but it was his own prudence that made him nervous.

"I...." He bit the inside of his lip. Part of him wanted to grasp the hand and abandon his trepidation. The other half wanted to turn and run away.

"I promise to lead you well."

It's just a simple dance, Brier told himself as he took Quintin's hand and stepped toward him. He was a king now, and he refused to let uncertainty rule.

Quintin led him to the middle of the floor, and Brier felt eyes on him. The heavy crown made his neck stiff, but Quintin's hand held his back steady. The violins started low, and Brier allowed himself to move with Quintin leading him across the dazzling floor. Brier flushed at the strength Quintin held him with, but fell into rhythm as the music enveloped him. He had never followed in a formal dance, but enjoyed the feeling of relinquishing control. Prince Quintin danced well, but Brier did not feel outshone or underdone. Quintin carried him through the song as though they'd rehearsed the spontaneous partnership. Brier danced into the next song and the next.

After all.... He lost himself in the man's sapphire-blue eyes. It was just a dance, and a dance would not hurt.

It took several ballads before they winded themselves, and Quintin led Brier back to the sideline.

"I must say, Prince Quintin, you kept your promise."

"But of course." Quintin smirked. "My mother insisted I come and pay my respects to the king of Lirend."

"Your respects?" Brier raised his brow. "Do you dance with all the kingdom's royalty?"

"Menlor treats her allies well," Quintin whispered and held the small of his back. Brier opened his mouth to respond when he heard a shrill call from the corner of the room.

"Quintin!" The woman waved her hands animatedly to get the man's attention. Brier cut his eyes toward the prince.

"Someone you know?" He gave the man a devious smile. Quintin gripped Brier's hand and pulled him under his arm to whisper in the side of his ear.

"That is Lady Y'vette," Quintin told Brier as his lips brushed Brier's ear. Brier shivered from the tingle up his spine. "She is the lady of Lord Wellish of Concord. Her father is a famous merchant. Has a ton of boats in Menlor. Do well for you to mention that with her." Quintin released him as they reached an elaborately dressed woman.

"Lady Y'vette." Quintin bowed his head slightly. "How long it has been since I've seen your radiant smile?"

"Oh stop it, you!" the woman exclaimed, but she blushed up to her ears and curtsied. "Thank you for the invitation, Your Majesty. It has been near ten years since we were invited to the palace for a ball. You were but a child then." She giggled.

"Good evening, Lady Y'vette. Thank you for accepting." He plastered on a polite smile. "Though I dare say you can't have been more than a child yourself, if at all over." He rested his hand lightly on the hilt of the ceremonial sword at his side, doing his best to imitate his royal companion. "I trust that you're enjoying yourself this evening?" The woman let out a sheepish chuckle and whipped out a patterned fan.

"I can see Prince Quintin has taught you his naughty charm already, King Brier." She laughed at the two of them and nodded. "My husband, Lord Wellish, and I knew your father long before his passing. He was a fine man and king, and I see he has a fine son as well." The mention of his father made him momentarily speechless, but he heard the warmth in Lady Y'vette's tone, and he thanked her for the compliment.

"If his dancing skills are anything like his kingship, he shall be fine at that too," Quintin added.

"Oh yes, but you two did look dashing on the floor together. People will think this is the making of a betrothal!" she joked, but Brier paled at the truth in her words. Parading around on the dance floor with a royal made fertile ground for rumors.

"Ahh, but if His Majesty would only have me." Brier narrowed his gaze at Quintin's words. "I'm afraid this one shall make me work for it, Lady Y'vette. I shall suffer yet before it is done."

"As you should," Lady Y'vette replied tersely. "Brier is a king and gentlemen, not some sea maiden to sweep off her feet. Isn't that right, Majesty?" Brier blushed slightly when he remembered Roland. The huntsman quite literally swept him off his feet.

"I'm not as easy to woo as that." Brier let out a mechanical laugh. A pang of guilt claimed his heart when he thought about how Roland had embraced him on *Yensira*. How he kissed Rolande under the lanterns and stars. "Please do excuse me." Brier bowed and turned away. He hurried toward the exit without stopping to breathe.

"Your Majesty!" Brier heard Quintin calling after him. He did not stop until he felt a firm grasp on his wrist. He flushed when he faced the handsome prince, winded though he'd only crossed half of the ballroom.

"You left before I could say good night." Quintin's forehead creased into a frown. "Is everything all right?" The hold on his wrist loosened, and Brier covered the place where Quintin's fingers touched his skin.

"Forgive me, but…." Brier shook his head and smiled. He thought he might be able to enjoy a night without thinking of his once lover, but that seemed impossible. "I think I should retire for the evening."

"So soon?" Brier had made it through the majority of the ball and spoke with every courtier in attendance. He did not think Lord Tamil would scold him if he left.

"You've exhausted me, Prince Quintin." Brier tried flattery instead.

"I do not believe I have heard those words before from mere dancing, King Brier, but I am happy with them nonetheless. Would His Majesty also allow me to escort him back to his suite? Or shall I count my luck thus far as spent?" Brier's smile faltered as the prince winked. Certainly this man did not think he would allow a stranger in his bed after a night of ballroom dancing.

"It is always best not to gamble on the whims of a king," Brier answered curtly to remind Quintin of his station. "But I'm sure there are plenty others who would love your company."

"Indeed." The man gazed around the room with a smug simper. "There are many here perhaps well more interested in me than His Majesty, though I dare say, not near as stunning." The more Quintin spoke, the more Brier tired of his narcissism.

"On the contrary, Prince Quintin, you dare say quite a lot, but no words with actual substance." Brier smiled sweetly and turned to walk away. "Now if you'll excuse me, I'll be going." Brier did not look back this time as he headed toward the main stairwell that led to his royal suite.

Finnas waited outside the ballroom to escort Brier to his suite at the top of the stairs. Brier sighed out as he eyed the long winding stairwell.

"Is everything all right, my king?"

"Fine, Finnas." His room was at the very top, and though he hadn't had the stomach for wine, he felt squeamish. Just as he began to walk, he heard Quintin call out to him.

"Your Majesty!" Brier tightened his jaw. He'd had more than his share of Aurelians tonight, and Prince Quintin was no exception. The only thing this man had to offer were compliments and gaudy smiles.

"Your persistence is admirable but it is for nothing, Prince Quintin," Brier called back and continued to climb the stairwell. "Please let me be."

"I understand. But please, let me say something before you depart for the night!" Quintin's desperate tone made Brier halt.

"Your Majesty?" Finnas waited for directives. Brier sighed. He had no intention of indulging Prince Quintin, but he should at least let him speak.

"Head to my suite, Finnas, I will be there shortly." He waited for the boy to get a right distance away before he spoke again. "Go ahead, Prince Quintin."

"I feel that I must explain my behavior." Quintin's haughty tone diminished. Brier turned to face Quintin and found him red faced and bowed.

"And why should you explain yourself to me?"

"I believe you have misunderstood me thus far, Your Majesty."

"Misunderstood you, have I?" He arched his brow, unimpressed. "Pray tell how, Prince Quintin."

"Well," he began. "In the first place I only meant to accompany you to your room, but not to enter it." Brier felt his face darken once more at the prince's bluntness, but he ignored his discomfort and countered Quintin's claim.

"Are you saying you have no impure intentions?"

"Of course not, Your Majesty." Quintin smirked as he stood upright. "But a dance, as lovely as it was, is not indicative of a lasting romance. I am not saying, nor will I say, that I have no intentions of hoping for more than just accompanying you, but not on this night."

Brier did not know how to respond, so he held the iron railing tighter and let Quintin continue.

"Furthermore, in the future, should a time come when you would have me, I would hope to spend more than just one night."

More than just one night?

Brier flushed fully. He spent only one full night of passion with Roland, but he knew the ecstasy from coupling with a man too well. "Is that all?"

"Wish that I ask for your forgiveness?" A hopeful smile made Brier purse his lips, amused. He hated to admit it, but the prince truly was handsome.

"And why should I forgive you, Prince Quintin?" The prince walked up the stairs toward him, and Brier held the rail.

"P-prince Quintin—" The prince touched his cheek and Brier stiffened. Quintin's touch was so unlike Roland's heavy calloused hands. Brier closed his eyes and tried to forget.

"Let us call it an indiscretion of my youth." Brier felt the man lean in, presumably to kiss him, but instead the prince released Brier's face and bowed. "Good night, King Brier." Quintin walked back down the steps and out of his sight. Brier let out a shaky breath before his eyes fluttered open from the unexpected trance.

SEVERAL DAYS after the coronation, Brier entered his suite to a bouquet of wildflowers on his wooden vanity. He thought of Marietta. By now the flowers in the garden had begun to bloom, but these were not taken from the palace. Mayhap from one of the courtiers, but it would be strange to send him such bedazzling flowers.

"My lord." Finnas knocked on Brier's bedroom door.

"Come in, Finnas," Brier replied. The vase that held the stems had an orange and red and white ribbon tied around the base. Though Brier did not know the sender, the colors seemed oddly familiar.

"Where did these flowers come from?"

Finnas set down a tray of milk and breaded sweet tarts from the kitchen. For the past few weeks, Brier had taken to late-night snacking before bed. Marietta scolded him, but the craving endured.

"They were given to me by a young serf when I fetched your clothes for the meeting with the courtiers." Brier bit off a piece of tart and nodded. "He said that he was sent by the Prince of Menlor. There is a card attached, I believe." Brier cut his eye to the flowers once more and saw a small envelope tied with the ribbon.

Greetings, King Brier Snow,

The writing had a light air. Looped and slanted on the page.

You're probably wondering who these flowers are from. I thought to send you three dozen red roses without a card, since who else could be so thoughtful, but then I came to the conclusion that I might elude you once more with my penchant for overexuberance, and that would defeat the purpose entirely.

In all honesty I do not even know why I am writing this letter. It is 3 a.m. I am thoroughly spent, and overdrunk I might add, and yet, the only thing I can think about at the moment is your uncontrollable laughter at my poor sister's expense.

Am I wasting my time? Probably. But it is rare that I take an actual interest in someone, and even rarer that they have such a lovely smile... I only hope that I might see it again?

With regards to you, King Brier, I humbly request an audience with you at Lord Renli's annual games party. I will save a spot for you.

Signed,

Prince Quintin Pascal

Brier stared at the letter blankly for several seconds before he spoke.

"Did Lord Renli send me an invitation to a party recently, Finnas?"

"Yes, Your Majesty. It is his gaming party held in the Aurelian Quads."

"A lively event?"

Finnas nodded with a smile. "He supplies the Quads and some of the wealthier Burges precincts, so many of the vendors attend. Lord Renli is one of the top Menlor merchants in Lirend."

"I see." So that's how Quintin knew Renli so well.

"Is everything all right, Your Majesty?" The boy spoke warily.

"Fine." When he glanced again he noticed Quintin's house colors wrapped around the silver base. Brier sighed and twisted his face. He honestly had not expected Quintin to seek him out, assuming the prince would have tired of his own game by now. If the rumors held true Quintin lacked decorum, but not bedmates.

Which is no concern of mine. He picked up the letter and wrote a small note declining the invitation. He had no intentions of fraternizing further.

"Take this to the boy who gave this to you, Finnas." He handed the note to Finnas and moved the flowers away from his bedside.

"Of course, Your Majesty." The young man bowed and left him. Brier stared at the note laid on his end table and scowled. He drank the entire cup of milk before he removed his clothes and lay in the large bed.

In Aire, Caite would spar with Brier in a field bursting with wildflowers. When he was too tired to move, Roland would come to carry him home.

Brier stared at the wildflowers across the room and clutched his bedspread tightly. Prince Quintin was nothing like Roland.

Chapter 17
The Aurelian Quad

"Your Majesty, I implore you," Lord Tamil begged him in the royal study as Brier read over Avenough's budget for infrastructure. He sat on a chair lined with silver on the back and arms, with a cushion lined in purple silk to soothe his ailing back. He'd commissioned the cushion specially since the queen's chair felt like a seat of thorns. "Lord Renli is one of our most important contributors to the market. The queen has always attended his events, it would be an insult for you to decline."

"I am not the queen," Brier answered simply. "I do not know Lord Renli, and I don't intend to attend an event on the basis of his relationship with Evelyn."

"I understand your concerns." Lord Tamil began again, though he seemed put out by Brier's casual use of the once queen's name. "But Lord Renli was also a constituent of your father's circle. He is most eager to get to know you as well." Lord Tamil paused to let Brier take in the new information. If there was anyone who could sway Brier, it was Braedon Snow. "It would be in your interest not to shun those who are loyal to the crown. Especially in this time of change."

Brier sighed and put down his quill next to the vial of ink. This was once his father's study. The dark wood bookcases lined the wall, and the forest green and cream sofa lounge sat directly across from his wardrobe-like desk. Similar to his father's throne, accents of iron leaves decorated his study as well. The desk lamp, the coffee table fixture, and the seal on the doors. Just beyond the window there was a seat Brier used to sit in and stare out over the Aurelian Quads. In the summers he could smell the smoke from fires at the more rambunctious parties. The most telling feature of the king's study lay dead center: a heavily embroidered rug fashioned from a map of Lirend. Everywhere he looked he could see Braedon Snow, beloved ruler of Lirend. Brier both loved and hated this room.

"He will be sorely disappointed if he believes I am like my father," Brier mumbled as he leaned back in the chair.

"You are more like your father than you know." Lord Tamil gave him an encouraging smile. He wished the lord's words were true, but he knew he had yet to prove himself. As far as opportunities went, this was as good as any.

"Lord Tamil." Brier picked up his quill and signed the budget for the infrastructure maintenance. Then he handed over the paper and said, "Let Lord Renli know I'll attend his party."

A MONTH after his coronation ball, Brier prepared to attend his first Aurelian party. Finnas had prepped his clothing, a deep blue suede coat with lace ties from the middle of the chest. Fine stitched rosettes bordered the neck of his royal coat. He chose simple black pants to tone down the showiness of his tailored jacket and cuffed black riding boots, which added some inches to his height. To finish his presentation, Marietta plaited his red hair into three fine pieces that met in the middle of a single straight braid.

"Are ya sure you'll be all right?" Marietta watched as Finnas fastened a black belt around Brier's waist. He winced from the leather and asked the man to loosen it some.

"I'll be fine, Marietta." He'd been feeling nauseous that morning, but attributed his sickness to nerves and overwork. Since the coronation Lord Tamil had versed him in every detail of running the kingdom. Holding court, presiding over noble events, rides through Avenough, leases to sign, treaties to sign, loans to sign. It seemed that nothing could be done without his final word and decree. As much as he enjoyed his duties, he also felt overtired many days. Lord Tamil promised things would get easier once he chose another advisor, but he had no one in mind yet, and the prospective courtiers did not interest him in the slightest.

"You look marvelous." She leaned in to hug Brier with some delicacy.

"I feel a bit stuffy." He pulled at the jacket. Although he'd just had the royal tailor make the coat especially for tonight, his midriff felt tight.

"Haven't I told you about those sweet tarts in the wee hours?" She shot him a reproachful stare. "You'll be fatter than that, mind you, if ya keep at it."

"I'll keep that in mind." Brier leaned in to kiss her cheek. Before leaving he gave Finnas a once over to make sure he looked stately enough to join him for the evening. "Come, Finnas, we mustn't be too late or people will whisper."

"You're taking the guard, right?" Marietta asked.

"I do not think we'll need a show as big as that, Marietta." Brier refused to have them within ten feet of his suite, and only Finnas and Marietta were permitted inside his bedchamber. His aversion to guards worried not only Marietta, but also Lord Tamil. "It will just be Finnas and I this evening."

"What if something happens and you need an escort?"

"Then I'll have Finnas here to escort me." Brier slapped the middle of the man's back and Finnas flushed deeply.

"You should bring a guard. There's no telling what might happen, King Snow. It's not like when you were a prince. There's danger in traveling alone." Marietta's coddling so reminded him of Leighis that Brier gave her a whimsical smile. Then he thought of Roland and the smile vanished.

"I will bring a guard, but they'll not escort me inside the gates of Lord Renli's estate."

"That seems reasonable." Marietta gave in without a fuss, knowing Brier would not be swayed further.

The ride toward Renli's was as uneventful as Brier assumed. The guards followed him and Finnas on horseback some yards behind their carriage. Lord Renli's party was for exactly one week, and although he'd invited the king to stay for the entire length, Brier hastily declined. One night was more than enough. He'd visited the Aurelian Quads several times since taking the throne, and the more he visited, the more he disliked them. In the first place, the homes took up a large part of Avenough's land but did not pay their fair share of taxes to the crown. When he asked Lord Tamil about this practice, he'd cited that many of the Aurelians had business within Avenough. They employed the Burges that lived farther inland, and some in the suburbs. The queen pardoned a fair share of taxes as reward for hiring more working-class citizens. Less unemployment meant the people could not complain about commerce, but the Aurelians in charge hired the Burges at lower wages, and higher tax rates, to compensate for their pardons.

Then there was the matter of the way they treated their servants. While the Burges worked for their living, many of the Aurelians still had Prolit families that worked for them through generations as per the law of passage. If a father worked for an Aurelian, his firstborn sons would eventually work for the same Aurelian family. Thus the family could not escape their slavery-like servitude, and some of the lords and ladies treated them as such.

The nepotism in Lirend was just as Roland had said; no, it was worse. Brier did not have the means to change the heinous system yet, but he had every intention to do so.

"King Brier." Several of Lord Renli's servants met him outside of the house along with a few of Renli's Burges acquaintances. They bowed and curtsied as Brier smiled and acknowledged them. Renli met him in the atrium along with his wife, Portia, and his daughter, Elena.

"It is a pleasure to have His Majesty grace my home."

"The pleasure is all mine." Brier met Lord Renli's bow. "Thank you for inviting me." He turned to Finnas holding his luggage. "Where should Finnas put my things?"

"Ah—please forgive me, Your Majesty." Portia snapped her fingers and a lanky man with wide shoulders came over. "See to the king's belongings at once," she barked. The man hurried to grab the bags from the king's retainer.

"Do you need anything from me, Your Majesty?" Finnas asked tensely. "If not I shall go and prepare your room for this evening." Brier peered up at the winding stairwell that most likely led to the mansion's bedrooms. Unlike the palace, where opulent iron gleamed, Lord Renli preferred gold, and lots of it. Even the railing of his grand staircase glinted gold.

"Yes, Finnas. That will be fine. Thank you," Brier added pointedly. Finnas left the hallway and moved to head up the stairs with the earlier servant.

"Your attendant is so vigilant," Portia commented as she led Brier through the vast atrium. They walked several paces with Elena and Renli following close behind them.

"Finnas is a good and trustworthy lad. My nursemaid recommended him to me."

"Your nursemaid?" Elena crooked her brow. "His Majesty still employs a nursemaid?" The girl chuckled. She had brown-and-gold hair like her mother's, but

Brier stared overlong at her light hazel eyes. Though Brier was sure they'd never met, something about her was familiar to him.

"Forgive my wording, Lady Elena." Brier laughed. "Marietta was once my nursemaid. But she no longer fulfills that duty."

"Whatever for do you keep her, then?" the girl said offhandedly.

Lady Portia tried to clean up the question by adding: "Perhaps King Brier hopes to employ her in the future, Elena. It is so hard to find good help. I should think if this Marietta is worthy of the king's praise, then she is worthy to look after his own children." Brier's boots halted on the gray marble floors.

"I keep her close because she is dear to me," he explained in a calm voice. "She took care of me when I was a boy, practically raised me from birth. I've known her longer than any courtier, and I trust her with my life. If there is anyone who I should keep in my circle, it is her." Lady Portia shot a glance to her husband before she bowed her head in apology.

"I am sorry, my king." Renli spoke to diffuse the situation. "My wife sometimes speaks without thinking when she is nervous. I assure you, she meant no offense."

"No offense taken." Brier smiled and tried to feign aloofness. They continued toward Renli's ballroom. He hoped Lord Renli's wife was just nervous in his presence, but something told him this was not the case.

Luckily for Brier, the night wore on quickly. Lord Renli's countless parties had fine-tuned his hosting skills almost to perfection. After they mingled over drinks in the ballrooms, the lord supplied row tables with place settings for goblets or plates of food. Servants stood at the ready, and hired musicians played light keys and harps. The vast space held almost thirty attendees. Every goblet had wine and every game seat had a player. For Brier's part, he did not play very many card games, but he enjoyed the impeccable wine and the banter between the lords and ladies. He even challenged one of the lords to a game of darts, which he easily won due to Caite's dagger training.

"You are quite good." Brier heard the rich accent and his smile faltered. He tried to ignore the man, but he spoke again more loudly the second time. "Good evening, Your Majesty. It is good to see you again."

Brier placed the dart on the table and turned toward Quintin, smiling. By now the women had gone to bed and left the men to their bottomless drinking. Brier thought of sneaking away with them, and now that the prince had arrived, he wished he had.

"Good evening, Prince Quintin." He inclined his head. "It is, as always, a pleasure to see you as well." He moved over to Lord Renli's table hoping to avoid further small talk, but Prince Quintin followed him immediately.

"Quin." Lord Renli held the gold goblet in his hand. "How nice of you to join us. Late. As ever." He sipped from the cup.

"I apologize. I got held up with some business in my suite." Brier could not help but notice Quintin's gleaming smile and the luxurious jacket he wore. The trim around his collar looked as though it'd been freshly stitched around the prince's neck.

"Business you say?" Lord Renli gave Quintin a knowing look. "Is that what we're calling it these days?" The lord let out a crude laugh, which the others followed. Brier just stared as the tension between Quintin and Lord Renli unfolded.

"Whether business or pleasure, I always see it through to the end. You of all people should know that."

Renli shifted in his seat. "Of that much I am aware." He peered up from his cards. "You don't keep your excursions a secret."

"I've no need to. Unlike yourself I am unmarried and unattached." Quintin turned pale blue eyes toward Brier. Even though he tried to ignore the Prince of Menlor, the man's gaze made Brier instantly uncomfortable.

"But not unchanging."

Quintin snorted, but Brier's keen ears noticed the vexation in Renli's words.

"Now, now, Alex," one of the older lords said. "You mustn't tease young men for having fun."

"I wouldn't dream of it." Renli shook his head theatrically. "I've had more than my fair share."

"I couldn't agree more. Now. What are we playing?" Quintin asked.

"Ruff." Renli held his cards possessively. Brier folded his hands under the table and watched in silence. In the game of Ruff, a pack of fifty-two cards was used and twelve cards dealt to each player, with the first of the remaining four cards turned over to determine the trump suit. The last several times Lord Renli had taken the game, but Quintin seemed ready to break the streak.

Four of spades was the first trump, and Brier watched the men pile their cards one atop the other until Lord Renli took the suit. Brier exhaled, relieved for some reason, as it seemed the night would carry on as it had before Quintin's arrival. That is until the prince took the next suit, the suit after, and the next.

"Quintin, are you planning to take everything from me?" Lord Renli was clearly drunk, and Brier could see his game getting sloppy. Quintin drank his fill, but Lord Renli played all night, and it seemed he had eyes much bigger than his tolerance.

"Only if you let me." The prince turned to Brier and winked. Quintin's smug grin made Brier's stomach churn.

"I'll let you if you promise not to rush like last time," Renli audaciously replied.

Brier was sure the men were no longer speaking about Ruff. He moved back from the table and prepared to leave for the evening.

"Going so soon?" The prince eyed him as he stood.

"Yes, I think I've had enough of cards."

And enough of the crude exchange between Quintin and Renli.

"But you've not played one hand."

"Not with you." Brier forced a smile. "You missed most of it with your tardiness, but it's been a long night." Renli chuckled at Brier's quip, and Quintin smirked.

"Let His Majesty retire if he sees fit. I, for one, say the night is still young!" Renli lifted his goblet and drank. When he stopped to breathe, one of the servers came to refill the cup. "There's plenty more fare and wine." Brier tired of the smell of stringent ale and meat. Everyone else at the table had their sixth and seventh glass of alcohol, but Brier still nursed his first cup of wine.

"Perhaps you have had enough, Alex." Quintin smiled and shook his head. "Remember Adeline's after-party in the port town? Don't want you passing out again."

"Nonsense!" Renli frowned. "We'll drink till dawn!" Renli raised the goblet once more in his enthusiasm, and fresh ale drenched the servant who stood beside him. The woman froze with her dress dripping and her bosom wet. Lord Renli staggered to turn toward her. The man appeared only momentarily shocked before he burst into laughter.

Brier moved to assist the woman when he heard Renli's boorish voice exclaim: "This one is ready for the after-party, hmm, Quintin?" Lord Renli raised his hand as if to strike her rear and Brier clasped the lord's wrist in a tight grip.

"I think not." Brier's authoritative tone resonated through the game room. The music stopped. The men at the table who laughed now sat tight-mouthed and wide-eyed and ogled Brier. Lord Renli appeared flabbergasted at the king's admonition, but he managed to regain himself before Brier released his arm. Brier moved over to the woman, who was soaked in alcohol, and touched her shoulder.

"Are you all right?" he asked the maiden with every eye still on him. She nodded apprehensively before a servant handed her a towel. Brier turned to Renli and glared.

"I believe you owe this young woman an apology, Lord Renli." Renli let out a nervous chuckle, which no one joined.

"King Brier is right, Renli. You've soiled her completely with your antics." Brier was surprised to hear Quintin scold his friend, but he did not let it show on his face. If the lord seemed stricken by Brier's censure, Quintin's words drove him over the edge.

"Surely you jest?" Lord Renli scoffed.

"Do I appear as a jester to you?" Brier's eyebrow arched. "Do your king's words amuse you, Lord Renli?" The group shifted uncomfortably and looked to Renli for reaction. Brier's heart thudded hard.

"No, Your Majesty," Renli answered grudgingly.

"Good." He waited for Lord Renli to compose his obvious fury, and the man turned to the young woman.

"Apologies, my lady," Renli sneered. "It was my mistake." Brier could feel the woman shaking in his hold.

"Take this woman to get cleaned up," Brier told the lanky man who'd assisted Finnas earlier. "I suspect Lord Renli won't need her services for the rest of night." The man bowed and guided her out of the game room at once. Brier turned to the remaining guests and they all stood in either fear or deference.

"Thank you for the lovely party, Lord Renli. As always, it is a pleasure to visit the Aurelian Quads. I hope that you will invite me again."

"Of course, Your Majesty." Renli bowed stiffly. Brier exited the ballroom without another word, and the silence permeated.

CHAPTER 18
THE COURTING OF THE COURTIERS

BRIER DID not know what to expect after his show in the Aurelian Quads. Lord Tamil had heard about the incident before he even arrived back at the palace somehow, but his advisor did not reprimand him. Brier either had made his thoughts on the Aurelians clear enough to his advisor, or Lord Tamil saw him now as a lost cause where they were concerned.

Zhennal, Ranolf, and Nieraeth were Lirend's closest allies and rather than sending ambassadors to his coronation, the three kings planned to visit in the cusp of spring. Lord Tamil stressed the importance of the amalgamate, but Brier did not need coaching in this regard. He'd been groomed since birth in the workings of foreign policy. As a child he learned the dialects and nuances distinct to each region. Mostly everyone in power knew the common tongue so it was more for semblance than pragmatism.

Brier concluded his interview with another prospective advisor when Lord Tamil announced Quintin's scheduled appointment. "And what is this appointment for?" The prince continued to send him flowers, now daily, and ask for his company, but Brier was too busy over the last several months to entertain Quintin's antics.

"He says that he would like to speak to you about possibly opening up trade on some of the more popular items from Menlor."

"He should speak with the Master of Trade about that. I believe Lord Emery is more than capable of cutting a deal with Menlor."

"He necessitated an audience with Your Majesty."

Brier let out a vexed sigh. "See him in, Lord Tamil." The man bowed and opened the door to let Quintin into the royal study. Brier did not fully look up from the documents, but skimmed Quintin's heavily embroidered jacket and tailored riding pants. Brier wore a simple green oversized tunic and plain black leggings. He probably should have dressed more prominently, but nothing fit him properly anymore. His jackets bound his stomach and waist, and his fitted pants did not come past the knee. When he complained to Marietta, she changed her initial diagnoses of weight gain to an impending, and untimely, growth spurt.

"Good evening, King Brier." Quintin bowed in Brier's peripheral.

"Evening." Brier finally gazed upward. "Lord Tamil, you may leave us." The advisor cut his gaze to the prince before giving a polite nod and exiting the study.

"You're a hard man to meet with," Quintin informed him as he relaxed in the seat across from the king. Brier noticed the prince did not ask for his permission to sit, but the prince's entitlement in that regard did not bother Brier. He rather liked not having to command people every second of the hour.

"I'm aware." Brier nodded. "I'm also a very busy man. Was there something you needed, Prince Quintin?"

"Straight to the point, are we?" The prince smirked.

"I apologize for my briskness, but I really don't have time to indulge your penchant for loquacity. I still need to go over the menu for the banquet with the caterer and make sure the kings' rooms are specially prepared."

"Sounds like you need more help."

"Yes, well… that is another job." Brier peered up expectantly. The prince's tenacity made him almost impossible to spurn.

"I came here to talk to you about two things. One business related, the other more personal."

"Start with the aforementioned." And he could skip the latter as far as Brier was concerned.

"Right. Well. I'm sure you're familiar with the relationship I have with Lord Renli." Brier pursed his lips. "Regarding the import and export of Aurelian goods," Quintin clarified.

"I'm familiar." He took the prince's bait. "Lord Renli has monopolized imports and exports out of Lirend."

"And why do you suppose that is?" Quintin inquired.

"Aren't you the one who does business with him? Why don't you tell me?" Brier challenged.

"Heh—" Quintin chuckled. "It is because Lord Renli held the contracts for many of the cities' trades. Even our allies, the Divine Three. His family owns the most ships in Avenough. Even more than the crown."

"Why are you telling me this?" He did not trust Quintin for a moment, and the last thing he wanted was to be in the middle of a lovers' spat.

"Because. I want to offer you, the crown, a contract to exclusive goods."

"What kind of exclusive goods?" Brier's thin brow raised.

"We have things in Menlor that Lirend does not."

"For example?"

"For example, our raw materials. Silver and oil. Also, our paper." Brier eyed Quintin carefully. Menlor's paper was made from the Lau tree. Soft and delicate like textured cotton, impractical and expensive. Aurelians would clamor to buy it. Brier tried to keep his face passive, but he knew his eyes gleamed at the prospect.

"Lirend can stiffen the sanctions around the trade market. In the past it was required for the crown to approve any foreign trades, but the queen suspended those regulations."

"Because we tax the merchants directly."

"Who tax the Prolit and Burges to make up for their losses. For all your preponderance, Lirend is a free trade market." Brier's head buzzed with all the information. He'd never considered the liability of relying on the Aurelians to run the foreign trade market, but Quintin's resolution made sense.

"Anything else?"

"I have a proposition for you regarding your current situation with the Aurelians." At these words Brier tensed.

"What current situation is that?" Brier probed. He had not made his plans for the Aurelians known to anyone. Not even Marietta.

"You wish to disperse the power in Lirend equally, do you not?" Had he been so translucent with his desires? Or did Quintin know something he didn't?

"I don't know what you're talking about." Brier narrowed his eyes.

"Don't you?" Quintin crossed his legs. "I don't pride myself as a political strategist, but I've seen the way you've been running this regime. You've passed several laws on sanctions in the work mines, and made it illegal for the Prolit to work more than fifty hours a week."

"You object?"

"Not in the slightest." Quintin shook his head. "Work is important, but I am under the impression that the gods put us here for a greater purpose. The pleasures of life are not exclusionary to Aurelians."

Brier's lip tightened. "What is your proposition, Prince Quintin?" He neither accepted nor denied the prince's claim, but he found himself more interested in the prince's proposal.

"Invest in the Prolit and Burges well-being. No offense, but the health care centers and schools are severely lacking."

"I'm aware of this." Brier glared at the prince.

"Yet you take offense to my words?"

"The public schools are a joke in Lirend. Any Burges who show aptitude as a scholar don't have the money to afford the university, and the Prolit don't even attend. There are too few health care centers and too many private Aurelian healers. The Burges cannot get an appointment for weeks out, and the Prolit cannot afford to take off to see a healer." Not to mention those that lived outside of the capital. The influx of disease and plague in the farmlands had mostly to do with inaccessible health care. "Nevertheless, this is my kingdom, Prince Quintin. I don't intend to muse over the quandaries with no solutions."

"I see." Quintin smirked at Brier's admonition. "Straight to the point after all."

"What are you proposing?"

"I will stand by you in the meeting with the allies, introduce you to the people sympathetic to your cause."

"I cannot help the Burges and Prolit with sympathy," Brier countered.

"As *I* am aware," Quintin remarked patiently. "While I find your efforts valiant, at the rate you are going, you will not succeed. Menlor will give you tools you can use in the hospitals you build. Offer incentives to those healers who work in them. Increase wages for those willing to teach in lower income precincts. In the meantime, free public university to lessen the burden of those hoping to advance in their education."

"And why should I rely on Menlor to help my people?"

"You have no allies in the court, you have no standing with the Divine Three, and you have no favor among the Aurelians."

"I don't want favor with the Aurelians," Brier cut in.

"Ah, but the Aurelians are the ones who will change things. Do you think Lord Renli is the only one who has taken advantage of the crown's vulnerability since your father's passing? They have influence in the courts, more than you know." Brier pressed his lips together, but he knew the prince's words rang true. Even if he managed to stabilize the trade lines, he could not govern a country that despised him.

"Do not be so quick to cut out the Aurelians. After all, they are still citizens of Lirend. They are not all like Lord Renli," Quintin assured him. "And of course, you always have the people to back you up. You need them as much as they need you. You cannot do it alone, King Brier."

Brier considered Quintin's words and then gave the man a slow nod. For a moment Quintin's words reminded him of Roland's. When he told Brier to trust the people of Lirend to stand beside him when he ruled. Even if he did not trust Quintin, he still trusted Roland.

"Reach out to the other allies. They will help you for the right price. I believe your coveted colur gems will catch the eye of the Divine Three, and Menlor of course." Brier did not doubt for a second the three kings would hesitate in helping him rebuild his working class if he offered them colur gems. Suppression made them almost unattainable in the market.

"Why would you help me?" Brier questioned, still leery of the man's motives.

"Menlor has been Lirend's ally for years. I believe it was your father, King Braedon, who hoped to wed our countries once upon a time. That is how you met my sister, Princess Adeline."

Braedon's plans for a marriage between Menlor and Lirend had thankfully gone unfulfilled.

"My father hopes to maintain these ties through solid trade lines."

"And you? What cause do you have to help my people?" Even if the King of Menlor wanted to establish good business decorum, that had nothing to do with Quintin's assistance with the Aurelians.

Quintin beamed before he bit his lip. "For now I will just say, I have a personal interest in your success, King Brier."

A FORTNIGHT later the kings of the Divine Three arrived. Brier stood pomp in his brilliant green jacket made of fine silk. Lord Tamil gave him a matching embroidered cloak to wear with the leaf insignia of his house, but the humid summer air took its toll on Brier. He'd finally kicked the mysterious nausea, but the remnants of fever still lingered. Marietta urged him to see a healer, and he promised her he would after the Divine Three departed. Until then, Brier consumed himself in running Avenough.

"My king, I humbly announce King Eduard of Ranolf, King Fiete of Zhennal, and King Askel of Nieraeth." Lord Tamil bowed from the neck and stood at their side. Brier rose from his throne to give the kings a rigid bow.

"Welcome." He plastered on an inviting smile. "Though I know you have all had long journeys, I am grateful that you have come all this way. Prince Quintin arrived some time ago, and I believe he has found the hospitality of my palace agreeable."

"Indeed." Prince Quintin winked, and Brier had the impulse to roll his eyes.

"It is a pleasure to once again have you standing in the halls of Lirend."

"The pleasure is ours." King Eduard was an older man with a crooked back and a long hooked nose. Brier did not stare overlong. Then to King Fiete. Much younger than Eduard, though not nearly as kind-looking. He wore a pretentious smile and draped linen across his chest. The final, King Askel, stood out amongst the three. He was the youngest and also, as far as Brier could tell, the sharpest.

During the first round of negotiations, he waited for Brier to lead the conversation before bolstering through with ingratiating proposals like Eduard and Fiete. Now that the rightful king was on the throne, they had a plethora of ideas. However, for ten years, since Braedon's passing, the Divine Three voided or vetoed all negotiations and propositions; a point Brier would not let them omit. He wanted to build schools, restore power amongst the Prolit and Burges, but most importantly, drain the pus-filled sac that'd become his Aurelian class.

"Forgive my impudence, King Brier, but why should we help you restore order in your lands?" King Askel boldly asked.

"Mostly because you have helped to disorder it, King Askel. Your dealings with the Aurelians and not the crown directly have caused a spike both in power and wealth in my country."

"We had no desire to negotiate with that vile woman," King Eduard spoke. "She was a pox on the crown."

"And yet you did not go through the courts."

"We did, Your Majesty," Feite said "Otherwise, how do you think we have kept the trading lines intact all these years?"

"By trading with the Aurelians, I suppose." Brier smiled and nodded. "Prince Quintin of Menlor has a contract with Lord Renli of the Quads. I suppose you all have similar contracts with Aurelian merchants to move your resources." Feite stared gobsmacked by Brier's perceptive assumption. All the while Quintin sat at Brier's side, watching in silence.

"No ill intentions were conceived, Your Majesty." Askel decided to intervene when Feite lost his words. "The queen made it difficult to keep the trade lines strong."

"I did not think anything untoward, King Askel, lest I would not have invited you thus. I commend you all for the fluidity when the success of the trade lines depended on your ability to adapt." Brier felt the men calm at his praise. "However, now that I have taken the reins, I hope that you will turn your attentions and dealings back to where they belong."

"Of course, Your Majesty," Askel agreed.

They sat down after the first round of negotiations to a grandiose banquet. Brier loaded his plate with thinly sliced cheese and salted bread native to Zhennal. For Nieraeth's dish, they scooped out the middle of a coconut and added squeezed lime juice. Then a redmelon salad from Menlor with mint and sundried tomatoes. After he'd finished his first plate, Finnas loaded him with more. For dessert the servers added rum to a white cream Bundt cake, a dish from Ranolf that made Brier's mouth water. The only thing missing for Brier was the meat. Finnas offered him a tray of skinned and boned salmon, but the smell made Brier's stomach churn. He longed for a slab of goat ribs, or some of the guild's pulled pork over the open fire. After the banquet Brier bid farewell to the kings and made himself another plate of food to scarf before bed.

"I'm glad to see you enjoy Menlor's redmelon." Prince Quintin took the seat beside Brier. Brier averted his gaze but felt too full to move away from him.

"It was very good, thank you."

"No thanks needed." Quintin shook his head. "Unless you want to thank me tonight. In which case I have several ideas in mind."

"All depraved, I'm sure."

"You're as astute as ever." Quintin let out a chuckle, and Brier sighed.

"And you remain steadfast as ever, Prince Quintin."

"Absolutely."

"Despite the fact that I've expressed my disinterest several times."

"Yes."

"And why is that?" Brier turned fully toward the prince. "What is it that you hope to accomplish with this pursuance?"

"Perhaps friendship. Perhaps something more. Is it so bad to be unsure of one's desires?" Quintin's white smile dazzled against the sapphire-blue of his eyes. Brier did not know whether he liked being considered desirable by a man other than Roland.

"I told you, I have an interest in you. Even if you could consider me a friend, I'd be more than happy with that arrangement."

"Friends?" Brier quirked his brow.

"Yes, my king."

"Like you and Lord Renli, I presume." Quintin gave him a probing stare. Brier did not know why the thought of Quintin and Renli's friendship miffed him, but he told himself it was due to the sordid trades that ensued between them.

"I enjoy Alex's company, but I do not consider him a friend."

"Well what do you consider him?"

"Hmm…." The man paused before answering. "Something to pass the time in Lirend."

"And me?" Brier startled himself with the question and felt his face burn.

"You, King Brier, are an enigma."

Brier shook his head, laughing "And you, Prince Quintin, you are exhausting."

"As I've been told before."

Brier forked a piece of redmelon. "Though I suppose friendship would not be so bad." He chewed, still snickering. "After all, your counseling with the Divine Three has been invaluable. Your support made the negotiations run smoothly. For that I am truly grateful."

"Then do you think that my generosity warrants a cup of coffee alone together?"

Brier did not answer right away. Quintin always made him feel uneasy, as though he was breaking a promise.

A promise to do what? Brier thought as he stared at Quintin. *More importantly, a promise to whom?*

"Very well, Prince Quintin." Brier gave the prince a hesitant smile. "But let us wait until the Divine Three depart."

THE DIVINE Three departed one week later, and Brier and Quintin breakfasted together for the first time on Brier's parlor veranda. Brier gazed out at blue cloudless skies and placid ponds on the grounds before the scape of Avenough. Lush trees dotted the city's dusty roads. Summer had come, and Brier's chest ached from the ping of nostalgia. One year since he met him. One year since he journeyed with Roland, from Avenough to Aire.

"It is a beautiful view," Quintin remarked.

"And a beautiful day." Brier stared at the mountains where the mines were located. He enjoyed the hawkeyed view of his kingdom, but sometimes he longed for the garden of his childhood suite. He could only imagine lazing away right now under the largest oak tree and reading a new novel. Brier yawned and stretched at the mere prospect.

"Are you tired, Your Majesty?" Quintin asked, chewing a poached egg.

"Not overtired." Brier smiled. "Though I am in no hurry to negotiate with the Divine Three anytime soon."

Quintin chuckled and nodded. "I am surprised this is your first meeting with them to be honest. Did the queen not involve you at all?"

"No." Brier shook his head. "She held the impression that I lacked the competence to rule." Quintin let out a scoff, and Brier peered up from his granola with honey and milk.

"Nonsense. You've more competence than the lot of the courtiers, and certainly more than Queen Evelyn."

Brier gave Quintin a hesitant smile. "Thank you for saying that, but in some regards her assumption is true. I have very little experience. What I know is from Lord Tamil's guidance, and now your own."

"What you know is your kindness and desire for equal opportunity. I cannot take credit for that." Quintin poured water into his white-leafed teacup and stirred. "Things are progressing well. Even the Aurelians seem less restless, though that is not unexpected. The queen has ruled since your father's passing. People grow restless when the monarchy is hindered. I suspect it is why having children, and so many, is considered a good omen among royalty," he uttered before sipping his tea.

"Then I suppose they will consider my rule an ill omen," Brier replied pointedly. "I don't intend to marry for politics." And certainly not to a woman.

"Then you don't intend to have an heir?" Quintin tilted his cup in disbelief.

"No. I do not. If Lirend demands a successor, I will adopt a child in name only."

"I see…." Quintin avoided Brier's gaze for a moment, as if considering his next words carefully, and then decided to speak. "May I ask you another question, Your Majesty?"

"That depends," Brier answered warily. Marriage talk did not suit him, especially since he had no prospect in sight. Perhaps at one time he could see himself wedded, but the topic had become too painful.

"Well, it is more of an observation than question." Brier nodded for Quintin to continue. "Correct me if I am wrong, but in the intimate sense, I had the feeling that you prefer the company of men?" The question more surprised than offended Brier. He did not expect Quintin to be so candid, though in the scheme of things, he should have.

"What makes you say that?" Brier asked with feigned innocence.

"Well you did stare rather hard at King Askel's ass when we went riding."

"I did not!" Brier retorted. Quintin smirked, and Brier rolled his eyes, laughing. "Oh all right, I suppose if I had to say, I prefer men. But that is of no concern to the crown. It's no one's business what I do in my bedchamber."

"I couldn't agree more." Brier expected a prurient reply, but Quintin only nodded once. He'd felt nervous, unsure of what to expect from the prince, but Quintin's arrogant air seemed to dissipate in their time alone.

"And you?" Brier asked cautiously. "Do you also prefer men?"

"Not particularly." Quintin shrugged. Again the answer surprised Brier. He was sure that Quintin and Renli had an affair. "Sometimes I like women. And sometimes I like men," Quintin further explained.

"Is that common in Menlor?" Brier continued to probe the man. "I only ask because you seem rather open in your affairs."

"Are you referring to Alex?"

Brier's face heated at the mention of the man he'd just pondered.

"Yes, Lord Renli. And others." Brier stared down at the dregs in his cup, but he could feel Quintin's sky-blue gaze still on him.

"It is not common in Menlor, nor is it particularly frowned upon. I don't make my preference an issue, so no one else does."

"Perhaps not openly." Brier reached for the teapot. "But don't you worry what they might say behind your back?"

"Why would I worry about the words of cowards who speak behind my back?" Quintin's bemused stare made Brier anxious. His whole life he'd worried about his image and his kingdom. To ignore the whispers about his scars, and his kingship? He'd never thought of it that way.

"Well I do not have the luxury of being a charming, albeit arrogant, secborn, Prince Quintin." The prince laughed, and Brier smirked.

"Glad that you find me charming." Quintin finished his third cup of tea. Brier knew they had stalled through their breakfast, but he found himself actually enjoying the man's company. It was refreshing to dine with someone who spoke without pretense.

"Does that mean I may join you again, King Brier?" Quintin glanced at him with apprehensive eyes. Brier smiled at the vulnerable expression on the prince's handsome face.

"Call me Brier, please." Brier nodded.

"All right, Brier." Quintin reached out to grab the king's fingertips. Brier felt a real tingle creep up the pale veins in his hand, and this time, he did not pull away.

CHAPTER 19
CONCORD

BRIER TORE through the open road with Frieling's feet pummeling the earth beneath him. A long fiery braid suspended in the air while his eyes focused on the dirt path before him. Quintin had a small lead in their unofficial race, but Brier could see the horse's hind legs dashing right in front of him. The race was to the south end of Balmur, a district just outside of Lirend's capital. They rode toward the farmlands, wide-open space with wheat and corn stalks that grew up to Brier's shoulders. They whipped over open fields and parched hills until they'd traveled well into the suburbs of the lush green province. Balmur was scarcely inhabited, despite its proximity to Avenough. The rustics had no desire to live so near the vivacious capital, and the Aurelians had no desire to live on undeveloped land.

Brier lagged behind the prince until they reached the edge of Balmur's forest, where the leaves cascaded down from the barren willow trees. Brier watched as Quintin slowed his horse to a stop, and he followed the man's lead. He walked lightly to cool Frieling down before he dismounted the horse and stood near the prince.

"I won, you know." Quintin unhooked a parcel on the side of his saddle.

"Who said we were racing?" Brier arched his brow, though he knew Quintin understood his childish game. They often visited this spot during their leisure time together. If he won, it was a race. If Quintin won it was merely a friendly ride to the country.

Quintin spread out a blanket next to the placid lake. The breeze cooled Brier's sweating forehead and neck. Quintin donned a beige jerkin while Brier wore a cranberry tunic cut just above his wrist to hide the scars on his skin.

After they laid out the blanket, Quintin set up a picnic for lunch. The prince packed boiled potatoes and cabbage with a loaf of cheese bread to fill them. Brier was famished, and they finished the food with a large bottle of wine and redmelon for dessert.

"You know, I think I enjoy Lirend in the fall better than Menlor," Quintin proclaimed as he sipped the sweet wine.

"Oh really?" Brier lay out on the blanket and watched the horses graze. He felt full, but not tired. Contemplative, but for a change, not melancholy. "What makes you say that?"

"Everything changes color." Quintin smiled playfully.

"Trees don't change in Menlor?" Brier twisted his head to face the prince.

"No. It's warm there most of the time. We get a heavy breeze and rain from time to time." Quintin rolled his shoulders and leaned back. "It is good sailing weather, but nothing as beautiful as this."

"I would love to go sailing!" Brier exclaimed.

"You've never been?" Quintin frowned.

"Never." The queen would never let him near a ship, and he'd not had the opportunity since his return to Avenough.

"Then I shall take you one day. Just us two. In Menlor we have ships almost as big as the mountains in Aire!"

"And you sail them?" Brier's eyes widened. He knew firsthand how gigantic the mountain lands were.

"I have been on the water since my fourth year."

"You must be quite the sea captain, then." Quintin smiled. Brier could tell the man wanted to boast, but consciously chose not to.

Brier peered up at the willow trees' hanging leaves. "The fall is beautiful, but come winter the lake will freeze, the snow will fall, and this tree will be bare. The sun will set earlier, and the earth will chill… everything is dying." He repeated his once master's words. Quintin did not speak at once, but Brier felt Quintin's intense stare.

"I've heard the snow is lovely." Quintin countered Brier's words. "And what better time to snuggle with you by the fireside than when the air freezes."

"Ever the optimist," Brier playfully chided.

"I'm looking forward to a white solstice here in Lirend." The prince wiggled his brows and Brier chuckled. "So let us say, it is a beautiful death?"

"Yes." Brier grimaced. "It is very beautiful."

But winter reminded him of a time he wanted to forget.

"Beautiful and yet…." The prince paused. "I remain convinced, nothing is as beautiful as you are, my king."

Brier squirmed at the compliment, aware of the blue eyes even in the shade of the willow tree.

"Thank you." He lifted up and gazed into the pond. The sun's reflection shimmered in the blue water.

"Is it wrong?" Quintin asked him.

"Is what wrong?"

"For me to find you desirable?"

"No." A vulnerable look in Quintin's eyes made Brier reach out and touch Quintin's wrist. "It's not wrong. I just…." He did not know how to react to another man's attention. Roland had always shied away from him romantically, but Quintin openly adored him. "I've never had anyone to view me in such a way."

"The men you've laid with never desired you?"

"The only man I've lain with viewed me as a child." Brier flushed and shook his head. Roland always pushed him away or coddled his feelings. "I was just a pupil to indulge," he whispered.

"You are not a child." Quintin shook his head disdainfully. "You are a man to love. Anyone who cannot see that is a fool."

Brier lowered his burning gaze. “It is I who am the fool. I wished for love when there was none.”

“Then we are both the fool.” Brier’s heart thudded at Quintin’s subtle confession.

“Quintin, I….” Brier’s brittle voice shook. “I don’t know what to say.”

“You don’t have to say anything, my king.” Quintin took hold of Brier’s hand and placed a tingling kiss on his knuckles. “The days I’ve spent with you, I’ve grown a great deal of affection for you, Brier.”

“And I you, Quintin,” Brier assured him. He enjoyed their days riding out to the countryside and making sport in the fields. They sparred together, dined together. Quintin even helped him run the kingdom. But they were friends. Friends and not lovers, and deep down Brier knew the reason why.

Rolande.

Even the thought of the huntsman made his chest thrum painfully.

“I don’t know… if I can give you my heart.”

“And I don’t want you to give me your heart.”

“You don’t?”

“No. Don’t give me your heart.” Quintin breathed inches away from his pink lips. Brier’s entire body shivered as Quintin placed a gentle kiss on his lips. The heat prickled Brier’s skin like warm summer rain. “Let me earn your affection.”

BRIER STOOD undressed in front of the mirror and held the underside of his belly. The once flat abdomen bulged out as if he’d swallowed a football. He inspected his body carefully. His face had rounded from his large portions of food, three meals, plus three snacks in between. Brier could never remember eating so much, but the matter of his scars was most disconcerting. They’d changed from a hoary silver to the color of black steel. And had his chest began to swell? Brier gripped his shirt when Marietta entered his suite without knocking.

“By the gods!” Brier clutched his nightshirt. “You scared me.”

“What are ya gawking in the mirror for?” She narrowed her gaze.

“It’s nothing.” He turned away from her and tried to hide the growing bump, but Marietta walked toward him.

“Nothing is it?” She ripped the shirt from his hands and crossed her chubby arms. “Let’s see it, then.”

Brier cursed under his breath as he turned to face her. She’d urged him to call a healer when he felt nauseous before, and then when his stomach began to swell, she reminded him once more.

“Brier,” she croaked out and stepped toward him. He expected a verbal lashing, but only silence came.

“You’re….” She stared at him, half-dumb and half-timid. She touched the middle of his stomach where the skin was most taut and trailed her fingertips around. It tickled, but Brier had no desire to laugh. “It can’t be,” Marietta whispered as she scrutinized his scars and chest.

“What can’t it be?” Brier mumbled uneasily. Marietta’s reaction made him more anxious than the oversized lump in his stomach.

"I don't know…." She shook her head, but Brier felt her hesitancy. "You need to call the healer, immediately."

"I knew that much," Brier grumbled. "He'll be coming tomorrow."

"How do you feel?" the woman asked deliberately.

"Mostly tired," Brier answered, moving to dress himself for the evening. He opted for a deep violet cotton robe instead of trousers, and a tunic that bound his stomach.

"You should stay in and rest, my king. I feel a storm coming." Brier wanted to point out that often times Marietta's predictions held no truth, but he did not have the heart or the patience to disprove her.

"I'll wear a parka just in case." Brier tied a light cloak around his neck before heading toward the door. Although the weather was intermittently warm or cool during the seasons' changes, he did not want to catch cold along with everything else. "I told Quintin I would meet him at the stables. I presume he wants to go for an evening ride."

"You shouldn't go riding." Marietta shook her head. "It's not safe in that condition."

"How can you say such a thing when we don't even know what the condition is?" Brier chuckled lightly at his nursemaid's coddling. The woman meant well, but there was no changing her ways. Brier leaned in to kiss her cheek, and Marietta held his shoulder.

"Promise me that you won't go riding." She grimaced.

Brier frowned and shook his head. "Honestly, Marietta. I feel fi—"

"Promise me." Brier stared at her quizzically. His nursemaid knew more than she'd revealed. It was something she wasn't saying. "Please?" Something she was hiding.

"All right, Marietta." Brier nodded slowly and exited through the door with Finnas waiting to accompany him.

"GOOD EVENING." Brier could not help the smile when he saw Quintin dressed as impeccably as always. The dark blue tunic contrasted the light blue of his eyes and his curly blond hair lay just above his shoulders. "Pardon my lateness. Marietta was having a fit."

"Oh?" Quintin began walking with Brier to the stables. "Is everything all right?"

"She's all right." Brier nodded. "She urged me not to ride until I take care of something tomorrow."

"Everything all right with Frie?"

"Yes." Brier nodded again. Quintin did not notice the weight gain, or, if he did, he did not mention it to Brier. "But I hope I haven't ruined any plans you had for us this evening."

"I have a surprise for you actually!" Quintin's face gleamed as he continued to lead them toward the stalls.

"What is it?" Brier mimicked the man's enthusiasm. He hastened his steps to follow the prince more closely.

"A good sailor never spoils the catch." Quintin shook his head.

"All right, sailor, but don't think I've forgotten about your promise to take me on a ship with you," Brier replied. Along with the advice, he gave Brier assistance in administration. With two hands they got the work done in half the time, and Brier had more time to spend with Quintin. "That puny rowboat we fished from doesn't count."

"If you ever take a break from your throne, I would gladly whisk you away to Menlor," Quintin proposed. "Then I can introduce you to my mother, and reunite you with sweet Adeline. I'm sure she would remember you."

"Hopefully not." Brier cackled at Quintin's tease. "But I've heard Queen Vivian is charming and beautiful."

"Indeed." Quintin smirked. "Only slightly less enchanting than you."

Brier snickered at Quintin's praise before he grabbed his hand. "I don't think your mother would agree with your taste."

"And why not? You are a fine Aurelian King."

"Because you are expected to marry a fine Aurelian woman, and have fine Aurelian children," Brier quipped. "Men don't marry men, Prince Quintin."

"You're wrong, you know." Quintin stopped walking and Brier tensed. "I would marry the person who makes my heart race when I hold their hand, my chest ache when I cannot be near them, and my body burn with desire," Quintin whispered. "Man or woman. It matters not to me."

"Quintin." Brier opened his mouth to apologize, but the prince gripped his arm and they continued to walk.

The more time they spent, the deeper Quintin seemed to fall, but Brier could not shed the burden in his heart. Even now he thought of the guild. Would Sasta, Dur, and Caite cut firewood to prepare for the winter? Would Umhal set to making firestones?

And what of Roland.... Rolande.... Ronan....

Brier always wanted to know.

They continued to walk until Quintin squeezed Brier's fingertips. They stopped in front of the royal horse stalls where he kept Frieling. "Is she doing all right?" Quintin asked the stableboys. They seemed to have expected Quintin's arrival because they were not startled by Brier's sudden appearance. They bowed at him before replying to Quintin.

"She's fine, Your Grace," one of the boys answered. "We just watered her and checked."

Quintin nodded before he grasped Brier's hand and led him down a long row of stalls. The crown had the largest supply of horses in the entire capital and therefore a huge stable to keep them. They used thick pine to reinforce the walls and built high ceilings to circulate the musky air. Brier did not know what Quintin intended. He'd told the prince he could not ride, and the sun had already set, so no horses still ranged the open fields. When they reached a stable at the far end, Quintin stopped and crept slowly toward the enclosure.

"Is everything all right?"

"Shhh...." Quintin put his finger to his mouth and led Brier toward the pen. Brier frowned, not fond of being quieted, but he followed Quintin's lead and glided toward the stall. His eyes widened before they gleamed at the sight of a pure white mare and a grayish colt nursing beneath her.

"This was the horse I used when I first arrived at the palace. Shortly afterwards they told me she was with foal."

"They didn't know she was pregnant?"

"I guess not." Quintin shrugged. Brier did not see how that was possible since he knew that horse breeding in the palace was strictly monitored. They only allowed their mares to breed with other royal horses.

"But look at the foal's coat." Quintin pointed to the foal's fluffy coat associated with the Coloured Cob breed.

"He's beautiful." Like a reverse dalmatian, the foal had white spots through his dark coloring.

"They said she got loose from the stables for a while, but came back on her own. They think she might have bred with a wild stallion," Quintin remarked. "I'm not sure what their plans are now that she's had the colt."

"I hope he'll be all right. In Avenough, only purebred horses lead the carriages or carry Aurelians on their backs." Would they separate the foal and sell him to the farmlands? Or maybe they would get rid of both of them. Brier did not know why, but he felt an impulse to cry. He shook his head and cleared his throat, stepping away from the pen to wipe his eyes before Quintin noticed.

"Are you all right?" Quintin stood behind him and held his shoulder.

"I'm fine." Brier felt like he'd said that too many times today.

"I'm sorry, I didn't realize about the regulations on breeding here. I remember that you said you liked horses. I thought you would enjoy this."

"I do—I mean, I am." Brier shook his head. He was stronger than tears over a damn sold horse. "The smell is getting to me." Only a partial lie.

"Let's go." Quintin held out his hand and Brier took hold once more.

AFTER THEIR stint at the stables, they ate dinner in the main hall and walked through the garden until Brier's feet began to ache. He wanted to continue the evening, but Brier could not remember ever feeling so tired.

"Thank you, Quintin, for a lovely evening," he said once they reached the door of his suite.

"Perhaps next time no tears?" Quintin teased him gently. He leaned in and pressed Brier's back on the gold and green door. Brier chuckled and nodded slowly.

"Despite the tears, I enjoyed myself. And you?"

"I always enjoy myself when I am with you." The prince reached up and touched the bottom of Brier's lip before he placed a chaste kiss. "May I?" Brier nodded before he felt Quintin's warm hands brace his mouth for the scorching kiss. Brier's tongue twisted and his body tensed as he heard Quintin purr. Roland had never made a sound like that, but Brier found that he liked the prince's thirsty moans.

Quintin pressed him more firmly against the door and Brier's body liquefied in the pleasant embrace. Quintin curled his fingers into his red hair and slid his hand up Brier's thigh-length robe.

"Mm—" Brier's eyes widened when Quintin's hand crept up to his groin. *How had they gone this far?* Quintin squeezed his sac. *This fast?*

"Do you want me to stop?" Quintin whispered against his ear. Brier felt the prince's tongue glide over the edge of his ear before Quintin trailed down his flushed neck. "Or do you want me to take you into your suite." He sucked Brier's pale skin lightly. "And show you just how much I desire you, Brier."

"Quintin…." He breathed out the man's name, desperate for a chance to think. His body responded to Quintin's touch with throbbing impatience. However, his mind wavered between tempting lust and palpable uncertainty. Brier's bicep tensed as he reached up to hold Quintin's chest. He stared into Brier's eyes, the passion of their kiss laboring Quintin's breath.

"I can't do this," Brier panted. "Not yet, I'm not ready. I'm sorry—"

"It's all right." Quintin shook his head and held Brier's face. "We don't have to do anything yet, my king. I told you, I will wait until you are sure." Quintin leaned so that their foreheads touched, and Brier felt a wave of relief wash over him.

"Just know, I would never hurt you, Brier." Quintin's blue eyes creased sympathetically.

"I know you would not." Brier lowered his gaze. "I'm sorry."

"There is no need to be." Quintin kissed his forehead. Brier let out a shaky exhale.

BRIER SAT in his empty bedroom running his hands through crimson, unbraided hair. His shoulders hunched over an opened letter from the King of Menlor, with ink and parchment adjacent.

It seemed that the first shipment of supplies for the newly built hospital would arrive in a fortnight. Brier thought to visit Quintin's suite to inform him of the letter from his father, but decided against it. He enjoyed Quintin's company and their friendship, but Quintin wanted more…. That much was evident. He could still feel the spot where Quintin's lips and tongue sucked his neck. Brier barely managed to pull himself away from the prince's heated embrace. And maybe he shouldn't have.

A subtle breeze swept against his back when that thought crossed his mind, and Brier shivered. He stood to close his parlor door.

To couple with Quintin… to give myself to another man….

Brier turned to dim the oil lamp, but froze in his step as heavy boots crossed the wood floors.

"*Venur*, little prince." The voice rumbled in the pit of Brier's gut and made his heart unsteady. Brier turned to see a man dressed in a thick wintery cloak fit for the autumn air. Fear skulked up his spine then, and he swallowed hard, standing tall.

"What are you doing here, Roland?"

CHAPTER 20
REBOUND

"*VENUR*, LITTLE prince."

Roland watched as Brier stood in his violet-blue robe. The collar covered up to his neck while the sleeves covered where Roland knew the silver swirls marked the king's pale skin. Fabric draped like a sash across his stomach and chest. He'd let the hair grow down from his sideburns toward his jaw. So different was Brier from the boy he'd taken in over a year ago. The king appeared as a man. As an Aurelian man.

"Or should I say, my king." Roland bowed with his face still hidden. "You look well. I am glad." He stepped forward, and the king slid back to keep the distance.

"You shouldn't be here."

The words held more truth than Brier knew. By now he should have been across the narrow sea, away from Aire and Avenough.

"I need to talk to you."

"If you must, then wait until tomorrow." Anger simmered beneath Brier's callous words, but Roland refused to give up that easily.

"What I need to say cannot wait until dawn." Roland kept his voice steady. The king did not answer, but stepped toward his canopy bed and began to turn down his blankets.

"I'm getting ready for bed, Roland." Brier pressed his name harshly. "If you would like to speak to me, I advise you make an appointment."

"I never needed to make an appointment to speak with you in Aire…."

"That was a long time ago." Brier whipped around to face him. Roland watched Brier's Adam's apple quiver as he swallowed. "And this is not Aire."

"Aye, I forgot this is Avenough," Roland jeered. "And you've found an Aurelian to replace me." He watched the king stiffen before Brier raised his chin.

"If you are referring to Prince Quintin, he is a friend. Nothing more."

A prince? Roland's heart squeezed. Brier had fallen not just for an Aurelian, but a prince. Someone of equal station to stand by his side. The realization struck Roland like an arrow. He'd tried to calm down after seeing the two men wrapped together in the passionate embrace, but Roland's temper began to boil at Brier's disclosure.

"You kiss mere friends like that?" Roland scoffed.

"Funny, I did not take you for a quidnunc, Roland. How long did you spy on us?"

"Long enough to see him practically mount you outside of your bedchamber. You've found yourself a 'fine Aurelian man.' I'm sure your father would be proud!" Brier shot him a loathsome glare before narrowing his emerald eyes.

"And so what if I did find someone to love me?" Brier sneered. "Who I fuck has nothing to do with you!"

"It has everything to do with me!" Roland retorted. "You think I would let another man take the man I love so freely?"

The words sputtered out before he had a chance to temperate them. Roland watched Brier arch his thin eyebrow. "The man you love?"

"I mean it." Roland swallowed Brier's diffidence and spoke more calmly. "I love you, Brier." He let the confession still the air, praying for the king to relieve him from the listless silence.

"That's unfortunate," Brier whispered, barely audible. "But I cannot help you." Brier moved to turn away, but Roland shoved Brier down on the canopy bed and pinned his arms. He could hear Brier's inhale of alarmed breath as he melded their bodies together. Then they lay in the moonlight that gleamed against Brier's golden framed window. Roland could see the marks on Brier's neck gleam on his pale skin.

"Let go of me and stop this nonsense, Roland." Brier tightened his mouth and turned his face away. Roland stared at Brier's familiar pink lips. He writhed between desire to kiss his once pupil and outrage at the king's raw disposition. "You're making a fool of yourself!"

"If I am a fool, then let me be ridiculed for it! I love you! And I don't care who you're with! I'm not going to let you throw me away!"

"Let me?" The man's eyes cut through Roland like the tip of a sword. "Do not misunderstand your position, Roland. I have no intention of asking your consent." The icy gaze froze Roland into awed silence. "Now. If you've nothing more to say, unhand me and leave my sight, Xeno-Ah—!"

Roland yanked Brier's deep red hair, and he craned his head up to escape the sharp metal. "Oh, I have something to say," Roland snarled in Brier's ear. The dagger was at Brier's throat before his last abasing words.

"I came to say good-bye to you, Your Majesty. But since you don't seem to have the time, perhaps I should let my knife bid you farewell." Roland pressed the knife closer to Brier's pale neck and watched the blood trickle down the king's collar. Brier clenched his jaw, but lay perfectly restrained.

"If you think that is best," Brier croaked out before the hilt of the dagger slapped his jaw. Brier's head twisted from the force of the blow, and he turned toward Roland with his teeth clenched and stained red with blood.

"Does it please you to look down on me? To appease your Aurelian pride?" Roland's eyes dilated as he yelled and pointed the tip of the blade to the man's throat. Brier clenched his eyes shut, rigid with fear, but he did not speak. "Or is it so lowly to be loved by a Thenian?" The anger seeped through him.

Has he changed so much?

So much in just a short time?

But then Roland heard the king's shaking voice.

"To be loved by a man who left me with nothing? Is that what you mean, Roland?" Brier grimaced, and Roland's hand clenched around the salient dagger. "You abandoned me when I had no one, and you think killing me would be worse?" Brier let out a caustic laugh before his chest convulsed with harsh sobs.

"I wished for death the first days without you," Brier whined as his breath hastened. "I wished to die because it hurt not to have you near me!" The blood on Brier's lip mingled with the tears that flowed over his temples and into his hair. "So if you want to kill me, kill me...." Brier sniffed and wiped the tears from his eyes. "But what you see before you is not pride but emptiness."

Emptiness?

Roland slid the knife away from Brier's neck and tensed in his dead gaze. Brier was but a shadow of himself.

The tears welled in Roland's tired eyes.

He'd left him without thinking of the consuming loneliness and the pain of desolation.

"Forgive me, Brinan, I...." He touched Brier's bleeding mouth, and the king's lip quivered with fresh tears. "I never meant to hurt you."

Not in this way....

"I came to apologize for the way we parted—I thought if I let you go, you would find happiness." Roland thought if he saw the king one last time that he could let his little prince go. "Forgive me...." Helenas died because he was too late to save her.

I refuse.

Roland leaned in and brushed his lips against Brier's forehead, and the king froze under him like ice.

I refuse.

"I'm sorry but... I love you." Brier would not discard him because he was too late to beg for Brier's forgiveness. He refused to let Brier go. He could not live with "too late" again.

"I love you, I know I've waited too long to tell you." Roland collapsed against Brier's warm chest. "But I won't let you forget me... I can't." Brier was all he had. Roland wept in Brier's arms before he felt delicate fingertips filter through his coarse hair. How could a touch soothe the burden he carried in his heart so effortlessly?

"If you don't want me to forget you," the king whispered, "then... don't let me forget you...." Roland raised his head to make sure he'd heard Brier speak.

"Did you hear my words, Brinan? I said I cannot let you go—" The kiss took Roland's words and the pain for seconds of pure bliss. Brier's warm tongue skated against his, and he let out a strangled moan, starved for the contact. Even a kiss would suffice. Even a kiss could heat his entirety.

The fierce kiss turned animalistic, biting lips and licking tongues mingling their spit. Brier clung to Roland's heavy cloak and let out a breathy shudder. Brier's fingers gripped a large chunk of black hair, and Roland let out a guttural moan. Brier did not speak, and nor did Roland. Instead they teetered on the edge of fear and excruciating hunger, ripping the seams of their tunics and jerkins. Roland removed his cloak and shirt without pause, desperate to feel the heat of Brier's pale skin, but the king pushed his hands away. He watched as Brier yanked down his trousers and exposed a stiff erection.

"Bri—" Brier mashed their lips together before he could sputter words. Roland sucked Brier's tongue with deliberate fervor. Their pants turned to moans as Brier's hands trailed down to his breeches to untie them. Roland's brow creased as Brier gripped him in a smooth stroke. Brier's hand twisted around the base before pressing his tip lightly into a squeeze.

"Ngh—" Roland shuddered at the soft touch, and his mouth hung open. Brier's technique had improved, and Roland wondered whether that was due to the prince's ministrations.

Roland gripped Brier's hand at the mere thought and pinned his wrist above his head. Brier's brow creased in confusion until Roland sucked his bottom lip into another wet kiss. Brier gripped Roland's shirt with his free hand, and Roland hiked up the robe to Brier's waist. The supple skin on his fingertips made him ripe with need, and he kissed Brier's neck before mouthing the ingrained marks on his shoulder. Roland trailed his tongue around the lines that swirled and shimmered in the faint moonlight.

"Nngn...." Brier's face reddened at the exposure, but Roland continued to lick his once lover. He did not think twice before lowering his head down to Brier's throbbing shaft and licking the pink tip. Brier whined before he shivered and enclosed Roland's head between muscular thighs. Brier's scent ensnared him like a deadly vine, strangling the last of his patience. Roland spread the man's legs and flicked his tongue up from the center of Brier's cleft, mouth watering from the taste.

"Haah-haah!" Brier's breathless pant made Roland delirious. He twisted his tongue underneath Brier's sac before he slid his mouth to Brier's member. The first taste of precum made Roland's cock go from half-mast to full hard in seconds. Roland slurped Brier's shaft and probed his entrance with his thumb, still teasing the underside of Brier's crown. When Roland slid a finger inside, he gulped down Brier's member simultaneously.

"Hgnh!" The pleasure choked Brier's whine. Roland shivered when he felt Brier's ass tense around his finger. "Ahh!" Roland's throat loosened as Brier thrust his hips impatiently.

"Mghm!" Roland gurgled as he pulled off the pink mass. The spittle pooled on his tongue as he soaked the king's cleft in saliva. Brier's fingers clenched in Roland's hair.

Gods....

Roland's head swam as Brier's fingers melded through his mane. Roland's eyes fluttered and then shut before his shaft gave an ardent throb. He skulked his fingertips up Brier's raised thighs. The waist-level slits in the robe revealed the underside of Brier's pale asscheeks.

Roland slavered his palm and stroked his hanging member. By the end he'd drenched his shaft in spit, and Brier watched him intensely, face flushed with legs spread. Ready. Roland didn't pause or think before he pressed the tip of his member into the taut hole.

Brier's eyes widened before he gasped. Roland dragged Brier toward him and—"Ahh-!"—bare bottom met pelvis. He slammed into Brier's ass, making the wooden frame thump against the wall. He leaned in to sate the pain of penetration with a kiss, but moaned into Brier's mouth when the king rolled his hips upward. Roland could still taste the coppery blood from Brier's bruised lip, but Brier exchanged the jagged kiss, wrapping his tongue frantically. Nails clawed into Roland's biceps, and he felt the familiar sting of broken flesh.

"Brinan." Roland rammed his hips into tight heat, trembling from the fingers that traced his ribs. Roland raised up from Brier's stomach and stared at him: tear-pinched emerald eyes, skin damp with sweat, the blush of his cheeks fused with the desire to explode.

"Ro—ahh—close!" Roland slapped against his ass harder, and Brier's member pulsed with another dribble of precum. He held Brier's chest and pounded him into the canopy bed. Roland's chest dripped with perspiration as the heat entangled between Brier's rear and Roland's thighs. He could feel Brier's hole stretching around his thickness and swallowing him up for more.

"Ah-haaah!"

The cries were Brier's plea.

The pain was Roland's mercy.

"Right—haah—there—!" Brier's mewling moans contorted into severe heaves. Brier reached out to stroke his stiff member. Brier had a titillating thirst, and Roland was determined to quench him.

"Ahh—there—!" Roland doused the man once. Twice. And the cum spurted on Brier's robe. Brier raised his knees and spread his ass, thirsty for Roland's seed.

Did that man teach him that too?

"Ahhh!" Brier shuddered as Roland hammered him with the need to possess. He gripped Brier's mouth and engulfed him in a kiss. Roland couldn't let go—he wouldn't let go. He slammed his palm against the headboard and let out a moan akin to a howl. Whatever it took. Brier was his.

"Fuck!" Roland groaned as he felt the pressure in his groin. "I'm coming!" Roland barely managed to sputter before he tensed to explode. He gnashed his teeth and let out a hiss as the cum spurted out of him. Roland sucked his tongue, tasting blood, sweat, and tears.

Roland wheezed out, his face and chest damp with perspiration. Brier's hands trailed from Roland's abs to his chest. He felt Brier's fingers massage the rough-hewn hair.

"I like your chest…." Brier whispered. Roland leaned in and kissed the man, still seated deep within him.

"I like your lips." He slid out his limp member and Brier whimpered. "And your neck." Roland nipped the man's collar. "And everything about you." Brier's arms wrapped around his broad back, and Roland relaxed in his embrace.

"*Venur*…. Ronan…." Brier's hushed voice made Roland's skin tingle. He gazed at the moonlight on Brier's peaceful face until he heard the rhythm of light breath. The hold around him slackened. Roland clung to Brier like a spoiled child and slept soundly for the first time in months, within his king's arms.

"ROLANDE…." THE sultry voice and warm air made Roland stall to open his eyes. This was only a dream. One he'd had many times. Brier held him and whispered his name after they'd made love.

Roland felt a caress on the back of his neck, and his eyes blinked open to drawn curtains and piercing sunlight.

"Good morning." Brier beamed. Roland grinned and nuzzled Brier's neck with his grainy beard. Brier winced when his weight settled.

"Are you all right?" Roland frowned at Brier's discomfort.

"Yeah…." Brier nodded though his eyes were still slits. Roland rolled to his side and watched as Brier held his stomach.

"You're not." Roland's brow wrinkled. "Did I hurt you?"

"It's fine, really." Brier shook his head. "I told Finnas to run my bath. I'm probably just tired from last night."

"One of your servants?" Roland asked. "Is it safe that he sees us like this?"

"Finnas is the only servant allowed in my bedroom."

Roland's frown grew more pronounced.

"Because he is the only one, save for Marietta, that I trust wholeheartedly," Brier explained. He lifted up and cupped the underside of his belly. It was then Roland noticed the heavy bulge. He tried not to stare, but Brier's full form came into view as he stood and began to strip. It seemed Brier had lost weight, or maybe that was due to the disproportionate way his weight spread. Arms and chest were thin, but Brier filled out toward his stomach, and around the man's hips and thighs. Brier caught Roland's gaze and held the robe against his stomach and chest.

"Does it disgust you?"

"Of course not." Roland frowned. As if Brier could ever disgust him. "But—is it because of last night?"

"No." Brier shook his head. "I've been feeling ill for weeks." Brier stepped toward the bath chamber and Roland followed. He watched as Brier shed the remnants of his clothing and stood in front of a full-length mirror. Despite the man's protrusion, Brier was still exquisite. The usually braided red hair fell just above the dimples in his plump ass.

Roland traced Brier's steps as he finally removed the covering and stepped into the tub. His shoulders were round, and yet his chest seemed puffy, almost swollen. Everything looked swollen to Roland, up to Brier's tired face. The patterned leaves still peppered his skin, however their color had changed to the color of iron. "What illness is this, I wonder?"

"I'm not sure, but it's inconsistent, save for my stomach." Brier exhaled deep as the water hid his body. "I was nauseous about three months back, but that has more or less faded."

Roland could remember seeing something like this in his past, but he could not recall. Perhaps Brier had gotten an infection of some kind? Or an ailment from something he'd eaten since coming back to Avenough? The most telling symptom remained Brier's stomach protrusion. Though it did not yet overwhelm his lean figure, it bulged like a man too fat for his knickers, or like a woman carrying her….

An image struck Roland, and he remembered where he'd seen such a bump, when he'd heard of the symptoms, and from whom. Roland stared at Brier's placid face. He reminded Roland of Helenas, full with their child.

It was as if….

Roland scrutinized the markings on Brier's pale skin more closely.

But it couldn't be....

Roland shook his head to free his mind of even the notion. Things like that did not happen, and rightly so, should they find themselves in such a predicament.

"These days I'm overtired and sore just from a day's ride!" Brier slid deeper under the water and dampened the ends of his red locks. Roland assumed he ogled the king overmuch because Brier smiled to encourage him. "Don't worry, I called the doctor last night. He should arrive here shortly."

"Why have you avoided it this long?" Roland scolded.

"I've been busy."

"With that prince?" Brier's face flushed and Roland arched his brow. He nodded once but said nothing more. "Who else knows about this?"

"Only Marietta... and Quintin," Brier mumbled. "I've canceled breakfast with him before when I did not feel well. He knows nothing about the recent symptoms."

"And you and this man...." Roland breathed out to calm his temper. He did not want to think of Brier with another man, but he needed to know. "You have not... he has not laid with you."

"Never," Brier answered simply.

"You swear it?" Roland demanded, but he regretted immediately. Brier narrowed his gaze and scowled.

"Would it matter if I had slept with him? You abandoned me, Rolande. You left me, alone. I had... every right to couple with him."

"So you did sleep with him?"

"Do you still doubt me?" Brier glared right through him, and Roland lowered his gaze. It was not that he doubted Brier, but his self-doubt threatened to drive him insane.

"Forgive me," Roland whispered. "I have no right to ask you such a thing." Brier continued to wash himself in silence, and Roland chastised his tongue. He did not peer upward until Brier grunted. Brier reached his arm out of the marble tub and tried to grab a plush robe with his fingertips.

"*Mmph*!" Brier slipped and almost fell forward before Roland jumped and caught the front of his chest. He steadied Brier on his feet before securing the small of his back. Brier glared and stretched his arm past Roland to grab the robe.

"By the gods, will you just stop?" Roland spat. "I'll get the damn robe!" Brier finally stood still, except for his gaze. Roland shook his head and sighed before he grabbed the robe.

"I'm sorry, all right?" He wrapped the robe around Brier. "I shouldn't have doubted your word." Roland's heart squeezed at the memory of the passionate kiss they'd shared, but he tried to push it out of his mind.

"We've only kissed," Brier confessed as though he could read Roland's mind. "He wanted more, but I wasn't ready to give myself to him. He's been... patient while I tried to get over you."

"I see." Even though Roland understood, the words still stung.

"And now that you're here, I don't want to get over you," Brier mumbled and lowered his head.

Roland lifted Brier's chin before he spoke. "I just want you to be happy, Brinan." He grazed the blanched skin with his fingertips until he reached the bruise on Brier's lip. "Perhaps you *should* find someone more worthy to love you."

"You believe the prince worthy?" Brier challenged Roland's words. Roland swallowed the lump in his throat as Brier brushed back a strand of his thick hair.

"You're what makes me happy. All I want, and have ever wanted, is you." Brier's lips pressed against his own. "It's only been you," he murmured before Roland tasted Brier's wet tongue. He grabbed the king's lower back out of the water and suspended him above the tub before placing Brier on the solid ground. Brier stood on tiptoes to reach his lips.

"Did you get shorter?" Roland teased Brier before he guided him to the bed.

"Did you get older?" Brier stroked his graying beard. He chuckled before the robe fell between them.

"Most assuredly." Roland licked Brier's upper lip and slid his finger between the crease of the man's ass. "Pining for you is making me gray." He palmed Brier's ass cheeks with both hands and spread his hole.

"Mgh…." Brier instantly flushed but dragged Roland's hips closer. They pressed together with the heads of their members practically kissing.

"Have me?" Brier gripped Roland's ass and ground hard flesh against his thigh.

"*Mana el man'*." Roland slid his finger up Brier's hole, and he shuddered.

Knock. Knock.

"Shit," Brier hissed, and Roland shook his head.

"I believe the guild did rub off on you after all."

"One moment!" Brier called and pulled on his robe. Roland pulled on his pants and waited in the lounge chair by the king's vanity.

"Your Majesty." The young servant bowed. "The healer is here. Shall I let him in?"

"Yes, Finnas." Brier began to braid his hair. "Let him know I'll be just a moment." The boy exited the chamber, and Roland watched as Brier tied his robe. "Will you stay?" Brier leaned in to kiss him.

"Is it all right if I do?" If the Aurelians found out that Brier had slept with a Thenian, they would run for torches.

"It is all right if I say it is all right," Brier quipped.

"Then I do as you bid, my king." Roland stood and mimicked an ingratiating bow.

"MY KING," the gray-haired doctor said in a dry voice, lightened by the friendliness in his eyes. Brier sat against the leaf-printed lounge in his suite, flushed to his ears with discomfort. Brier allowed the man to check his heart, take his temperature, and check his pressure, but the instant the doctor asked Brier to untie his robe he tensed. "I cannot examine you if you do not allow me to see your body."

"Just from the symptoms he has mentioned, is there anything it could be?" Roland asked the doctor.

"Could be?" the man repeated sarcastically. "Why yes, I dare say it could be anything."

"Like?" The doctor narrowed his gaze in confusion. "What's the worst-case scenario?"

"Well of the more deadly causes, it could be a condition in which blood or fluids fill the space between the sac that encases the heart and the heart muscle." The doctor held his hand into a fist. "This places extreme pressure on your heart. The pressure prevents the heart's chambers from expanding fully and keeps your heart from functioning properly."

"And what happens then?" Roland urged the doctor to continue.

"Your heart can't pump enough blood to the rest of your body when this happens."

"And then?" Brier paled.

"And then you die," the doctor replied simply. Brier shot Roland a tentative glance before his hold loosened on the robe ties.

"Listen, I'm aware that sometimes things of this nature can be embarrassing. But your health is a priority. More so because you are the king of Lirend."

Roland met Brier's gaze and nodded to give him assurance. "We need to know, Brinan. Good or bad."

"All right." Brier sighed out and opened the robe.

Roland watched as the healer poked and prodded Brier's stomach for several minutes. He kept his eyes on the doctor's hands though he could hear the old man muttering to himself about "curious" and "very strange."

"How long have you been in this condition?" the doctor asked, pressing his hand against Brier's stomach.

"A little over six months," Brier answered apprehensively. "It started shortly after I returned from Aire, but only noticeably since the third month." Brier winced as the doctor kneaded against the hardest spot on his stomach. Roland saw a jump in Brier's skin that made him grip the arm of the chair. Brier reached for Roland's hand and held it tightly.

"Did you feel that, King Brier?" The doctor peered upward.

"Aye." Brier nodded with his eyes wide. "It felt as though… as though something kicked from inside of me," he admitted, still flushed. "Like a bass in my stomach." The doctor smiled knowingly, but Roland squirmed.

"Well?" Roland demanded when the doctor continued the examination. "What is it?"

"Well I cannot be sure. I have only read about such a thing in books. In my own time it has not been confirmed. But it appears you have a condition known as gravidity."

"Gravidity?" Roland said, tilting his head.

"Procreation, or the process of producing one's heirs. Though admittedly this way is unconventional." The healer chuckled.

When Roland still did not understand, the doctor patted his shoulder and said, "The king is to be a father." Then he looked down at their hands conjoined. "And I suspect you will too."

"Father?" Brier stared at the man, incredulous. The doctor grabbed a white tape measure out of his bag and began to mark the circumference around Brier's belly.

"Ha-have I gone mad?"

"I would say you've gone about twenty-four weeks? Give or take a few days."

"My Lord." Brier crunched Roland's hand. "As you can clearly see, I am a man. Therefore, I cannot be pregnant. It is impossible."

"Impossible?" the doctor answered, flummoxed. "I dare say it is possible, lest we see it before our own eyes." Brier opened his mouth to speak before the man scratched his white goatee. "Though I will admit the how is curious indeed. I have a guess only, and I don't know it to be right."

"What is it?" Roland ignored Brier's dangerous eyes.

"These marks." The doctor touched Brier's shoulder. "Have you noticed any changes of late?" Roland peered down at the marks on Brier's skin.

"They are darker since I last saw him," Roland replied calmly. Brier would not accept the possibility, but Roland accepted the reality.

"How long has he had them?"

"His whole life."

"I would wager they've something to do with this."

"No, this cannot be the answer!" Brier suddenly snapped. He snatched the robe shut before he shot them both a threatening glare. "They're just scars!"

"Not scars, symbols." The doctor pointed to the new leaf budding on Brier's still visible chest. "A sign that you have this gift. Else how would you know?"

"I wouldn't know." Brier held his temple and shook his head. "I mean… I didn't know I could." Roland rubbed the inside of Brier's wrist to soothe the anxiety.

"Any other changes?"

"When we—" Roland paused. He did not want to embarrass Brier, but he remembered something else. "When Brier and I did—"

"Conceive," the healer filled in.

"Yes. On the night we conceived, the symbols glowed gold."

That night….

Brier's marks glowed gold as Roland thrust into him slowly, but when they had awoken, the symbols went back to the silver from before.

"And before your suitor—Lord umm—"

"Roland," Roland filled in.

"Yes, before Lord Roland, there were no others I presume?" The healer turned to Brier again, but now his ears were the color of blood.

"No one before or after," Roland answered to quell their earlier argument entirely. He wanted Brier to know that he took full responsibility. He watched Brier sit up fully on the lounge, and the king's expression shifted from uncertainty to concern.

"If this is true," Brier contemplated. "What is going to happen?"

"Well to be completely honest, I am not sure," the man told them both, now looking grave.

"What do you mean?" Roland widened his eyes before he scowled. "Do you mean to say you're not sure what to do?"

"With a normal pregnancy? Yes. But as I've said before, I have not seen this in my lifetime, and I know little of the effects pregnancy will have on Brier." He turned to Brier then. "My suggestion is to rest as much as possible, and do not overexert yourself. I will do more research in this matter, and of course, give you all the information I find."

"And…. What of the child?" Brier mumbled.

"Kicking like a buck in the womb, which is a good sign. Your pressure is a little high. I'll prescribe something for that."

"So then, the baby will be all right?" Roland further inquired.

"I don't know." The doctor shook his head. "The same goes for the babe as for the king. I cannot guarantee its safety. If the pregnancy or birth endangers the king's life, then we will have to act."

"Have to act?" Brier whispered.

"To consider termination," the doctor told them.

Brier covered his eyes with his hand and let out a shuddering exhale. "Thank you," he said softly. "You may leave now. If anything happens, I'll call for you. I only ask that you don't tell anyone what you have seen here today, Doctor Kupetz."

"Please call me Meade." The doctor bowed smoothly. "And I have sworn the crown my complete confidentiality, Your Majesty."

"That includes the former queen," Brier added. The doctor inclined his head but said nothing more as he moved toward the exit. Finnas stood in the waiting parlor to let him out. The door closed with a snap and the air hung heavy with "what if."

What if Brier didn't make it? What if the baby did not survive? With so little to go on, both Brier and the child could meet a tragic end.

"I do not know what to say," Brier uttered, eerily calm. Roland turned toward Brier and brought the man's ashen knuckles to his lips.

"What are you thinking?" He reached up to massage the back of Brier's scalp.

"I guess, I'm having a baby?" Roland could see the fear and apprehension crease Brier's brow.

"*We're* having a baby," Roland corrected him. He stared into Brier's watery eyes. "Yet you look close to tears."

"What if I cannot take care of the child? What if I'm not a good father? What if something happens to the baby, Ronan?" Brier pummeled him with questions that he did not have answers to, but Roland kissed his forehead to smooth the lines.

"We will take care of this child together. You will be as wonderful a father as you are a person. A child could not ask for a better person to give it life."

"And the baby? What if it does not make it?" Brier's breath hitched. "What if—if I do not make it? I don't want to die, Ro!"

"And you won't." Roland frowned. "I don't care what has to be done, I promise you." He wiped the tears from Brier's cheek. "Didn't I tell you I cannot let you go?" Brier nodded with a watery smile. The man reached out to hug Roland, but then jerked in surprise.

"I felt it again!" Brier beamed and grabbed Roland's wrist to place his hand.

"Is this the first time you've felt it?"

"Of course I felt her moving before this, but I thought that it was only my stomach upset."

"Her?" Roland arched his brow with a grin.

"Well, we can't very well keep calling it 'it.'" Brier's face colored. Roland nodded and continued to rub Brier's stretched skin. It was amazing. Inside this belly Brier carried his child, their child.

"I think it will be a she," Brier admitted sheepishly as they waited for the baby to kick again. "What do you think?" For all Brier's skepticism and worry, Brier's face lit up each time the baby wiggled within him. Roland opened his mouth to reply when he felt a hard jump in Brier's skin.

"I think he or she, our child will be perfect." Roland stood and held out his hand for Brier to grab hold. He leveraged Brier to his feet and guided him toward the canopy-tiered bed.

Even after the men woke from a tense nap, they lay in silence. Roland could hear the gentle plink of rain against the glass on the gold-framed window near Brier's bed. Finnas tied the canopy linen around the large tiers on either side of the bed so that nothing obstructed the view of dusty gray skies. Roland rubbed the king's back for a while before Brier nuzzled against his chest. "Are you okay? Do you need anything? Are you hungry?" Roland asked.

"I'm fine," Brier answered. "I'm tired, but I suppose I'll need to start my day rather sooner than later."

"Not yet." Roland held Brier tightly. Then Roland slid his hand to his stomach and rested it against his naval. "I have not had my fill of holding you thus." He kissed Brier's neck.

"I would love to stay with you all day, but if you keep me in bed too long, Marietta is going to skin us both."

"I've worse causes to die." Roland slid a hand over Brier's to twine their fingers together over the bump. "I've only two reasons to live." Brier tensed in his arms before he spoke.

"Were you not here, I don't think I would be able to bear this load."

"You are stronger than you think." Roland kissed the top of the red hair. "You have more power in you than you will probably ever know, Brier." Their child would only test his lover's strength, not break it.

"I hope you are right, Roland." Brier squeezed his hand. "For all our sakes, I hope you are right."

WHEN THEY rose officially, the men took a light lunch in the parlor since the weather worsened in the late afternoon. Brier refused to eat the salmon Finnas served, but he finished an entire bowl of pickled hummus and bread. Roland just stared. He did not mention the obvious increase in his appetite, but he could clearly see the effects their child had on Brier.

"What?" Brier peered up to catch his stare. Roland smiled and shook his head.

"I was just thinking how handsome you were." He sipped his wine and evaded Brier's gaze.

"Liar." Brier grinned. "You're probably thinking I eat like a horse." He chuckled before he took a sip of water.

"More or less." Roland snorted. "I also think I've never seen you more stunning," he said simply. There was no jeer in his words. When he gazed at Brier's rounded face and wide hips, he only appreciated Brier's strength.

"And you are very handsome." Roland smirked as he watched Brier rise from the table holding the underside of his belly. Soft lips grazed his own before Roland held Brier's chin.

"Do not flatter me overmuch, or I will put an end to your hunger, king."

"This is no mere craving, master." Roland leaned into the next kiss, ready to make good on his threat, when he heard a gentle knock at the king's door.

"By the gods, I wish people would stop doing that." Brier let out an impatient huff before settling himself and returning to his food. "Come in." Finnas came in with a swift bow to the king, and then toward Roland.

"Your Majesty." The boy kept his head lowered as if he knew the news was unwelcome. "Prince Quintin awaits your company. I informed him that you were currently busy, but he insisted he see you." Roland clenched his jaw when he heard the prince's name. He watched as Brier hesitated before replying.

"See him in, Finnas." Roland could sense Brier's apprehension, but he did his best to remain neutral. He'd made enough of a scene last night without the provocation of the prince's introduction.

Quintin stepped in with blond curls that fell just above his green-padded shoulders. The tunic he wore fit him like a glove, tight around his chest but loose around Quintin's waist and flat stomach. He was more muscular than Brier, though less so than Roland. The leggings he wore under the layered tunic made Roland aware how different Aurelians dressed. He would never wear breeches that tight or revealing. In the end the prince's clothes gave Roland the impression of a peacock: wild in its colors and clamoring for attention.

"Good afternoon, Brier." Quintin smiled. His face was handsome enough, but the jutting characteristic was certainly the prince's sapphire-blue eyes. Iridescently blue. Unshakably confident.

"Good afternoon, Quintin." Brier spoke his name casually. "Are you all right? Finnas spoke as though you needed me in earnest." Quintin's smile faltered when he finally noticed Roland sitting across from Brier. The prince puffed his chest and refocused.

"I came to see that you were well, but it looks as though I am interrupting something."

"Just a late lunch. Please feel free to join us." Brier turned toward Roland and stood to adjust his seating. Roland watched Brier conspicuously hide the bulge with the tablecloth. "Prince Quintin Pascal, this is Roland Archer." Quintin nodded once as he took a seat Finnas offered him.

"Good afternoon, Lord Roland." Roland could taste the sarcasm in Quintin's voice.

"I am no lord," Roland corrected him bluntly. "Roland is fine."

"Pardon." Quintin bowed his head with a smirk. He cut a piece of the salmon Finnas served him. "Incidentally, I do not think I have seen you at the palace, Roland. Are you just arrived?"

"Last night actually," Roland answered, not taking his eyes off the other man. "Brier was kind enough to give me refuge after my long travels."

"Oh?" Quintin's eyes narrowed toward Brier at the implication. Brier cut his gaze to Roland, but did not refute him. Roland knew Quintin had never entered Brier's bedchamber, yet here he was, a seeming stranger, boasting of their night together. "And where are you from, might I ask?"

"Aire." Quintin blinked twice before he smiled and then let out a hearty laugh. "Surely you jest!" He turned toward Brier for confirmation of the supposed joke.

"Does my companion's origin amuse you, Prince Quintin?" Brier answered after swallowing. His solemn response made Quintin's light shine slightly dimmer. "He is from Aire, where I spent the better part of a year."

"His Majesty was in Aire?" He gaped at Brier, awestruck. "Good gods! What for?"

"I had my own business," Brier answered with ease. He held up his cup for Finnas to refill his tea. Brier tried to smooth away the animosity, but Roland's jaw tensed with every word Quintin uttered.

"In that dump?"

"Aire is a part of Lirend," Brier replied pointedly. "Lirend exiles our criminals to Aire instead of sentencing them properly in court. Of course it has gone to ruin." Roland's chest swelled at the pride in Brier's voice.

"No offense to you, Roland." But Roland was sure Quintin meant it offensively. "But Aire is an overrun wasteland."

"And so is any other land without proper vigilance. 'Tis not all crime and ruin, Prince Quintin. Refugees inhabit that land as well," explained Brier.

"Those Thenians?" Quintin scoffed as though Thenians belonged in the dregs of the tea he sipped. "They are worse than the criminals to boot." Roland glared at Quintin, and he knew Brier could feel his rage surface. "I'm sure you have your reasons, but why a king should live there I do not know."

"A king would not live there." Roland cut off Quintin's rambling. He was tired of listening to the syrupy voice. "But Brier was a prince only months ago. He was my pupil for almost a year there."

"And what do you do, Roland, that a prince of Lirend would follow you?"

"I am only a huntsman." Roland seethed. "A Thenian huntsman." Quintin did not show an ounce of remorse from his earlier comment but glared more consciously.

"Should the king hunt his own food before he eats it?" Quintin sneered. "What could a hunter teach him?"

Roland reached over and gripped Brier's face, and before Brier could protest, he kissed him deeply. At first Brier stiffened, but either by habit or longing, the king's need melted any resistance. When their lips parted, Brier gasped out both furious and flushed.

"A hunter could teach him many things, I think."

Chapter 21
The King's Guard

THE AIR stilled then shattered as Brier felt Roland's heated lips touch his own. He tried to fight it, but the hand on his jaw and the strength of Roland's tongue sent him into a stupor. He licked Roland's tongue, still riled from the broken kiss before Quintin's arrival. He could not quell the lingering heat since last night's raw coupling. Roland finally released his head, and Brier let out an exasperated breath.

"A hunter could teach him many things, I think."

The words coiled around Brier and his passion turned to rage. He shoved Roland's shoulder and stood from the table.

"Enough of this foolishness!" Brier shouted at Roland. He turned toward Quintin, whose eyes had gone shock wide. "Both of you are behaving like children. I don't intend to be made into sport!" He was no pawn in this petty game, and he refused to let either one of them use him for their amusement.

"Who is this man, Brier?" Quintin's words were frostbitten. Brier swallowed before he answered firmly.

"He is my lover."

"The one who abandoned you?" Quintin's piercing glare almost drove Brier to silence, but he kept his voice steady.

"Yes," Brier answered in a hushed whisper. He had to be strong. Quintin deserved at least his resolution. "He let me go in Aire, but the past is in the past." Brier unwittingly smoothed a hand on his stomach. "There are more important things between us."

"Like what?" Quintin challenged. "What hold does he have over you?"

"That is none of your concern," Roland grumbled. Brier stared between the two men. If he did not do something, they would come to blows.

"Quintin," Brier uttered calmly. "For now, I think you should go—" Quintin stood up and slammed his fist on the table. Brier jumped, but Roland stood with his hand at his waist.

"I'm not going anywhere until you talk to me! Alone!" Quintin yelled. "You owe me that much, my *king*." He pressed Brier's title. Brier walked over to Roland who still held the dagger Brier knew hung at his waist.

"*Acai*, Ronan." Brier felt the tension ease in Roland's shoulder as he spoke in Thenian. He peered up into Roland's slate-blue eyes and gave him a knowing gaze. He needed to talk to Quintin.

Roland did not fight his words, though Brier knew he wanted to. Roland gave him a rough peck before he gave Quintin a warning glare. Brier watched Roland as he turned to walk away and disappeared into his bedchamber.

"What is it that you wish of me, Prince Quintin?" Brier stared at Quintin. Though he'd only just arrived, Quintin looked exhausted. His usually buoyant eyes creased as he spoke softly.

"Is that all you have to say to me? Last night we shared… we shared what I thought was something real." He shook his head in disbelief. "Today you regard me as a stranger?"

"I have always regarded you as a dear friend, Quintin." Brier shook his head feeling the weight of the accusation. "I should not have kissed you last night. It was a mistake. I apologize for that."

"Our kiss was no mistake! *He* is the mistake!" Quintin pointed to the embellished bedchamber door. "He who left you while you coddled your broken heart! He is the one who has ruined you for yourself and for any man who would hold you dear!"

"No. It's not like that anymore." Brier shook his head. "Ronan has opened his heart to me. He loves me." Quintin held his face and touched the bruise on Brier's lip.

"Is this the way he shows you his love? By striking you like a work mule?" Quintin gritted through his teeth.

"He was only jealous because—" Brier winced at Quintin's touch. "Because he thought that I had laid with you."

"*He* is a savage brute!"

"Your prejudice of his Thenian blood blinds you—"

"Damn his blood, Brier! It does not matter! I would never hurt you!" Quintin screamed. The prince's winded plea shook Brier to his marrow. His words had truth, but Brier could not stop his heart from longing for Roland.

"Have you ever loved someone?" Brier stared at Quintin's watery eyes. "Truly loved them?"

"You dare ask me that, King Brier?" Quintin's muted tone made Brier's stomach ache with guilt. Brier's eyes fell as he leaned against the door. "I love you, Brier. Can you honestly say you feel nothing for me? Was I just a way to pass your time?"

"I do love you, Quintin, just not in the way you want me to." He knew that Quintin had grown fond of him, even held affection for him, but Brier would never yearn for Quintin the way he yearned for Roland. "You deserve someone else. Someone who can give themselves to you wholly."

"I don't want anyone else, Brier!" Quintin screamed. He let out a deep sigh and whispered, "I love you."

"I'm uncertain what you want me to say." Brier's voice shook when he felt the hot tears well under his lids. "I can't let him go. I'm very sorry, sorrier than I have ever been…." Brier felt warm hands slide under his bruised neck.

"He's not the right man for you. You are a king. You should be with someone who understands what it means to have power, someone who you can share your life with—"

"Quintin—" Brier protested, but the prince continued to speak.

"You think that this is the right thing to do because you are blinded by whatever it is you think you share, but I won't give up." Gentle fingertips grazed the bruise on Brier's lip once more. "I would never hurt you. I would love you, and protect you," Quintin repeated seriously.

"I know you would, Quintin." Brier's breath hitched before he wept. "I'm sorry." He knew Quintin would never hurt him, never break him, never turn him away, and yet… Brier did not know how to sate his or Quintin's breaking heart. Quintin's weight shifted as he stood tall. "Please, do not hate me."

"I couldn't." Quintin shook his head and smiled sadly. "Because when he breaks your heart again, Brier, I'll be here to pick up the pieces." Brier squeezed his eyes shut as he slid his hand over his stomach. He could hear Quintin's steps before he exited the parlor.

Brier let out a shuddering breath, trying to keep the tears from falling. He swallowed the knot in his throat and wiped his face as he entered the chamber.

"I'm sorry for the wait." He kept his teary gaze hidden. "Are you still hungry?"

"What's happened to you?" Roland met Brier at the door and pinned him against the wall. "Tell me." Brier relaxed into the huntsman's warmth. He clung to the tattered jerkin and buried his face in Roland's chest.

"Why are tears all I ever have to offer?" Quintin's words echoed in his desolate mind. "I'm sorry for hurting him. I don't know what to do." Brier sniffed. "I understand I led him on, but I didn't know you would come back to me. Is it wrong to want to be with the one you love?"

"No, Brinan, it's not wrong." Roland shook head.

"He says we are not meant to be. He says you will hurt me again."

"I wouldn't."

"But how do I know that?"

"Because I love you with every broken part of me." Roland held his face, and Brier gazed at him. "Because even though Prince Quintin might be better for you, there is no one, no one who loves you more than I love you, Brier." Roland's soft kiss made his heart ache.

"You love me?" Brier despised the helplessness in his voice, but he could not veil his longing for Roland.

"With every fragment of my heart, Brier. With whatever is left in me to give you. For you and this child, I will willingly do anything."

"Even marry me?" Brier piped. He did not even know where the request derived from, but hope consumed his heart. Roland's gaze faltered.

"When I closed my eyes and held you, I saw only you and our child, safe and happy in my cabin in Aire. There is nothing and no one who could thwart this contentment. Would that I could make my dream a reality, but I am not an Aurelian."

"I could still marry you," Brier whispered. "You are free from your contract now. You could marry me and take my name."

"I am still a Thenian," Roland reminded him bitterly. "Your court does not recognize me as a citizen of Lirend." He sighed out, and Brier could feel the anguish of Roland's words. "Be it in my power, I'd marry you tomorrow. You must know this."

Brier nodded slowly. Be it in Brier's power, he would have never left Aire. Never left the Black Forest where only they could find comfort. "If I were not king of Lirend…." But Brier knew he could never leave his people. He'd stirred up so much in his short time on the throne, he had to see it through. He owed it to himself and his father. Brier wrapped his arms around the huntsman and let the tension drain out of him.

"Sometimes I wish you were not king of Lirend. Sometimes I wish I could lock you away and never let you go." Roland's voice grew black, and a tinge of titillating fear crept up Brier's spine.

"Aye, Rolande. Don't let me go." Brier pressed his lips against his lover's to quell the tension in his heart. It did not matter who doubted them as long as he had this man's love.

ROLAND LOUNGED in the chaise and gazed outside to the mountainous sky. The king's suite was at the peak of the palace and peered down from the veranda across the expanse of Avenough. Roland could see the grandiose mansions located only a few miles away, and beyond that, the illustrious city. Beyond that lay the suburbs, and beyond that, Aire.

Roland found himself alone again. Brier needed to make up for the time he'd missed, forgoing his kingship for his lover. Roland tried not to mind, but Brier's suite did not suit him. He thought of taking a trip to the square, but he did not have proper clothes to sport. One look at him, and the guards would arrest him. He had his voided contract on hand, but he doubted that would matter in a predominately Aurelian city.

He tried to remember his life in Aire before Brier, what he'd done to pass his time alone. Mostly whittling, some sculpting and playing the light keys. Brier had rows of books on the shelves lining the study adjacent to the king's bedchamber, but Roland never had a predilection for reading. He gazed at his crossbow in the corner of the grand bedroom. The crown molding had shimmering gold, leaf-green, and cream-white leaves painted intricately. The king's suite, fit for a king. Roland let out a deep sigh. In his plans for returning, he did not consider his own uselessness. In Aire he had a purpose; in Lirend's capital, he was a worthless Thenian.

Knock knock.

He heard familiar rapping at the king's bedchamber and opened his eyes from an impromptu snooze. "Come in," he answered in a gruff voice. He did not bother sitting up. Most likely it was Finnas with his lunch and an apology from the king. Over the past weeks Brier tried to have lunch with him, but it seemed his schedule did not warrant much time for them together during the day. At night Brier was exhausted, and it was all Roland could do to massage him, hold him, kiss his cheek, and send him to bed.

"What's for lunch today, Finnas?" Roland asked in his Thenian drawl. He did not mind Brier's young servant. The boy was mild mannered and did not ask too many questions.

"A bunch of nothing." A woman's voice rang in his ears. Roland sat up off the chaise and peered up to a portly woman with a large bosom. "Get up with ya now, it's nearly noon." She stepped past the veranda and grabbed his clothes hanging up on the wardrobe. Then she stomped back toward him and threw him the cloak, tunic, and breeches.

"Up. Up." Roland stood on command, but frowned when he realized he had no cause to. "Put yer clothes on and come on with me." She headed toward Brier's parlor to wait, but Roland called after her.

"And where are we going?" he asked, frowning. He had not left the suite in over a week. Even though Brier lived in the palace, the vast building did not feel like a home to Roland.

"Out with ya." The woman shut the door behind her, and Roland held his clothes in his hands, dumbstruck.

AVENOUGH DID not resemble Aire in the least. Roland had visited the Aurelian Quads twice when his contract remained, but never ventured this deep into the city. The cobblestone streets made the handcarts rumble as they roamed to and from either side of the walkway. Those streets leading to the center of the shopping district were narrow with tiny shops side by side like townhomes. Roland tried to read the names of them, but some of them were in the different dialects of Lirend. "Excuse me, ma'am." Roland tried to keep up with the woman who navigated through Avenough streets with purpose. "Where are we going?"

"Not ma'am, Marietta," she corrected, bustling along. Roland clicked his tongue impatiently, but followed the woman down the busy roads. They came to what Roland assumed was the central hub of the business district in Lirend's capital. A blush marble fountain with a true to life sculpture of Braedon Snow stood directly in the center of the square. The late king stood tall holding a colur-gem-embedded shield, with iron lining the grand stone. The fountain spurted water in intricate designs, and a number of musicians and dancers entertaining for coin. Around the entertainers Roland could see children laughing and dancing while their parents bartered with vegetable vendors selling their wares before the start of the harvest season. He stopped to watch a redheaded lass with wide eyes and a curly mane, barefoot and laughing loudly. A smile tightened his lips as he wondered who his and Brier's child would favor most.

Bread shops and stalls for meat caught his eye. In Aire they did not have such things, and the village in Thenia was too quaint for such luxuries. Each home instead made their own bread, or gifted it to their neighbors. It was considered unseemly to use meat not killed, skinned, and cooked in one's own abode. Therefore, Roland was thoroughly taken aback to see open dealings, on the street no less.

"Come on with ya." Marietta poked his side and Roland crossed his arms, brooding. There was no way he was going to be led around by an old woman with no cause.

"Not until you tell me where we're going." He had not spoken more than two words to the woman since his return to the capital, but he knew Marietta did not care for him. She did not openly express her distaste, but Roland overheard the discussion when she found out Brier was pregnant. At first she berated him for waiting so long to meet with the doctor, something Roland too conceded, but then she proceeded to caution Brier in regards to his affection. Roland could not blame the former nursemaid for her prudence, but he did not take favor to anyone intercepting his and Brier's love.

"We're getting you proper clothes," she told Roland simply. "You can't roam about the castle in naught but a cloak and homemade breeches."

"I don't plan on roaming the castle," Roland quipped. He had no cause to leave Brier's suite. He took his meals in the parlor's veranda, or if he felt especially lazy, right in the bedchamber.

"Yes well, it might suit you not to see the king all day, but he's a right mess without seeing you till dusk." Roland cut his gaze toward the woman suspiciously. He hadn't found a place in Lirend's capital, and the king's limited time agitated him. While Roland did not wish for Brier's disquiet through the day, it comforted him to know he did not suffer alone.

"It does not suit me at all. I'm not used to being holed up in a room for days, and I don't enjoy missing King Brier's company," he admitted, still following her lead. "But what can I do? He is the king. I am a Thenian. I knew the implications when I returned to Avenough."

"Indeed, you are a Thenian, and yet Brier needs you," she replied. "And why do you think that is?" Roland stood silent. He knew the reasons he needed Brier, but he still could not think of one reason a king would need or want him.

"I do not know," Roland answered honestly.

"If you do not know your worth, why should any Aurelian consider you worthy? This capital doesn't take kindly to refugees. Free or otherwise." She turned to walk away, but Roland called to her.

"I do not care what anyone in this capital thinks of me, including you," Roland added for good measure. He could never compare to an Aurelian in wealth, status, or charm, but no one could equal his love for the king. "The only ones who matter to me are Brier and the babe within him. I will do whatever it takes to make sure they are happy and safe."

Marietta stared at him before she placed her hand on her hip and chuckled. "Not as gutless as I thought, then." Roland's brow creased. Marietta began to walk again, but Roland noticed her pace slowed.

The autumn air agreed with him, despite the number of people in the business district. In addition to the shops, he noticed the fashion even the common folk wore. In Aire, naught was needed but a heavy cloak, long-sleeved tunic, sturdy boots, and perhaps a pair of cow or deer hide gloves to protect one's hands from hard manual labor. However, the citizens of Lirend made a point to dress stylishly and don their fancily laced britches with shined boots and garish-looking collared shirts. When he first saw the prince who'd taken to Brier, he thought Quintin dressed a slight batty, but seeing his lower counterparts dress in even more frivolous wears made Roland cringe at his prospects.

They stepped into a corner shop with a weathered sign and several loiterers smoking something acrid. Roland held his face but did not protest as they entered the cramped store. He peered around at the fabric-covered walls and the floors with bits of old wool and silk. The man reading behind the counter wore a pair of chalky spectacles.

He peered up from the book and beamed at Marietta. Roland could see where several teeth were missing.

"Afternoon." The man stood and bowed. "What brings you here, my lovely lady?"

"Enough of that." She clamored into the room and sat down on an idle stool. "We're here on business. Got a job for you." She pointed to Roland.

"I see." The man nodded. He ogled Roland closely before he smirked. "It has been a long time since I've seen a Thenian in my shop."

Roland tightened his jaw. "Problem with that?"

The man shook his head and smiled. "What's your name, young man?" he asked Roland.

"Roland Archer."

"Rolande." The tailor stepped from behind the counter and held a long strip of measuring tape. "My name is Ser, but my given name is Serven." The man began to measure the width of Roland's back. "*Venur*."

Roland turned to Marietta when he heard the common greeting. Marietta smiled but did not acknowledge the exchange. Was this man a Thenian too?

"So what are we looking for today?" Ser posed.

"I need something so that I won't stand out so much," Roland answered. His eyes darted to a mannequin with an intricately laced jerkin of patterned lilies. "Preferably something not too gaudy."

"Mm." Ser nodded. "I think the best way to go about this is to tell me exactly what you don't want, so that I may find something that suits you better." He'd never thought too much about the way he presented himself. His clothes were functional, not fashionable, but in Avenough they made him recognizable. Anyone with sense knew he did not belong.

"Do not put me in anything that constricts or binds me," Roland told the man with a commanding tone. "I do not want any frill, no lace, and for the gods' sake, do not put me in any color that makes me think of a babe's nursery." The tailor looked warily and expectedly at Marietta before he let out an amused chuckle.

"I think we can manage that."

After he was properly fitted for his new wardrobe and put in garb more fitting of Avenough, Roland stared at his reflection. He wore a dark forest-green tunic, rather plain except for the leather embellishments on his shoulders and around the collar. There were gold buttons that columned the front and an armored belt to hold his dagger. Ser fitted him in black trousers that did not bind him so that he could move freely. Marietta left and came back with a pair of new leather boots to wear with his ensemble. Roland protested, saying his shoes were fine, but Marietta insisted they match the new clothes.

"Now you look like you belong in a palace." Marietta inspected the garb before she turned to Ser. "Thank you. Send the bill to the palace. I'll send Finnas to pick up the wardrobe when it is completed."

Ser bowed graciously. "*Diole'*, Marietta, Lord Rolande." Roland thought to correct him, but he changed his mind at the last moment. If he was dressed like an Aurelian, then he should act like one.

"*Diole'*, Ser." He inclined his head and followed Marietta out of the shop.

MARIETTA ENTERED the king's study with a carriage bag and Roland at her heels. She eventually schlepped him to several stores in the city, including one to fit him for a proper belt with royal tassels. The one he now wore bespoke of his station in the palace, not as a servant, but something similar to a guard.

"Evening, Brier." Marietta plopped down into the seat across from Brier, unloading the bags into the chair adjacent.

"Good evening, Marietta." Brier did not peer up from the large desk he scribbled on. Roland had never entered the royal study. The walls, similar to Brier's room, were a leaf-green color that shimmered against an intricate thornli..e chandelier above him. Finnas stood by his side, swapping signed documents for those that still needed the king's seal.

"Busy?"

"Very," Brier snapped back. "I'm signing off on the budget for the new incentive program, and several of the courtiers have decided to pull their support at the last minute." Roland watched Brier run his fingers through the red locks.

"I see." The woman nodded.

"They're complaining because they aren't receiving the same tax cuts or money from the crown."

"Uh-huh."

"But the reason I've got to do this in the first place is because they refuse to open their practices to anyone but the Aurelians!"

"Mm…."

Roland frowned at Brier's obvious frustration, but Marietta only provoked him.

"Do ya think you can put that down for two seconds to look up?"

Brier scoffed before he slapped the table. "No, Marietta, I ca—" But the protest died on his lips. Brier stared at Roland as though he'd seen a ghost or phantom.

"*Venur*, King Brier." He gave the king a small bow, a grin on his face.

"*V-venur*." Brier stood and inclined his head. Green eyes trailed from his now ear-length black hair and shaven face. The clothes Roland wore accented his chest and shoulders perfectly, and the black trousers did little to hide his bulge. Brier opened his mouth to speak before he clammed up once more.

"Still busy?" Marietta asked Brier smugly. He flicked his head toward her with an indignant glare before she stood and grabbed Finnas's arm. "Come on lad, the king won't get much done with his mouth hanging open." Finnas turned toward Brier who nodded once and dismissed him for the day. When the door closed, Brier moved away from his desk and flushed deeply.

"Well?" Roland stepped closer. "Do you like it?"

"Gods, yes," Brier replied hurriedly. "I mean, yes you look lovely. Handsome or—" Brier shook his head laughing. "I don't know why I'm so embarrassed right now." Roland leaned in and kissed his lips lightly. Brier swooned from his touch.

"I'm glad you like it." His gruff voice cut the tension in the air. Brier held the leather on his biceps and smoothed down the suede on his chest. He thumbed the gold buttons before Brier's fingers filtered through Roland's hair.

"You cut your hair?" Brier sounded surprised.

"Aye, your nursemaid felt it would be more appropriate for someone of my station." Roland had felt more than a little self-conscious at the salon where they'd shaved his beard and cut his wavy hair, but Marietta assured him the change would suit him.

"Someone of your station?" Brier frowned.

Roland smirked and pulled out a sword with a gold hilt from his waist. "As your personal guard of course." He showed Brier the weighty metal, inscribed with the king's seal, before sheathing it once more.

"Oh, but this is a wondrous idea!" Brier let out a noise akin to a squeak. "You can come with me to court now, and escort me to those awful hearings."

Roland nodded. His slight hesitance for the notion washed away at Brier's conviction. "And I'll be with you at all times, just in case something happens with the baby. If you need me, I'll be right there." Brier nodded and unknowingly held the bulge where the babe would rest. He gave Roland a smirk before he moved toward the study door and locked it. Roland watched Brier untie the draped robe to reveal a demure shoulder, riddled with blazing marks.

"And if I need you thus?" Brier raised his thin brow, and Roland smirked.

"*Mana el man'*, Brinan." Roland bowed. "If you wish it, my king."

WHEN ROLAND woke, Brier hunched on the edge of the bed. Brier wore a sheer robe to cover the marks on his skin, out of habit or weariness Roland could not tell. And yet they remained visible, darker still in the silvery hue.

"Brier?" Roland reached out to smooth Brier's shoulders.

"Mm?" He twisted to meet Roland's gaze.

"Are you all right, my king?"

Brier nodded and held the top of his stomach. "I'm sorry to wake you. I was just… considering," Brier whispered.

"What ails you?" Roland asked.

"Not pain." Brier hesitated. "I was considering…. I should tell the kingdom about the pregnancy." Roland gazed warily at him. He was glad Brier now openly acknowledged their child, but he was also prudent in Meade's caution.

"You do not think so?" Brier's face fell.

"I think we should wait a bit longer," Roland told Brier calmly. "I think it would be imprudent to make the announcement before we are sure that you won't…." He paused attempting to cushion the harshness of his words. "That you will be able to carry the babe to term."

"You don't think I will?"

"I didn't say that, Brinan, but…." Roland thought then of Helenas. How he waited for a child that never came. "The child may not make it."

"I know she may not make it." Roland watched the king's spirit wane as he spoke. "But I pray to the gods she will."

"Meade seems hopeful." He tried to comfort Brier. "Every day that goes by both of you grow stronger. Let us wait a month more. By that time the chances are better," Roland added.

"Mayhap…." Brier let out a soft sigh, and he drew his robe in closer. "But would we love her any less? If she faded, she would still be a part of us. Something we cherish. Something that is only our own…."

Roland listened to Brier's poignant affirmation and his heart ached. "I will love her more every day, just as I love her father more every day." Just as he loved his lost Helenas and their child. He leaned in and kissed Brier's neck. "She may not have my name, but she will know me as her *aida*."

"Father?"

"Aye." Roland pulled the man into the king-size bed, and they lazed side by side. He reached in front of Brier and began to rub his stomach idly. Even if the child did make it, she would never be recognized as his seed. An Aurelian could not marry a Thenian under Lirend's law. Their child would only be a bastard in the court's eyes. Still, Roland prayed their child to be healthy, to see the world, to see the light in their eyes when the babe arrived. Most importantly, to feel the love he knew only Brier could give.

"Be well, *nan*," Roland whispered to their child. He smiled and tried to rouse Brier when he felt the babe moving in his belly, but by the time their child returned his touch with a kick, the king had already unburdened his worries and fallen asleep.

CHAPTER 22
THE TREE OF LIFE

"IN THE first place, there's too many holes in this plan," Lord Tauftor drawled. Roland watched as the fief lord of Bedlorn leaned over the rail aisle. His stomach protruded almost as far as Brier's.

"What holes are you speaking about?" Brier questioned him. "Specifically."

"What happens after the five years when Menlor decides to no longer assist us?"

"By then we'll have instituted our own regime," Brier answered. "The purpose of educating the lower class is not to have them work as serfs for the rest of their lives, Lord Tauftor. The intention is for them to branch out with the skills they've learned and start their own practices, schools, businesses."

"And let our farmlands rot," the man countered.

"I doubt you will find a shortage of help in your suburbs. The unemployment in Bedlorn is not nil. For a good wage, there is always someone willing to work."

"Where Aurelians will suffer that cost as well." The courtiers murmured their consent to the lord's words.

"The Aurelians in Lirend make more than their fair share, Lord Tauftor. I'm sure they can part with some coin to give a worker a decent wage. In Bedlorn you made thrice the amount of the crown. No doubt your dealings with Zhennal had something to do with that." Roland had to stifle a chuckle as the lord's face reddened.

"I've done nothing untoward. Before your regulations I had every right to—"

"Have I accused you of wrongdoing?" Brier's brow rose. Roland shifted in his seat. He could feel Brier's tension next to him. "I only ask that Aurelians pay their workers a fair wage. I only ask that the lower and middle class be granted an opportunity to get an education beyond a field and plow."

"Your great-grandfather enacted the law of passage to prevent this very thing. Prolits and Burges abandoning their post for the colur gem mines, forgetting their places in our society. We've lasted as long as we have because we've kept social order in Lirend. I don't see how this benefits her."

"You don't see because you don't want to see," Brier admonished him. "Prince Quintin and I have outlined everything you need to know in the missive. Our allies have backed us both financially and domestically. If you have any more objections about the taxes on Bedlorn's merchandise, I suggest you make an appointment with Lord Somran, the treasurer of Lirend." Brier did not wait for the lord's reply before he continued. "Now if there's nothing more, I propose we vote on this next week. I would rather not be waylaid further in this proposition." Brier stood and the court followed. Roland stood by Brier's side, peering over the twisted faces: most of the fief representatives, but not the lords of the districts beyond ten miles of Avenough. They shuffled out in deep conversation, though Roland could not hear more than clips.

"He's nothing like King Braedon...."

"The line has definitely changed...."

"Well if the Divine Three have agreed...."

Roland tried to ignore them, but he noticed one man stayed back to speak with Brier directly. He smiled before he bowed low. "Your Majesty, it is an honor to finally make your acquaintance." The man wore black spectacles and a brown tweed jacket. His style and demeanor had a maturity, but the wispy strawberry blond hair made the man appear younger.

Brier inclined his head before he spoke. "It is a pleasure. Lord Yaris, is it?"

"Yes!" the man exclaimed. "You know my name?"

"Of course." Brier smiled. "You were one of the few Aurelian doctors who volunteered to work in the new university." Brier began to walk and Roland trailed their steps. "I appreciate your generosity and your time." Brier bowed again. "You have no idea how much you've helped."

"Oh my goodness." Roland noticed the man's blush. "Well, I've only done my fair share. My father was a healer, so naturally with the law of passage, I became a healer as well you know. Well, of course you know," the man rambled. "Anyway, my father worked in the south districts of Avenough. He used to help homeless Prolits. He even traveled to the countryside a few times."

"He sounds like a very benevolent man."

"He is—was," Lord Yaris corrected. "He died six months ago."

"Sorry for your loss. May the gods keep him," Brier whispered.

"It is all right. He led a good life, Your Majesty. He spent his last days in this court. He hoped that one day, he would be able to see things change. Something like your proposition for the Prolit and Burges—some change in this country! I think he would have backed your efforts tenfold."

"Th-thank you," Brier stammered. Apparently Brier never learned how to deal with this type of person. Sasta often times overwhelmed Brier with his overexuberance.

"No thanks needed. I'm here to offer you my support." They stopped when they reached the open atrium.

"What do you mean, Lord Yaris? Your accepting a position in the university is more than enough."

"Not nearly. But I plan to do more," Lord Yaris replied. Brier gazed at Lord Yaris curiously. "What if in addition to the university and health centers, we create mobile health units, for those who live in the countryside?"

Brier blinked before he stopped at the atrium's stairs. "That is a grand idea. It would decrease the mortality rate, the spread of sickness, and encourage wellness, but unfortunately the crown cannot afford something like that at the moment. We are able to enact the plans for the school and health centers through the increase of taxes on the Aurelians and the new regulations set on trade."

"I'm aware." Lord Yaris chuckled. "I actually *did* read the missive, Your Majesty." Roland heard Brier's soft laugh. "No—what I'm proposing would be from my own doing. Something in coordination with your own efforts."

"In coordination?"

"Yes. I think the people will respond well to your plans. Even the Aurelians will eventually come to see how much more they will profit from healthy workers. If we could generate interest in the university, I think the young people would see the opportunities in education. Even the Prolit."

"Yes," Brier agreed. "The only way this will work is if we get the Prolit and Burges on board, but I couldn't ask you to fund a program like this, Lord Yaris."

"You're not asking me." Lord Yaris shook his head. "I'm more than happy to help. As I've said, my father waited for this moment."

Brier glanced at Roland, and he smiled lightly. He did not expect an Aurelian courtier to donate to Brier's cause.

"I—" Brier grinned. "Well I don't know what to say. This is more than generous, Lord Yaris, thank you."

"No thanks needed, Your Majesty." The lord bowed. "It would be an honor to help in a worthy cause."

Roland fell back a step as the men continued to talk over plans and arranged a meeting for the next day. He wondered how many other courtiers were like Lord Yaris, waiting for someone to lead them in the social reformation of Lirend.

Roland and Brier walked toward the gardens. The weather had officially evened out to a cool autumn crisp. The leaves on the oak trees shed, and the flowers began to wilt.

"Are you going to the premiere in Avenough next week?" Roland asked Brier. Roland heard Lord Yaris invite Brier along with his wife.

"Mayhap. It's been a while since I've seen a live show."

"Do you enjoy them?"

"Oh yes. Very much." Brier nodded. "They invite me whenever a new show debuts. I've gone several times since I returned to Avenough."

"With Quintin?" Roland asked. Brier halted in his step and turned toward him.

"Aye," Brier answered sheepishly. "With Quintin." Brier reached up to touch his smooth chin. Roland peered around to make sure they were alone. "Does it bother you?"

"I've no cause to speak about it," Roland whispered. During the few times he and Quintin crossed paths, he could feel the prince's animosity. "But I think if you'd like to go to the play, you should. You deserve a break, Brinan. You've been working yourself ragged." He leaned down and kissed Brier's forehead.

"Will you escort me?" Brier asked. Roland gazed into the hopeful eyes and shook his head.

"You know I cannot accompany you as a suitor."

"Then come as my personal guard?" Brier offered. "Captain Galer accompanies Evelyn all the time. No one will suspect there is more between us. You could sit next to me." Of course. They would not suspect him as anything more than a guard to protect the king. He was not an Aurelian like Quintin who naturally garnered Brier's attention.

"*Acai*?"

Roland stared down into the emerald eyes and felt his hesitance dissipate. He could not refuse this man anything. Leastways his company.

"All right, Brinan." Roland nodded. "*Mana el man'*."

ROLAND VENTURED into Avenough often now with his guardianship, but he never attended formal events. Despite his clothes and shaved face, Roland still felt put out when Brier donned his more luxurious garb—not that the theater was exclusive to Aurelians. Burges attended Avenough shows as well, but when someone let slip that the king would be in attendance, the square buzzed with excitement.

They met at Lord Yaris's house, some miles away from the Aurelian Quads. Even the lord's home spoke of a modesty that, according to Brier, did not fit Lord Yaris's worth or wealth.

They rode in a champagne-colored carriage with white accents around the frame of the windows and gold wheels. Brier held his stomach several times as they bumped along the cobblestone but assured Roland that he was all right.

"How sweet." Lady Yaris smiled. "Your guard is very protective of you."

"Overmuch at times." Brier chuckled nervously. "I'm still not used to traveling so often by carriage, but we can't very well travel by horseback to the grand theater." The woman laughed at Brier's joke, but Roland knew the truth. At his last visit, Meade forbid Brier to ride horseback for fear of falling or the horse throwing him off. The child inside him grew more each day, and he could see the effects on Brier's lean body. The markings that once glowed gold now glinted black on his skin. His hips filled out more in his tailored robes, and his nipples had spread and enlarged. Of course Roland did not mention the transformation to Brier, lest he grow insecure about the change in his body.

When they stepped out of the carriage, Roland held out his hand for Brier and then for Lady Yaris as a courtesy of sorts. After the woman thanked him, she joined Brier and Lord Yaris at the foot of the grand marble staircase. The theater had a stone front with two sculptured globes resting in the gods' fingertips. He trailed behind the three of them, careful not to pace himself too far or too close. When they entered the theater, green velvet lined the floors with gold candelabras, rails, and seats. Roland could not take in the splendor fast enough. He blinked when Brier touched his fingertips.

"*L'tyva el*?" Brier whispered as they walked toward their seats. Roland opened his mouth to reply when he heard a man's booming voice.

"Amory, Trish. I expected I'd see you here today, but not in such company." The man wore a military jacket, but with garnish and medals hanging from his heart and decorated tassels at his waist. "It is an honor to be in your presence once more." The man bowed and Brier stiffened.

"General Hilburn." Brier inclined his head.

"How are you, Jannon?" Lord Yaris asked. "Doing well I hope."

"Oh yes, yes. I'm actually on leave at the moment. Whitley is due for our eighth any day now." Roland tried to pay attention to the conversation Yaris and the general had, but he could not ignore Brier's agitation when he saw the general's face. How did Brier know this man?

"Your eighth." Yaris blinked. "Goodness, congratulations."

"Congratulations, Jannon," Lady Yaris echoed.

"Thank you, thank you. The gods bless us. Hope that I'll get the same news from you soon." He patted Yaris's back, but the doctor only feigned a smile.

"Are you here by yourself?" Lord Yaris asked.

"No, Renli is here with—"

"Jannon." A man of his age came to stand by the general's side. Roland stared at the man's smiling face and for a moment, experienced a flash of déjà vu. Renli's dark hair clashed almost eerily with his cool hazel eyes. "What have you gotten into so quickly?"

"Amory is here with his wife and His Majesty," the general explained. Renli glanced at Brier, and Roland continued to examine his face.

"I see." Lord Renli smirked before he bowed low. "Good evening, Your Majesty."

"Good evening, Lord Renli." There was no denying Brier's distaste this time, etched in his stony expression.

"It is a pleasure to see you again."

"The pleasure is, as always, mine." Though Brier's tone told Roland it was anything but.

"After the show we should all go and grab dinner together." Lord Renli glanced at Brier once more. "That is if His Majesty is free. I know how *precious* the king's time is."

"No more precious than anyone else's," Brier answered stalely. "Dinner would be fine."

"Yes, dinner sounds lovely," Lady Yaris replied.

"I've one more companion with me."

"Oh yes, where is he?" The general turned toward the stairwell, but Roland continued to stare at Renli.

It was as if....

But they couldn't have met before.

"Brier." The king blinked. Roland stared so long at Lord Renli that he did not immediately recognize the blond curls and airy voice.

"Quintin."

Roland caught Brier's anxious gaze.

"What are you doing here?"

"He's accompanying me." Renli patted Quintin's back. "Amory, Trish, this is Prince Quintin of Menlor."

"Hello." Lord Yaris bowed along with his wife. "Greetings, Your Grace."

"Please, call me Quintin."

"And of course you know His Majesty, King Brier." Renli's smirk grew wider.

"Of course." The prince smiled and then turned back to Brier. "You look well, Brier."

"Umm, thank you...."

Roland glared at the prince and the tension sizzled the air. The lights flickered, and Lord Yaris gazed around the hall.

"Looks like the show is starting. We better take our seats." The three men nodded and walked some ways down the same row. Roland watched the three men as they left them and cursed under his breath. The last thing he wanted was to suffer a dinner with that silly-haired prince.

"Have you ever been to the theater, Lord Roland?" Lord Yaris asked him.

"No," he answered. "This is my first time attending."

"Oh, well you're in for a treat."

"I've heard good things about this play," Lady Yaris said, taking the seat between Lord Yaris and Brier. Roland sat at the king's right in the middle of the second row. He could hear the violins and wind pipes tuning. The strings screeched against the walls and ceilings. "The musicians are from all over, but the main character comes from Menlor, I believe."

"Oh yes, he has a beautiful voice," Lord Yaris told them. "I saw him in *Cards in Hands*."

"What is this play called?" Roland asked in a hushed voice as the lights began to flicker and then dim.

"*The Tree of Life*."

STILL WORDS unspoken.

Please let them be forgiven.

My only true wish.

Roland stared at the stage, mouth open and chest stiff from the ache. The actor sang the last lines in a vibrating tenor. The sound of lightning crashed, and Brier clutched his hand. The curtain raised to show a decorative tree made from prop wood and fashioned leaves. The drums started low and increased until they rumbled through the theater.

Boom!

Lightning struck, and the man fell to the ground in a melodramatic death, and the audience gasped.

The music stopped before a sleepy violin played a lament. The man crouched into a ball before he danced into a cutout in the tree and the tree's branches glowed. Roland's eyes stung from staring so intently, but he could not move his gaze. Then the curtain closed, and he heard the sound of raucous applause.

THEY SAT in a spacious dining room with glass vases and marble tabletops. Instead of standing upright, the candles floated in the large vase of magenta-colored water. The lively chatter on their side of the bistro did not suit the intimate tone. Lord Yaris ran into two more friends outside of the hall, and after some fuss over his acquaintanceship with Brier, they decided, all eight of them, excluding Roland, to walk over to the nearest restaurant worthy of Aurelian patrons.

Roland held the door for Brier and the several behind him who neglected to thank him. They took their seats farthest from the door, in a nook where Brier sat at the head of the table. Lord Yaris sat on his right, and Quintin sat in Roland's seat to Brier's left. Roland sat instead on the end of the table. He stretched his arms inconspicuously and gazed around the cramped table in the vast space. Lord Yaris pulled his wispy hair back this evening to counter his perpetual scatterbrained guise, but still failed. As for Lady Yaris, her breast-length black hair and sharp features endowed her husband with the seriousness his appearance lacked. The woman next to her, Lady Iris, wore a low-cut gown to accentuate both her long neck and bosom. Roland avoided the direction entirely after he ogled overlong and the woman winked at him. Then her husband, Lord Iris, sat beside her, a short man with spectacles and a white mustache. He owned several plantations south of Avenough. General Jannon Hilburn, who sat beside Renli, knew Lord Yaris due to his work in the military. Lord Renli was a merchant out of Menlor, and he sat beside Prince Quintin Pascal. Two women, six men, and they all catered to his lover's attentions. Everyone, it seemed, wanted to be near King Brier Snow.

"I am no connoisseur where art is concerned, but that was the most splendid play I've ever seen," the general said. "What did you think, Your Majesty?"

"I would have to agree, though I've not seen enough plays to compare it to. Do you come to the theater often, General?" Brier asked. Roland noticed Brier had warmed up in mutual company.

"Not as often as I'd like." The general leaned in closer. "If it is a matter of opinion, though, it is Lord Yaris whom we should seek."

"You frequent, Lord Yaris?"

"I am familiar with Avenough's playhouse," Lord Yaris answered noncommittally.

"As usual my husband minimizes his talents. He is on the board of artistry in Avenough, Your Majesty. He doesn't miss a show."

"Is that so?" Brier chuckled. "I didn't realize I was in the company of an aesthete. Thank you for humbling yourself in our presence this eve."

"I—it is nothing all that extravagant, Majesty." The man shook his head.

"Come now, Amory, don't be modest," Renli jeered. "We sang together in that play when we were in grade school."

Lord Yaris flushed. "I only enjoy the theater, but I am no singer."

"I assure you, my husband has a beautiful voice."

"I don't doubt it." Brier smiled.

"Well, if I was not a prince I might have taken to the stage in lieu of a seat in the audience," Quintin proclaimed after Brier's praise.

"That you might rise to a seat of already assumed importance?" Brier teased the overproud man.

"That I might grace the world with my talent, of course." Quintin began to sing, and the table laughed. Roland stifled a scoff.

"Better that you continue to enjoy the life of an actor vicariously," Renli said tersely. He sipped a good swig of ale. "Lest we be cursed with your crooning."

"I admit my voice needs work, but His Majesty sings beautifully."

"Oh?" Renli turned toward Brier. Roland watched his lover jerk his head toward Quintin before he flushed. "I did not know our king had a penchant for singing."

"I do not," Brier uttered.

"Oh, but I've heard you sing. It's lovely really."

"Oh, Majesty," Lord Yaris clamored. "You must sing something for us."

"Quintin esteems me overmuch," Brier mumbled.

"I don't doubt that," Renli replied with a fake smile.

Roland ignored the man's obvious snub, but bristled when Quintin said, "Come now, how does the song go again?" Quintin bit his lip as he tried to recall the words. "I've walked afar, and grazed the skies?"

Roland gazed at the now pale king as Quintin searched his memory.

I combed the stars,

And walked afar,

To see a sea calm blue....

"Would that Lirend be a playhouse instead of a sovereign country, then His Majesty could sing to our enemies." From another man at the table, Roland might have assumed the taunt friendly, but Roland understood Renli's attitude from the beginning. He did not care for Brier in the slightest, and the longer they dined, the greater the man's animosity shown through.

"Your pardon, Lord Renli. It sounded as if you doubt my ability to deal with Lirend's threats?" Brier scowled.

"Apologies if it sounded that way, Your Majesty. I'm confident you have talent beyond singing. After all, you wooed Menlor's prince into an exclusive contract with the crown."

"I merely fortified the lines between Lirend, Menlor, and the Divine Three. If there are *any* threats to the sovereign or king, Lirend and her allies will personally see to them," Brier assured Renli. Roland watched in awe as Brier tactfully put Renli in his place.

"His Majesty certainly has a way with words." Renli smirked before he turned toward Roland. "And with men." Roland narrowed his gaze at the brown-haired man and tightened his lip.

"I think that's enough talk of politics," Lady Yaris announced. "Come now, dinner is coming." The servers came to their table in a straight line with food dished on silver plates. Roland stared at the polished forks, spoons, and knives, gleaming against the candlelight.

"Hunting season is fast approaching," General Hilburn said. "I'm planning a trip through Balmur soon. You two should come with us."

"No, thank you." Quintin shook his head. "I'm not fond of hunting."

"Renli?" The general turned.

"I'll pass." The man yawned. "There's something so utterly pedestrian about camping in the wilderness."

"Your prissiness endures," the general laughed. "What about you, Lord Roland? Are you a hunting man?"

"He hunts just outside of Aire in Sherdoe," Brier answered for Roland.

"Oh really? I've heard that Sherdoe has the most game right before winter. Is that true, Lord Roland?"

"It is." Roland nodded, grateful for the change in conversation. It seemed General Hilburn had an archery and hunting club in Avenough. "We catch enough in the fall to last me and six men the whole of winter."

"Incredible," General Hilburn answered. "And the weather?"

"Freezing," Roland replied. "Or very nearly. Aire grows frigid in the winter."

"And you still manage to hunt?"

"Oh yes." Roland nodded once more. "Foxes, deer, rabbits. We even caught a bear last year." The general's eyes widened to twice their size.

"You jest?" he whispered, amazed.

"I wish I did." Roland laughed at the man's wide-open mouth. "It nearly killed King Brier in the process."

"What?" Prince Quintin turned to Brier. "You never told me that."

"It was a long time ago." Brier glanced at Roland. "Over a year ago."

"So it's true?" General Hilburn turned back to Roland. "Well that settles it. You've got to come with us our next trip south."

"Oh, I'm sorry." Roland shook his head. "But I really don't have the time to—"

"Nonsense. Even the king's guard needs a bit of free time."

Roland began to shake his head to decline again, but this time Prince Quintin's voice rang out.

"I thought that club was exclusive for premier citizens of Lirend?"

"It is." The general glanced over to Roland. "But certainly allowances can be made."

"I think not," Quintin answered. "Wouldn't want people to get the wrong impression of the club. You've already turned down a number of qualified Aurelians and Burges on account of their reputation."

"Lord Roland is the king's guard. Surely that qualifies him."

"Is that what you plan to tell your patrons?" Quintin asked with a smirk.

"They'll be no need to tell them anything, because I'm declining the invitation," Roland answered briskly. He stood from the table and bowed. "Lord Yaris, Lady Yaris, thank you again for a lovely evening."

"Where are you going, Roland?" Brier asked when he grabbed his cloak.

"We should prepare to leave, Your Majesty. Remember you have that appointment tomorrow." He paused. "With Meade."

"Oh, yes." Brier nodded. "Yes, I'd almost forgotten. It's getting late. We should go."

"So soon?" Quintin asked.

"It's an important appointment," Roland answered for Brier. "He cannot miss it."

"Pardon, but are you by chance talking about Doctor Meade Kupetz?" Lord Yaris questioned.

"Yes…." Brier nodded warily.

"Is it your stomach? Still getting sick in the mornings?" Quintin asked. Roland growled lowly, and Brier threw him a furtive glance.

"It's nothing to worry about." Brier avoided the prince's question and stood. "I should get going. Just let me use the wash before we go." He skirted past Quintin and the rest of the table before he disappeared into the restroom.

Quintin's chair screeched away from the table, and he followed Brier without a word to anyone.

"The prince is smitten." Renli yawned loudly and the wave of familiarity washed over Roland once more.

"Oh?" Lord Yaris looked toward the washroom. "How can you tell?"

"It's painfully obvious to anyone who can read the signs." Renli smirked, and Roland caught the man's gaze. "How a man looks when he's completely enamored. How a man looks when he's desperately in love."

"And why shouldn't he be?" the general asked Renli. "Despite their gender, they make a fine couple. Better than the trulls he usually takes to."

"Indeed. Both their tastes seemed most improved." Roland glared at Renli, and the lord let out a dark chuckle.

"Let His Majesty know I'll be waiting in the carriage for when he's ready." Roland bowed before he turned as if headed toward the exit door, but he headed to the washroom instead. He did not trust Prince Quintin for one moment.

Roland leaned back against the wall silently. After several minutes of waiting, he decided to go in and get Brier himself.

"Quintin…." Roland paused when he heard Brier whisper. He watched the two figures as shadows on the wall. Brier's lengthy hair at his waist. The prince's high collar to the nape of his loose curls. "We can't… I'm sorry… but I can't."

"You honestly feel nothing for me? Truly?"

"I… I do love you," Brier whispered.

"I love you too!"

"But not… in the same way that you love me."

"You do, Brier. You just don't know it yet. You just haven't given yourself the chance to—"

"Quintin, please—"

"No, just listen to me." Quintin's voice shook as he spoke. "If he was not here. If he'd never come back, I would have earned your love."

Roland waited for Brier to refute the man's claim, but the king was silent.

"You can tell me that you do not love me in the same way I feel for you, but when we kissed that night, there was more than friendship in that kiss, Brier."

"Quintin." Brier's hastened breath startled Roland. He watched the two shadows meld together as Quintin hugged him.

"I love him," Brier whispered when the man's hold slackened.

Roland stood, eyes wide. He held the hilt of his sword, hands shaking. He wanted to kill the prince.

"I won't give up."

Roland breathed slowly and stepped back to calm his fury. Without another word Roland stomped through the restaurant with his heavy boots and walked toward the palace, as always, cold and alone.

ROLAND LISTENED to the sound of Meade's counting. He used a thick stethoscope over Brier's ripening belly, only blinking and murmuring every so often.

"About 145 beats per minute," the doctor said.

"That fast?" Brier blinked.

"Normal," Meade replied. "The medicine seems to be helping with your pressure. How are you eating? Sleeping."

"Eating well," Brier replied. "Sleeping… somewhat. I can't seem to get comfortable anymore. The heartburn doesn't help."

"Do you have any pain?" The doctor grabbed a leather bound notebook and began to scribble.

"Everywhere," Brier answered.

"Could you be more specific?"

"My shoulders, back, legs, thighs, feet."

"Okay, so everywhere," Meade replied. Roland snorted and shook his head. "Any anal bleeding, nausea, constipation?"

"No," Brier murmured. "Nothing like that."

"Tightness in your stomach?"

"Everything feels tight," Brier argued.

"This is more like an internal squeezing. It might even feel numb for a while."

"Oh yes." Brier nodded. "I've felt that a few times."

"When does it happen?" Meade questioned.

"Throughout the day I suppose. It doesn't last very long, though."

"How long?"

"One, maybe two minutes," Brier replied. Roland could sense the doctor's concern, and he questioned the healer.

"Something wrong, Meade?"

"In a normal circumstance, I would say no. It's common for women to experience prelabor contractions. Practicing for birth in a sense. In this case, I don't have much to go on as to what to expect, but I did find something in my research." The man set down the notebook and pulled out a thick volume and a thin binder from his bag. He placed the text on the table and opened it. Roland noticed the leaf emblem on the spine immediately.

"I had to search the royal archives. Thank you for granting me access by the way."

"Of course." Brier nodded. "We're as eager as you are to get more information."

"Aye." Roland agreed. "What were you able to find?"

"Well, I searched the royal family tree first," Meade told them. "I looked for anything similar to Brier's own genetics. Red hair, freckles, green eyes, similar birth weights, heights, etc. Well, I could eliminate most of those traits. Brier's mother had red hair, and so did his father King Braedon. The green eyes could also be from his mother or grandfather, King Braun. The only anomaly is the symbols on his skin."

"Naturally," Brier replied.

"Well, I had to confirm my hypothesis," the doctor explained. "At that point I went through to look for any records similar to your own. When Brier was born, they noted a single silver mark on the back of his neck."

"Only one?" Roland asked.

"Yes. Only one. And I found three others in the royal line with this distinction."

Roland could tell Brier had never heard this information before. He stared at Meade with keen eyes.

"The first one recorded was over two hundred years ago. His name was Austine. Then the next one, about one hundred years after that named Moran. Unfortunately there's not much about them. They were secborns and only distant cousins of the crown. Seems they cut ties from Avenough when they were old enough and lived outside of the court."

"So they wouldn't have been known," Roland deduced.

"Not at all." Meade shook his head. "I searched the records for them, but they stayed virtually off the map. Most likely to protect themselves."

"So then… there's nothing." Brier deflated.

"Not exactly," Meade continued. "Remember I told you. There were three cases of the distinction. The third, and the most recent, was only seventy-five years ago."

"But that would have been in Grandfather Braun's time."

"Yes. His nephew, first son of your great uncle Aengus. King Braun would have at least known about the lad. His name was Elrique. He too had the single silver mark on his neck, and I presume yours spread each year?"

"Yes." Brier nodded slowly. "How did you know that?"

"Well, that's the first thing Elrique wrote in his journal." Meade unwrapped the thin binder filled with tattered pages and scrawled writing.

"A journal?"

"Yes. A medical journal actually. Seems your cousin was a doctor."

"In Avenough?" Brier asked.

"No. He and his partner lived in a home outside of Avenough. Most likely in one of the more prominent smaller districts. Nonetheless, Elrique did have the same marks on his skin." Meade showed them the drawings Brier's cousin made. They mirrored the symbols almost identically. "If you're like Elrique your ejaculate is probably clear."

"I've never inspected it," Brier mumbled.

"It is," Roland answered for Brier. "So what does that mean?"

"It means that Brier, like Elrique, cannot sire children of his own."

"I can never have children with a woman?" Roland struggled to keep his face passive at Brier's question.

"I'm sorry Your Majesty, but no."

"Then…." Brier smiled and held the middle of his belly. "This is the only way I can have a child."

"Yes. Elrique noted in the journal how incredibly delicate the timing was. To have conceived your first time trying…well let's just say it's a rarity."

"It was unintentional, I assure you." Brier pursed his lips, but kept his smile. "No one told me I could get pregnant. Not even Father."

"Well, generally anal intercourse wouldn't lead to procreation."

"Then how is it possible?" Roland asked still bemused.

"At this point I have only Elrique's theories to go on."

"Which are?" Brier replied.

"Well, Elrique theorized that there must be an opening hidden *inside* the anus."

"Inside the anus?" Brier frowned. "Connected to what?"

"It starts from something like a seed, and grows every year. Elrique called it a tree. The tree of life, actually."

"Arrogant one wasn't he?" Roland snorted.

"Indeed." Meade chuckled.

"And leaves from this 'tree' are on my skin?" Brier asked, ignoring Roland's remark.

"Exactly. The roots of which lie deep inside of you, Brier."

"But how is it that he can become pregnant?"

"Because like every tree, when it reached full maturity, it released seeds. When the leaves on Brier's skin glow gold, the vessel where this tree lies is fertile, waiting for, let's say, 'nourishment' to make it grow."

"My contribution."

"Heh, yes, Roland." Meade answered nodding.

"And then the seed inside of me grows," Brier whispered.

"Yes, Your Majesty."

"This is amazing." Roland stared incredulous. "You're amazing." He turned toward Brier, grinning.

"More amazing are Elrique's actual entries. He chronicles his growth, the mark's progression and—" Meade smiled. "—his births."

"His births?" Roland clung to Meade's words. "You mean he actually gave birth to a child?"

"Three, actually," Meade told them.

"Then—" Brier's breath hitched. "Then that means—"

"That there's a possibility things will work out." Roland's heart raced.

"More than a possibility, Ronan!" Brier squeaked. "It means our child will be all right."

"It means we have something to go on," Meade corrected them both. "We still don't know what the result will be, but Elrique has at least given us a guide."

"Yes, and hope," Brier added, still beaming.

"Yes, well." Meade continued the examination. "The main things he marked were the changes in his body. From what you've both told me Brier's are mirroring Elrique's observations."

"And that's good, right?" Roland asked.

"That's very good," the man said, but then frowned. "Although I'm worried about the contractions. Elrique doesn't experience that until later months. Have you been under any stress lately? Physical or otherwise?"

"I am the king of Lirend. Every day is stressful," Brier answered caustically. "Rightly so, I should think."

"Rightly so or otherwise, you need to slow down, King Snow. At twenty-seven weeks you're in your third trimester. You should think about delegating more to your advisors. Take time to rest. You'll need your strength for the delivery."

"I rest," Brier retorted. "I even take naps sometimes during the day."

"When I force you to," Roland amended. Brier gave him a look of betrayal before Meade continued.

"I understand that you're under a lot of pressure right now, but it's essential that you take this seriously. I've told you the similarities between you and Elrique, but the difference in your lives is vast. Elrique worked as a private doctor for wealthy Aurelians. His singular job when with child was documenting the experience."

"I understand." Brier nodded. "I promise, I'll take better care."

"All right." Meade packed up his belongings. He went to grab the journal when Brier stopped him.

"Please, Meade. I know you're still researching, but is it all right if I hold Elrique's journal for a few days?"

The doctor blinked before he chuckled and nodded. "Of course, my king. By rights, it belongs to you. I only borrowed it for my own observation."

"Thank you." Brier grinned. "I appreciate everything you have done thus far."

"Aye, *Diole'*." Roland stood and bowed. "We owe you more than you know."

"It is a pleasure as always." The doctor bowed and then walked toward the door. Brier sat up off the chaise and pulled his robe over his shoulders and chest. He picked up the book and walked over to the small desk in the corner of his bedchamber. Roland could not help but smile as he watched his lover pore into the journal. Page after tattered page, Brier's green eyes scanned the journal as he grimaced and grinned.

"This is amazing," Brier said some hours later. Roland had begun whittling a piece of wood he bought in the square some days prior to occupy him. "Elrique's marks are just like my own. He says that they glowed gold each time he conceived."

"Is that the only time?"

"*Na*." Brier's face grew red. "When he was particularly aroused they would as well."

"I see." Roland chuckled. He avoided the urge to ask Brier if he'd ever experienced that trait before.

"Heh—" Brier giggled. "My whole entire life I've thought that only I endured this."

"It must feel good to know that you share a similar fate with your cousins," Roland replied. Brier had always felt like an outcast in his family. Having proof that there were other Aurelians like him might quell some of Brier's anxiety.

"It feels good to know that I am not alone," Brier said wistfully. "That my worries, fears, dreams… are not for nothing."

Roland paused when he heard the dejection in Brier's tone. He set down the wood and stepped over to where Brier still sat. "Of course they are not for nothing." Roland closed the journal and Brier peered up at him. "Your worries, your fears, your dreams. They are all a part of you." He leaned in and kissed Brier's forehead. "A part of you I hope to never see tarnished, Brinan." Roland kissed him once more, but this time on his supple lips.

"I wish we could disappear like Elrique and the others," Brier whispered. "I wish that I could love you openly, and not hidden in this suite."

Like he'd loved Prince Quintin? Roland tried not to let envy darken his thoughts.

"Lord Yaris was right in what he said, Brinan. Lirend needs you. Your heart. Your rule."

"And I need you," Brier countered. He held Roland's wrist and entwined their fingers. "Last night, I wanted to tell them that *you* were my lover."

Last night....

"Even a king's guard does not suit His Majesty."

The memory of the prince whispering his love to Brier made Roland's skin prickle with acrimony.

"I don't care." Brier squeezed Roland's hand. "I don't care if you suit me in station, Rolande, I can't imagine my life without you."

"I know, Brinan. I feel the same." Like a numbed bruise, the ache in his chest began to ebb with Brier's words.

"We cannot marry, I know this, but what if we got our own place?"

"What do you mean?" Roland eyed Brier warily.

"Well, I mean. All three of them, my cousins, found peace after they'd cut ties with the royal line. Of course, I cannot do that, but what if we found our own place to live? Together."

"Away from the palace?"

"Aye. Away from the palace. Away from the courtiers. Away from the Aurelians and everything else that disturbs us."

"But—don't you have to live in the palace? You are the king of Lirend."

"Aye. And nowhere does it state that I must live in Avenough. There are other districts near enough that I can still govern effectively." Roland gave Brier a dubious stare. He doubted Lord Tamil, Prince Quintin, or even Marietta would agree.

"I don't know, Brinan. Wouldn't they suspect something untoward? With you away from your home?" As much as Roland wanted to claim Brier as his, the king's sovereignty and happiness remained Roland's ultimate concern.

"This isn't my home, Ronan." Brier shook his head. "Verily, I felt more at home in your cabin than I've ever felt here in Avenough." It was the first time Brier spoke of their time together in Aire so candidly. Despite the good times, there were memories there that still pained Brier. And Roland.

"You're sure you want to do this?"

"I'm sure." Roland watched Brier's determined face and he knew he'd already lost. Brier's stubbornness would far outlast Roland's skepticism.

"We can go to Balmur," he told Brier with a smile. "There is a property some ways south of here. An old villa."

"By the willow creek?"

"Aye. You know it?"

"Yes, of course. It's not more than five miles from here."

"Less than an hour's ride on horseback. Close enough that you can come and go to Avenough."

"And far enough that we won't need to endear ourselves to anyone." Brier beamed. "I love it. I can have someone survey that land by tomorrow."

"*Na.*" Roland shook his head. "I want to do it."

"Do what? Survey the land?" Brier frowned.

"Rehabilitate it from the foundation," Roland answered. "I want to build us a home that is our own." He reached down and touched Brier's stomach. "And our child's." Brier placed a hand overtop his, and Roland entwined their fingers. "What say you, my king?"

"*Mana el man'.*" Brier leaned against his arm. "If you wish it."

CHAPTER 23
HEIR

BRIER WALKED toward the west wing with Finnas on his heels. He had not told his retainer anything about Meade's frequent visits over the past weeks, though he knew his time was running out. Eventually everyone would know. It was not something he would be able to hide forever with draped robes. Even now his bump had become noticeable, albeit explainable if anyone asked.

The chamber appeared dark when Brier entered, though he could see a light at the far corner of the room glowing. The rounded wooden table acted as a centerpiece for the vast space. The former queen graced the head, seemingly alone, with an embellished goblet beside her.

"Your Grace." Brier inclined his head slightly. Today he needn't worry about lying because revealing the truth to the former queen was exactly what he intended to do. "Good evening." She did not stand when he entered as customary, but lifted the cup and took a deep gulp.

"King Snow." Her smile was both acerbic and alluring. "To what do I owe the pleasure of an impromptu visit?"

"I tried to inform your guard I would be around, but Lord Tamil says he could not locate him." A burly guard stepped from the shadows, and Brier tightened his jaw. He had not actually seen Captain Galer since he'd dismissed him some months back. Brier had gotten over the expulsion to Aire, but the punch to his gut still simmered in his mind. The captain bowed, and Brier returned a stiff nod. "This is a private conversation, Captain Galer. Please excuse yourself with my retainer." The captain turned toward the queen, who considered the order before she complied. Brier followed the guard with his eyes until the man disappeared from view and the door snapped shut.

"What is so important that you need to interrupt my leisure time, King Brier?"

"I'm sure you have no lack of unused time, Your Grace," Brier pointed out. "Nevertheless, I am here because you are my closest official kin, and this news concerns you, more or less." He watched the woman raise one of her blonde brows, but she did not speak.

"In one week I will make an announcement in the square." He walked over to stand closer to her.

"About?" the woman simpered.

"About the succession of the throne." Brier took a deep breath before he continued. "To let the kingdom know I will have an heir."

"Heh—" The queen shook her head. "Once again you demonstrate your ignorance of Lirend's laws. Even if you have gotten some poor woman saddled with your seed, it does not matter. A bastard of a king is not granted succession of the throne."

"Only if a maiden carries his seed," Brier corrected her. Then he cupped his hands under his enlarged stomach. "But I am the one with child." The queen's eyes widened first in disbelief, and then in disdain.

"So it is true."

"You knew about this?"

"That you were born with a curse? Oh yes. It's been all I could do to sustain your father's lineage."

Brier stood with his chin level and his eyes fixed. He expected yelling, cursing, perhaps even for the woman to try to throw him out, but he did not anticipate the queen's perceptive glare.

"And who, pray tell, have you spread yourself?"

"That is none of your concern." Brier was unable to say if the erstwhile queen simply loathed him or derided him for sport. She had tended to his basic needs, certainly, but he doubted it was out of affection for him and was most likely due to the remnants of whatever affection she had for his late father. Now King Braedon was gone and Brier remained.

The woman chuckled. "What, does he not even want you after getting you with child? Or do you simply not have the gall to tell him about your accursed condition?"

Brier bristled but did not let her goad him into revealing Roland. Blessing or curse, she could not steal this from him.

"I only came to inform you, Your Grace."

"And why should I care? You are no longer my concern," she scoffed. "Do as you wish. King," she added caustically.

"I plan to," Brier answered calmly and began to walk away. "In the meantime, I would advise you to make yourself more accessible. There is no reason to have you present on the palace grounds and unavailable."

Brier stepped out of the red chamber, past Captain Galer, and toward his suite. Finnas scurried behind Brier, holding the king's agenda.

"Your Majesty, you have an appointment with Lord Tamil in an hour."

"Cancel it."

Brier walked into the suite expecting to see Roland's smile, but found an empty bedchamber instead. He lay out on the bed, tired from nothing. He hadn't even made it to lunch, but he strained from the burden of the day.

"Where is Roland?" He let out an impatient sigh.

"I believe he is meeting with the contractors. They're putting the foundation up for your estate."

"How long ago did he leave?"

"I'm not sure, Your Majesty," Finnas answered. "I know that he was invited to a game of archery earlier in the day."

"Outside of the palace?"

"Yes." Finnas hesitated.

Brier's heart sped nervously. "With who?"

"General Hilburn called for him, but he made no mention of attending the match, Your Majesty."

"I see." Brier knew Roland's station would make him more accessible to the people of Lirend. At the events he and Roland attended, it was obvious that General Hilburn and Lord Yaris enjoyed the huntsman's company, and others would as well. Still, Brier had not considered that Lord Roland might enjoy their company.

Finnas stood by the bed silently. Brier turned to his side with a sense of longing. Roland had not played any sport since he came to Avenough, and the first time was without him. Of course Brier could not hold himself upright, let alone a bow. He told himself it did not matter, but he could not help the twinge of jealousy he felt for Roland's time. And what if the queen was right? What if Roland grew bored of him or found someone else to love? The larger he grew, the clumsier and more burdensome he became. Brier covered his head with the satin-laced pillow and dismissed Finnas for the rest of the day.

BRIER SLEPT, but for how long he did not know. The cool air flushed his round face, but his tired eyes stirred when someone touched his temple.

"*Venur*." The rough voice burned through him like lit kindling. All at once the tension of the day began to dissipate.

"*Venur*, Ronan," Brier breathed out. He yawned with his eyes still shut, and Roland leaned in to kiss his lips.

"Good evening." Roland smirked as he pulled back from the kiss. "You must be tired if you're resting before bed."

Brier shook his head and sat up fully. "I came to see you." He chuckled. "Though I guess I drifted waiting for you."

"I rode out late this morning to the countryside. The shipment of alderwood came in at dawn for the doors." Roland's dark brow creased. "Is everything all right with the baby?" Roland touched his stomach.

"Everything is fine. I just… wanted to see you." He lowered his gaze. The days when Roland busied himself with other things, Brier held unfair resentment. He did not want to share Roland's time with anyone, leastways an Aurelian. Roland frowned before a pensive smile pursed his lips.

"Aye, so that means you miss me." Brier considered Roland's words. When Roland let him go, there was a petulant longing to be near his master once more. The despondency consumed him. Yet here now, he missed the lover who held him every night. How could he want another person so completely?

"Yes…." Brier averted his gaze. The truth settled between them, and Brier shifted uncomfortably in the silence. "Is it wrong that I missed you?"

"How could your desire to see me be wrong?" Brier felt the full lips on his creased forehead. "I missed you too, Brier."

"You did?" He peered up into the slate-blue gaze.

"So much that it hurt." Brier leaned his cheek against Roland's chest and sighed out, basking in Roland's rare transparency.

"I know I am silly. I have responsibilities at court, and I know you are busy building the house and entertaining others, but I feel like I've not seen you in forever."

"Who are these others?" Roland questioned him.

"Lord Yaris's friend. That Aurelian general," Brier mumbled. "Finnas told me he invited you for a round of archery." Brier heard the deep chuckle in Roland's chest as he shook his head.

"He only harkens me for your favor," Roland answered. "Because he sees how hopelessly devoted I am to my king." Roland winked, and Brier's stomach clenched. He was a king jealous over a mere general.

"Forgive me." Brier closed his eyes and exhaled. "You should be allowed to see who you wish."

"You are the only one I wish to see, King Brier." Brier's heart thudded listening to Roland's admission. "I told you, I will lock you away so that you belong only to me."

"You're the only one I belong to." Relief washed over him, and he lazed on the bed under Roland's caress. The bright red hair had grown somehow longer, though the freckles on his nose and cheek remained constant. His hips had not spread more, but his stomach grew fuller every day.

"She seems to enjoy when I rub your stomach thus." Brier watched Roland curiously as he smoothed a hand over his taut skin and leaned in to kiss his belly.

"Do you think I'm still attractive?" Brier suddenly asked. Roland frowned at the seemingly ambiguous question, unaware of the exchange Brier had with the queen earlier in the day.

Still, Roland did not hesitate before he answered, "I think you more than attractive. I think you the fairest in all of Lirend." Roland leaned down to kiss his stomach once more, but this time Brier grabbed a chunk of Roland's dark hair.

"Then why do you not take me?"

Roland slid out of his grasp and let out a bark of laughter. "Come again, Your Majesty?" Brier pouted to fight the fierce red in his cheeks. He realized too late that the question sounded more like a demand, but he did not want Roland to indulge him… or maybe he did.

"It's just that, we haven't slept with each other in the last month, and I want you… that is if—"

"If I want to have you?" Roland ogled him, incredulous. Brier tried to avert his gaze, but Roland held his chin firmly. "You know, sometimes I think this babe does touch your mind a bit." The wrinkles creased Brier's brow.

"Not only do I think you attractive, I think you charming and exquisite. I think you intelligent and wise beyond your twenty years. I think you elegant and sexy, Your Majesty." Roland leaned in and kissed his pout. "And I would stake my head for someone to refute my claim," he added crudely.

"Please do not." Brier shook his head, still flushed. "I am monstrous."

"You dare to challenge me?" Roland narrowed his gaze.

Brier pursed his lips, annoyed, before he shifted his gaze and mumbled, "No." He both hated and loved how effortlessly Roland eased his worries.

"Good." Roland caught Brier's mouth in a heated kiss and pressed him into the bed. Brier tried to speak, but Roland sucked his throat to draw out only breathy moans.

"I know you're exhausted, my king. It's the only reason I've resisted the urge to have you." Goose bumps erupted on his skin from Roland's husky tone. "But I crave the taste of you."

Roland stripped Brier down to nakedness. He whimpered as Roland licked every inch of bare skin. Roland's tongue swirled against Brier's enlarged nipples and pleasure pinched the crown of his stiff member.

"Don't, Roland." Brier pushed Roland's chest, embarrassed by the changes in his body, but Roland continued to suck and fondle his pink perk. "Mhmm!" Brier gasped as Roland lifted his leg gingerly. Brier twined his fingers through dark hair before he pushed into Roland's mouth, desperate to be owned.

"Impatient," Roland whispered, and Brier ground his hips up to show Roland his true need. He doubted he was the fairest in his current state of enormity, but Roland desired him, and that thought made Brier ache for his touch. Roland tried to mollify his urge with a pressurized stroke, but Brier's need surmounted the pleasure.

"Will you calm yourself?" Roland nosed the inside of Brier's thigh and his tongue trailed to the underside of Brier's sac. Brier twisted like a corkscrew, praying to the gods their child did not stir within him.

"I can't." Brier fumbled over to the vanity beside them and procured a small white jar. He dipped his fingers into the cream-like gel before he lifted his legs and spread them wide. "You've made me wait too long." Brier traced his fingers around the space between his taut member and sac, and Roland watched mesmerized.

"Can you forgive me?" Roland's heavy hands enclosed his shaft completely and Brier slid two fingers deep without a wince.

"Aye," Brier panted. He could feel Roland's eyes on him as he slid a third finger to prepare for Roland's length and girth. He trembled from the heat of Roland's caress and the probe of his own fingers. "If you hurry and mount me."

Roland kissed the crown of his member before Brier felt a fourth finger puncture his ripe ass. He shut his eyes, gasped out, and nearly coughed as Roland stretched his cleft. "Ahh—Ronan!" Like a man possessed, Brier bucked toward Roland's fist and writhed from the prickling pleasure that coursed through his skin. His body begged Roland to finally spear him, but Roland's flesh hung heavy between his thighs. At the first sign of Brier's undoing, Roland latched on like a thirsty desert wretch.

"Mgnn...." Roland's mouth consumed him with heat. "Ronan...." Roland hollowed his cheeks to taste Brier's saccharine seed. Roland curled four fingers deep, and Brier whined to the sound of squelching white cream.

"I'm—Rolande—!" Brier screamed, either desperate for more or release—which, he could not even tell. Roland inhaled the whole of his shaft and in the next moment, Brier's chest tightened. "Ah—!" He held his breath as his member twitched in a surge of cum. Brier's mind blanked for several seconds while Roland swallowed the remnants of his bliss. When he came to, Roland released Brier's rod with a loud pop, slid his fingers out, and peppered kisses on each of his sweaty thighs. Brier's body remained tense, legs suspended in air as if directed with a string.

"Better, Brinan?" Brier violently shook his head. Roland had barely shunted the ache within him, but the lack of the man's heated mouth turned Brier from king to beggar.

"Have me, please, Ronan, I need you!" His lips quivered as he pleaded. "*Acai*!"

Brier felt the man's teeth sink deep into his thigh, and he jolted so vehemently the bed rattled in its frame.

"Don't worry, I will."

Roland flipped Brier to his side and positioned him to all fours like a cur in heat. Brier steadied his knees and arched his back, braced for penetration. He listened as Roland uncapped the jar of cream. Roland pressed in only the tip of his member, but Brier wriggled anxiously. He felt Roland's hand wrap around his neck and Brier's mouth watered in foretaste of the eventual plunge. The waiting was unbearable.

"Relax, Brinan." Roland's hands grazed the back of his thighs and sac. Brier let out a deep breath, and his ass melted around Roland's stiff flesh.

"Ah—yes!" Brier gasped with the first shuddering thrust. Roland's hand tightened on his neck and the strength sent shivers down his spine. "Gods...." Brier moaned from his seeming weightlessness in Roland's grasp.

"Harder." He pushed back against Roland's pole, and his eyes fluttered from the pleasure. "Please, Ronan."

Roland cursed and held Brier's waist to restrain him.

"I don't want to hurt you." Brier knew Roland's reasoning, but Roland moved too slow, or as it were, too gingerly.

"It's all right, *acai*." Brier needed the pith of Roland, and the raw passion to release his burdens: running the kingdom, Prince Quintin's relentless advances, his insecurities, this pregnancy, and the crushing realization that he and Roland would never be accepted in Lirend.

"If you wish it."

Brier howled out in pleasure as Roland's thick shaft rammed inside of him.

"Aye!" He wished it. He wanted it. His hands shook as his member throbbed viciously and Roland pummeled Brier's sensitive gland. Tears pricked his eyes, but he absorbed Roland's tension and pulsed for more.

"Ahh—coming—!" Brier reached down and wrapped his fingers around the base to hold back his own climax. "There!" He used every ounce of strength in his body to ride back against his former master, gasping for air. "There. Yes—!" Roland prepared him, filled him, and wrung him with every thrust. The grip around his neck strengthened, and Roland's words melded into incoherent murmurs of Thenian, curses and prayers. Brier removed the hand that held his base and readied himself for Roland's load.

"Mmmgghh!" Roland let out a vibrating moan, and Brier shrieked at the force of his slams.

"Ngh—ngh—" Brier buried his face in the satin and silk of his bedding, succumbing to the sweet thrill of his second climax. Sharp gasps strained Brier's lungs as he emptied his load between the sheets and the bulge of his stomach. Roland growled, and Brier shuddered as the man's cum gushed.

"Gods," he mewled out, dazed from the shock of their simultaneous release. Roland pumped until Brier's member went limp. Roland pulled out slowly and helped Brier to his side.

"Are you well?" Roland still fought to gain his breath.

"Of course…." Though sudden exhaustion overwhelmed him and he fought to keep his eyes open, Roland's hands began to soothe the ache in his legs. "I've almost everything I want."

"Almost everything?" Roland frowned, and Brier gave him a heady smile.

"I think I want some redmelon pie…." His eyes closed once more.

"Thank the gods it's only pie. You've worn me out, Brinan." Roland let out a relieved sigh, and Brier chuckled darkly. "I saw some chocolate mousse cake as well. Shall I fetch it now or will you sleep first?"

"Mm… chocolate mousse then pie. Or pie, chocolate mousse, and then sleep…." Brier considered in limbo.

"Milk could be good too," Roland added.

"Aye definitely," Brier whispered. "Don't forget… the milk…." But Brier could only taste it in his dreams. Roland's massage dragged him into such a deep slumber that he barely felt the warm kiss on his cheek.

"I FEEL as though I'm going to be sick," Brier told Marietta as she braided his hair. She'd washed his red locks with a honey-based shampoo, and the smell made him nauseous. He sat in his bedchamber on a lone stool and tapped his foot to ignore the bubble in his gut. His face felt warm. He could feel the dabs of sweat curling his red sideburns.

"Sorry, I'd forgotten how sensitive ya are." It was midfall, but Brier perspired as if midsummer. "You're white as a board. Are ya sure you're up to it today, King Snow?" Brier nodded, but Marietta crossed her arms, unconvinced. "I still think you should wait." She helped Brier into the velvet emerald robe. "I understand the courtiers, but there's no reason to the citizens."

"There's no reason not to tell them either." Brier wiped his forehead with a gold-colored kerchief. "The people of Avenough have stood by me in all my endeavors this past year. They deserve to know the truth. If I took a wife and she was with child, we would announce it."

"But you have not taken a wife, and you are to have the child," Marietta countered. "Presumably with no partner." Brier pursed his lips. He knew Marietta was trying to help, but the woman's words only aggravated his current unrest. "If it was Prince Quintin then—"

"If it was Prince Quintin, then there would be no child to speak of. I'll not be ashamed of Rolande. Bastard or not, this child is our own."

"Our child is no bastard." Roland's gruff voice startled Brier, but the declaration assuaged his apprehension. "With or without my name, he or she will know me." Brier heard the pride in Roland's voice, and his chest swelled.

"*Venur*, Ronan." Brier twisted to kiss his lover.

"*Venur*." Roland grimaced. "*L'tyva el*?"

Brier nodded. "I'm fine, though I feel a little uneasy."

"Well, you are a vision." Brier chose a robe that would conceal much of the added weight. The emerald accented the fiery red of his hair, adorned with a golden circlet. A smaller version of the crown he wore during formal occasions.

"Thank you." Brier beamed at the compliment. "We're heading to the square now." Roland nodded and turned to Finnas.

"Ready the carriage, please. I'll check the stairwell to make sure Lord Tamil does not ambush us." Roland jested, but the words held truth. Ever since his meeting with Evelyn, the lord had made it his mission to find out what the king concealed.

Finnas and Roland disappeared, leaving Brier alone with Marietta once more.

"This is it," Marietta whispered. Brier pulled on a white fur coat that hid his shoulders and bulge. "After this announcement nothing will be the same."

"Things have not been the same for a while yet, Mar'. My life has not been the same since I journeyed to Aire." Brier held his stomach. "I love him. I wish you could be happy for me."

"I am happy for you," Marietta answered wistfully. "I wish things were easier, for the both of you, but I am overjoyed, King Snow." The woman leaned in and kissed Brier's cheek. "Now, let us go announce your child to Lirend."

WHEN THEY reached the square, Brier finally composed himself. The cool air helped with his mild fever, and Roland's presence assured him. While they usually held Avenough's festivals in the square, the solstice was still weeks away, so Brier decided to blockade the space around the ornate fountain. The guards surrounded him, with Finnas standing behind him, Roland on his left, and Marietta on his right. He stared across the gathered mass of people, adorned in their best robes, dresses, and jackets; he had decreed a feast be given afterward for the people to celebrate the news of Lirend's heir. Even the Aurelians congregated amongst the Prolit and Burges, segregated but present. He knew they would assume Prince Quintin the father, and all he could do was let them. Brier learned long ago he could not control gossip and in the end, it did not matter. This child belonged to him and the love of his life. No one could take that from them. Brier stepped forward and let out a deep breath before he began.

"Good evening. Firstly, I'd like to thank you for coming. I know how busy your lives are. That you would take time out of your day to indulge me, I appreciate the effort. In return, I trust you to enjoy the feast afterwards," Brier called, earning a cheer before silence fell. Then he could only hear the sound of the spurting fountainhead and his heart thudding noisily. "For a long time, a stomach sickness befell on me. I thought that I was ill. I thought I might leave you before my time, and the thought filled my heart with sorrow." He paused, watching the countless men and women. "I am pleased to say that it is not an illness that ails me, but something we have never seen before. At least not in this lifetime," he added, smiling.

"The truth is that I was born with marks upon my body. I have kept them hidden all my life. I disdained them, and yet, they are why I am here before you." Brier cleared his throat and breathed deep. He had remained hidden all his life. First by his queen stepmother, and then of his own volition. He hid from the stares, from the whispers, and then from the weight of his crown, but now he could not hide or run.

"I am with child." Brier spread his white fur to reveal his stomach. "The child is due in a few short weeks, and I pray that you can join me in celebration of its arrival." The whispers grew until the square broke out into full-fledged commotion.

The guards moved inward to protect him, and Brier noticed Roland's hoary eyes scan the nonplussed crowd.

"It is just as the queen foretold! A curse!" a man's voice bellowed and the crowd turned his way. "She warned us!" The man walked to the front of the crowd, and Brier recognized him at once. Lord Alexander Renli. Some of the Aurelians nodded with indignant expressions though most appeared fearful of Renli's obscenities. "His body has the mark of darkness!"

"Is it a curse to be able to conceive young that would have otherwise not been born? A curse to bring forth an heir to inherit the throne and continue prosperity and peace?"

"A curse for our king to take the seed of another man."

"Perhaps you should not be so quick to berate your king, Lord Renli, since it was my grandfather who took the throne, and dragged your line from the very depths of squalor." Renli's eyes widened in shock before his face flushed with anger. Brier had not intended to belittle him in the square, but the man's outburst incensed him.

"Who is the father, Your Majesty?" a maiden holding a young child asked. Brier fought not to gaze at Roland.

"He wishes to be kept a secret, as we are not wed." Brier feigned a smile.

"The gods will scourge the whole of Lirend for this!" Renli called out once more. "We will all be punished in the next life for this abomination!"

"You will be punished in this life if you do not hold your tongue!" Roland's heated voice refuted. Brier stared at Roland's pained face before the man lowered his head. Brier shifted his weight and raised his chin to speak clearly.

"It is a fool who believes that bringing forth life is a curse. The gods have given Lirend this blessing, and they make no mistakes. Now, if you will excuse me." Brier turned away from the murmuring crowd. "Please, enjoy the feast." Marietta held his back and led him to the carriage, and Roland trailed them with the guards. The instant the door closed, his lover gripped him into a tight hug. Brier's shoulders slackened in the warm embrace.

"That could have gone a lot worse," Roland assured him. "You did well, Brinan."

"He's right," Marietta agreed as the carriage jutted them forward.

"I heard the Aurelians whispering," Brier replied hesitantly. "They believe Prince Quintin is the father."

"Let them believe what they want." Roland's words rang out in the carriage. "We know the truth." Brier nodded, though he could feel the tension in Roland's voice.

"I hope that they can come to accept this."

"They will, they just need time." Roland kissed the top of his forehead and Brier smiled gently. "Trust your people, King Brier. They have not forsaken you." Brier wanted to believe Roland's encouragement, but he could sense trepidation within him.

"Aye," Brier whispered as he leaned back in the carriage seat. Roland reached out to entwine their fingers, and Brier braced himself for the impending storm.

BRIER REMOVED the crown on his head before he settled in the chair of his father's study. He donned a smug smile as he watched Aurelians traipsing back from the square, those too pretentious to eat with the Prolits and Burges.

Well, let them eat of their own hand, he thought as he closed his eyes. He'd sent Roland to fetch him dinner with Finnas for a chance to be alone with his thoughts. Lord Tamil had not found him, yet, but he was sure his advisor would seek him eventually.

Brier raised his hand absentmindedly and thumbed the iron music box on his desk. If his father was still alive, he could have sought his counsel. He would ask King Braedon how to be strong when he felt like breaking. How to stand for love when love knocked him down.

"Brier…." He inhaled at the sound of his name spoken so softly. When he opened his eyes, the prince stood before him, clad in royal blue and Menlor's orange tassels.

"Quintin." Brier stood from the wooden-backed chair. Quintin did not speak, but scrutinized Brier's body with piercing blue eyes. "I'm sure you've heard." Brier held his swollen belly. "Lirend will have an heir." He tried to smile, but it came as a grimace.

"How?" Quintin asked. "How is this possible?"

Brier unbuttoned the top of his robe to show Quintin the silver swirls on his skin. "It is because of these that I am able."

"And I am to assume that man, Roland, is the father?" It never dawned on him that Quintin might think himself the father, especially since they had never coupled.

"Aye," Brier whispered. "I cannot name him, but he is the father of this child."

"I see." Quintin cleared his throat with a false smile. "Then this visit is as good a time as any to bid you farewell."

"Farewell?"

"Yes, I am returning to Menlor. This evening on the next ship heading southeast." Brier swallowed as Quintin's words seeped through him.

"Must you go?" Brier mumbled.

"You expect me to stay?" Quintin glared. "After everything?" He scoffed and shook his head.

Brier knew he'd hurt Quintin, but as selfish as it was, he never wanted their friendship to end. Quintin had helped him, cared for him… mayhap even loved him. Yet he chose now to bare himself to Quintin. Now when he knew they had no future.

"I'm sorry I hurt you, Quintin." Brier pressed his lips together. "But it is as I've said before. I love him. I cannot let him go."

"I know that!" Quintin yelled, and Brier flinched at the outburst. He clenched his hands into a trembling fist.

"I know that you love him…." Quintin whispered. "But that does not mean I can bear witness to it anymore." The prince stepped closer to him, and Brier lowered his gaze. He did not know what to do when his words held no meaning.

"Quintin, I—"

"Your Majesty!" Lord Tamil burst into the king's study. Brier composed himself and stepped to Quintin's side. "We've just heard the news!" Lord Tamil exclaimed, and to Brier's surprise the man smiled. "We are so happy for His Majesty, and of course for you, Prince Quintin. When will you two wed?" Brier's eyes widened as the prince grappled with the question.

"Prince Quintin is not—" Brier began to speak, but Quintin's voice overpowered his own.

"We're not—" Quintin clenched his jaw firmly. Quintin held Brier's bicep before he gripped his waist. "That is to say, we're not sure when the wedding will be."

If Brier's eyes grew wide at Lord Tamil's exuberance, they nearly popped when Prince Quintin attuned the lord's claim.

"Well, it must be soon. Brier is nearly sprung." Lord Tamil laughed heartily.

"Yes." Prince Quintin echoed the laugh. "We cannot have the first heir born a bastard." Brier could not think to refute either of them. If he told Lord Tamil Quintin was not the father, the advisor would browbeat him into confessing Roland's identity. If he hid the truth, his admission in the square would be for nothing.

"Quintin." His voice came out hoarse. "You—"

"Are the happy father." Quintin smiled sweetly. "Now, if you'll please excuse us, Lord Tamil. Brier is very tired, and he needs to keep his strength up."

"Oh, of course, naturally," Lord Tamil answered before he bowed. Brier watched Lord Tamil disappear behind the oak doors with a loud thud.

"By the gods, what have you done?" Brier shoved Quintin away from him.

"I saved your ass," Quintin bit back. "You said you did not want him to be named, so I named myself instead."

"As my intended?" Brier yelled, frantic. "I told you, Quintin, you are not the father!"

"I know that," Quintin exhaled. "But what would you have me do?"

"What would I have you—" Brier raised his brow, incredulous. "You should have told him the truth!"

"Did you not just say that you did not want them to know?"

"I did, but—"

"But you did not think the court would want to know whose blood runs through the heir of Lirend's veins?" Brier paled at the slap of reality. He hoped that he could pawn it off on a distant royal, some unknown Aurelian who could disappear before the child was born. How foolish he was not to consider the ramifications of Lirend's heir. Brier staggered into the chair across from his father's desk. Quintin stepped toward Brier and kneeled down to sit at eye level.

"Is it so bad that they believe the child belongs to me? At least until it is born? The court will be so enthralled that they will not care if we do not marry."

"What about your own family, Quintin?"

"I will return to Menlor after the child is born and inform everyone of the misunderstanding."

Brier bit the inside of his lip. There was no way he could conceal Roland's identity without Quintin. However amiss Quintin's plan seemed, Brier needed him once more.

"You shouldn't have to deal with this." Brier held a pulsing vein in his head. "I just have no idea how to get the court to accept a Thenian. I can't just tell them Roland is the father."

"You don't have to tell them yet." Quintin grasped his hand and held it gently. "Let me buy you some time. We will not announce anything publicly. If Lord Tamil does tell others I am the father, then let him. Later we will simply say it was a misunderstanding. Right now it is about showing the people you can handle this pressure, my king. They will not care who the father is if your kingdom continues to flourish."

"But why?" Brier whispered. "Why would you… this is… too much, Quintin."

"It is not too much for the man I love." Quintin held his hand. "I love you. Trust me, Brier." He leaned in and gave Brier's forehead a gentle kiss. Brier's eyes fluttered shut before he heard a plate shatter to the ground. He peered up to see Roland in a full run toward Quintin.

"Ronan!"

Before Brier could react, Roland bolted toward them. Brier watched in horror as the huntsman slammed Quintin's head onto his father's mahogany desk. The papers slid and scattered across the floor. Brier rushed to stop Roland, but Quintin's face bulged, shock red, as Roland's hands wrapped around his neck.

"It is clear that you did not understand our first meeting, so let me explain this to you better, prince." Brier heard Roland's words through grit teeth. Roland stared at Quintin with his eyes cinched to slits, and Brier saw the wild beast. Terror spindled like a web through his chest, but Brier ignored his urge to run and continued to shove Roland's bearlike frame. "If you talk to him, if you touch him, if you come near him again, I will end you!"

"I'm trying to—" Quintin kicked his legs and wheezed. Spittle dripped from under his trembling lips. "Guhh—to help—!"

"Let go, Ronan!" Brier shouted to the huntsman. He pulled the leather collar of Roland's jacket, trying to yank him. "He's trying to help us, nothing more!" Quintin fell to the floor like a coin piece. Brier rushed to Quintin's side, but blanched when Roland turned to him with that murderous gaze instead.

"Help us? By confessing his love to you?" Roland grabbed Brier's wrist and faced him away from Quintin who still struggled to catch his breath. "By putting his fucking hands on you?" Brier tugged his hand back viciously, and a ripple of pain shot through his body.

"By protecting our child!" Brier screamed. "Because you're unable to come forward as the father, Quintin had to—" Brier faltered at the sudden tightening in his stomach. "Had to—say he was the father."

"I don't see how this helps! That he confirms a rumor that the people of Lirend spread!"

"He is giving us cover and safety until our child is born." Brier sank down into the chair, breath hastening.

"It is the only way to hold the courtiers off!" Quintin finally regained his hoarse voice. "They will want to know who sired this child. And since you will not, or shall I say cannot, I took the charge to stand in."

"It is not your place to stand in!" Roland bellowed to Quintin.

"*Acai.*" Brier squeezed his eyes shut as he felt the painful tightening once more. Roland could not understand his friendship for Quintin. Quintin could not understand his love for Roland. He never wanted to hurt either of them, and yet, his actions only caused them both pain. "*Acai*, Ronan… leave him be." Brier felt someone's hands on his back, and then on his shoulder.

"Brinan, are you okay?" Roland whispered.

"*Na.*" Brier shook his head as the contraction gripped him tighter. He shivered from the fear, but warm blood stained his breeches, and hot tears clouded his vision. "Get Meade. Now."

CHAPTER 24
UNDONE

ROLAND WAITED at Brier's side while Marietta dabbed Brier's head with a cool cloth. Watching Brier whine and cry from pain made Roland aware that he had not seen him suffer since their trip to Sherdoe one year prior.

Roland paced the king's bedchamber but kept his eyes on Brier lest he fade. The prince sat on the chaise some feet away, but Roland could not even care about his presence.

Acai.... Brinan....

When Meade showed up, Roland clamored to Brier's side.

"Everyone but the father should leave." The doctor spoke, visibly ruffled, but not frantic. Roland cut his gaze to Quintin, but the prince did not argue. He turned his gaze away, looking solemn, and walked with Marietta out of the suite.

Roland turned toward Brier when he heard fabric rip. Meade sheared the emerald velvet with large scissors.

"How long ago?" the man asked mechanically.

"About an hour," Roland stuttered. "He just—keeled over and then the blood started." He swallowed when Meade draped a sheet around Brier's bottom half and began to examine the king. Brier whimpered, but Meade did not let it deter him.

"He's in labor," Meade informed Roland. "I'm going to try to stop the contractions, but if I can't, we'll have to take the baby."

"It's too early." Brier let out a wail and shook his head, sobbing. "She won't survive this early, Ronan." The doctor stood up and Roland gripped Brier's hand.

"Shhh...." Roland kissed Brier's knuckles. "Let us save our tears for the outcome, and not the possibility."

Brier's breath grew rapid as he fought to keep their child. Sweat clung to Brier's frail body and the color left his skin, but Roland could feel a sturdy grip on his hand.

"I shouldn't have told anyone." Brier shivered when he spoke. "I should have disappeared with you when you came back to Avenough."

"Hush, Brinan." Roland tried to keep Brier calm even though he inwardly reeled from fear. He could not do anything to help Brier keep the babe, but he was sure to watch for signs that his lover was fading. That he wouldn't let happen. He'd already made up his mind. "There is nothing for regret. We are here together. That is all that matters."

"It's ready." Meade returned holding a lengthy syringe.

"What is it?" Roland frowned.

"A medicine to stop the contractions," the doctor explained. "I'm using a concoction for preterm labor. The dosage corresponds to his weight and height. It should work."

"And if it does not?"

Meade picked up another needle. "I will take the child so that Brier will not lose more blood. Better we lose the babe than the king."

"Stop waiting!" Brier commanded, though tears stained his red face. Roland nodded almost in a trance.

"Ronan." Brier's hold tightened on his hand, and Roland observed him intensely. Even then the possibility of losing Brier remained. At the sight of the bloodstained sheets, he thought of Helenas and the memory of his first babe who never saw the light of day. Tears beaded in the corners of Roland's eyes, but he choked out a breath and wiped them before Brier noticed. It felt like hours, though Roland was sure mere minutes passed. The healer kept a hand on Brier's stomach and raised his watch to time the errant contractions. Brier's skin still paled, but his breath soon evened, and Roland felt the grip steadily loosen.

"The contractions have stopped." Meade pulled away his hand and let out a deep sigh.

"Ronan…." Roland held Brier's cheek. The king smiled sleepily before his eyes lolled from white to closed.

"Brier!" Roland's voice rose in terror.

"It is all right," Meade assured Roland. "I laced that potion with a sedative. Just in case we needed to…." The doctor trailed, but Roland understood. "He'll sleep for some hours."

"Thank you." Roland nodded with a surge of respect for the old Aurelian. He'd prepared to save Brier from the torment of the worst outcome. The loss of Brier's first child.

"I'm ordering him to bed rest until the child is born, and I would advise keeping stress to a minimum. This is not a normal pregnancy. Brier is very young, and though his body has adapted to carry a child, physically he is strained, and more so mentally."

"It's my fault. I knew he was stressed from the announcement, and yet I quarreled with Prince Quintin and Brier." Roland lowered his gaze before he ran his fingers through his wavy black hair. "At the pressure from the courtiers, Prince Quintin has claimed my child as his own. I was just… so angry."

"So I've surmised," the doctor replied with some understanding. "But you must control your anger, Roland. Tempers are dangerous vices, especially around young ones."

"I know." Roland clenched his fist. "Brier turns to the prince because I cannot stand by his side. I will never be an Aurelian." No matter what he did, he would never be a king's equal in this world.

"The king has very few people in his corner, Roland. He turns to the prince because he is a friend, one of the few he has right now."

"And I lashed out at him for it…," Roland whispered. "Of my own jealousy. I caused this."

"No." Meade shook his head and patted his back gently. "Brier's current state is caused by high risk, high stress, and overexertion. It was only a matter of time. The baby will likely come early no matter what we do."

"So?" Roland's brow creased. "The child will not make it?"

"I have stopped the labor for now, and the further along he gets, the chances of both he and the babe surviving increase. He only need hold on a few more weeks, and you only need to support him."

"I will." Roland nodded once. "I swear it."

"I trust that you will," Meade answered as he packed away his bag before Finnas came in to change the soiled sheets. Roland lifted Brier up and held him in his arms. "I will leave something to help him sleep," Meade informed Roland before he exited the bedchamber. When Finnas left them, Roland filled the basin with hot water and began to clean his lover's skin.

"Ronan…." Brier whimpered but did not wake.

Even in exhaustion Brier called to Roland. The thought both contented and saddened him. He wanted to make this burden easier. He wanted to take away Brier's worries, but as it stood, he only seemed to make them worse.

"RONAN…." ROLAND stared at Brier's restless feet. He raised his head gingerly and peered up at Brier's tired eyes.

"Thank the gods you're awake." Roland sat at Brier's side the entire day, and then when night fell, he laid his head on the man's thigh. So afraid was he that the labor pains would start again or that Brier would fade in his sleep from so much lost blood. Meade had assured him Brier would recover, but he could not erase the image of trickling blood from his mind.

Roland stood up to grab the pitcher of water on the vanity and handed a cup to Brier. "*Acai*, drink." Brier sipped from the cup. "Meade says you should at least keep hydrated. If you think you can eat, I can fetch some warm broth."

"What about the baby?" Brier demanded. "Is she all right?"

"Fine." Roland tipped the cup to Brier's mouth once more. "If you rest and keep the stress down, which we will. He's put you on bed rest until our child is ready to be born."

"Am I able to move?"

"You are not to get up save for the restroom. I talked him into letting you eat your meals in the parlor, but mostly you need to make sure you are in bed. I have already let Lord Tamil know you will be absent in court for a while. I did not tell him the reason."

"And what of my duties?" Worry creased Brier's brow. "How can I run the kingdom from my bedchamber?" Roland averted his gaze before he mumbled the prince's name under his breath.

"What?" Brier leaned in to hear him.

"I told Lord Tamil that you requested Quintin to rule in your stead," Roland uttered clearly. Brier stared at him nonplussed, and Roland had the childish urge to suck his teeth.

"Why?" Brier bit the inside of his lip. "I mean—why would you—when you—"

"I saw you two talking in the bathroom, and I ignored it," Roland confessed. "When I saw you two again, I acted rashly out of anger."

"Is that why you left early that night?" Brier frowned. "I thought that Lord Renli had driven you out."

"Well, his antagonism did not help," Roland admitted. "But seeing you in that man's arms. Listening to him confess his love."

"*Acai*, Ronan. I swear to you. I regard him only as a friend."

"I know, Brinan. Prince Quintin is your friend." Roland swallowed the distaste of the man's name. "And if you trust him, I will not refute you." Brier did not reply so Roland continued to ramble. "He loves you, of course he would. The worst part, though, is knowing that he's right about us. You are far better off with him than you'll ever be with me. You suit each other. He is an Aurelian prince. You are the king of Lirend, and I'm—"

"The only man I will ever love." Brier's declaration cut Roland's stream. He stared into the emerald eyes and grimaced.

"I know you love me, Brinan. It is not lack of love that makes me this way, but my own fears." He was afraid that Brier would see him for the wretch he truly was, and then he would lose everything. His king, his child, his reason for living. "I am sorry for hurting him, and you. When I saw him touching you again… I just… lost it."

"I should have told Lord Tamil the truth." Brier shook his head. "Then none of this would have happened."

"*Acai*, Brier." He rubbed the top of Brier's head. "Regret is for nothing. You are here and well." He slid next to Brier and held the man's back against his chest. "Just think, in a few more weeks we will hold our child, in our new home." He kissed Brier's flushed cheek.

"Is it ready?" Brier squeaked.

"Almost. Perhaps by the solstice." Brier let out a delighted chuckle, and Roland marveled still at the man's unimpeachable innocence. Despite the harshness of the day, Brier could still laugh.

"It will be wonderful. Right on the outskirts of Avenough," Brier mused.

"A quick ride by horseback."

"And it's so quiet near the farmlands. The tenants lead a simple life." Brier nuzzled against his chest. "Oh, and we should get horses too, Ronan! We can breed our own since the palace only allows purebloods."

"Horses?" Roland chuckled lightly.

"I don't see why not with all that land. We can just watch our family grow." Brier yawned sleepily. "I think we should have several."

"Horses?" Roland repeated, perplexed.

"Children…." Brier answered as his eyes slid shut.

Something akin to fire fluttered inside Roland's chest. The king battled with fate's uncertainty and self-doubt, but when it came to him, when it came to Roland, Rolande, Ronan, Brier was fearless.

"We will see, Brinan." Roland held him tighter.

"Aye… I can't wait." Brier sighed out sleepily. "Somewhere safe and quaint."

"Home," Roland whispered.

ROLAND POURED cold milk from a pitcher and watched Brier propped on his bed eating a frozen sweet tart. His belly aligned with the tip of his chin. "We should put a cow in here," Brier declared when Roland handed him the glass of milk. "Then I wouldn't keep sending you for milk." The bed rest agreed with Brier, and he no longer had the tired bags under his brilliant green eyes.

"Better that we move you to the cow, I think." Roland sat a reserve glass on the vanity. "And hopefully you would not pick up the smell." He kissed Brier's forehead and smiled.

"It wouldn't smell if we cleaned it," Brier finished the tart and milk. There were no signs of contractions since his preterm labor several weeks prior. Roland watched Brier ruffle through a mountain of papers while he fixed the armored belt around his trousers. Brier prepared to meet with Lord Tamil and Prince Quintin, while Roland prepared to visit their home in Balmur.

"I don't understand it. Why have the plans for winter festival been delayed?" Brier searched through the pile.

"Perhaps Prince Quintin can help. Have you talked with him today?"

"No, I haven't, but he should be here around five." Brier let out a puff of air. "I'm supposed to meet with both he and Lord Tamil to discuss the plans for my extended leave." Roland nodded silently, unprovoked. He'd done his best these past weeks to ignore Quintin's presence. He said hello when they met and good-bye when he left. It was icy, but cordial nonetheless. He despised all the time Brier and the prince spent together, but he consoled himself with the realization that Brier would soon have their child. After that, they planned to spend six weeks away from Avenough while Brier recovered at their home in Balmur. Roland would have Brier and their babe all to himself, and that prospect remained his solace. "Marietta is on her way to discuss plans for the baby's nursery here."

"I will take my leave, then." Roland leaned down to kiss the man's cheek.

"How dare you leave me with her to discuss wall colors while you gallivant in Balmur?" Brier teased as he wrapped his arms around Roland's neck. Roland could not stifle the deep laugh that rose in his chest.

"Forgive me, my king, but we Thenians do not pride ourselves on home decor." Roland smirked.

"A likely story." Brier bit Roland's lip and a thrilling twinge rolled through him. Meade expressly forbade intercourse, so they'd found pleasure through their mouths and hands instead. Brier would slide Roland's breeches down right below the curve of his ass cheek and expose the throbbing stiff flesh. Then Brier would lap him gradually before slurping the tip, letting his mouth salivate. Brier's throat would loosen to take Roland deep and "*Mmh….*" There was nothing like the tingling of the back of Brier's wet mouth.

"Ngh…." Roland licked Brier's tongue hungrily before pinning his arms to his side. He twisted his tongue around Brier's, tasting sweet tart and milk. Brier panted into his mouth and Roland sucked his lover's air before he flicked his tongue to intimate his lewd intentions.

"Mmph.... Ronan...." Brier mouthed his name between kisses. Roland parted from Brier's lips and began to nibble his collar. Brier stretched his neck to feel more of the teasing. Never the one to deny his king, Roland quickly gave in. He unclasped the layered silk robe and slid his tongue down the king's exposed nipples and chest. Brier arched off the canopy bed and shivered as Roland trailed soft kisses toward his stiffening member.

Knock. Knock.

Brier groaned and pulled back. Roland watched as Brier closed his eyes and shook his head, dejected.

"A king's duty is never done," Roland told Brier, standing up. "I'll be back by seven." He kissed Brier's cheek and left his lover to conceal a sizable erection.

ROLAND FOUND that building suited him well. His muscles enjoyed the strenuous work, and his mind felt more at ease away from the fuss of Avenough.

There was plenty of land for the horse stalls Brier requested. The huge estate had a two-mile radius on either side with woods covering the majority. There were shallow ponds to keep the soil fertile and bigger lakes to swim in during the hot season. The pine trees would stay green all year. Perhaps one day he could even take his child with him to Aire. Slowly but surely Roland allowed his life with Brier to take shape in his mind.

"Lord Roland." Roland turned to the burly contractor who helped him with the renovations in Balmur. "Did King Brier say whether he'd like the path in blue stone or limestone?"

Roland just installed the columns on the expansive, freshly built patio. The sturdy wooden beams crisscrossed over an open fountain of granulated stones. The walkway in question led to the outdoor patio where Roland anticipated warm summer nights and intimate dinners with his lover.

"I'd say go with the blue." It would add to the natural hue of the beryl lakes plastered through the estate. The contractor nodded and directed his men to begin laying the tiled stones.

Even though they still had at least four weeks ahead of them, Roland marveled at the work they'd done so far. He could not wait for Brier to see the suburban estate. A home fit to welcome the heir of Lirend.

Roland's forehead began to sweat as the sun's glare blinded him. He held his hand like a visor over his eyes before he bent the shovel into the earth. The men were packing up to leave, but he wanted to finish digging the hole for the fire pit he planned to install tomorrow.

"*Venur*." Roland stopped at the airy voice. He held the grip of the shovel and gazed at the pile of dirt adjacent. He whipped his head around and beamed at the man with silvery blond hair and pale green eyes.

"*Venur*, Leighis." He raised his arm and waited. Lei walked toward him and crossed his forearm to make the symbolic *X* of the disbanded Ceve guild. "*L'tyva el*?"

"I'm well, Ronan." Lei flashed him a grin, and Roland dropped the shovel.

He crushed the man into a hug and laughed as the warmth spread through him. Though they were no longer brothers in guild, Lei would always be his brother in bond. "What are you doing here?"

"I asked Umhal to watch over your star, but I didn't expect you to be here of all places." Lei gazed at the brick villa.

"What of the others? Sasta and Durham? I left them before we reached Sasel."

"They're both great." Lei nodded. "They took passage on a ship heading to Menlor. I thought you'd went with them, but when they wrote they told me you didn't board the ship. When you did not return to Aire I thought—" Lei paused.

At that time Roland was so destitute, he could not even function. In that state he knew what the healer most likely assumed.

"I knew you were still alive since Umhal said the light had not faded from your star, but I was worried you'd been captured." Guilt knotted Roland's stomach. He had not written to Lei or Umhal, despite their attentions in Aire. "Why didn't you tell me you were returning?"

"I did not know I would return." Roland pulled away from Lei and stood up straight. "I hadn't planned to come back to Avenough, but I just…." That night when Sasta and Dur went west, he'd had every intention to follow. However, when the three reached the boats docked in Sasel's waters, he could not board. "I had to see him, Lei."

"I understand." Lei nodded with a knowing smile. "You love him."

"More than I ever thought I could." Roland grinned sheepishly. Lei did not tease him, but flashed him a smirk.

"So what's all this?" Lei nodded toward the house.

"This is King Brier's Balmur estate." He gripped Lei's shoulder and led him toward the freshly laid walkway. As he suspected the blue stone fit well against the still fresh-colored grass. "I'm sort of building us a house."

"Sort of?" Lei's eyes went wide as they entered the huge parlor. He gave Lei a tour of the house with all the custom additions: the banister with alabaster stone and the strenuously laid pinewood floors, the door knobs carved with intricate leaf work, the verandas framed with tinted glass to keep out the sun's open glare. With the foundation reinforced weeks ago, they only needed to paint and add furniture to the inside of the house.

They stopped at the stairs, and Roland held the railing. The light pinewood complimented the pure white of the stone. "It's not finished, obviously, but we're hoping to have it done by the time she gets here."

"She?" Lei frowned. For a moment Roland felt like Brier as he could not contain his excitement. He grabbed Lei's hand and led him upstairs through the wide hallway and past his and Brier's bedroom. He opened the door to a tiny room adjacent to the master: the nursery.

Plush cream carpet lined these floors, along with a dyed brown fox fur rug. The ivory armoire spread from the entryway wall to the doors of the veranda. To shut out the natural light, they added thick curtains the color of copper champagne. This was the room Roland had spent the most time in, carving intricate petals in the dark wood panels. He then painted the walls with a deep amethyst purple and the crown molding antique white. Satin ribbon held a mobile overhead with iron lapwings that dangled where the authentic Thenian crib, when he eventually built it, would be.

"The wall color is a tad premature, but he thinks it will be a girl."

Lei stood bemused, taking in the lavish decor before he turned toward Roland. "But who is this room for? Is Brier to be wed?"

"Not any time soon." Roland grinned. Lei continued to peer at him confused, and Roland chuckled lightly. "Brier is with child, Lei. My child."

"I don't understand."

Roland momentarily forgot how strange the whole predicament sounded to someone unfamiliar. He exhaled to gather his thoughts. "You remember, when Brier was attacked by that black bear in Sherdoe. When you stripped him, you saw the markings on his skin?" Lei nodded slowly. "Well they're not markings from a curse. They're fertility symbols, Lei."

"Like the ones of the Goddess Arion?"

"Exactly like that." Roland had never been so grateful for his best friend's perception.

"How far along is he?"

"At this point, nigh thirty-four weeks."

"Dear gods…." Lei's eyes widened. "Have there been any complications?"

"A few actually." Roland nodded gravely. "He went into labor several weeks ago, but the healer was able to stop the contractions. He's on bed rest now." They did not speak for a while then. Roland gave Lei a moment to process all that he'd said.

"You said that he is thirty-four weeks?"

"Aye…." Roland answered apprehensively.

"Then he was already… when he left Aire." Roland shifted, visibly uncomfortable.

"He was of age when we coupled, Lei," Roland assured his friend. "I swear it."

"It doesn't matter to me if he was or wasn't." Lei shrugged.

"It matters to me," Roland grumbled. "I am an old man compared to Brier."

Lei let out snort and shook his head. "And I've told you before, Brier does not care about the difference in your age, Rolande."

"Regardless. It is shameful to take advantage of someone so young."

Lei laughed. "Oh, Ronan. You are a true fool if you believe you are the one who seduced Brier." He took another glance around the room. Compared to his intimate cabin, Roland dipped this room in elegance and grandeur.

"Are you saying he planned to couple with me?"

Lei smirked. He patted Roland's shoulder and headed out of the room, leaving Roland utterly baffled.

"SO… WHAT about the others?" They shared Roland's horse and rode out to an inn called Draughons on the selvage of Balmur. As inns near Avenough went, the townhome was a shanty. Fissured windows with dust that made the glass gray, and a lump of a bed in the corner of the cramped room. No dressers, no vanities, no four-poster bed. Its only solace was the pub below where Roland insisted they share a drink. Lei tried to excuse himself to bed, but Roland dragged Lei down by his shoulders and plastered him onto a teetering bar stool.

"Caite is taking freelance work in Aire. He's picked up a huge contract from some Aurelian. Making serious coin these days."

"How much?" Roland inquired.

"I heard about five thousand a job."

"Five thousand?" Roland's eyebrows shot up. They didn't get half that much when they did jobs for Aurelians, and that was split seven ways by the guild.

"Aye, and he does not disclose the nature of the jobs to anyone… not even Botcht."

Roland blinked but did not question Lei further. He did not want to know what kind of jobs the boy was doing to make that much unsolicited.

"Umhal's alone a lot these days," Lei informed him. His soft eyes and silver hair seemed out of place for the dingy tavern, but Roland did not question his choice of accommodation. Lei still dressed in his weathered gear from Aire, and any capital native could pick him out as a foreigner if he tried to stay within the city. He was probably safer in this shack than in Avenough's square. "He holes up in his cabin for days unless I come see to him. I think he took it the hardest when the guild split up. We were like family to him."

"We're still like family." Lei shot him a wary glance but did not refute him. Even though they'd formally disbanded, he still wanted to have his brothers in his life. Seeing Lei made him realize that. "And Botcht?"

"What about him?" Lei's shaky voice retorted. The man held out the mug to the barkeep to refill. He'd already drank half his weight.

"He's not here with you?" Roland tentatively asked.

"Should he be?" Lei sipped his ale.

"I would think so…." Roland trailed. "I thought that once we absolved our contract, you two would… well to be honest I thought that you two would wed."

"*Na.*" Lei scoffed before he lowered his head. "I don't think I will ever marry."

"Oh?"

"I'm not… the marrying type I guess." Roland traced the somber lines around Lei's mouth as he spoke the words.

"I guess I'm not either," Roland admitted with a sigh.

"Brier asked you?"

"More or less…."

"Have you told him yet, Ronan?" Lei's calm tone clashed with the weight of his question. He shook his head and gazed at the foam at the bottom of his mug.

"*Na*, I can't tell him about the contract. It would crush him."

"It would crush him more to know you hide things from him. Something like this will only end in heartbreak for the both of you."

"If I tell him the truth, he will never trust me again," Roland said. He thought of the turmoil in Brier's heart when he'd returned, and he promised to never hurt Brier again. "After all that I've put him through, I couldn't ask him to trust me again."

"You could ask… but you are afraid of what the answer will be." Roland stared at Lei's muted face.

"Ever is your perception unrivaled." Roland chuckled at his longtime friend. "It is true. I am a coward when it comes to love."

"*Na.*" Lei sighed. "It is not love we cower from… but rejection."

Roland sighed out once more and finished his ale. The thought of Brier refusing him terrified him as much as the thought of revealing the truth.

"BRINAN…." THE dim light made the gold on the king's door feel less gaudy. Roland's night with Lei went overlong, and the sun had long set when he returned to the palace. Roland bathed off the grime of the day and crept into the king's darkened bedchamber. Brier slept, unmoving. It was only a quarter past nine, but Brier rested more than he ate these days. They had a mild winter, with no flurries and very seldom rain. Still, Roland lit a fire to keep him warm from the late bath.

Brier's stomach bulged under the crease of his full chest and over where his hips had spread. The dark symbols blazed bright on his skin, shining like the temple beacon. Roland stripped off his bathrobe and sidled up to his lover's warmth. Brier melded against his chest, and Roland grinned when Brier opened his eyes.

"Ro?" Brier whispered before he lifted. "Rolande." He hugged Roland's chest tightly.

"What's wrong?" Roland frowned when he felt the strength of his hug. "What's happened?" He heard Brier's soft cries.

"Oh, Ronan. It's horrible."

"The baby? Is everything all right? Should I get Meade?"

"*Na.*" Brier sniffed and shook his head. "It's not the baby—it's Lord Yaris." Brier choked out a sob. "Lord Yaris is missing."

"Missing?" Roland could feel the blood drain from his face. "What do you mean?"

"Remember I told you the preparations for the winter festival had been delayed?"

Roland nodded slowly.

"Quintin told me there've been a slew of crimes in Avenough lately. Someone ransacked some stores in the square and even set a store on fire."

"What?" Roland's brow creased. "Why?"

"I don't know." Brier shook his head, still weeping. "But Quintin thought it would be best to delay the plans."

"Of course, of course, but what about Lord Yaris?"

"No one has seen or heard from him. Not for several days."

"When did he go missing?"

"About a week ago, according to Lady Yaris. He made a house call in Ridgeport and did not return. Quintin thinks it might have something to do with the season's changing. It is not unheard of for peasants to cause mayhem in the winter. But Lord Yaris is missing. What if something's happened to him? We've got to find him!"

"Don't worry, Brinan. We'll find him." Roland nodded and rubbed the back of Brier's head. Lord Yaris missing? Unrest in Avenough?

"What happened to you?" Brier sighed, still clutching his jacket. "I tried to wait up, but you didn't come back. I was so scared after I heard how dangerous the city is right now."

"Forgive me." Roland kissed Brier's temple. "Lei sought me out, and we shared a drink."

"Leighis?" The teary eyes bulged wide. "He's here? In Avenough?"

"Not far." Roland wiped Brier's tears. "At an inn near the gates."

"How long?"

"Only for a short while. He came to make sure I was all right."

Brier's brow creased. "Does he think you in danger with me?"

"*Na*." Roland shook his head and smoothed over the king's disposition. "But I told no one I was returning to you, Brier. I was planning to go to Menlor with Dur and Sasta." Brier listened but did not speak. He never told Brier about his time in Aire alone, but he wanted Brier to know about the discontent and the suffering. "When you left…." He started, but rephrased. "When I let you go, my world crumbled, Brinan. I shut myself away in my cabin for weeks, and I ignored everyone. Even Leighis."

"You could have sought me. I waited for you to come after me," Brier admitted.

Roland sighed out and rolled to his bare back. He stared up at the leaf emblazoned with colur gems. "I should have, but once I'd let go of my crippling pride, all I felt was shame, Brier."

"What shame is there in love?" Brier asked him wistfully.

"None," Roland whispered.

Only in my own actions….

"I told myself every day that I had awakened something in you that I could not see through to the end, but the truth is that I was only afraid." Brier levied his weight on his elbow and gazed at Roland.

"Afraid? Of what, Ronan? I love you."

"I know you do." He finally turned back to face Brier. Now was the time, if any, to tell him about the real reason he let Brier go.

"I wonder sometimes if simply loving is enough." Roland could not see Brier's full expression, but the gaze was both sleepy and bewildered.

"It is enough for me," Brier stated absolutely. "That you give yourself wholly, what more can a man ask of his partner?"

Roland grazed his fingertips across supple lips, and Brier leaned into kiss them. "Promise me, Brinan, that you will never leave me." Brier's intense gaze both calmed and disquieted his heart.

"What is it, Ronan?" Brier's soft voice pleaded. "Tell me…." Roland wanted to tell him. The deep thud in his chest foretold the strain of his mind and his heart.

"Lei and Botcht split up," he lied to placate Brier's suspicions.

"But why?" He watched Brier bite his lip. "They seemed happy… I thought that they would—"

"Wed?" Roland finished his sentence.

"Aye," Brier answered, crestfallen. "I know Lei loves him."

"Yes, but Botcht never made his feelings quite clear to Leighis. True they coupled and had what I would call an intimate friendship, but outside of that, nothing." He pulled Brier into the crook of his arm and breathed deep. "I love you more than anything, Brier. Just the thought of losing you makes me restless."

"You will never lose me. I'm here, Rolande. I promise you." Brier leaned in and kissed the tip of his nose. The light peck made him stiffen as the guilt seeped through him. Roland did not turn to face him, but Brier nuzzled against his chest nonetheless.

"I've wasted so much time…." Roland whispered. "I am a true fool. Forgive me."

"There is nothing to forgive." Lithe fingers traced the coarse hair on his chest. "Leave the past where it belongs, and look to the future, always." Brier spoke the words of the guild and Roland's heart raced. The past, where his nightmares prevailed and perhaps where the truth belonged.

WINTER SETTLED over Lirend like a slow and moody fog. Misty at first, but then the mountains creaked from the implacable rain. The winter plans should have been well underway, but due to a series of supposedly unrelated crimes, they'd called off the festivities. While more than six Aurelian merchants had their property ransacked, two of Avenough's Aurelian lords died mysteriously. The first, a scholar from the precinct Bedlorn, who worked with Brier in the plans for the university, died in a house fire set directly in the square. The fire reached several of the townhomes and neighboring stores, and set the entire village on end.

The second Aurelian, by the account of his wife and daughter, choked on a chunk of an apple lodged in his throat. Of course no one could implicate the crown's negligence, but the citizens talked nonetheless.

Then finally, the matter of Lord Yaris, who disappeared in Ridgeport. The man vanished without word or notice.

The Aurelians whispered about the obvious curse on Lirend that Lord Renli had warned them of. The Burges took a more practical approach, citing the change in weather and the seasonal temperament of gods. It did not take much to spook peasants, but the Prolit reassured themselves with the fact that no one in their lowly stations had died. Yet Brier could not decide which was worse: the fact that someone may have hurt others to conspire against the crown, or the fact that the Aurelians considered the birth of his first child a bad omen for Lirend.

At officially thirty-six weeks and two days, Meade had moved into one of the palace suites, on call for Brier's anticipated delivery. Brier tried to concentrate on the long list of palace preparations for winter, but the wind jittered the iron clasp on his windows, and his mind toiled over Lord Yaris's disappearance and the strange deaths.

"King Brier?" Quintin's airy voice rang through his worrying. "Are you okay?"

Brier nodded and tried to shuffle the papers as if he'd casually begun to tidy his spread, but Quintin excused his lethargy.

"I think that's enough paperwork for today." They'd gotten through most of the open court requests and laid plans for next year's meeting with the Divine Three, whose trade lines ran unhindered since their last encounter. Quintin's suggestions for strengthening the lower classes, combined with Brier's regulations and welfare, were in no way a small success. In half a year they'd seen a 20 percent increase in productivity in the mines, along with the highest enrollment rating of mostly Burges, but even some

Prolit, in the newly built university. In reality, the only bad news to speak of was the deaths of high-class Aurelians and one missing. Naturally the kingdom spoke of it obsessively.

Quintin scooped the loose parchment on the lap table he used to take dictation from Brier and held it under his arm firmly. "Lastly, Lord Tamil continues to pester me about plans for our wedding."

"And how should I plan a wedding when I cannot move from this bed?" Brier quipped. He knew Lord Tamil would be more than happy to take over the proceedings, but he found it opportune to use his obligatory bed rest as an excuse for his disinterest in wedding plans.

"A fair question." Quintin smirked. "Perhaps he expects me to roll you into court," Quintin teased. Brier let out a soft chuckle before he leaned his head against the white of his bedspread and pillows.

"I do not think the court worries overmuch. You have done a wonderful job in my stead, and I thank you." Brier inclined his head.

"No thanks needed, Your Majesty. It is an honor to assist Lirend in her time of need. As for the wedding…," Quintin began more hesitantly. "I think Lord Tamil would have the heir born into a marriage."

"Obviously that is the most desirable course. But what is desirable is not always feasible, Quintin." Brier sighed out. He did not want to discuss marriage with Quintin when he knew their arrangement for the hoax it was.

"That much you don't need to dictate to me, King Brier. I most of all know the truth of that sentiment." Quintin had started using his title once more. After affection came to blows with Roland, Quintin had taken stringent precautions to keep their relationship neutral.

"I think I'll take my leave." Quintin grimaced before he bowed stiffly. Brier held the duvet and pressed his lips together. Would they ever regain the normalcy of their friendship?

"Oh. One more thing." Quintin paused at the door.

"Yes?" Brier glanced at Quintin's tensed back.

"The queen sends her regards." He turned the golden knob and disappeared from Brier's bedchamber.

BRIER STOOD at his veranda and watched the snow flurries land on his sill. He lifted his hand over the condensed glass and marked the letter *X*. Leighis left Avenough without saying good-bye to Roland, and never even sought Brier. He thought he and Leighis had formed a friendship during his time in Aire, but Leighis's slight told him otherwise. Perhaps to Leighis, like his queen stepmother, he was only a burden.

Brier heard his parlor door open but did not turn when someone entered his bedchamber. Hefty boots stomped on his wooden floors, and he recognized the emphatic gait instantly.

"*Venur*, Brinan." Roland shuffled his heavy cloak, and groaned as he sat to remove his boots.

"*Venur*," Brier whispered. He leaned his head forward to the frigid glass. He breathed out to add to the cloud of smoke.

"Are you well?" Roland asked him. Brier did not know the answer to that question. A numbness washed over him. Just when he thought he had a hold on his fate, reality came to rip the reins from his grasp. Brier opened his mouth to reply, but a warm body stilled his tongue. "*L'tyva el*?" The man's Thenian tongue wrapped around him like his weighted hands, and tears pricked Brier's eyes.

"I don't know…," he replied honestly. Roland twisted him around so swift that his breath hitched.

"What ails you?" he whispered. "Is it the baby?"

"The baby is fine." Brier lowered his gaze.

"Then what is it, Brinan?"

How could he explain the lingering loneliness in his heart to the man who utterly fulfilled him? Roland accepted him, loved him, cherished him, and yet happiness eluded him. The tears rolled down, and he covered his face to hide.

"I don't know." He shook his head and rested it against Roland's chest. "I hate crying so much, but the tears won't stop falling. I feel useless in this bed. I feel alone when there are naught but books and servants to keep me company." He thought he had made friends in Leighis and Quintin, but they abandoned him when it suited them best. "Am I so worthless that I cannot even keep those who are dear to me?"

"Who can you not keep?" Roland demanded.

"Mother, Father, Prince Quintin, Leighis…." Brier thought of their good-bye, when Roland ignored his desperate plea. His heart squeezed as the memory ensnared him. "Even you." No matter what he did or said, they all let him go.

"Keep me? Brier, I would give my beating heart for you."

He heard Roland's words, but he did not meet his gaze. "For our child and for our future, but for the me who existed before—"

"The *you* who existed before is the reason I exist today!" Roland grabbed his jaw and forced his eyes upward. "Hear me now, Brier. Because I am not going to say it once more." Brier stared at Roland, his face creased between anger and concern.

"Think of a man who has lived with his worthlessness his whole life, suddenly to have a boy with naught but kindness love him unconditionally. I did not accept our union because I knew that I did not deserve you. In truth, I still don't." Roland kissed him softly, and Brier squeezed Roland's arms. "And yet you love me in spite of everything. And yet the gods saw fit to have you love me. To bear this child."

"Our child." Brier smoothed his hands down Roland's taut skin.

"Our child." Roland held his gaze. "Your parents loved you as much as we love our unborn. They did not leave you; they were taken away, fighting for every second they had to be near you. As we would fight to be near our own. Can you not see that?"

"Of course I can." Brier nodded.

"That man, Quintin, wants your heart. I cannot blame him, and yet I can't let you go," Roland proclaimed.

"You're the only one I've ever wanted." Brier gazed into slate-blue eyes that smiled at his words. The man leaned in to kiss the crease of his mouth once more.

"You are more than worthy to be loved." Roland leaned in to kiss Brier again before he paused and gazed at him wide-eyed.

"What is it?" Brier asked. Roland gave him a smile before he let out a moderate chuckle and pulled away.

"I was just thinking, Lei did give me a message to give you after all." Brier walked with Roland as he led him to the dinner table and filled their glasses with wine. Brier hoped his face did not redden when he heard that Leighis had sent him a message through Roland. He did not want his lover to think something amiss. Brier only craved his and Leighis's bond.

"He congratulated us both, and said that he wishes for your swift recovery. He also told me to tell you that you are close to your heart's desire, whatever that means."

Warmth spread through his fingers even though they held the cool bronze goblet. "If he thinks so, then I suppose I shall have to do my best." He sipped the nectarous wine. Leighis did still care for him, and he'd remembered their exchange during *Yensira*. Roland studied him, but Brier made his face passive enough so the huntsman could not surmise the cryptic message.

"Lei garners such a reaction from my lover?"

"Leighis is very wise." Brier smirked at Roland's transparency. "As are you, Master Roland." He winked before he pursed his lips.

"And yet it is his words that have assured you." Roland's brow quirked.

"Wherefore this reaction?" Brier feigned surprise. "Can it be? The valiant leader of the Ceve guild jealous of his underling?"

Roland pressed his lips together before he finished the wine in his goblet and stood. "I would be jealous of a mere vermin if it took my place in your heart."

Brier muted the grin to a subtle smile and shook his head. "Nothing takes your place in my heart." He clumsily rose from his seat. "You are mine to the end of all things." He took Roland's lips in a breathy kiss, letting the mild wine lure out his wanton desire. When Brier pulled back, Roland wore a wicked smirk before he guided him to the bed.

"*Mana el man'*." Brier drowned in the heated kiss and caressed the huntsman's broad chest. If he wished it, Roland would give him the stars. Still—Brier felt Roland's teeth draw the breath from his throat—this man remained his only invocation.

AT FIRST Brier thought he'd woken due to the sudden sweltering heat. Roland had grown so accustomed to the cold temperatures in Aire that Lirend's capital felt especially warm. Therefore, Brier oftentimes woke to a mountain of silk and satin bed linen piled at his back. He would normally manage with the layers, but with the added weight of the pregnancy, and the hormonal changes in temperature, Brier could not tolerate the warmth. Indeed, he thought the fever plucked him from his sleep until a familiar pang roused him. The tightness crept through his hips and gripped his stomach like a crushing wave. He breathed out steadily to allay the ache, making sure to keep count of the seconds that passed. Meade told him the contractions would start mild and grow each hour with intensity. Should he wait to call for Meade? He'd felt the restlessness in his sleep for the past several hours, but not enough to stir him officially. When he reached the five-minute mark and the next contraction did not come, he decided to wait a bit longer. No sense rousing the entire palace for what could be a false alarm. Brier laid his head down and closed his eyes. His heart fluttered like a dancing leaf in the wind. He reached down to rub the stretched skin on his belly and smiled at the prospect of finally meeting their babe.

CHAPTER 25
SEEDS

EVEN THOUGH Brier only wore a light robe, the feverish pain made him sweat as the contractions pummeled his worn form. Brier grew used to the paralyzing jolts, but then they morphed into agony. Roland wiped his brow with a warm cloth that Brier wished were cool, though he could not focus enough to verbalize his request. Roland faltered between abnormally close proximity and lingering aloofness. When Meade finally arrived, Roland intended to leave before Brier cut Roland a dangerous gaze.

"You leave me and I'll neuter you," Brier threatened through painful breaths. Marietta might have chastised him for the unorthodox idea, but Brier demanded Roland's presence.

"How close are the contractions?" Meade asked a nurse attendant. He'd never seen the mousy-looking woman, but Brier had no qualms about her. Whatever Meade needed, he had.

"Two minutes, if that," the woman answered briskly. "Water hasn't broken." Brier did not understand half of the doctor's exchange and still could not master the process his cousin outlined in the journal.

The roots of the leaves that flowered his skin lay dormant within him until his adolescence. From then on, the bed flourished with every passing year to create a fertile vessel. Of course, Brier's body unknowingly indicated the possibility of conception: when his usually silver scars glistened gold, when he bathed the marks raised like shed scales, and when most fruitful his sexual desire increased tenfold. Brier paled when Meade told him about the birthing process, but Elrique's research assured Meade that the opening within Brier would stretch to accommodate the babe.

"Dear gods!" Brier whined. He doubted everything Meade told him as the relentless cramps and spasms crippled him.

"It's almost time. Brier, are you okay?" Brier barely avoided the scoff in his throat, and he grunted out an affirmative.

"How do you feel?" Meade continued to probe him.

"Like I am being continuously run over by a carriage." He replied caustically before grimacing in pain. His feet pressed into the bed as his back arched disjointedly. "*Acai…*," he begged to Roland.

"Brinan." Roland answered his plea instantly. "You're doing so good. Just hold on a little longer." Brier knew Roland had no clue how long before their child would greet them, but nonetheless, Brier clutched the assurance and held Roland's steady hand. He felt Meade's hand probe the opening between his legs before a warm gush heated his bottom and thighs. At first Brier felt relieving pressure as fluid trickled beneath him. That was until a stab of agony winded him.

"*Na*!" Brier wept and harsh tears burned his irises. Before, the contractions tightened and released him, but this pain crushed him. "Something's wrong, Ronan!" He screamed out in terror.

"Dear gods, what is it?" Roland's temper flared at Brier's suffering. Like a barbed wire whip, the pain slashed through the king's last resolve.

Brier caught the doctor's weary face as the white beneath him soiled with blackened blood. Fear pulverized any hope Brier had of ever seeing his child's face.

"He's losing too much blood. Cut the gown!" Meade demanded.

Brier's vision grew blurred as he trembled against the fine cream silk and embroidered pillows. He panted through his tears and whimpers.

"Brier!"

He heard his name faintly. He tried to reply but before he could exhale, his breath hitched from a stopper in his throat. He tried to inhale, but his lungs constricted painfully.

"He's hyperventilating. Get a mask!"

No mask would save her, Brier thought as the nurse covered his face in an enclosed tube. Air forced its way into his lungs, but Brier lost the urge to breathe.

Will she die?

"Save him!"

Will I die?

"Brier!"

Was that his name?

He could marginally see a lengthy syringe before Meade inserted the needle into a vein in the crook of his elbow. A strange numbness crept up his chest, through his body, out toward his limbs, and then the pain dissipated like crumbled stone. Meade tugged the skin on his stomach, pulling something, and then Brier saw her. A blue-faced babe drenched in bile. Despite the mask he wore, Brier's breath stilled. He could see his daughter, and yet he heard naught but Meade's tensed voice. No infant's cries. No sounds. Harrowing silence. Death.

Brier turned toward Roland and used his last strength before he croaked, "Save her, Ronan." His vision grew dim before he waned. "*Acai….*"

BRIER WOKE to the sound of mumbled orders and hushed replies. He blinked away the grogginess and sleep that sealed his eyes, conscious of the rising and falling of his chest. Brier watched Roland with Meade, Finnas, and Marietta through his glassy gaze. They all four sat at the tea table with a kettle. Meade, an Aurelian doctor, Marietta, a Burges nursemaid, Finnas, a young Prolit, and Roland, a Thenian huntsman.

Brier twisted his lips, though he could not manage a full smile, and adjusted his arm to test its stability. He could move it, but not much, and the strength it took discouraged him.

"R—" Brier's voice ached as he spoke. "Ronan," he strained out softly. The room stilled.

"Did he speak?" Marietta tried to whisper, but her boorish voice rang out. The others waited for Brier to speak again, but the hassle made him weary. When it seemed they had not heard him, he closed his eyes and prepared to speak out once more, but when he opened them Roland stood above him.

"Good morning, Brinan." Roland's gruff voice eased the tension in Brier's chest. "*L'tyva el?*"

"Aye." He closed his heavy eyes and nodded. "Though it hurts to speak," he wheezed.

"That is because you went into shock and hyperventilated." Meade came beside him. The doctor sat on the edge of the canopy bed and stuffed the buds of a stethoscope in his ears. Brier vaguely remembered struggling to breathe during labor, but the specifics eluded him. "Open your mouth." Brier did so, albeit grudgingly, with three additional sets of eyes on him. Marietta appeared too anxious to speak, and Finnas looked frightened. Only Roland stared directly at him with eyes like the sea's calm blue.

"Your fever is down a great deal, but you're still warm." Meade touched his temple. He continued to go over the long list of ailments while Brier's head spun from dizziness and exhaustion. He did not care one iota about his own standing. The only thing that mattered was—

"Where is she?" Brier demanded in the frail voice. His kin exchanged queer looks before he hardened his gaze and tightened his jaw. Was she gone? He lowered his head to stifle the brimming tears in his eyes. He would not cry in front of them. He refused to cry when he knew the potential risk.

It was all right, he had said, if they never met her. If they never held her thus.

It was all right if she could not see the world because she lived in his heart.

It was all right if she never saw her own *Yensira* lantern, because he would share his own with her in the endless sky.

It was all right.... So why did he feel his soul fading?

"Mm...." Brier's heart ceased in his chest when he heard the light whimper. He peered up slowly and saw the bundle of lilac terry wool.

"She's here, Brinan." Roland settled beside him gingerly. Brier's bulged eyes burned as the singular tear slid down his cheek. His chest tightened, but this time with all-consuming warmth. "Do you want to hold her?" Roland whispered.

Brier nodded so hard his teeth clicked. He wanted to hold her, to touch her, to love her for infinities. Roland leaned in closer to him and held the child's neck and head with her body cradled beneath Brier's ribs. When Roland finally settled her, the baby's mouth twitched, but she did not stir. Brier gazed at his child. He gazed at her as though he'd never seen a babe in his twenty years. He gazed at the sleeping babe like the resplendent star she was, shining in his eyes, sparkling before him. Roland reached up to pull a strand of loose red hair, but Brier just stared in a potent daze.

"Let's all of us go." Marietta's voice cut through his awe. "Give 'em some time alone." The three gathered and headed to leave before Meade turned to him and spoke.

"I'll be back to check on you in a bit." Then he turned to Roland. "Don't let him ogle the child all day. Coax him to eat if you can." The Aurelian doctor talked business, but Brier could see the smile in the crease of his lips. Brier heard the door shut before he turned to Roland with a watery smile.

"She's here," he mouthed to Roland so as not to stir her. Roland nodded with a grin and went to fetch him a glass of water.

IT TOOK some persuasion, but Brier finally agreed to eat while the child slept in a circular bassinet beside him. Roland fed him temperate broth, and then he drank more water to hydrate. Roland then explained to him, in his limited proficiency, what had happened during labor. Everything progressed naturally and without complication until Brier's water broke and the child forced its way out too quickly. The cord that attached baby to vessel wrapped around her neck and caused her nigh suffocation.

"He nearly sliced you in two to get her out. A casares section or something like that."

"Caesarean," Brier corrected him. "Meade informed me it might happen."

"Well, no one informed me." Brier opened his mouth to the spoon waiting at his lip. "I nearly shit myself when I saw your innards placed against your chest."

"Thank you for both of those images," Brier teased, but Roland did not laugh. He placed the bowl of chicken broth on Brier's vanity and hunched over, drawing his palm over his knuckle.

Brier grimaced. He wanted to wrap his arms around his lover's wide back to shield him from the memory. "*L'tyva el?*"

As always Brier's use of the Thenian's natural tongue eased some of Roland's tension. "By the gods, you scared me. I almost lost you, Brinan," Roland whispered. "Had Meade not been there, I would have lost both of you."

Brier listened but did not speak.

"I don't know… what I would have done."

"No need to know as we are both well, Ronan," Brier assured his lover. He turned his head instinctively to the bassinet beside him. "Even now the princess sleeps soundly." The moment he'd said the words, a banshee wail skirled through his bedchamber. Brier's brow knit in confusion and then worry as the babe cried out.

"Ro—" He whipped his head to Roland who'd already risen from the bed to grab a bottle off the dining table, halfway back to their daughter. He held the premature babe almost fully in his palm, cradling her head as before and cocooning her in his elbow. He uncapped the top of a glass bottle of formula and corked the babe's mouth with a nude nipple. Their daughter latched on and drank with her hungry whimpers quieted. All the while Brier gaped at the scene, utterly speechless.

"What in the gods' names was that?" Brier deadpanned. Roland let out a hearty chuckle but did not shift the bottle once.

"That would be your beautiful daughter, and princess of Lirend." He continued to snicker. "I had the pleasure of staying with her through the night. I can tell you her howl outdoes Veti's."

"By far." Brier shook his head, still reeling. "What is that you feed her?" he asked, now curious about his daughter's first night without him.

"Formula that Meade prepared. She is a little underweight, but Meade says he expected an early delivery."

"How often does she eat?" Brier asked.

"Every two to three hours so far," Roland replied. Brier stared at the babe, but he could not evade Roland's suddenly sheepish gaze.

"Wherefore this look?"

"Meade said that… if you wanted to… if you desired it—that is…." Brier continued to stare bemused at Roland until he saw the man's eyes directed at his chest.

Brier flushed darkly at Roland's assertion. He had in fact discussed the possibility of nursing their child with Meade, but the exchange became a distant memory when the threat on his life became evident.

"I—" Brier began, but did not finish. He stared down at his chest and realized that someone had bound him firmly with a wrap of cotton and latex rubber. His chest felt tight and uncomfortable.

"Meade had the nurse bind you before Marietta washed and clothed you."

"Why?" Brier lifted his head to see his two-hundred-plus-pound lover wince when he answered.

"That is because… your chest spilled earlier."

Brier cringed and lowered his gaze, but he wished he could hide his face. His ears tingled from embarrassment, and he imagined his head looked like a ripened redmelon.

"I didn't know you were able to."

The assumed result of pregnancy was a child, but despite Meade's instruction, Brier did not consider the aftereffects. "By the gods. Why did he have to tell you this?"

"Why wouldn't he tell me?" Roland queried. "I am the father of your child. I am your lover."

"Aye, and it is that reason I don't want you to see me this way!" Brier spat childishly. Roland peered down at their child who continued to drink, content in her gradual pace.

"Is it so bad that I see you this way?"

"Aye," Brier retorted.

"Why?" Roland demanded.

"Because."

"Because what?" The man grunted.

"Because—" Brier paused and bit his lip. He met Roland's fixed gaze and his resolve waned. "Because I don't…." Brier gritted through his teeth. "I don't want you to lose desire for me." He hated admitting the truth, but the main reason for his reluctance was simply his want to be held by his lover once more. Nothing could trump the love Brier felt for his daughter, but Roland left him with a need so vast it made him feel helpless.

"Tell me something." Roland's tone evened. "Is it your pride or your stubbornness that still makes you ashamed of your body?" Brier flicked his head up as the man popped out the empty bottle and lifted the babe to his shoulder. Roland rubbed the child's back in gentle circles. The babe burped seconds later, and Roland used one hand to cradle her back, while the other cradled her head in his palm.

"You're good at this," Brier mumbled. He could not even lift his arms, and Roland had mastered the feeding techniques.

"You will be too," Roland assured him with a smile. He placed the baby back in the bassinet. Brier peered over to catch a glimpse of her finally awake, but she'd already drifted back to sleep. Roland must have sensed Brier's disappointment because he followed up on his words. "She mostly sleeps, eats, and poops as I can tell. Oh, and wails." Brier did not take his eyes off the sleeping girl, but chuckled at Roland's words.

"Her hair is like yours," Brier noted, still smiling. "Are her eyes like yours too?" When Brier turned toward Roland, the man smirked and climbed onto the bed to lie beside him.

"I will let you discover that for yourself when she wakes." Roland entwined their fingers and Brier's fingertips tingled. "Presently, though, we're faced with a much bigger question than her eye color."

Brier creased his brow in confusion. "And what would that be?"

"Her name."

Brier's puzzlement turned to incredulous surprise. "You haven't named her yet?"

"It was not my place to do so alone," Roland answered. "She is the princess of Lirend. Verily, the king should have a say." Brier had not let himself think of names for a child they might have lost. He referred to the child as "her" to offset the logical detachment he might feel from losing the babe too early, but now she needed a real name.

"Do you have any ideas?"

"Hmm…." Roland stroked his chin. Brier could see the grainy whiskers grown in likely from the time Roland spent at his bedside. "Mayhap something that alludes to her delicate nature. Something to remind you of your father?"

"Something Thenian for sure," Brier mused. He wanted the child to carry Roland's name in some way, since she would not bear Roland's last.

"How about *Ryanne*?" His lover turned toward him, smiling. "It's a version of Ryan, which means little prince in Thenian."

"Ryanne." Brier smoothed the name over in his Aurelian tongue. The name had strength like her father's and spoke of her standing in Lirend. "I love it."

"And then for her midname?" The task fell back into Brier's hands. The only maiden's name that came to his mind represented beauty and grace, enchantment and kindness, memories and longing.

"Iines," Brier whispered. "For my late mother." He turned toward Roland for his blessing. Roland grinned and nodded. "Ryanne Iines Snow. What do you think?"

"I think that is a beautiful name for a beautiful princess." Roland lifted their hands and kissed his knuckles.

"She is beautiful," Brier conceded as he peered over into the bassinet. Even though she slept, Brier could not peer away for too long.

"Easily the fairest in Lirend." Roland pursed his lips smugly.

"Naturally." Brier smirked. "Though I do believe you are smitten, Master Rolande."

"When my lover is as exquisite as you, it is hard not to be." Brier's face heated, but he did not avert his gaze. He felt a twinge in his throat, but swallowed the urge to kiss Roland when Ryanne whimpered. The babe still slept in the cradle, but before his daughter drifted, she bewitched him with brilliant eyes. Ryanne's lush gaze reminded him of the willows of Balmur, the jade of a newly plucked colur gem, and of course, his own green irises.

"Her eyes are like my own."

"Green as Lirend's rolling hills," Roland whispered from behind him. "But she sleeps for only short spurts, and I crave your eyes on me." Roland grabbed Brier's face and demanded his undivided gaze. Roland mouthed his exposed neck and shoulder with thick moist lips. Brier's eyes slid to slits, though he fought to keep his attentions on the weary babe. Roland would have none of it, as the man pushed him down on the bed and enraptured his tongue with a yearning kiss.

"Heh—" he let out a breathy laugh when they parted. "I can hardly move, Ronan. Do you plan to take me thus?"

"If you could bear it, I would," Roland answered, the hunger in his voice transparent. "But Meade says it will be at least four weeks for you to recover."

"Four weeks?" A sudden realization hit him. "Then that means… I cannot ride to Balmur." The plan was to have Ryanne in the suburban home, but his daughter came nigh three weeks earlier than they anticipated. Now he would have to spend almost his entire leave here in Avenough. There was no way he could relax with the presentiment of his stepmother pulling Quintin's strings and Lord Tamil's pestering him about marriage. He still worried over the kingdom's unrest and Lord Yaris's disappearance. Even Marietta would fuss over Ryanne and possibly monopolize the babe's care. Roland leaned in and kissed the lines that formed on his brow at the prospect of his cut furlough.

"Do not worry overmuch, King Brier." Roland's use of his title sent a tangible thrill up his spine that made his stomach tighten. "Your guard will protect you and Ryanne from Avenough's burdens." Roland's deep voice made Brier squirm.

"I suppose I can behave for four weeks." Brier exhaled deep and used his conserved strength to clutch Roland's tunic. He smelled of Ryanne, and her scent instantly calmed Brier. Roland wrapped his arm around his bound chest. Brier tensed, but did not protest as Roland's breath heated the skin on the back of his neck.

"I love you, Brinan." Of all the assurances his lover had uttered, avowed love alleviated some of his anxiety.

"I love you too." He reached up to squeeze Roland closer, but accidentally ground against his lover's stiff bulge. Brier flushed, but Roland only smiled before he guilelessly spoke.

"Just so you are aware, King Snow." Roland closed his eyes. "Whether you are maimed with the use of one arm, swollen with our child, or spilling to feed her, as long as you are sound in mind and body, I will always take pleasure from you."

CHAPTER 26
BROTHERS

ALTHOUGH THE sun had set, the clouds made the day thick with a gray fog. Roland returned from working on the house in Balmur when he stumbled upon his lover in action. The man coddled a mewling babe with his lively song while he cleaned her bronze-tinged skin with a warm cloth.

Whistle whistle....

Calm your bristle....

The day is light and new....

The man pulled the crying child and exposed his chest to let the babe suckle.

I combed the stars,

And walked afar,

To see a sea calm blue....

Roland listened and watched but did not speak. He stared in a calm reverence, marveling at how well Brier had adapted. It was like observing a lapwing in its nest. Completely natural instinct.

Roland waited for Brier to finish nursing before he entered the bedchamber fully. Brier still felt wary about others' stares, but he no longer flushed anytime Roland mentioned her feedings every three hours. Their daughter had a self-imposed schedule they had no choice but to keep. Roland found the days exhausting, but Brier swiftly grew accustomed to their babe.

"YOU ARE late." Brier smiled as Roland revealed his presence. He did not have the heart to tell Brier he'd watched him candidly with their daughter.

"Apologies, my lord and savior." He bowed his head jeeringly low. "I had to make sure I'd succeeded in my task before returning to His Almighty Majesty, may the gods keep him."

Brier let out a soft chuckle at his ingratiating act and shook his head. "You jest, but I will tell you there are courtiers who behave so unctuously."

"I do not doubt it for a moment." Roland stepped toward the bassinet and squatted, eye level to the sleeping princess.

"I just fed and bathed her for the night. Hopefully she'll sleep for a while yet."

"Hope eludes me when it comes to Ryanne sleeping." Roland stood up and leaned in to kiss Brier lightly. "Although you may have the gods' favor today."

"Oh?" Brier stood from the bed and began to remove his chamber robe. "Good news?" His eyebrow quirked before he bent to retrieve a plush towel for cover. Roland could not help but stare at Brier's arched back and bare bottom. Though he knew they had at least a week more to wait, his natural desire had matured into an insatiable craving. Most likely from the taunting realization that Brier possessed something he wanted and could not have… not yet anyway.

"Indeed." He traced Brier's curved waist as he walked toward the bath. Roland followed like a trained dog at Brier's heels. He ogled the king as he finally exposed his stomach. Brier now wore a scar that cut straight down the middle. The wound started flesh pink but had healed considerably. Brier could walk and sit comfortably without pain from the incision.

"Thank the gods for this." Brier lowered himself in the heated tub and let out a deep sigh. "So what good news do you have for me?" Brier whispered and closed his eyes.

Roland hesitated before answering, just watching Brier unwind in the balmy tub. The boy who once covered himself head to toe in fabric now lay bare before him.

"Ronan?" Brier's puzzled voice broke his nostalgia.

"Oh yes." Roland beamed. "The reason for my tardiness is that I made a short stop before I came back to the palace."

"Whatever for?" Brier reached over to grab a clear vial of honey-scented shampoo.

"To see Meade," he partially disclosed. "You wondered whether you could ride and spar soon, remember?"

"I remember!" Brier's voice rose in volume. "And what did he say?"

"He said that you should be able to in a fortnight."

"Really?" Brier grinned fully. "That is great news!"

"I agree, you'll be able to stretch your legs some," Roland answered, pleased with Brier's reaction. "Mayhap you and I can take the trail heading east if you'd like to go for a three-day hunt?"

"That sounds wonderful." Brier dunked his head into the water. Roland smirked, impressed with his supposed finesse. He and Brier would go out and hunt, eventually, after their erotic overture.

"Oh." Brier suddenly rose from the water. "But what of Ryanne?"

"Isn't that what we hired Victoria for?" Victoria was their new nursemaid and former apprentice to Meade. After Brier's wayward labor, the brown-haired woman resigned with the doctor. Then she applied the next morning, shaken and overwrought, for the open nursemaid position. With Marietta's approval, and Meade's blessing, the young Burges nurse became nursemaid to the first babe she delivered.

"Ryanne is too young to be without me for so long. I cannot nurse her if I'm away on a hunting trip," Brier explained, slipping into his clean robe.

"Well, she can't very well come hunting with us." Roland's bottom lip drooped.

"No." Brier giggled. "She cannot." The king almost glided past him before he reached out and gripped Brier's wrist.

"Then both of you come to Balmur," Roland proposed. "You and Ryanne." He pulled Brier closer. "Come to Balmur when you are fit to ride."

"Is the house finished?" Brier's brow arched skeptically.

"Nearly," Roland answered. In truth, their home had at least a month's more work to be done after his two-week hiatus after the birth of Ryanne. They were back on schedule, but he still needed time.

"Hmm…." Brier bit his bottom lip. Roland could see two minds. One here, safe in the palace with Ryanne, the other at their home, lounging in Balmur. A short holiday before he officially returned from his leave. "It is almost a two-hour ride by carriage to Balmur. Are you sure Ryanne will be okay?"

"She'll be with us. Safe." Roland watched Brier's shoulders untense at his assurance. He did not worry for their child, as she would be cared for properly no matter where they resided. "I want to give you a break, Brinan." A respite, however brief, from his duties as both father and king.

"All right." Brier nodded tentatively. "We'll go in a fortnight, but only if Ryanne is well."

"Of course." Roland leaned in and kissed his lover's pink lips. "If Ryanne is unwell, we smite the entire capital," he teased.

"For once your wrath is justified," Brier quipped. Roland let out a deep chuckle before he wrapped his arms around Brier's waist and kissed him once more.

THE DAY of their trip to Balmur, Roland helped to prep the carriage and load their weighty luggage. They were only spending one week in the country, but he insisted they have enough provisions to last them. He'd worked overmuch in the past weeks to make sure their home suited a king and princess, and now he only wanted to rest, or exhaust himself in a more carnal position.

"Do you think we bought enough cloth for the diapers?" Roland asked his lover, holding the small of Ryanne's back. She wore her tailored clothes that Marietta and Brier ordered, but Roland wrapped her in a warm fox fur to shield her from the cold.

"More than enough." Brier pursed his lips. "And we can always wash them out if need be."

"I'll leave that to you," Roland replied.

"You most certainly will not," Brier countered with a laugh. "You've no trouble filling her belly when I cannot nurse her, but I've noticed your aversion to her dirty bum."

"I've no talent in that regard." Roland smiled innocently.

"That does not exclude you from the task." Brier smirked. "Besides, how can you ignore her when she screeches like a cat?"

"Verily I can't. Which is why I'm glad you hired Victoria."

"Victoria is not here to save you," Brier replied pointedly. "It is only Ryanne, you, and I, for one week. Alone…." Perhaps he'd imagined it, but Roland thought he heard a tantalizing purr behind Brier's last word.

"How will I manage you both?"

"Effortlessly, I'm sure."

Roland knew he'd been beaten before he began. Brier and Ryanne had him wrapped around their fingers, and he would not have it any other way.

THE HOME was a farm villa style, two levels, equipped with a shed, patio, and a garden adjacent. The open lands exacted Brier's desire to breed horses, while the bordering forest contented Roland. In the interior, he'd pulled, cut, and shaved the wood to create the high arched ceilings and sturdy pillars to hold the humongous frame. They used heavy stone to fortify walls in case of high winds or floods and concrete for the foundation. The oversized bedrooms were five on one side and two larger master suites on the other, bathing rooms adjacent. His and Brier's suite held the nursery.

Brier nearly shrieked when Roland showed him Ryanne's nursery above the gardens. The winter had made the earth desolate, but in spring a nook of fresh rose beds and wildflowers would align with the open walkway.

In the backyard Roland built tables to accommodate many or a few, and a deep fire pit for open grilling and summer nights to snooze by the open fire. Their patio overlooked the ponds spread through five acres of flatland, and onward to the bordering forest.

"Now it's not completely finished yet," he warned Brier after the tour. Ryanne fell asleep midway through, but he held her nonetheless. "We still have to order the furniture for the sitting room and finish the stables, but the bulk is done. I didn't have time to build Ryanne's crib, so she'll have to sleep with us till then."

"Which is perfectly fine with me. This place is wonderful!" Brier exclaimed.

"Ryanne's nursery is right by our bedroom so we won't have to move far," Roland pointed out.

"Aye, and we can put a daybed for Victoria in the nursery when she keeps her," Brier added.

"And if Marietta decides to follow you here, which I'm sure she will, there is room enough for her."

"There is room enough for her and whoever else we might be expecting in the future." Brier winked before he gazed down at their child in Roland's arms. Roland twisted his lips.

"The bedrooms are for guests, Brier."

"And what guest do you expect to come here?" Brier snorted, but Roland frowned slightly at the insinuation. They had not discussed more children since before Ryanne's birth, and he had no desire to.

"We should move in soonest." Brier changed the subject. "I'd love to be settled before my birthday."

"We cannot move in just yet," Roland told Brier, but beamed at his enthusiasm. "I think you should still stay in the palace for a bit longer, just until you're officially cleared to begin work by Meade. Then of course you'll have your court duties and such. An hour's ride on horseback does not seem such a burden when you have not been governing all day, but will you not feel exhausted if you make the trip every day?"

"Not if I came home to you and Ryanne every day." Brier brushed the babe's dark tuft of hair. "If I am overtired, I will rest before I ride home."

Roland heard the obstinacy in Brier's voice and knew he could not sway his lover. "I would be happy to wait for you in our new home." He caught Brier's lips in a swift peck. "Come, let me put her down and I'll show you the bath."

After they laid Ryanne to sleep, they took a drink in the parlor and lounged on the compact love seat. The quiet living room, sweet wine, and warm sage of the walls easily settled both he and Brier.

Knock. Knock. Knock.

A heavy hand on wood stirred them from their nap. Roland blinked, surprised he'd drifted so easily, before he realized he'd woken due to the hammer-like pound on their door.

"Who could that be?" Brier murmured with a frown. Roland honestly did not know, but he stood from the couch and instructed Brier to check on Ryanne. Before he opened the door, he bent down to grip the steel hilt of the dagger in his boot cuff.

"Who's there?" he barked out.

"*Con l'ellar*?" The deep voice rang out in Thenian.

"Who does he think it is, Leighis?" a light melody echoed.

Roland wrenched the door open and stared upward to the giant Dur.

"Dur!" He opened his arms as the crushing hug raised him off the ground. Before Dur pulled away, three other smiling faces popped out from the side of the giant. "Sasta, Umhal!" He wheezed as Dur continued to squeeze him.

"Let him go, Dur, you'll suffocate him." Sasta laughed out loud as Dur finally put Roland's feet back on the wood floors.

"*Venur*! Rolande! *L'tyva el*?"

"*Aye, diolenan*, Sastania." He crossed his forearms with the members of his guild. "When did you get back?"

"Only two weeks ago for *Yensira*. We were going to head east, but then Leighis told us of you and Brier. And then we'd heard from Umhal that you'd be coming this way!" The boy was as enthusiastic as ever, unable to control the pace of his words.

"So you came before heading out on your next adventure?"

"Aye," Dur answered in a slower pace.

"Are you going to invite us in, Ronan? Or must we idle in your foyer?" Lei asked him.

"Of course, forgive me." He ushered the men into the parlor. The once quiet house quickly filled with chatter as the five of them spoke over top of each other in a mix of Thenian and common tongue.

"And we couldn't believe it when Leighis told us you'd gone back to Brier in Avenough. Well honestly it was more, I could not believe he would have you after what happened in Aire."

"Yes, well," Roland rubbed his neck, feeling sheepish. "Circumstances being what they were." He chuckled before he turned toward low creaking on the stairs. Brier stood at the top, looking both bewildered and elated at the guild's presence.

"Brier!" Sasta's high-pitched voice echoed in a room with such high ceilings. Brier smiled at the man, though Roland could see him clutch Ryanne cautiously. Sasta was known for his turbulent hugs. "By the gods, you look different!"

Brier's smile faltered, but he inclined his head politely. "*Venur*, Sanan. *L'tyva el*?" Sasta's eyes widened as he heard Brier speak perfect Thenian.

"*Aye, Venur*." He bowed. "*Na'saan el*."

"Indeed," Brier answered in common tongue. "But you come most unexpectedly. I'm afraid we haven't prepared enough to host you properly. Mayhap Rolande can ride towards Avenough to grab more food," Brier informed them, coming down the stairs. Roland watched Ryanne grip the man's robed chest. Most likely he'd just finished nursing her.

"Do you think we would come empty-handed?" Lei stepped toward Brier, evermore lanky with his silver hair tied and braided. "We've come with enough provisions and gifts for a true housewarming party."

Roland looked toward Brier. He knew how hectic parties with the guild could become.

"What do you think?" Brier defaulted to him.

"I think it's fine, as long as you guys mind yourselves," Roland added reproachfully. "Our babe is newborn and unused to the noise." Though the girl's own screams rivaled Veti's howls, he and Brier tried to maintain calm around her.

"With Thenian blood she'll learn the thrill of a good rouse!" Sasta piped. Roland showed them to the kitchen to prepare the food as Lei went over to coax Brier into holding Ryanne.

Though Roland did not expect the guild's company, the affair turned out rather lively. The men had prepared more than enough in the cart they used for travel. The smell of roasted sausage and fried potatoes filled the villa's vast space. Sasta cooked a pot of brussels sprouts, a favorite of Roland's, along with a boiling pot of fertilized quail eggs. When the smell made nearly everyone faint, Roland sent them outside to the fire pit. Nonetheless, they ate the plentiful meal in good spirits. As with any Thenian soiree, they played music to break the silence. Sasta played his small flute, while the rest poured the alcohol in globs, filling the colur-gem-encrusted goblets full of homemade shine and aged wine.

By the end of the night, Roland leaned back against the couch, properly liquored. The others sat around the coffee table playing cards. He heard the faint whirl of a spinning top and Ryanne's low whimpers as Brier coaxed her to finally sleep. Brier seemed to enjoy himself, but his practiced charm and amicable smile made him difficult to read in others' company.

Roland sifted through the crowd until he met Umhal's pensive gaze. Though Umhal usually did not speak more than a few words, Roland felt the weight of his stare as he stood and walked toward the atrium. He did not hear footsteps, but he could sense Umhal's presence.

"*Venur*." He turned to face the frail frame. "I wanted to personally give you my regards. Lei told me you were the one who helped him make sure I was all right." Umhal nodded silently before his eye locked on Brier and Ryanne.

"She was born under the eleventh star. Though she should have been born under the twelfth." Perhaps Roland imagined the man's cryptic tone, but he tried to keep his face passive. "Her birth was a difficult one," Umhal stated. "She almost killed the king of Lirend."

"Not purposefully…." Roland gazed warily. "Yes, Brier had a difficult birth, but Ryanne had naught to do but be born."

"I don't blame the child." Umhal shook his head. "But just as the stars align, there is a reason for everything."

"There is no reason for it."

"A father's atonement?" Umhal questioned him.

He narrowed his gaze before he whispered, "Brier has done nothing wrong."

"Brier is not her only father." Umhal gave him a knowing look, and Roland stiffened before he glanced at Brier. "If you continue this way, I see the blackening of your heart, Ronan," Umhal warned him. "Your deceit will undo you both."

"Aye, I know this!" Roland turned back toward Umhal and whispered harshly. He did not need a seer to tell the consequences of his chicanery. Like a defrosting lake, Roland could see the cracks in the ice he glided over. However, he'd slithered so far from the bank he could not get back safely. "I'm going to tell Brier soon, I just—"

"Tell me what soon?" Brier's firm voice chimed. Roland whipped his head toward his lover. His heart thudded madly. Lei's pale eyes locked, and Roland tensed when the man pursed his lips reprovingly.

"That we're out of wine." Lei gripped Roland's shoulder. "We're going to run to the carriage to grab the replenishments." Roland twisted his head back toward the puzzled king, and Lei dragged him toward the overstuffed cart.

"Are you an idiot?" Lei asked as he released Roland's shoulder and moved to unlock the hatch chord.

"Not officially," Roland answered and helped Lei unload the jugs of wine.

"You must be if you haven't told Brier the truth yet." Lei hopped off the cart and began to untie a rope on the side.

"I'm going to tell him," Roland repeated, sighing.

"When?"

"Soon."

"When the whole thing blows up in your face?"

"Just a few moments before that, hopefully." The man scoffed before he fiddled with the rope more.

"What the hell are you doing anyway? I've got the wine. Let's go back before Brier questions me further."

"Calm yourself, Ronan." Lei exhaled as he finally unhitched the tarp. He ripped the heavy cloth off a huge piece of wooden furniture. Long bars with painted leaves shielded a white feather bed with a fur-lined dust ruffle. The carving stood out the most, with a silver shield in the shape of a leaf on one side of the base, and a deeply carved bow on the other. Roland slid his hand over the bow and the painted leaves glowed gold on the bars. Though the sun sunk low, it did not take Roland long to recognize it as a crib.

"You built this?" Roland asked, hoarse from the sentiment.

"We all did. I remembered you didn't have one yet." Lei called the other members of the guild, and they all traipsed out. Roland went and wrapped his arm around the king's waist while Brier tilted his head, puzzled.

"What's going on?" Brier whispered through his teeth.

"The guild has a gift for us." He beamed at Brier. The wind had picked up and blew the tarp over the cart and on the slate-blue patio. The orange dusk swept over the villa's expanse as all six men huddled on the patio.

"We're a little late," Lei conceded as he chuckled.

"As usual," Roland quipped.

"But we'd like to congratulate you on the birth of Princess Ryanne Snow."

"*Diole'*, Leinan." Brier's mouth twisted into a grateful smile and inclined his head to thank Lei for the kind words. "But Ryanne is more than just the firstborn of Ronan and I. She represents the union of two countries that long since should have been one. She is a reminder to me that the Thenians have a place in Lirend, just as any other citizen in this land."

"Indeed, Brinan." Lei nodded. "We should have put down our animosity and learned to love one another long ago."

"I plan to make amends for the hardships your people face in Lirend. For the hardships, I admit, my own daughter may face. But hopefully, with the cooperation of the willing and the condemnation of the unwilling, we can move on, without hate and prejudice to hinder progress. Without resentment for our past sins. Yours and mine."

Roland gazed at his lover. As Sasta had said, he did look different. The boy who once faltered with every step had taken his throne and strode gracefully into ancestral power. The timid boy he'd met huddled before the former queen had become a symbol of parity. Like his father before him, he'd become a man of substance. A man the Thenians could be proud to pledge their fealty to. A man Roland was proud to love.

ON THE first day Brier took Frieling for a three-hour ride around the grounds. Brier left after lunch and did not return until Roland finished dinner. In Aire the weather had likely reached below freezing, but Avenough remained a wintry mix of rain, fog, and snow. The weather in Balmur chilled, but Roland did not mind the cooler temperatures. Ryanne, like any Thenian, adapted well to the change of surroundings.

On the second day, Brier took a stroll by himself in the gardens, and on the third day, he read in the nursery by his lonesome. Roland made sure to keep Ryanne fed and happy while Brier took a much needed rest. The solitude did his lover well. Brier unwound in the confines of their new home, away from Marietta, Quintin, and Lord Tamil.

On the fourth night, when Roland expected Brier to take personal time alone, he came to his side instead. Roland had laid Ryanne in the nursery while he whittled a rough piece of alderwood. He wanted to give Ryanne a present of some kind, but he hadn't decided what to carve her yet. He peered up when he heard the door creak, and in stepped his lover with a coy smile. Roland quirked his eye, puzzled at the wanton expression before Brier leaned in to whisper in his ear.

"Meet me in the bath in ten minutes."

WHEN ROLAND stepped into the bathing room, he expected to find Brier fully immersed. He often followed his lover when he bathed, but rarely did he join him.

Tonight however, Brier had aligned the candles on the border of their deep marble tub and dimmed the hanging light fixtures. The foam bubbles and wild lilies floated above the clear water. Brier sat with his feet submerged, but the rest of his naked body exposed on the berm of the tub. He twisted his head when the door opened.

"Close the door," Brier whispered. "I don't want Ryanne to wake up." Roland swallowed the thirst in his throat and inched forward after closing the door. Brier had certainly set the mood, but he did not want to assume too much.

"She's in the nursery."

"Good." Brier stood from the tub, sloshing the water, and stepped toward him. "I don't want to be interrupted."

"I'll listen out for her while you bathe."

"I appreciate that, but what I have in mind requires your presence."

"Oh really?" Roland smirked as he wrapped his arms around Brier's bare waist. "And what, pray tell, does that entail?"

"I could tell you…." Brier began to unbutton the gold clasp on his leather jerkin. "But why don't I show you instead." Brier raised the twill to reveal the fine hair on his lower abdomen. Roland strained to keep himself passive, though he stiffened from Brier's caress. Smooth hands glided across his stomach before Brier's hand dipped into his waistband. The king eased down Roland's trousers to reveal his mass.

"But you seem to know what it entails right enough."

Roland cleared his throat, abashed from his obvious stimulation. His aversion to masturbation and his overzealous will to finish their villa in time made his patience raw and his hunger ripe. Brier kissed down his stomach and sank to his knees.

"It's been a while since I tasted you." Brier swiped his tongue over the slit of his member and slurped his tip.

"Aye." Brier's tongue tickled down the side of his shaft. "It's been over a month since I had you," Roland grunted. And three months since they'd fully coupled. His mouth went dry as Brier kissed the head of his shaft. Roland wanted to thrust his hips into his lover's mouth, but he waited for Brier to lead him across this pleasurable slope.

"Brinan." Roland shivered as Brier pooled spit around the opening and ridge of his crown. "*Acai….*" Roland whined from the succulent lave. When Brier pulled back, spittle dripped down the side of his gleaming member. All the while Brier's eyes glowed upward to stare at his twisted face. Brier rubbed Roland's hung member on his upper lip, lower lip, everywhere except the king's outstretched tongue.

"Do not rile me up overmuch, King Brier." Roland grit his teeth and grabbed a chunk of red hair.

"Ngh—" Brier clutched his waist. "What if I like riling you up, Master Rolande?" To answer, Roland thrust his hips against Brier's waiting throat, and Brier devoured Roland with one gulp.

"Mghn." Roland pressed his tongue to the roof of his mouth and let out a shaky breath as Brier bobbed and swallowed his thick shaft. His hand slid up Roland's leg and began to massage between his sac and meaty thighs.

"Haaah-mgghnn!" Roland's voice echoed. He could feel his abstinent days and nights culminating. Then Brier gripped his sac and Roland lost his resolve. He bucked his hips and watched the king's face redden as he assaulted the back of Brier's throat.

Brier gagged slightly but did not pull away, claiming Roland's member. This time Brier's tongue flicked over his tip as the man slurped simultaneously. Roland crumpled under his tongue, fingers clenched in the red strands of loose hair.

"If you don't want me to spill in your mouth, you better stop now, Brinan!" His shaft oozed precum in warning, but Brier only pulled back momentarily before he barraged Roland once more. When he realized Brier had not shied away, he released a deep exhale that made him shudder.

Gods....

His chest tightened at the rhythmic slosh of his member in Brier's mouth. His knees grew numb as Brier's throat absorbed his flesh. Then all at once the pressure reached its limit and his shaft spasmed.

"Hggnn... coming!" Roland held Brier's head as his member thrummed against his lover's coated tongue. Brier dribbled the semen before he guzzled Roland like scrumptious redmelon, the man's lips smacking for more. Twisted ecstasy pulsed through Roland like a charged current, and he clawed Brier's shoulder, yielding utterly to the stimulation.

"*Acai*, Brinan!" Roland begged when Brier continued to suck him. Brier peered up with an almost chaste expression as the drool and cum stained his mouth and chin. Roland reached down to wipe the juice with his palm. His heart pounded maniacally as Brier leaned in to lick even his fingers clean of cum.

"Nn... tas' guud...." Brier's words slurred over Roland's digits. The heat from Brier's mouth made Roland's sleepy member jolt.

"You're going to be the death of me," Roland panted out.

"You can't die yet." Brier licked those lips and stood, his pink-tinged member fully erect. "I'm not nearly finished with you." Brier stepped across the tiled marble and into the tub.

CHAPTER 27
PROPOSAL

THEY KISSED longer than any time Brier could readily recall. Roland's tongue found every crevice of his mouth to lick. Brier ground his hips against Roland's member, eager to ride, but willing to wait. He savored the scalding tongue that marked his neck, caressed his shoulder, and trailed to his hypersensitive nipples.

"Hggnnn! Ronan." Brier flushed at his own plaintive cry. Roland lapped at his nipples and Brier's back arched, beckoning the sensation and cringing from the overstimulation. Roland understood his unspoken dilemma and reached between them to stroke Brier's member. Ecstasy coursed through Brier's body, and he twined his fingers in Roland's coarse hair. "Ah—ah—" He swiveled his hips upward into Roland's grasp.

"Stop.... Ronan." Brier's skin flushed full red when he felt the milk drawn from his engorged nipples. "*Acai*!" Brier buried his face in Roland's neck, knowing his lover could taste him, but the huntsman's mouth only grew more ravenous. He shivered under the assault as Roland ripped wanton moans from his throat. "Ahh!" His body rolled in the water, and he pressed into Roland's groin. Roland controlled his spastic waist with a firm grip.

"Have me," Brier whispered. He lifted his ass above the water before he savored his milk on Roland's tongue. He reached out to squeeze Roland's girth, but he only held Brier tighter.

"Not yet." Roland dipped his free hand in the jar of cream-like lubricant. Roland's fingers crept under him, and Brier inhaled at the first slick plug that breeched him. "This hasn't been used in a while." Roland began to dig him out and Brier's eyes misted over.

"I'm all right, Ronan, please," Brier pleaded, ready to feel the split of his lover's sword.

"Do you think me overly cautious, King Brier?" Roland mumbled against Brier's reddened ears. Brier shook his head before he answered.

"*Na*, I—" Brier heaved when the second finger slid within him. "I think you a sweet master."

"Hmph—I'm not nearly as sweet as you believe." Brier caught Roland's narrowed gaze. "For example...." The man snatched Brier's hips. "If you keep looking at me like that I'll rip right through you." Brier choked as three fingers stretched him. "Or maybe I'll just watch you spend your seed from just my hand."

"Haaaannhh!" Roland's fingertips crushed his spot. "*Na—acai*!" Brier screamed.

"Would you think me sweet still, then?"

"Ahh!" Roland's mouth found his nipples once more, and Brier clawed his shoulders.

"Tell me, king." Roland's tone grew dark and Brier whimpered. His eyes flecked with tears as he gasped to reply.

"I would—think you cruel, master." Brier's sharp breaths overlapped Roland's merciless laugh.

"Honest as always."

"Ngh—!" The slick tongue encircled Brier's nipple, and he yanked Roland's hair to hold his head. "*Acai* Master! S-stop!" He craved this man's incomparable sword, but could not last under Roland's tongue massage. "Ngh… I'm gonna come." But the hand on Brier's base gripped him.

"Not yet," Roland huffed into his ear. His husky voice made Brier tremble. "Let me fill you up first, Brinan." Brier clenched his eyes and bared down as Roland shifted to pierce him.

"Hurry." Roland's head slid in without pain, but tears rolled down Brier's cheeks as the man's length and girth entered him.

"Ahhh—shhhh!" Brier hissed out a moan before he took Roland's mouth into a fevered kiss. Roland licked against Brier's tongue and bit the tip playfully.

"Don't try to muffle your voice, Brinan." Roland lunged upward, and Brier's lubed ass quaffed. "Show me everything."

Brier cried out as Roland spread him with another plunge. His body opened and gripped Roland's thick flesh. The water cooled his skin, but not his fire as he clawed Roland's bronze-tinged shoulders. Roland let out a guttural groan before Brier felt the euphoric pace quicken. He rode Roland voraciously, blinded from his own desperation.

"Ahh, aye!" Brier reached between them to stroke his hungry flesh, but Roland held his wrists.

"*Na*. Not with your hand," Roland commanded.

"I need to come!" Brier pleaded. Roland entwined their fingers, and Brier squeezed Roland's hands. The bestial hump made him cringe.

"You can come without your hand, Brinan." Roland licked the bottom of his lip. "You almost spilled from my mouth, didn't you?" Brier flushed at Roland's lewd words, but did not shy from them.

"Aye, I did but—"

"Then come. Now. Just like this." Brier wrapped his legs around Roland's waist. Roland slammed up, and pleasure spiked up his spine. His eyes fluttered before they shut, and he focused on Roland's rigid member. The burning penetration melded into a thrilling rush. Roland took his mouth into a kiss, and Brier's breath hastened with each pump.

"Feel good, Brinan?" Roland teased Brier's tongue.

"It's—good—ah—soooo good," he puffed out through their kisses. Roland slapped into his cream-filled ass, and lilac-scented lube ensnared him. The candles formed lewd shadows on the wall adjacent. The water splashed and Brier's back bowed in the tub as he wheezed and thrashed. "Close, Ro!" Heat pooled in his groin as his stomach tightened.

"Ahhh-ahhh!" Roland slid out slow, and his orgasm stuttered right on the brink. "*Acai.*" Roland's shaft slammed deep and Brier erupted. "Mgghnn—yes! Give it to me," he cried. He jerked his hips in rhythm to Roland's thrusts.

"*O ta a'min,*" Brier whispered with their lips still grazed from the kiss. Roland's thick cum seeped into his raw hole. He shuddered as Roland's shaft spasmed within him. Bliss skulked up Brier's spine, and he clung to naked skin. He shut his eyes and kissed Roland's wet shoulder. He'd almost forgotten how fulfilled Roland made him. Almost.

BRIER COLLAPSED into their bed, over Roland's unshorn chest. Roland's hands wrapped around him to cover the peeled nerves, and then blanketed him with the bed's layers. It took Brier more than a moment to calm as he came down from the buzz of his third orgasm of the night. Even under the heavy fur, he shivered.

"Is that better?" Roland's hoarse pant gratified him more than even the skillful rod.

"For the moment," he whispered with a smug smile.

"You are insatiable as ever I see." But Roland did not seem to mind his libido. He smirked before he kissed the silver marks spreading on Brier's shoulder and collar.

"Aye," Brier whispered before he lifted his neck for Roland's tongue.

"But that's okay… I'm not going to let you sleep tonigh—"

Brier blinked his eyes open when he heard Ryanne's muffled cries. Roland let out a curse before he slumped against the feathered pillows, and Brier burst into a fit of laughter.

"I don't think she'll let me sleep either," he answered, amused. "Why don't you go get her, and I can dress so she can eat?"

"I don't want to." Roland kissed his smiling lips. "Just a little bit more." But the baby's cries grew louder and his lover sighed longingly.

"She won't go back to sleep, Ronan." Brier chuckled at Roland's lethargy. "She's hungry."

"I'm hungry too," Roland groaned. Brier laughed once more as Roland squeezed his waist before he rolled out of bed.

"You are terrible, Master Roland." Brier grinned as he watched the man dress.

"I thought I was good, 'sooo good.'" Roland mimicked his shameless moans. Brier ignored the heat in his cheeks and pursed his lips.

"Will you fetch your daughter before she wakes the gods?"

"Aye, I will get Ryanne so she can eat." Roland paused at the nursery door before Brier eyed his lewd smirk. "And hopefully there's something left."

Brier wore a cozy velvet robe to feed Ryanne as Roland stoked the dying fire. Brier peered upward, and Roland inched toward the bed apprehensively.

"Is it okay if I sit with you?"

"It's all right," Brier mumbled. He nourished his daughter and pleased his lover with the same chest, yet the two felt nothing alike. "No point in hiding when you've already seen me thus."

"*Na.*" Roland shook his head. "This way is more beautiful." Roland kissed his forehead, and Brier glowed from the tender words.

AFTER HE fed Ryanne, they commenced their usual coddling. Roland gushed over his daughter, kissing her nose and stroking the tuft of black hair on her smooth brow. In the summer they'd plant peonies and trim the willows planted throughout their land. When the weather broke, mayhap he could buy the stray foal and her mother for their stable. It would be fun to take Ryanne for her first ride to swim in the shallow ponds before letting her stretch out in the main lake less than a mile south.

"I wonder if she knows how beautiful she is," Roland asked.

"You tell her every day…." Roland sounded foolish questioning the mind of an infant, but Brier found Roland's doting rather cute.

"If I don't, some pompous Aurelian will steal her away from me."

Brier laughed out loud, noting Roland's context, and shook his head. "You have a long time yet for that, Rolande. No one would even expect her to marry until she comes of age." Brier's smile faltered. He had not thought about his marriage prospects since he came to Balmur. He'd enjoyed his time away from the bustle of Avenough, away from Quintin, away from even Marietta. Brier stared at his lover and felt a small pang in his heart.

He only wished….

"Do you think she knows she broke up our alone time?" Roland peered up at him and grinned. Roland was completely smitten.

"Her?" Brier leaned down and kissed Ryanne's forehead. "No, she's innocent. Perfect little angel."

"Like her father." Roland reached out to grab his hand, and Brier's heart thudded with uncertainty.

"Rolande…."

"Hmm?" Roland kissed his knuckles.

He only wished this dream was not temporary.

"I want you to be my lover," Brier uttered clearly. Roland's forehead creased before he smiled, bemused.

"I thought that I already was." He chuckled lightly. "Or is there something you need to tell me?"

"*Na.*" Brier shook his head and hardened his resolve. "I want you to be my lover, not only in flesh, but also in name." Brier gave Roland several moments to surmise the meaning behind his words.

"Are you proposing to me?" Roland asked, slightly breathless.

"Yes." Brier had not said those words specifically, but the general idea was the same. "I want you to be my husband." Roland stared at him wide-eyed until Ryanne squeezed Roland's outstretched finger and he cleared his throat.

"The court will never allow us to wed," he immediately countered. "A consort is not only a lover, Brinan. If you should die, it would be I, your lawfully wedded spouse, who would rule Lirend."

"*If* I should die, I would want you to take the throne," Brier offered. Roland opened his mouth to speak, but Ryanne burped, and Brier pressed on. "Through the law of passage, our daughter will inherit my throne. Ryanne will rule Lirend when she is ready. Unlike my stepmother, I know you would step down in our daughter's stead." He could see Roland's lip tighten at the last words but he did not speak, so Brier continued. "In the event that I expire, I need someone who will continue the policies I laid in place."

"They will never let a full-blood Thenian rule a piss pot!" Roland's voice rose. "Let alone the great Braedon Snow's kingdom." Brier bristled at Roland's implication, but calmed when he saw the hopelessness in Roland's lowered gaze.

"Braedon Snow is not the king of Lirend." Brier reached out to raise Roland's chin. "I am." He stared into Roland's cool eyes, calm and blue like the sea, yet filled with so much longing.

"Our daughter cannot rule with me named as her father, Brier. You know this. The law of passage marks her as having Thenian blood and would bind her to our contract with the Aurelians."

"When Leighis comes back to Balmur, I will show him the work I've done with the Prolits. We will map out a plan for the Thenians' recompense, and I will sever the contract your people once signed with my father. I planned to do so anyway. It was foolish to begin with, though I understand now the desperation that claimed the Thenians at that time. Then you can stand by me as my husband, and if I should die you—"

"Just stop, Brinan," Roland snapped. He lowered his gaze. "I have you… I have Ryanne…." He shook his head. "How can I beg the gods for more when they have blessed me thus? Even after everything I've done. After all the sins I've committed." Brier stared as Roland's eyes glistened with tears. "I cannot rule Lirend." Brier touched the crease of Roland's weary eyes.

"Then don't rule Lirend," Brier whispered. "Just be mine. Just love me, and our daughter. I do not care who you are. I do not care what you've done. You are my everything, Ronan. I won't live without you by my side." Brier leaned in to kiss Roland's lips and felt his lover stiffen against him. When they parted he only gave Roland an inch of space between their faces.

"I am an old man, Brier," Roland grunted. "Are you certain you want to marry me?"

"There is no one I would rather share a bed with, raise our daughter with, spend my life with." He smirked and fingered through Roland's graying hair. "Old man or not, if you are willing, I would have you as my husband." Roland had captured his heart long before he'd had time to think about their stations or age differences. He loved Roland, Rolande, Ronan. He loved this daring ride where at times he felt as though he might break without Roland by his side. "Marry me," he repeated firmly before Roland nodded, and Brier watched the man's lips turn into a timid smile.

THEIR TIME in Balmur passed much too quickly for Brier's liking. He helped the coachmen pack the cart while Roland tended to Ryanne's dirty diaper and coaxed

Frieling into joining the lead horse of Avenough's carriage. The guards waited stiff-necked and ever silent as Brier rubbed the horse's blond mane.

"And that's Papa's other spouse," he overheard his lover tell their daughter. "He loves that horse more than he does your poor *aida*." Brier rolled his eyes before he pursed his lips.

"Isn't it time to end your silly feud with Frieling?" Brier grabbed Ryanne from Roland so he could enter the carriage first.

"I don't know how good *your* memory is, but that horse almost got us killed," Roland said loud enough for Frieling to hear.

"But we didn't die." Brier handed Ryanne back to Roland. "And I remember that night well enough. Before then you were rather cold towards me." He climbed into the carriage and shut the curtained door. Roland let out a grunt to answer him and spoke to Ryanne in Thenian instead. The driver stalled before Brier felt the carriage rock and the horses traipsed down the paved road.

That night....

When he'd almost fallen from the cliffs. He sat in Roland's presence bare for the first time. He'd never felt more alone and vulnerable, and Roland made him laugh despite his circumstances—despite his hopelessness. Brier smiled at Roland as the man shifted their daughter's bonnet.

"Wherefore this look?" Roland questioned him. "I'll not have two sets of green eyes on me on the whole of this journey."

"*Mana el man'*, Ronan." Brier closed his eyes and leaned his head back with content on his lips. Roland acquainted him with a feeling Brier could not name at the time, but what he certainly knew now.

Love.

CHAPTER 28
CLANDESTINE

ROLAND STOOD in a pressed white tunic with gray slacks and black leather around his waist. Marietta poked and prodded him for hours. He'd shaved the shadow on his face he'd grown in Balmur and cut his hair once more. Despite the salon's clippers, the gray on his sideburns remained stubborn.

"I swear to gods." Brier bustled past him. Roland saw the brilliant red of Brier's hair and bare chest reflected in the same glass.

"Lord Tamil has followed me through every corridor since we arrived home. I understand the man expects Quintin and me to marry, but who is king? He or I?" Roland pulled on his jacket. "And Marietta has practically made me sick with her worrying every time I leave Ryanne with Victoria. She is her nursemaid after all."

"Perhaps she wants the job?" Roland considered.

"She goes on about how much she enjoys her retirement and then chastises me for doing my job." Roland ogled Brier as he bound his chest to keep the milk from leaking. "I will be glad when I am free to move to our villa in Balmur."

"Do not scold them overmuch, Brier. They are just glad to have their king back in Avenough. It's clear that Marietta missed your presence," Roland replied.

"I missed her too," Brier exhaled. "But honestly, you would think Ryanne cannot function without Marietta there to dote on her."

Roland listened to his lover idly. He sat in the chair adjacent and noticed Brier's mother's music box in the corner of the desk. He'd taken on a stoic mood since they returned to the palace, calm but pensive. Brier decided that they should marry, despite his station, and yet he'd never felt so secluded. How could he tell him? After so long? How could he destroy his lover's trust so completely? He gazed at the iron-made box and remembered the wooden one he'd gifted to Brier a year prior. When he broke his heart the first time. When he'd let Brier go.

"Ronan?" Brier held the hilt of the decorative sword on his waist. His white jacket clasped neatly with green stripes on the front and side. Roland gaped at Brier and felt the weight of their stations once more. "Are you all right?" Brier's frown made Roland smile wistfully.

"Aye. Just thinking." He gripped the clasp of the belt and pulled Brier to his lap.

"What are you thinking, I wonder, to make your face so somber?"

"Am I not a somber man?" Roland raised his brow half smiling.

"Not lately," Brier answered honestly. Green eyes probed him before Roland spoke.

"I was thinking how lucky I am to have you, Brier." How lucky he was to know and love this man, this king who'd helped so many and planned to help more. And here he was, full of darkness and deceit. Full of naught but lies and heartache.

"I was thinking I don't know what I would do without you and Ryanne by my side."

When he thought he'd lost Brier, his world faded to black. No guild member or god could save him from the wretchedness that consumed his soul. And yet, here was. He'd come full circle without a will or a way to redemption.

"I was thinking I can't live without you."

"And why should you?" Brier questioned him. "This marriage guarantees at least that I'm not going anywhere. I'm yours for eternity." Brier kissed Roland's forehead and smoothed the lines. "Do not worry so much, Master Roland. You're already gray enough." Brier stood from his lap to finish dressing, but Roland reached out to grab his wrist.

"Brier." Roland lowered his head. His chest constricted as he tried to think of the proper words, or improper words. What did one say to break their lover's heart?

I'm sorry?

Forgive me?

Please love me?

Hadn't he already begged for Brier's forgiveness one too many times? Roland tried to form words, but they died on his quivering lips.

"What is it?" Brier's gaze turned fearful.

"I love you," he whispered in a painfully hoarse voice. "I love you more than anything. You know this, right?"

"Of course I do." Brier's frown deepened. "Rolande, I—"

"Your Majesty." Roland heard Lord Tamil's tenor before a light knock.

"Come in." Brier struggled to gain his passive countenance as Lord Tamil entered the parlor.

"The court is assembled for your announcement. They await your presence."

"Thank you, Lord Tamil. We'll be there in a moment."

"Yes, Your Majesty. Prince Quintin has already arrived. I can only presume this is the news we've all anticipated?"

"Rather presumptuous of you, for sure," Brier replied with some vexation. "But I don't recall inviting Prince Quintin to this council." Roland understood Brier's concerns. As much as Brier tried to revive his and the prince's friendship, their relationship grew ever stale.

"I apologize, Your Majesty." Lord Tamil bowed. "Prince Quintin said that he had an announcement regarding your assembly. I assumed it was the same as your own." Brier's gaze flew upward before the man shot Roland an anxious gaze.

"Let us go before the court revolts in your absence." Roland wore a false smile to mask the turmoil in his heart. They could not let Quintin share the news before the king. Brier gazed at him for several moments before he nodded once.

"We will finish our discussion later."

THE ROYAL court had never boded well for Roland. In the days before Brier's competence, his father, King Braedon Snow, held a court similar to this one in order to constitute the contract that legally bound the Thenians to the ruling class of Lirend. The antiqued walls and red curtains gave the court the appearance of a grandiose theater, and the proceedings oftentimes matched that guise. Several rows with polished wood and gold banisters held the court's overflow while the main floor held at least a hundred chairs. Most of the Aurelians came to make sure their names and bloodlines remained reputable, and the others had nothing more entertaining to do. Given the king's imperative announcement today, every seat was full.

When the king entered the iron doors, the court stood. Brier set a durable pace to reach the court hall stairs, but Roland could see every eye on Brier. He settled on his throne and all the Aurelians followed suit. All but one, Roland noticed. Prince Quintin Pascal remained standing on the right of Brier. Perhaps Roland imagined it, but Quintin glared daggers across the expansive hall.

Brier sat at the top of the rowed aisle in a stiff-backed chair Roland knew Brier detested. He tried to smile through his nerves, but Roland could see the apprehension that creased Brier's eyes.

"Welcome." Brier's once timid voice now reverberated through the hall. "I am glad to see that the announcement of my betrothal interests so many. I expect to see the same attendance when I pass a new edict regarding our Thenian brethren." The court murmured, but not loud enough to interrupt. Brier continued unfazed.

"As you know, I welcomed my first child, Ryanne Iines Snow, two months ago. I trust the rumors of her beauty have met your trained ears, and I assure you, she is every bit as stunning as they say." At this some of the Aurelians smiled, though most of them just looked miffed.

"To those of you who have sent your regards, I thank you. To those of you who have sent my daughter gifts, I am deeply moved by your generosity. However, for those who have chosen not to celebrate my daughter's birth, but to shun her, please know that your disdain does not go unnoticed."

Roland saw several of the Aurelians shift in their seats and heard faint coughs from the balcony.

"In the year since I have taken the throne, I have seen this court up in arms over the meager abetment given to the most destitute, to the most forlorn, to our citizens who need us the most. This year's crown coin has more than doubled, and yet some of you postulated Lirend's demise. Even if we did not see a gross return on our investment, I would continue to help the Prolit and Burges share in our wealth and prosperity. Today is not the time to outline our court's upcoming docket, but I will say again to those who wish to oppose me." Green eyes gazed at the courtroom of lavishly dressed nobles. "Your discord in this kingdom does not go unnoticed."

Roland stared at his lover awestruck. It had become a habit for him to lose himself in the king's eloquent speech. Brier turned toward him and gave him a sly wink before he pressed on.

"Now, in regards to my betrothal, I'd like to commend Lord Tamil for his employ. I know marriage between two men is not common in Lirend. Were it not for my dear advisor's persistence, I would not have had the courage to ask the love of my life for his hand."

As if on cue, Lord Tamil approached the king's throne. "Thank you for your praise." Lord Tamil feigned modesty. "That our kingdom is prosperous, that Princess Ryanne's legacy is ensured.... My only concern has ever been His Majesty and the Kingdom of Lirend."

"Of course." Brier nodded. "Ryanne's father and my concern has only ever been our daughter, and that will remain a constant. With that said, I apologize for any trouble my ambivalence has caused. The truth is, as much we all love Princess Ryanne, her birth was not planned. I can see where this might appear reckless to you all, but it was not my intention to have my first child unwed."

"Naturally." Lord Tamil bowed once more. "Circumstances being what they are, we understand, Your Majesty."

"Indeed. Circumstances as they were, Ryanne's father was not aware of my pregnancy, nor was he present during the first six months." Lord Tamil raised his bald head and flicked his eyes toward the prince.

"But my king, Prince Pascal has been here since the beginning."

"True, but Ryanne's father is not Prince Pascal." Lord Tamil's face turned a putrid shade of blue before he paled completely.

"Then who is the father?" he mumbled as if he hoped the king was playing an ill-intended joke.

"You remember Roland, don't you, Lord Tamil?" Roland felt a twinge of fear in his gut, but he stood next to Brier anyway to assert the claim. He was not going to let Brier bear the brunt of the court's disdain. "Ryanne's father is my guard."

It took several moments for the shock of Brier's words to disperse in the crowd. Whispers turned to loud imprecations, and Lord Tamil looked personally stricken. Prince Quintin met the questioning stares with a glare before Lord Tamil found his outrage.

"A mere palace guard?" Lord Tamil's voice rang out.

"A Thenian palace guard, from Aire," Brier corrected. "One who is to be my husband. So I suggest you watch your tongue, Lord Tamil."

"It is an insult to your father's name—"

"Oh, speak not to me of insults, Lord Tamil." Brier's tone grew harsh. "It was my father who indentured the Thenians into lifelong servitude."

"Your father built the wealth in this land!"

"On the back of the poor and downtrodden!" Brier stood and the room went silent. Roland held his breath as Brier regained his poise. "Despite this court's protest, I will marry Roland Archer at the first sign of spring."

"You cannot marry a Thenian!" Lord Tamil screamed.

"Lord Tamil is right." Roland watched the Prince of Menlor approach King Brier's throne. Quintin's usual springy voice had turned to ice. "You cannot marry that man."

"And why not?" Brier demanded.

"Because you cannot marry a man who is to be charged with treason and conspiracy," Quintin uttered clearly. Roland inhaled and tightened his jaw. If he had not seen the color drain from his lover's face, he would have thought he imagined the prince's words.

"What are you talking about?" Roland gritted through his teeth. He was not going to admit anything, lest he be tricked into revealing himself to Lirend's entire court.

"Oh, so you have not told your supposed fiancé about your past?" Quintin scoffed.

"I know about his past!" Brier spat. "You presume too little about our bond, just as you presumed too much of our own!"

"That may be," Quintin seethed from the king's snub. "But at least I am not a murderer."

"No." Brier's jaw tensed. "You are a coward to bring up the past with no just reason."

"There is a just reason!" Quintin yelled with his eyes flashing. "His entire village was decimated in Thenia under his order! He led his people to go up against the king to gain more riches, and they were exterminated like rats. Then when King Onas rose up against him, he killed him in his sleep like a true coward, King Brier!" Quintin shook his head in disgust. "And this is the man you choose to marry? One who would sacrifice his own for his own greed and ego? One who would kill his own family?" Roland lunged at Quintin but the waiting guards held him back. "Oh yes, Lord Roland, I have heard many tales. How you waited after your men fought and died to come and look upon their burning bodies. You are nothing more than a blackguard. I would die before I see Brier yours."

"If you continue to spout naught but lies, you will die here and now!" Roland howled. "I will have your tongue first and then your life!"

"A lie is it?" Quintin glared. "Then is it also a lie that you were contracted to kill the king of Lirend?"

Roland looked at Quintin with his eyes widened. All of a sudden, he felt as though a carriage had bowled him over and the blood drained from his face.

Not this way.

"It is a lie," Brier answered for him. "He was contracted, by Queen Evelyn, to teach me at my father's request."

The king turned toward him, and Roland stared at Brier helpless. He prayed to the gods.

Not this way.

"Tell him, Ronan," Brier whispered. "Tell him about you and the guild." Roland lowered his head, clenching his fist. He could not face the green eyes upon him.

Please.... Not this way.

"Brier...." Roland swallowed his shame. The thought of using Brier's trust to deceive him made Roland unable to sleep at night. And now the look in Brier's eyes... the confidence with which Brier spoke when he talked of Roland's loyalty. It made him sick to his stomach.

"Answer your king!" Quintin shouted madly. "Tell him how you conspired against him!"

"Ronan?" Brier's voice quivered.

Roland felt the tears well in his throat and he choked out a hallow reply. "Brinan… let me explain." He tried to reach out to Brier, but the man recoiled and the guards held Roland back.

"Explain?" Brier's voice trembled.

"We were offered, all of us, a chance to void our contract with the Aurelians. I—I admit that at first I considered it, but in the end I couldn't go through with it."

"So you were contracted to kill me?" Brier gaped at him with disbelief in his hard eyes. "How could you? How could you agree to kill someone you didn't even know, Ronan?"

"I—" Roland swallowed. "Brier—I was a broken man… after Helenas died, I had no reason to live. The queen knew about my past. That is why she chose me to train you."

"Now you will drag our queen into your blasphemous lies? Have you no honor?" Quintin handed Brier a tattered parchment. "It says he was to gain your trust and then use that to assassinate you! I wouldn't be surprised if they paid him to bed you as well! This was never about love!"

"That is a lie!" Roland yelled. "I cannot live without you! You and Ryanne are my heart! You know that, Brier!"

"Even… even if this letter were not true… why would you not tell me?" Brier's voice choked with the unshed tears. "Why wouldn't you trust my heart?"

"I should have told you—I wanted to tell you so many times!" Roland could feel the aged court walls crumbling around him. "If you only knew the guilt I felt, the guilt I still hold in my heart now!" His voice hushed to a whisper. "I was afraid that you would not… that you could not love me if you knew the truth. And then we found out about Ryanne."

Roland thought of his precious girl. Innocent Ryanne.

Afraid to lose her….

He raised his head and met Brier's wounded gaze.

Afraid to lose my king….

"I wanted to tell you… so many times, beloved. I swear to you, but I was afraid to lose you both!"

"You didn't trust me!" Brier hissed out, eyes flashing in anger. "You didn't love me enough to tell me the truth!"

"I tried!" Roland retorted. "I wanted to!"

"Wanted to what, Roland? To fuck me? To use me like everyone else? Is this why you had me?" Brier's face paled as he exhaled. "To… to make a fool of me?"

"Never!" Roland yelled. "When I took you to my bed, it was because I wanted you. I wanted you. Brinan I—"

"Enough!" Brier cut off his words. "Enough of this foolishness." The faint freckles on Brier's nose flared red before the king straightened his back. He stared at the letter with cold eyes.

"This. This is what me and your daughter are worth to you." Roland watched Brier crush the letter in his hands. "Then take your fee, Thenian." Brier threw the crunched paper at Roland's feet before the guards made their way through the crowd of nobles. "Escort him out of this courtroom."

"*Acai....*" Roland whispered harshly.

"Allow him to retrieve his things and...." Brier trailed as Roland spoke.

"You promised me, Brinan."

"And ride him to the gates."

"You promised you wouldn't leave me... *acai,*" Roland begged, but Brier ignored his desperate pleas.

"Make sure he does not step foot in this capital again."

"Ryanne!" Roland screamed. "Ryanne is my—!"

"Do not speak her name!" Brier whipped back to face Roland and his voice echoed in the great hall. "Don't you dare try to use her—" The king's breath hitched. "To justify your treachery!"

Roland's heart squeezed in his hollow chest. "*You and Ryanne are all I have,*" Roland whispered in Thenian. "*You can leave me, but that will not change the truth.*"

"*The truth means nothing to you,* Roland...."

"*You're right. I have no honor. No trust, even my heart is not my own,* Brinan." Roland bowed his head. "*It belongs to you. Will you take it?*"

Please.

"*I don't have anything else to give....*"

Please.

If Brier refused him, he would truly have nothing. It was the reason he'd come back and the reason he knew he could never leave again.

"*Acai.*"

Roland begged, but Brier's silence permeated. Then Brier's chest heaved, and he turned away.

"I'm sorry," he answered in the common tongue. "I can't." Brier cut through the guards barricading the stairs.

"Brier!" Roland cried. But the man did not stop to turn back this time.

"Brinan." Roland watched the love of his life slip through the whole of a stunned congregation.

CHAPTER 29
NAMESAKE

"BRIER!" THE name echoed in the corridor. Brier hurried down the hall with several guards buffering the crowd.

"My king!"

Brier did not know who called him, and he did not care. For now, he just needed to be alone.

"My king!"

Brier fought the tears that burned his eyes. Two corridors from his chamber. He just needed to hold on a little longer. Just a little more and he could succumb to the agony of his breaking heart. In a few seconds he could drown in his tears.

"Brier!" Someone gripped his wrist and he turned to yell, but the sound vanished when he saw Quintin's maddened glare. "Are you all right? Did they hurt you?" he asked, referring to the crowd.

"*Na*—I mean no." Brier shook his head. "I'm fine. I just want to get to my room." He tugged his wrist. "Release me, please."

"I will come with you."

"No." Brier feigned a smile. "I'm fine."

"You're not fine!" Quintin yelled. "Stop saying you're fine when you're clearly…." Quintin squeezed his palm. "Your hands are shaking."

Brier's smile faltered. "I'm just nervous." He tried to pull his hand away, but Quintin held him.

"Let go!" Brier tried to shove the man, but Quintin grabbed hold of his arm and dragged him into a stiff hug.

"Stop fighting," Quintin whispered in his ear. Brier blinked back the hot tears. "You don't have to pretend you're all right. It's okay to let it out." The hug sapped the last of Brier's power, and he slumped against Quintin's chest.

"Why?" Brier whispered as he clutched the gold trim of Quintin's jacket.

Why would Roland lie to him?

Betray him?

Use him?

"Why?" Brier cried out. "Why does it—" He wound his fingers in the back of the prince's jacket as the tears gushed. "Have to be this way?" He held tight to Quintin as he sobbed against the man. Brier's small frame shook until his legs gave way, and he fell to his knees. Quintin rubbed his head, not speaking a word, and Brier wept for his loss, as if the silence gave him permission to let go.

BRIER RAISED his knees to his chin and stared out the condensation-covered window. The tears dried by the time he entered Quintin's bedchamber hours ago. The snow dusted the windowsill, but Brier could not see beyond the haze of fog and darkness. When the sun set fully, Quintin tried to rouse him.

"You should eat something. It will make you feel better." Quintin offered him a tray of biscuits with the tea.

"No thank you." He did not want to think, or drink, or eat. He just wanted to sit here and revile his own folly.

"Your nursemaid asked for you. I told her you were resting."

"Thank you," Brier replied. "I don't want to see anyone right now."

"I understand." Quintin nodded. "Take as much time as you need. I'll tend to the others." He seated himself behind an oak desk at the corner of the room. Smaller than Brier's and of different wood, but of the same style. The parlor walls had fine linens draped over several couches, including the lounge Brier rested on. A giant crimson and orange rug covered the entire floor, while Quintin had repainted the walls a pale saffron. Unlike Brier's own suite, this room fit Quintin Pascal like a tailored glove.

"Something wrong?" Quintin's airy voice called. Brier shook his head before he smoothed his hand over the decorative throw pillow.

"This is the first time I've ever entered your suite," Brier replied.

"I took some liberty with the designs. I hope you don't mind."

"Not at all," he whispered. "It's lovely. I wish my own suite reflected my taste better."

"Interior reconstruction is sometimes a lost art, but I find that one's surroundings oftentimes dictate comfort." Quintin smiled.

"You have a knack for it."

"Thank you, Your Majesty."

"Please…." Brier lowered his head. "I know that you could not view me as a friend and mayhap we've lost the familiarity we once shared, but I would have you at least call me by my name." Quintin was a loyal advisor, but he didn't need an advisor. Right now he needed a friend.

"Brier…." Quintin stood. Brier watched the tall blond stride toward him. "I never stopped viewing you as a friend. It was for my own heart that I distanced myself from you. I can't pretend that I don't…." Quintin paused and sat beside him. "This may not be the right time to say this, but I never stopped loving you, Brier." Brier's heart raced, but he did not take his gaze off Quintin's pale blue eyes. "You can talk to me about anything, and I will listen."

The pain in his chest spread to form a tight knot of guilt in his stomach.

"Quintin…." The tears slid down to Brier's chin. "My heart hurts. It feels like someone has ripped a hole right through me." He held his chest. "I cannot understand how… why he would do such a thing." He scrunched his hands over the silk fabric. "Why?"

"I don't know," Quintin whispered. "That man is a fool for hurting you."

"He said that the queen knew about this, mayhap she—"

"Brier." Quintin squeezed his hand and exhaled. "Queen Evelyn is the one who told me about his treachery."

Brier's eyes went wide.

"The Ceve guild had a contract merely to teach you. But someone else hired Roland to kill you."

"Who?" Brier demanded.

"I'm not sure, Brier. I started investigating Roland when the queen revealed his past to me. She was worried for your safety."

"But she sent me to live with him!"

"Because she did not know his past then. The instant she heard about his involvement with the Thenian massacre, she sent Lord Tamil to retrieve you." Brier tightened his lip but did not reply. He did not need to tell Quintin how cruel his stepmother had been to him since his father's death. It was for nothing if the queen actually tried to protect him. "He killed an entire fleet of soldiers. Slaughtered the King of Thenia in his sleep! The man is a monster, Brier."

"Not to me," Brier refuted. "He's been with me this long and nothing has happened. Ryanne and I were alone with Roland in Balmur. And I was with him for almost a year in Aire. If he really wanted to kill me, he could have done so… more than once."

Quintin chose not to respond to this point of contingency. "The fact remains he bound himself to a contract to take your life! How can you still defend him?"

"Because I don't want to believe the father of my child is nothing more than a cold-blooded murderer!" The ire vanished from Quintin's eyes.

"Brier—"

"Please leave me, Quintin. I think I'll sleep after all." He turned from Quintin's gaze. Brier held the cushion against his chest and leaned his head against the arm of the chaise.

"I know right now it does not seem like it, but the gods have a journey for you, Brier."

"Don't speak to me about the gods. From my first breath they have scorned the very steps I take."

"Then perhaps this is a chance for you to walk down a different path… you and little Ryanne." Quintin covered Brier with a heavy leopard skin fur.

What now? Though he stared out the window his gaze was soft and unseeing.

A different path, Quintin had said, deviating from the one he knew and loved. Brier squeezed his eyes shut as the tears started to fall once more.

"WHAT ARE you doing here?"

"I need to speak with the king. Marietta told me he was here."

Brier's eyes fluttered open and he gazed through the darkness. The soft feather pillows and heavy quilt let him know he no longer slept on the lounge in Quintin's parlor. Curtains draped around the four-poster bed, but he could see a faint light coming from Quintin's bedecked parlor.

"Speak with him?" Quintin replied. "You will never see him again!"

"If he'd let me explain—"

"Explain what? You are an exile! Had King Brier not given his punishment, you would be sentenced and hung by the court!"

"He does not understand. It was before I ever met Brier that I considered the contract!"

"Stop these lies! Would that you find your wits and flee before the current ruler of Thenia hears of your capture. I personally will see to it that a bounty be set upon your head!"

"For what crime?" Roland demanded.

"For the crimes against Lirend's king and princess!" Brier stared at the shadows on Quintin's wall.

"The only crime I've committed is loving Brier! One that you would hang me for long before you found out about my past. I dishonored myself to protect him from the truth!" Brier clenched the blanket that covered him. "I love him, with everything in me. I never meant… to hurt him." Roland's desperate voice trembled.

"But you have hurt him! You publicly humiliated him in front of his court!"

"You were the one who humiliated Brier today, not me!"

"He suffers by your actions! He weeps now for his loss and for Ryanne's. That she will not know you!" Quintin countered. "Do not make him suffer for you any longer."

"Wish that I could make it so he never suffered."

"Then you should have never come back," Quintin told Roland. "I love Brier."

"I know you do, but Brier loves me."

"Does he love the real you who betrayed him?" Quintin challenged. "Or does he love a fanciful idea of you?" The tears oozed out of Brier's eyes. For all this time he'd idolized a man who did not exist. A lover who would never harm him, a strong master and honorable guild leader. All of it was a lie.

"I will take care of him," Quintin said.

"So he can fall in love with you?"

"If the gods will it," Quintin answered honestly. "If you never returned, we would have married by now. I would have loved Ryanne like she was my own. I do love her, like she is my own." The shadow shifted, and Roland pulled something from his bag.

"I need to see him. I have to give him something."

"If he sees you now it will only hurt him, Roland." There was a long pause then. Brier waited for Roland to refute Quintin, but the huntsman did not.

"Will you give this to him, then?"

"You dare ask me to—"

"Please. Just—just please give this to him. I will go without a fight if you do." The shadows moved again as Quintin took something from Brier's once lover.

"I will give it to him, but do not show your face here again," Quintin hissed. "Do not come back. Let him live his life. You owe him at least a chance at happiness."

Brier watched the shadow of his lover vanish from the wall, but he did not go after him. He waited for Quintin to check on him in bed, before the chamber door closed completely and he was left alone. Roland was gone, Quintin was gone, and there was nothing he wanted more than for this nightmare to end.

BRIER'S DAYS turned to weeks, until weeks passed by in obscurity. The news of Brier's affair spread through Avenough, from Aurelian to Burges to Prolit, and eventually into foreign lands. The Divine Three requested his presence at Zhennal's annual ball. The invitation was cordial, but Brier could tell the request was obligatory. They wanted to apperceive the political strength in Lirend. Two weeks after the missive, Brier arranged a meeting with Lord Tamil and Prince Quintin in order to assess the damage.

"Well, it's a disaster is what it is!" Lord Tamil paced Brier's parlor.

"We've surmised that much, Lord Tamil," Brier answered, annoyed at his advisor's pessimism. "I understand where we stand in the eyes of the Aurelians." Lord Renli made his point at Brier's announcement of his pregnancy and continued to unite the Aurelians against him. "But what of the Divine Three?"

"Our ambassadors tell us the news has traveled as far west as Ranolf's Wilshire. No threats to disrupt the trade lines, but I imagine they don't feel much confidence in the situation."

"Because Ryanne was born out of wedlock?"

"That, and her parentage. The Divine Three strictly adhere to their own blood. I've heard several of them married their own cousins in order to keep the lines pure. Not only would they assume discord in the royal line, but it is a disgrace to Lirend."

"What do you mean?" Quintin questioned. "King Snow has done nothing wrong. It is mere misfortune that he met the likes of Lord Roland."

"That he would be enticed by a man like that says enough!" Lord Tamil let slip. Quintin's eyes darted to Brier apologetically, but he did not let the cheek affect him. There were more important matters than Lord Tamil's prejudice.

"What news have you heard from Menlor, Prince Quintin?"

"No news, Your Majesty, only questions. For once the rumor mill does you a kindness. Aurelian gossip is so exaggerated, they cannot fathom the truth from fiction."

"What did they ask? Specifically?"

"Whether you are well. Reports say you fell ill after the court hearing since they've seen so little of you since then. They ask, of course, about this mysterious guard who was under your employment, and...." Quintin halted.

"And?"

"And of course they ask about Ryanne's blood. Whether or not she is a full Aurelian. I did not answer."

The room grew silent before Lord Tamil piped, "Well, it matters not whether you do or don't. Her parentage is known in the court. They will never let her take the throne."

"As if they had a say," Quintin growled. "Ryanne's father has naught to do with her sovereignty. She is still Brier's daughter and still a princess of Lirend!"

"And a blight of His Majesty's lust!" Brier's eyes widened when Quintin gripped the lord's robe and slammed him against the wall. Tamil shouted a curse before he raised his hands in surrender.

"Quintin." Brier stood and touched the prince's back gently. "It is all right, really." He was used to the ridicule. The bite no longer left a sting.

"You will not speak disagreeably about Brier or Ryanne in my presence. Do you understand?"

"The truth remains, Ryanne will never be accepted with that man as her sire and King Brier's name," Lord Tamil said coldly.

"And who is to say she will have my name?" Brier's voice rang through the air. The two men gazed at him and Brier arched his brow. "Do you two want to fight? Or to listen?"

Quintin released Lord Tamil with a shove and wiped his jacket as if to ward off a foul stench. Brier walked toward the bassinet adjacent to his desk.

"Perhaps Ryanne would not be allowed to rule under the name Snow, but if I married Prince Quintin, I would take the name Pascal." The revelation seemed to still the air. Lord Tamil's eyes flicked between Prince Quintin and Brier.

"I am no crown prince," Quintin replied softly.

"Aye, but should we marry, I would shed the name Snow and take your own. That would ensure the trade lines are still intact through my marriage to Menlor while cementing my power in Lirend. No one will doubt Ryanne's claim to the throne if we marry."

"Brier—" Quintin frowned. "You don't need to do this."

Brier stared, indifference spread through his fine features.

"Of course he does!" Lord Tamil cut in. "It would solve the problem completely. Prince Quintin, you are the son of King Bastian of Menlor. Brier can go to Zhennal's ball as your intended. Once Brier marries you, he will be entitled to your inheritance and name. Any children Brier and you have will be rightful rulers of Lirend."

Quintin continued to stare at Brier reproachfully.

"And when Ryanne is old enough, she could marry Prince Quintin's sister's son and become queen of Menlor."

"No." Brier interjected. "I won't sell my daughter to Menlor's royalty like my father tried to do to me. My marriage would be a political one, I will accept that, but I will not implicate my daughter." He stared at Ryanne in her bassinet. "She will be free to marry whomever she wishes. Is that understood?"

Lord Tamil opened his mouth to argue, but seemed to think better of it when Brier narrowed his gaze.

"Yes, Your Majesty. I'm sure the court would be more than pleased with that compromise."

"Good." Brier turned toward his daughter. "If that is all, I'll send Finnas with the remaining drafts later this evening."

Lord Tamil bowed. "Of course, Your Majesty." Brier heard the man shuffle out, and then just he and Quintin remained.

"Care to tell me exactly what you are doing?" Quintin questioned him with a hardened gaze. Ryanne began to whimper from obvious hunger, but he could not feed her in Quintin's presence.

"I am saving face," Brier answered briskly. He picked Ryanne up from her crib. The babe wobbled only slightly before holding her head steady.

"Saving your face from whom?" Quintin followed him across the parlor as Brier placed Ryanne in her swing to calm her. "Or from what, I should say?"

"Not my own." Brier began to unbutton his suede jerkin. "My daughter's," he told Quintin, not looking up at him. "She is all that matters now."

"But to agree to marriage…." Quintin trailed.

"Is it so reckless?"

"You once said that you would not marry for politics. Am I to assume you've changed your mind?"

Brier paused at the string of his tunic and peered up to see Quintin's apprehension. "I allowed myself to believe that a marriage for love meant more, but in actuality, it is all the same."

"It is not the same," Quintin argued. "In the first place, a marriage for love means that you love the person and not just the idea of marriage."

"I don't have time for semantics." Brier pursed his lips. "Ryanne is my concern right now. Her future is all that matters to me."

"And what of your future, King Brier? Will you go on living this jaded existence?"

"If it will protect my daughter's future? Yes." Then Brier thought of the bronze-tinged man, and he felt a pang of regret. A future without Roland meant a future where Ryanne did not have a father. She would never know the way he spoiled her or the way he kissed her forehead when she slept. "I will do anything to protect her, including marry. Will you help me or not?" Brier asked simply.

The prince inhaled slowly before he let out a shaky breath. "You would all but marry a stranger, and you think that would appeal to me? If a loveless marriage is what you seek, then I cannot help you."

"Certainly, you are more than a stranger to me." He gazed into the man's honest eyes. "I hope I am more to you, than that."

"More to me than—" Quintin sighed and shook his head. "You are the most important person in my life."

"Then help me, please. This is the only way I know how to protect my daughter."

Quintin's jaw tensed.

"Please?" Brier repeated. Once again he needed Quintin.

Brier watched Quintin's eyes shift before he sighed and shook his head. "All right."

"All right?" Brier asked.

"All right," Quintin repeated. "I will do it."

"Thank you, Quintin." Brier smiled softly.

"I am not doing it for you. I am doing it for myself. This whole mess is in no small part due to my own actions. Of course I want Ryanne to be safe, and for her future to be secure. And beyond that… beyond that…."

"Beyond that?" Brier tilted his head. Quintin leaned in slowly and gave him a gradual kiss. "Quin…." Smooth hands raised to stroke his cheek. Brier pushed Quintin's chest to pause his lips, but Quintin leaned in farther and licked the tip of his timid tongue. The spark fizzled to a burnt end. He could not refuse a simple kiss from his betrothed. This was his life now. Brier closed his eyes to numb his apprehension, and he wondered whether he would ever feel pleasure from a kiss again.

CHAPTER 30
NEW PATH

THE CARRIAGE bounced down the cracked pavement and caused Ryanne to jostle in Brier's arms. After the late winter storm that hit the south of Lirend, the delicate roads farther south still needed mending. He worried the child would fuss over the bumpiness of their journey to Balmur, but she only laughed when the carriage hiccupped over dents in the earth.

"I do believe she's enjoying this," Quintin said, slightly pale in the face. Brier chuckled and nodded.

"She is a daredevil, most certainly. She already walks unassisted. Marietta says she is advanced, but I think she is more interested in exploring."

"You can certainly reach higher on two legs than four," Quintin noted.

"Exactly." Brier laughed again. "It is all to cause more mischief."

Quintin's laughter made Brier grin. "Mischievous and beautiful. A blight on us when she is old enough to court."

"The only blight will be on whomever she fancies, I would wager." Brier kissed the top of the girl's black hair. She was like her sire in color, but like Brier in every other way: small pointed nose with an angular jaw and round green eyes that outshone the brightest colur gem. She laughed when they rolled over another bump, but Quintin held the hanging lever.

"Mayhap she is old enough to try on a horse?" Brier pondered. "Not a full grown one of course. A little pony perhaps."

"Perhaps," Quintin answered. "But do you think she might be a little young?"

"I don't think so." Brier shook his head. "Like in Menlor you sail early, we in Lirend ride before our third year."

"Yes, and Ryanne is nigh one."

"Yes, but Marietta did say she was advanced."

"Of course." Quintin smiled at Brier's gentle boast.

"We can buy her a pony and keep it at the stables in Balmur."

"All right, but that means you'll have to visit this estate more." Quintin exhaled in relief when the carriage finally stopped.

Brier did not reply verbally, but he nodded as he gathered Ryanne's day bag. He'd avoided his estate in Balmur as much as possible since the last time he'd visited with Roland. If he needed to see to a maintenance issue, he sent Finnas, and if he had no choice but to tend to matters himself, he made a round trip.

The late summer heat lashed against them until they stepped into the shade of the willows just outside the villa's keep. Although the huntsman had vanished, Roland's print still lingered in this house. The stone the man laid fared well against the elements. The open plains with the backdrop of the summer sun looked as beautiful as they'd projected. Ryanne squirmed in his arms to get down and explore her new surroundings, but Brier held her firmly until they reached the double oak doors.

"Mmh!" His daughter whined and babbled.

"Let her down before she starts howling," Quintin told him under the cover from the hot sun. He pulled a handkerchief from his jacket to wipe the sweat on his brow. Ryanne's outbursts were more from frustration than hunger these days, but she could belt out a cringeworthy wail.

"If she does actually howl one day, perhaps we could put her in the capital square for show?" Brier teased. He barely had time to take her hat before the girl tottered out of his arms.

"Heh—we would lose her in the crowd." Brier heard Quintin say before Ryanne squealed from something she'd found.

"Not with a firm leash," Brier called to him.

"Between Victoria and Marietta, they would beat us both black and blue."

Brier laughed. It was true. Ryanne captivated any in her presence, and she did not insist on the coddling those who knew her bestowed. Her open smile and rambunctious nature made others cheerful. Even the sourest-faced Aurelian could not tame her spirit.

"Mama and Papa will love her too." Quintin bent down and kissed Ryanne's cheek gently. "And they'll be thrilled to have her at the palace when we visit after the wedding."

"Don't you mean thrilled to have their prince back?" Brier quirked his brow.

"Thrilled to have me, of course," Quintin admitted, unabashed. "But eager to meet you after I've boasted of your fairness against the whole of Menlor."

"You did not."

"Of course I did." Quintin smirked. "You should know by now that I am a vulgar man at heart, Brier. When I have something of value, I feel an urge to show it off." Quintin kissed his cheek this time, and Brier's face warmed. Despite his cavalier charm, Quintin always made Brier feel special.

They spent the day mostly in the garden watching the waterfall from the wooden beams overhead. In the spring the water would overflow and drain into a well Roland had installed underground. That water was used as storage reserve for irrigation in such an isolated area. As long as the servants ran the water frequently in the winter, the pipes would not freeze. As for the open fields, they tended themselves. Now that the summer had begun, Brier could see the wildflowers, green hills, bloomed peonies, and trimmed shrubs. Even the palace servants bickered over who should be in charge of the king's illustrious Balmur estate.

"You know this garden reminds me of the palace garden," Quintin mused.

"That does not surprise me." Brier watched Ryanne's eyes following a butterfly. "Since I planted this garden in the spring before the earth thawed."

"I see, so you have a green thumb."

"Hmm. More... I enjoy the gentle quietness." He remembered his days as a child in the gardens alone. He'd sing to the lapwings and the butterflies who accompanied him.

"Yes. I find that you are most peaceful in the midst of green things."

"You do?" Brier blinked.

"My room overlooks your garden. I have seen you many times...." Quintin chuckled, and Brier squirmed uncomfortably. He did not realize he'd exposed himself so unknowingly. "Though I must say, it is a pitiable act to just watch forever. One day I hope to have a place amongst your garden. To have more than your friendship."

Brier was glad when Ryanne stomped over to show them a mature dandelion she'd pulled from the earth.

"Mm!" The girl thrust the flower in Brier's face to inspect.

"That is a wishing flower, my love. You put your lips together and blow it to make a wish." The girl stared at him, confused until he searched for another to show her. "Look, Ryanne." He pursed his lips before blowing, and the pods fluttered in the air between them.

"Ahhh!" The girl's eyes went as wide as her grin. She immediately pursed his lips to try, but blew more drool than air.

Brier burst out laughing as his daughter searched for more dandelions to blow. He laughed so hard his cheeks hurt when he finally stopped and caught Quintin's quiet stare.

They ate a light dinner of fish and dried tomatoes on the patio, and by the time evening settled, Ryanne had tired herself to sleep. Brier wanted to go back to the palace, but Quintin insisted they stay at least for one night. Though the ride to Avenough was not overlong, the trip to Balmur rattled them. Brier couldn't expect a tired child to fare well in the back of a carriage, and so he agreed to spend the night in Balmur. His first night since his holiday with Roland.

He and Quintin shared a guest bedroom away from the main suite. Ryanne's room had long since transferred to one of the main bedrooms as opposed to the nursery adjacent to the master suite. That room held too many memories. Too many promises even. Mayhap Brier subconsciously thought sleeping there would taint whatever happiness he once shared with his erstwhile lover. Nevertheless, Brier laid his sleeping daughter to rest and shared a room with Prince Quintin Pascal for the first time.

"Wish that I'd brought my own day bag," He joked as he stepped out of the bath. "The summer's heat is brutal in Balmur."

"Indeed. By midday I long for the cool of the palace." Brier's eyes followed the shirtless prince.

"Yes, but not Lord Tamil." Quintin chuckled.

"Certainly not." Brier echoed Quintin's laughter. "Although if I recall, you are the one who incensed him in regards to our marriage."

"Had I known how hounding a man could be, I certainly would not have. He behaves more like my nagging wife than your chief advisor."

"He would be flattered, I think, that you called him your wife." Brier smirked.

"Ha-ha." Quintin crossed his arms. "And what have I done to deserve that punishment I wonder?"

Brier's head fell against the satin-cased pillows as he howled with laughter. Quintin's smile faltered before he uncrossed his arms slowly. Brier noticed the pause, and he peered up at Quintin's bare chest. "What's wrong?"

"Nothing." Quintin beamed. "It's just good to hear you laugh again." Brier stared mute before Quintin's gaze grew too intense and he cut his gaze away.

Quintin moved to Brier's wardrobe where he took his pick of unworn trousers. Brier gazed at Quintin's angular back and the low dip of his buttocks until his face flushed when he recalled the prince caught him staring at the king of Nieraeth's bum.

"Do they look okay?" Brier jerked his head up.

"Excuse me?" Brier stammered.

"The pants," Quintin replied with a frown. "Do the pants look all right?"

"Oh." Brier nodded. The pants Quintin wore were high knickers, which hid the short length. "Yes, fine." All day Brier sensed a strange energy emanating from Quintin. Not intimidating, but still primal. Or perhaps that was his own body adjusting. Ryanne nursed less and ate more from the table. The milk, which once leaked, now engorged his chest, and the scars on his skin lightened. Meade assured him that it was only his body regulating after having his first child, but Brier's uneasiness remained.

"Are you all right?" Quintin sat near him on the edge of the bed. Brier's heart raced as the weight shifted.

"Aye, I mean yes, I'm just… a little warm I think." A partial lie. He'd just gotten out of the bath and the stone walls kept the villa cool. However, Brier did feel heated, especially when Quintin sat so close to him.

"Yeah." Brier gasped when Quintin held his chin. "Your face is all red." Quintin licked his lips, and Brier inhaled before the man's tongue met his own. With Roland, the kisses were hard and passionate, burning Brier internally. However, Quintin's kisses tingled on the surface of his skin like a feather.

Brier squirmed at the slick tongue caressing him. He slid his hand down Quintin's lean chest and over his hard nipple. Unlike Roland's definitive lines and olive skin, Quintin's complexion was like warm cream.

Am I doing this?

Quintin pushed the center of his chest into the mattress.

I haven't prepared for this.

Of course eventually he would consummate their marriage, but right now?

In this house where I….

Quintin broke the kiss, and Brier could feel his eyes on him.

"Are you okay?" Quintin whispered. Brier peered upward, apprehension overflowing. "You're shaking."

"I'm sorry." Brier held Quintin's biceps. "I'm trying, but I don't know if I can do this. I haven't prepared, and it's been a while since I've done something like this."

"Perhaps this will work better if I yield to you?"

"Yield to me?" Brier raised his brow.

"Yes, Brier. There is more than one way to couple with a man." Quintin's hand skated down Brier's chest. Long thin fingers gripped his bulge through his fitted trousers. "This is for more than just show, Your Majesty."

"I know that," Brier mumbled, but his cheeks flared crimson. Roland was the only man he'd ever known. He and Leighis only ever discussed the idea of lovers switching positions.

"Then?" Quintin straddled him. Light kisses heated, then cooled over the skin on Brier's neck and collarbone.

Then what? Brier thought as Quintin's tongue slid southward. Brier's toes curled as Quintin lifted his shirt and exposed the marks hidden on the sides of his abdomen. He prayed to the gods they did not glow gold this night. Brier felt a pause when Quintin reached the vertical scar on his stomach from Ryanne's birth, and he reached down to hold the prince's head.

"You don't have to. I know it's not pretty."

Quintin gripped his wrist and stared at him. "What's not pretty?" His tongue skated down the heinous-looking scar, and Brier shuddered. "You're exquisite." Quintin's fingertips dug into his sides to slide his undergarment and trousers down. As always everything felt fast-paced with this man. Before Brier could think, his member throbbed from the attention. His head filled with doubts, but Quintin's tongue reassured him.

It's all right, Brier thought as Quintin palmed his stiff flesh. Heat coiled around the tip of Brier's member as the hand stroked him to hardness.

It's all right.

Quintin nuzzled the crimson fuzz between the base of his shaft and thighs.

"Haah!" Brier shivered as the heated breath made his sac tighten on Quintin's chin. He closed his eyes to relax, but that only made his muscles tense under Quintin's ministration.

"Brier." Quintin kissed the tip of his stiff rod and Brier swallowed the urge to stop him. "I promise, I'll make you feel good." How could he give in when right now all he could think of was Roland? How the man devoured his aching hardness. How his lover unraveled him inside and out. How the huntsman's hunger drove him to writhing ecstasy. "It's all right, just relax." But the affirmation did not soothe the disquiet in his heart.

"Quintin…." Brier gripped his shoulder. "I can't do this."

Quintin's eyes drooped before he glanced upward. "Because of him?"

Brier pressed his lips together.

Never take a man you do not love, Leighis's words rang. Brier could not understand the wisdom of Leighis's words then, but now they epitomized his current situation.

"I'm sorry."

"Please. Don't apologize, Brier." Quintin slid his knee off the bed and stood. "It doesn't make me feel better."

"It wouldn't be… right for me to do this right now."

"I get it," Quintin answered pulling over his tunic. "You can't fuck me because you love him."

"I won't fuck you because you deserve more than that!" Brier spat. Quintin scoffed before he gathered the rest of his clothes.

"Don't tell me what I deserve while you long for him, okay? Stop pretending to protect me, when we both know the reason you're rejecting me." His boots stomped over the hardwood toward the door. It wasn't as if he did not want Quintin physically, but how could he make love to one man when his heart belonged to another?

"Quintin." The prince paused on the door handle. "If you just give me time, I—" Brier clenched the silk on the duvet. "I'm trying… all right?"

"Well, you're not trying hard enough."

Brier opened his mouth to speak, but the door slammed before he could finish.

The next morning when he woke, Quintin had already prepared them breakfast in the dining room. Ryanne babbled her way through the meal, but the two men remained silent.

"Mmh!" The girl demanded off Brier's lap once she'd had her fill.

"All right, Ryanne." He sighed out as she squirmed out of his hands and half crawled, half ran out of the dining room.

"At least she is in a good mood," Quintin remarked as the child disappeared.

"Heh—it would take more than awkward silence to dampen Ryanne's spirit." Quintin chuckled at the joke before the room went still once more. Brier felt like Ryanne, about to fidget in his seat, when Quintin finally spoke.

"I'm sorry about last night," Quintin said ruefully. His tone made Brier squirm after all. "I acted like an ass. My behavior was completely uncalled for."

"No." Brier shook his head. "I shouldn't have pushed you away."

"You had every right to push me away." Brier looked up and Quintin gazed intently. "You're not ready. I understand that. It's just…." Quintin exhaled. "I love you, Brier. Wish that I could make you understand that better without cumbersome words."

"I do understand, Quintin," Brier whispered. "I—" Ryanne collapsed onto the ground. "Ryanne!" Brier called, but the girl struggled to her feet and disappeared into the kitchen once more.

"That child is tougher than me." Quintin frowned, and Brier laughed out.

"Honestly, I think she's tougher than both of us. Certainly more independent."

"I'm not too proud to admit that. I know it's hard to imagine, but I was a spoiled child. I spent my youth attached to my mother's hip."

Brier snorted. It was not hard to imagine the curly-headed youth clutching his mother's leg at all. "I probably would have been the same if my mother had not passed."

"Oh, yes." Quintin frowned. "I'd forgotten."

"It is all right, really. Marietta cared for me and raised me like her own."

"And she did a fine job."

"*That* is a matter of opinion. But I am blessed to have her, and Ryanne. Even when I am busy in court or dealing with crown matters, Ryanne finds her own way."

"Be grateful that you do not have a needy child." Quintin smirked. "Only a needy man."

"I am." Brier chuckled as he shook his head. "Honestly, who needs a son when Ryanne is more resilient than half of the lot her age?"

"A son?" Quintin blinked.

"Aye. Lord Tamil keeps going on about having a son just in case Ryanne marries into royalty. I think he still holds hope for your sister's son."

"I see." Quintin nodded slowly.

"It isn't as if I should have more children anytime soon. Meade would have my hide if I even thought about it."

"But you do want them?" Quintin asked suddenly. "That is to say, you want to have my children? Eventually?" He gazed at Brier expectantly as he mulled the idea over in his head. He always wanted more children with Roland, but Quintin was now his future. At some point he needed to accept that… right? Brier opened his mouth to speak when he heard a loud thud and then a crash from the kitchen. His chair scraped as he stood and called his daughter's name.

"Ryanne!" She came into the view from the parlor and stood before her father proudly. "Quintin, go see what's broken please," Brier said before he checked Ryanne for bruises. "By the gods," he said when he realized the child was uninjured. She twisted in his arms, but he refused to let her go as he walked toward the kitchen.

"Looks like a vase fell over." Quintin searched for the broom. "Best keep her out of here."

"Be careful with the glass. Don't cut yourself." Brier saw the glass and wildflowers littered on the slate tile floor. "How did it fall?"

"Probably just the wind." Quintin swept up the shards. "One of the servants left the window open maybe?" But Brier was sure that all the windows were sealed shut when they'd arrived. He followed the trail of water from the vase, which led to the wide open window.

"Someone was here." He clutched Ryanne closer to his hip before Quintin stood.

"How do you figure that?" He emptied the glass into a tin pail.

"The windows weren't open yesterday, Quintin."

"The servants this morning?"

"Are directed not to leave the windows open."

"Servants make mistakes, Brier," Quintin replied. He wrapped his hands around Brier to console him.

"That vase had a silver base," Brier added.

"I know. I gave it to you, remember?" Quintin kissed his forehead.

"A very heavy thing to suddenly fall."

"Perhaps Ryanne bumped into the counter."

"She was in the parlor when it fell."

"Well, then I default again to the wind." Quintin smiled and Brier pouted. "Do not worry overmuch, Brier. When we get back to Avenough, I'll tell Captain Galer to have guards stationed here while we're away. We should do that anyway since we'll be in Menlor for quite some time after the wedding. Then you two are all mine." Quintin nosed Ryanne's fingers. "Isn't that right, Ryanne?"

"*Aida*!" The girl pointed at the window with her lips pursed. Brier's ears perked at the Thenian tongue.

"Ha-ha!" Quintin chuckled, delighted at Ryanne's first word. "What did you say?"

"*Aida*! *Aida*!" she repeated.

"*Aida*?" The realization finally dawned on him. "I thought you said that she would call you Papa. Did you teach her *aida* then too?"

"I never taught her that," Brier said quietly and continued to stare out the open window as if he'd see something, or rather someone, appear from nothing.

Ryanne recited her first word till the carriage arrived, then as the footmen loaded the car, and then as they bid farewell to the Balmur estate. It would not concern Brier so much if the girl did not point insistently as if she knew something he did not.

Quintin must have noticed his uneasiness because the man held his thigh and said, "Don't worry, Brier. She probably picked it up from one of the servants." But Brier knew there were no Thenian servants employed in the palace. "She'll tire of it when she learns a new word to replace it."

"Of course." Brier tried to smile. He held Ryanne in his arms as he stepped out of the carriage with Quintin's shoulder for leverage.

"*Aida*!" Ryanne shouted.

"This is your Papa, Ryanne." Quintin pointed to Brier. "Papa." Ryanne ogled at Quintin's lips. "And I'm…." Quintin glanced at him. "I'm…."

Brier leaned in and kissed Quintin's chin. "You are my future husband," he whispered.

"Trying to pacify me, King Brier?" Quintin murmured.

"Of course," Brier answered as they continued to walk toward the atrium. "Though I suppose if we're to have more, they would call you Papa." He took hold of Quintin's thin fingers and held them tightly. Despite his feelings for Roland, he wanted the happiness Quintin could possibly give him. They entered the atrium, all three of them together, and Brier made a quiet promise to himself. He was going to make this work, not only for Quintin who'd given his all, but also for himself. And for Ryanne.

CHAPTER 31
UNREST

ALTHOUGH ROLAND spent his spring in Aire with Veti, he could not stay away from his lover. He thought to hide out in Avenough, but the risk was too high. The only other place he could think to catch a glimpse of Brier was a place he knew only they two shared. The villa where they lived their fairy-tale life.

Over the past months, he came to Balmur without warning but only encountered Brier twice. Once when Brier rode Frieling past the villa and up to the edge of the forest. The second time when he came to check on a hiccup with the villa's irrigation system. This time, though, Roland recognized the royal carriage at the front gate immediately. Had Brier come to spend the night? Roland slipped inside the patio door quietly. Perhaps if Brier was alone, he could finally have a chance to talk to him. To try to explain everything clearly without the hundreds of onlookers. To apologize or beg or whatever he needed to do to make things right.

"I love you, Brier. Wish that I could make you understand that better without cumbersome words."

Roland paused at Quintin's lofty voice. He could hear Brier's voice, but could not make out the muffled reply.

A sharp thud hit the alderwood floors, and Roland hid behind a pillar.

"Ryanne!"

Hollow footsteps pattered toward him, and his heart stopped. A child close to age one stood in front of him. She was Brier's likeness, but with his own bronze-tinged skin and wavy black hair. Roland held his mouth so he would not shout and scare the babe.

"Ryanne…." His voice went hoarse as he spoke. The girl stared at him unsure before he knelt down to her height. "*Cormin ele aida.*" The words babbled out. "Come, Ryanne. Come to *Aida*." Roland waved his hand to the girl, and she tilted her head. Then Roland held out his arms, and the babe's tentative walk became a full run into his arms.

"*Aida*!"

"Aye, Ryanne. *Aida*." The tears pricked the crease of his eyes, and Roland hugged her. He hugged her so tight he did not think he would be able to let go. "It's me, *Aida*," he whispered, kissing the girl's cheek and forehead, remembering the feel of his daughter in his arms and her smell, and her beautiful voice, and her soft hair, and the brilliant green of her eyes. "*Aida*," he told Ryanne, smiling through the tears.

His daughter squirmed in his arms at Brier's voice, and Roland released her.

"Who needs a son when Ryanne is more resilient than half of the lot her age?"

"A son?" Quintin questioned as Roland stepped closer to listen.

"Aye. Lord Tamil keeps going on about having a son just in case Ryanne marries into royalty. I think he still holds hope for your sister's son."

"I see...."

"It isn't as if I should have more children anytime soon. Meade would have my hide if I even thought about it."

"But you do want them?"

Roland felt his heart stop for the second time. He knew Brier wanted more children, but he never considered he'd have Quintin's children. Despite what had happened between them, Brier was his and only his. It didn't matter who he lay with; the king's heart belonged to him.

Right?

"That is to say, you want to have my children? Eventually?"

Of course... if they get married... then of course Brier would....

Roland slammed his hand on the counter and the glass vase wobbled and broke.

"Ryanne!" Brier yelled.

Roland climbed on the counter and jumped out of the alcove window into the garden below.

"How did it fall?"

"Probably just the wind. One of the servants left the window open maybe?"

"Someone was here."

Roland listened to the men's gentle squabble. Quintin tried to assuage Brier, but Roland noted the impatience in the king's voice.

"*Aida*!" Roland heard the child exclaim. He covered his mouth to stifle the chuckle and leaned his head against the wall. Roland heard Quintin's voice trail as they entered the atrium.

"Did you get everything you need, love? Lady Y'vette invited us to dine with her tonight."

"I have everything. Do we have time to lay Ryanne down for a nap?"

His lover.

"I think so."

His daughter.

"And if she sleeps past the time just let her...."

That man.

Roland watched the golden wheels pull through the gates and out on the main road. He stared down at the hand that'd held his daughter. How could he hold on to this feeling before it disappeared again?

THE COLD ale slid down his throat and settled in his belly. Ryanne had grown so big without him there. He'd thought they needed him, but the truth was they didn't. If he let them live without him and stayed away as Quintin had said, perhaps they could find true happiness.

He'd agreed to meet Lei at Draughons Inn, but regretted his decision. It was the closest place for a drink, just outside Avenough's keep, and he knew they accepted Thenians with no questions asked, but the longer he thought of his loss, the more his heart stung.

"How much for the liter?" Perhaps he could catch Lei and pitch a tent outside of the keep.

"For the king's wedding week, all drinks are half."

"The king's wedding week?" Roland's voice cracked.

"Aye, he'll be married in five days. And more than that, he's marrying some hoity-toity prince from Menlor. Twiggy blond fellow," the bartender answered matter-of-factly. "That country's huge, and they've got tons of money. The inns in the city are packed with visitors coming off ships by the dozens." Roland nodded slowly. He'd known they were due to wed, but not so soon. "Then of course you've got the looky-loos, just trying to catch a glimpse of the royal family. Been strange rumors floating around the whole business of the king's conception. Stranger than the whole bit of him being pregnant in the first place." The bartender laughed and Roland cringed at his toothless smile.

"Rumors like what?" Roland could not help but ask.

"Some say the prince isn't Princess Ryanne's father."

"Who says that?" Roland asked quietly though his heart banged in his chest.

"I don't know much on it, but from what I heard, the king lay with two men around the same time. One of them was his guard, big burly fellow, 'bout your size actually. Then when the truth came out, the guard had to flee so the prince would spare his hide. Rumor has it the babe is the guard's bastard, doesn't belong to the prince. She does favor our king, but her coloring is a bit different. I heard the queen was furious. Sent out a manhunt for the guard and everything." Roland did not reply but stared at the clear liquid in his glass feeling sick.

"But of course," the bartender said, noticing the expression Roland wore. "All this is just hearsay and rumors. No one knows what drove out the guard. Could have been a conspiracy or such. The king has a good head. Why, things haven't been so good since King Braedon Snow was alive. I thought it odd. First the whole queerness of men with men, and then the whole business of baby carrying. It worried me, figured people might see a small little country like ours and be on the warpath. But it looks like he's managed to snag himself a royal of Menlor and like I said, they're no country to have a go at."

Right. Brier marrying Quintin would unite two kingdoms with status equal to the Divine Three. Where Lirend had the money and Menlor had a modest army.

"Another one," Roland called, but the bartender had taken his silence for disinterest and moved to the other end of the bar.

Married in a week's time. Roland cursed under his breath. The worst part was that he could blame no one but himself.

"Ronan." Roland felt a hand clasp on the back of his shoulder.

"Lei." He smiled and pulled the silver-haired man into a stiff hug. "*Venur*," Roland whispered in his ear. They moved to a smaller table in the corner of the pub where they could not be easily overheard, and he explained to Lei what happened at the villa in Balmur. Lei gazed at him with pity before Roland sighed and shook his head.

"Maybe I should truly disappear," Roland thought aloud. "They seemed happy without me."

"And give up on your daughter? No, Ronan. That is exactly what they want you to do!"

"It doesn't matter, Lei. Even if Brier would have me, I still have Thenian blood in my veins."

"And so does your child," Lei argued.

"Aye, and that is already causing problems for her."

"It is not our blood, but the Aurelians who cause the problems! Had it not been for that prince's spite, this would have never happened to you!"

"They are not all bad." Roland's time in Avenough had given him the opportunity to meet noble lords and ladies who actually campaigned for the rights of his people. Lord Yaris, Meade, even Brier's father, in his misguided altruism, tried to help them.

"How can you say that when your blood forbids you to be with your own *baim*?"

Because Roland knew the cause of his ruin. It was his own dishonesty. His fear. His lack of trust in the only man who'd loved him despite his past. Despite everything. Roland stared at Lei, pensive in his thoughts.

"We shed our contract on paper, but we cannot escape the chains of Aurelian rule. It does not matter what we do," Lei whispered bitterly. Roland cast Leighis a concerned look.

"Of course it matters what we do, Leinan. Not for ourselves, but for the future generations. If not for me, for the sake of my daughter—"

"So she can be a plaything for the Aurelians as well?"

"Brier would never allow that," Roland whispered.

"As if he had a choice," Lei scoffed.

"He is the king." Roland gazed hard at Lei. "Of course he has a choice."

"Then why does he not free us all?" Lei demanded. "Why has he forsaken us out of his own resentment?"

"I told you. The whole of the Aurelian Quad was there when he revealed me as Ryanne's father. They saw what they believe is a betrayal of their king, by a Thenian man. They think I tried to kill the king of Lirend. Can you not see how bound his hands are?"

"I see only an accomplice in the tyranny that binds us! We cannot have families without fear they will be drafted for the Aurelians' petty tasks. They use us as whores and servants. We cannot marry freely or have any say in the rulings that affect our lives. Even now, we are shrouded in the darkness while their people continue to prosper. He has helped the Prolit and the Burges, but they refuse to help us because we are beneath them. When does it end? When do we say 'no more'?"

Roland's eyes widened at Lei's words. "You're starting to sound like Botcht, Leighis."

"I'm starting to think that's not such a bad thing." Lei downed the rest of his ale, and Roland gazed at him worriedly. He'd never heard his best friend speak of the Aurelians with so much malice.

"Botcht's message has not changed. He calls for unrest in the home we've lived in for years."

"He's tired, Rolande," Leighis whispered. "And by the gods, I'm tired of it too."

"Aye, we're all tired," Roland countered. "There are problems in Lirend, I will admit that. But a revolution? Our men will die by the hundreds."

"When we stand together as a unified group, they cannot match our skills and strength. Why think you they ambushed us like cowards that day? Used trickery and deceit to conquer us!" Lei clenched his jaw. "We were too few when we came here from Thenia. Too scattered and weary. But Botcht's message has spread through Aire. Even the outlanders have joined him for the fight."

"Even then we—" But Roland paused as Lei's words clicked into place. "What do you mean, joined him for the fight?" Lei tried to turn away, but Roland probed his pale eyes. "Tell me, Leighis."

"They're going to seize the palace," Lei muttered.

"What?" Roland exclaimed. He cut his eye to several of the patrons who looked over when he yelled. "What?" Roland hushed his tone. "How? When?"

"On the king's wedding day. Botcht already assembled them, Rolande. You can't stop it."

"I can and will stop it!" Roland whispered harshly. "Is this Botcht's plan? To have our people slaughtered like beasts?"

"He's making our people finally defend themselves!"

"And sentencing them to death," Roland gritted through his teeth.

"Like they did us?" Lei stared at him assuredly before Roland narrowed his eyes.

"My daughter is in that palace, Leighis. My child is in danger because you and Botcht choose to cling to this grudge against the Aurelians, and for what? Where has the hatred led us?" Roland yanked his traveling cloak and stood from the table.

"Where are you going?" Lei demanded.

"To find Botcht." Roland had to strain not to shout. "To put an end to this—this foolishness."

"There's no use trying to talk him out of it.... He won't listen."

"Then I'll stop him dead on!" Roland yelled again. The barkeep glared at him and Roland stormed away to head toward the exit. He only got a few paces from the inn before Lei called to him.

"Ronan. Wait!" But Roland did not pause in his step. When Lei reached him, he was out of breath. The heat from the sun bore down on the man's face, blotching his pale skin.

"I don't want our people to die," Lei panted. "You are right in all that you've said, but I don't know if he will listen. He and Caite." Leighis shook his head. "He and Caite have it in their minds that the crown is their enemy." That didn't surprise Roland in the least. Both of the men harbored animosity toward Aurelians, understandably so. But warranted or not, Roland refused to let them harm Ryanne and Brier.

"This isn't Brinan's fault, Leighis. Our struggle spans back before the king was even old enough to know our plight. Now that he does, he has sworn to help us. Brier will not go back on his word. Trust me." He reached over to hold Lei's shoulder. "Help him. Help me stop this before it begins."

"I'll do what I can to sway Botcht. In the meantime, you stay on the border. They'll be coming from the west, Ronan."

"Through the mountains?"

"Aye. They plan to go through the border towards Sasel and come in from there."

"How many?"

"I can't say for certain. Botcht seems confident, though. Enough to seize the palace, I know that much." Roland nodded firmly before Leighis bowed to him.

"You are like a brother to me. I don't want your daughter to die in this fight."

"Then help me save her." Roland stood Lei upright. "Convince Botcht to stop this madness."

"I will try. You have my word." Lei extended his hand to shake, and Roland pulled him into a hug. "*Te'na an'*, Rolande."

"Till then, my brother."

CHAPTER 32
BINDING

BRIER WOKE on his wedding day with a strange foreboding in his heart. Marietta pecked him ragged with the preparations for the event, but he felt disquiet as he rose from his canopy. Before Ryanne's howling cries could stop him, he stepped toward the full-length mirror and assessed himself. He'd had a child but for an accident of his unknown lineage, and now he would have a husband in namesake. For all his days he would never have guessed his current situation. He was marrying a prince, but not the love of his life.

Brier shuffled over to the veranda off his suite and opened the partition, allowing the spring air to greet him. He no longer had a view of the gardens, but a high vantage right above the entire kingdom. He could see the city's entire expanse from his cliff palace: the Aurelian Quads that bordered the palace's immediate terrain and the residential city townhomes that clustered before the sparse outskirts. The farther outland one traveled, the less houses and people there were. Just a five-mile ride out from Avenough stood the home Brier shared with a man he once knew. The huntsman Rolande; his master, his teacher, the father of his child, his first love.

Brier sighed and shook his head. Thoughts of Roland would only dampen his spirits this day. The wedding was to take place out in the gardens, beneath the copious branches of an oak tree. Quintin had suggested a more formal wedding, in the court hall or the temple, but Brier declined. The Aurelian temples were for sanctioned betrothals, and although the royal court accepted Prince Quintin Pascal as a consort, they did not agree to the means by which the engagement came into happenstance. A forced marriage due to a bastard child was never something anyone boasted, but Brier couldn't care less. Ryanne was the only solace in his loneliness, and he could not regret her birth if the gods personally asked him to.

"Paaapaaaaa!" The little princess's voice called out to him. Brier moved toward her nursery before his daughter grew restless. She openly grinned at the sight of him, the few teeth she had visible in her smile. He lifted his daughter out of the timber wood crib the guild made especially for her. Umhal's charm still worked. The carved leaves, similar to the marks that peppered his skin, glowed gold for her amusement.

"Good morning, Princess Ryanne." Brier kissed Ryanne's forehead and ogled his daughter as if to determine her actual likeness. He supposed she took after Roland. The sun kissed her olive skin. Her hair was thick like the dense forest and black like midnight in winter. Similar to Roland, her temper flared more oft than not. Ryanne decided at that moment to display this trait as Brier laid her down to change her. She wanted none of it and wriggled to get out of his arms, most likely to hassle either Victoria or Marietta for breakfast. She mewled as Brier chuckled at her stubbornness, unaware of how different their lives would soon be. She would be a princess of both Lirend and Menlor, likely expected one day to marry Prince Quintin's nephew.

"Heh—Rolande would say you should never marry, Ryanne." His daughter stared up at him with curious emerald eyes, unaware of what their lives might have been. Summers in Aire with the guild to protect her. Fall in Sherdoe riding the deer trails and chasing foxtails through the woodland. *Yensira*, where the stars glittered across the open fields, and in the deepest part of the forest where men confessed their love.

A wave of despondency washed over Brier and tears prickled the corners of his eyes. It was for nothing, truly. When the man he loved betrayed him, he betrayed their daughter, and Lirend. He could not forgive Roland because he could not forgive himself for his own foolish heart. Ryanne whimpered in a fit, and Brier rubbed the child's head lightly.

"Whistle whistle, calm your bristle...." He picked her up off the changing table and held her to his hip. "The day is bright and new."

A WHITE roller led up to the base of the tree and on either side of the lightly petaled walkway. Ribbon-backed chairs rowed out for the lords and ladies, while those with lesser stations stood to watch the garden ceremony. Brier had heard the citizens of Avenough had gathered around the high walls merely to gain proximity to the wondrous event. A king of Lirend marrying a prince of Menlor. It was the first time in Aurelian history and quite certainly the last.

The day did turn out bright, and the sun rose high in the sky over the expansive palace gardens. Brier's nerves bested him as he paced inside the east corridor. He wavered twice when Marietta asked after his agitated state, but eventually Brier settled down when Victoria brought Ryanne to his side. Like her father, she calmed him.

"Papa." The little girl grabbed his red hair and made a game of twisting the ends around her tiny fingers. He chuckled when she threatened to yank off his gold crown, and held her hands against his mouth to kiss them.

"This is for you, Little Ryanne," he whispered to his daughter. More than anything, even more than his love for Roland, he wanted his daughter's happiness. He would do anything to make sure she would have more than he ever did, more than her heart's desire. Marrying Quintin meant guaranteeing Ryanne's future and standing in Lirend. It was important for him to, as Lord Tamil had spelled it, "Cement the trust of the people." In addition to that, he did not want Ryanne to grow up in a single parent home. When Brier's father lived, he'd showered Brier with as much affection as he could bestow. However, Braedon, like Brier, had responsibilities to Lirend. Thus, Brier saw his nursemaid Marietta more than he did his own father. He refused to let Victoria and Marietta fill the role of parents for Ryanne. With Prince Quintin as his husband, he could share the load of his duty as king, and he knew the man would share the responsibility of raising Ryanne. Truthfully, Quintin already had.

"Brier."

He stood, exhaling.

"Are you ready?"

The question, so simple, and yet his resolve garbled in mixed emotions. Ready to be a husband to Quintin? Mayhap. He'd accepted their marriage, political or not, and thanked the gods he considered the prince a friend. As for coupling, he'd accepted that too. Sexual fulfillment was part of his role as Quintin's husband, and while he could refuse as mere friends, he did not stand much chance once they were officially wed. Mayhap he would enjoy warming Quintin's bed? The thought brought a chill up his spine, but Brier quickly shook it off. Quintin would not use him like a bed wench, and if Brier felt averse to receiving, the prince made it clear he did not mind yielding. Quintin wanted him, and despite Brier's own misgivings, Quintin actually did love him, and Ryanne for that matter. That much Brier knew. But whatever fate they met as a wedded couple remained unknown.

"I'm ready." Brier smiled at Ryanne as he lifted her up in his arms and carried her to the alabaster veranda that led out to the garden. He let Ryanne walk first on unsteady feet, with Victoria following. The curls Marietta set in the toddler's hair fell the instant they'd settled, but Ryanne still caught the eye of every attendee in her peony-pink-colored dress. Brier let out a chuckle as the girl bent to pick up the scattered roses. She threw the flowers above her head and watched with awe as they floated.

The violins began subdued and then increased in volume. Thankfully he remembered his cue from the rehearsals, and the preparation calmed some of his tension. He walked out at the sound of the viola's solo to a garden of standing guests. His white jacket, infused with the green and gold of his house, gleamed in the sun's luster. Prince Quintin Pascal stood at the end of the aisle, more handsome than Brier could easily recall, or perhaps it was his unhindered expression, similar to little Ryanne's in her wonderment at rose petals.

Brier stood before Quintin. He gripped the hilt of the sword on his waist and grinned sheepishly as he leaned in to tease his future husband. "You look as if you've seen the face of the gods," he whispered to Quintin before the priest began.

"The gods should wish to be as beautiful as you are today, my love," Quintin breathed in his ear. Brier's face flared at the unexpected praise. When Quintin leaned away, Brier stared into the prince's sapphire eyes and saw in them everything he lacked in his own. Happiness, passion, love.

"I—" But before he could fully begin, the priest turned to them both and commenced his oration.

"Dearly beloved, we are gathered here today in the presence of these witnesses, to join King Brier Ignacio Snow and Prince Quintin William Francis Pascal in matrimony commended to be honorable among all; and therefore is not to be entered into lightly but reverently, passionately, lovingly, and solemnly. Into this, these two persons present now come to be joined. If any person can show just cause why they may not be joined together, let them speak now or forever hold their peace." Brier held his quivering tongue, but the foreboding in his gut threatened to upend him.

"Quintin William Francis Pascal, wilt thou have this man to thy wedded spouse, to live together according to the gods' law of binding? Wilt thou love him, comfort him, honor and keep him, in plague and in vigor? And, forsaking all others, keep thee only unto him, so long as ye both shall live?"

"There is no one I want more to share my life with." The flame danced in Quintin's gaze, but Brier saw his own hope dying. "I will."

"Brier Ignacio Snow, wilt thou have this man to thy wedded spouse, to live together according to the gods' law of binding? Wilt thou love him, comfort him, honor and keep him, in plague and in vigor? And, forsaking all others, keep thee only unto him, so long as ye both shall live?"

"I...." Brier's heart thudded wildly. His fingers trembled on the sword as his calm morphed into shame. Even if Quintin knew he did not care for him in the same way, he still hoped for eventual happiness, eventual passion... eventual love. However, as Brier stared into the depths of Quintin, he knew that eventually would never come. His heart had decided long ago to belong to one man, and no matter how much time passed, that would not change.

Brier lowered his head and began to speak, but in the same breath an arrow cut directly between them. He jerked his head toward the direction the arrow came from and saw another arrow puncture the assailant's skull. The man screamed as he fell from the palace wall, and Brier's blood ran cold.

"Someone's attacking the palace!" Quintin tried to shield him from the flying arrows, but Brier darted toward Ryanne. The guests snowballed into a panicked mass. Brier heard screams and cries as arrows flew from the walls of the palace.

"Victoria!" He yelled to the nursemaid, but Victoria had already found him in the sea of people. "Take her inside! Don't let her out of your sight!" He wanted to stay with his daughter, but he needed to help the guards secure his castle from the now scattering men. Dozens of them climbed over the wall with ropes to harness, but Brier could tell they were not from Avenough. Their heavy boots and thick shoulder cloaks were made of wild elk fur.

"*Awwwoooo*!"

And then he heard it.

A wolf's howl.

Brier twisted his head to see the black wolf zip in front of him and sink his fangs into an enemy's leg.

"Veti...." Brier whispered as his chest tightened, but he could not be here. An arrow narrowly missed him through his desperate disbelief, but he finally composed himself and took cover on the wall of a gardening shed. He breathed out to steady his shaking hands, but Roland possibly being there unnerved him more than twenty armed men.

"Veti?" Veti came to his side when the beast released the mauled-to-death foe. The beast panted and gazed at him with black eyes and a crimson red muzzle. "Where's Roland?" He searched frantically in the mound of fighting, but he could not see Roland's towering figure. Mayhap he wasn't here. Mayhap he hadn't come.

"Where's Rolande, Veti?" But at that moment the sound of Roland's growl ensnared Brier, and he turned to watch as Roland fought two enemies at once. Roland's sword was as quick as his arrow. Veti launched to help, and Brier stared paralyzed as the wolf tore an armed man down to the ground. Roland stopped only to breathe but caught Brier's defeated gape from across the garden.

"My king!" Quintin ran to his side with his orange coat smeared in blood. Brier fixed his gaze on Quintin instead and opened his arms when he hugged him.

"Are you all right?" He squeezed Quintin's back. "You're shaking." Brier pulled away and nodded once.

"I'm fine. What about you? You're covered in blood."

"Not my own," Quintin snarled. "We're outnumbered, and they're heavily armed. Reinforcements are on the way."

"If they surrender, make sure you do not harm them. These men are not warriors, Quintin. They're from Aire."

"For them to slay us where we stand? These filthy beasts have no honor, Brier!" Brier flicked his gaze to the place where Roland just stood, but the man had vanished once more. "What about Ryanne?"

"She is safe. I saw her and Victoria into the palace myself."

"Good. Then you should stay here until the guards can reach you. I don't want you to get hurt in the fray."

"Are you mad? There are innocent people out there!"

"And they would see you dead before they risked their necks to save you!" Quintin spat. Brier frowned at Quintin's bitter retort. How could he ever think Brier would cower while his people fought for their lives? Ryanne was safe, but he would not abandon the Aurelians. Even if they did despise him.

"I'm staying." Brier gave him a glare that said he would not discuss it further. Quintin let out a frustrated sigh, and Brier felt his anguish. He could see the sweat beaded at the top of Quintin's forehead and the look of veritable anxiety in his eyes.

"Brier…." Quintin held his face, and Brier's body stiffened from the harrowing tone. Quintin leaned in and gave him a chaste kiss, one that made Brier's heart break with remorse. "Don't die."

Brier ran out into the clearing and accessed the destruction. They set fire to the shrubbery and capsized the stone sculptures. The culprits had traded their arrows for hand-to-hand combat, and Brier watched as his guards sparred with men in black cloaks, men worn not only from battle, but from strife. Brier did not have time to scrutinize it. An enemy charged at him with his sword ready to attack.

Brier's sword clanged, but he felt someone move at his back. He pivoted gracefully, but screamed as his face met the hilt of the other's sword. Brier winced as his nose bled from the hit, but did not falter as the blade met his foe's. He rebounded faster than his adversary and managed to hack off the man's sword hand with one swipe.

The enemy screamed out, but Brier had no time to breathe.

"I won't make it that easy!" He whipped backward to slash another enemy behind him between the arm and chest.

"Heh—" The man grabbed at his arm wound, his hood fell, and Brier saw the man's face. "*Venur*, little prince."

"You…." Brier froze in horror. A young man with a sly but handsome face stood before him, hazel eyes cool as ever. His dark hair fell to his shoulders, but the man wore it in a ponytail down his back. "Caite?" Brier called out in disbelief.

"Aye," the man called back and held the wound on his chest delicately.

"You're behind all of this?"

"Not all of this." Caite still wore the smirk that Brier had memorized from his time in Aire. "Just capitalizing on my brother's chaos."

Brier's jaw tensed. So it was Botcht who'd planned the raid. No surprise there really. The man had made his contempt known long before Roland came back to Avenough.

"I tried to do this much sooner—but after I took that Aurelian doctor—"

"You?" Brier whispered. "You took Lord Yaris?"

"Bull's-eye!" The man chuckled and twisted his sword like a baton. "And set the fire in the square."

The web unfolded before Brier. The fire in the square, Lord Yaris's disappearance, a bid for his life.... "Where is Lord Yaris?" Brier demanded.

"Unfortunately, Lord Yaris had to be dealt with," Caite answered.

"You." Brier's stomach churned. "You killed him?"

"That wasn't part of the plan," Caite admitted to Brier. "I was just supposed to capture him." He sighed. "But it turned out he had some pretty powerful friends. That general, for one, started sniffing the trail. I had to cut the loose ends."

"Why?" Brier yelled. "You killed innocent people!" The sword slumped to his side, but Caite stood ready.

"It's not personal," he told Brier with a shrug.

How could Caite say it was not personal when Brier assumed they were comrades... brothers? Roland had assured him the others in the guild had grown to accept him, even care for him. Had his whole existence in Aire been one big lie?

"I don't understand." Brier shook his head. "Why kill innocent people just to kill me?" Wrath coursed through his blood. If the guild resigned to kill him, they should have done so before he even came back to Avenough. Before he'd had Ryanne! Before he let Roland rip away the last part of his heart! "You should have killed me in Aire!"

"Don't think I didn't want to. You know I hate dramatic shit like this." Caite let out a dark chuckle. "But my employer was adamant your name be smeared before I killed you. I guess you pissed off the wrong Aurelian, Your Majesty." Caite smirked.

"So you've become a lapdog for the Aurelians you supposedly detest?"

Caite smirked. "I *might* have avoided all this had Rolande left you alone, but of course, you trapped him, getting pregnant and all. He's too gallant for his own good. He wouldn't leave you like my father left my mother."

"I didn't even know I could carry a child, Caite!"

"No matter." Caite yawned, but winced when he went to stretch his wounded arm. "I didn't expect you to tag me. You've gotten quite good." Brier stared at Caite as revulsion curled his thin lips.

"Save your praise for someone who cares." Brier used his white coat to wipe the blood from his nose and stood ready to battle.

"Oh, that hurts me, truly it does." Caite narrowed his gaze. "Especially since I taught you everything you know." Brier came at Caite midrant to catch him off guard. His plan might have worked, but Caite was a skilled swordsman, and easily met his charge.

"Trying to surprise me, hmm?" Caite leered as he struck Brier three times. His sword vibrated in his hand as he tried to match Caite's speed and accuracy, but he did not have the experience. He needed to end this. Fast. He rushed toward Caite, letting out a furious yell, and their swords met in midair. Caite was slower to defend, but Brier's strike did not have the power needed to bring him down with one blow.

"Come now, Brinan, you can't seriously think you're a match for me." Caite gritted his teeth. "You are nothing." Caite gazed at Brier with manic eyes. He began to put more force against Brier's sword, and Brier's face twisted in alarm. "You think these Aurelians love you? They don't!" Caite let out a caustic laugh. "No one loves you!" Brier had to strain against Caite's strength, but he refused to give up. He couldn't give up. Caite's words, as true as they once were, might have been, they were so wrong now.

"Is that what you think? That no one loves me?" Brier smirked as he pushed his sword steadily forward. He watched Caite's eyes shift in uncertainty. "Once that may have been true, but no longer," Brier uttered coldly. His life whirred by for nineteen years with only the love of his nursemaid and his deceased parents, but no longer. The boy who once stumbled down the unknown path alone now walked as a man impervious. Brier no longer feared his fate. He welcomed his praise, his failures, his joy, his sorrow. Caite's sword shook, and Brier stepped toward his once teacher to gain his footing.

"Ronan loves me."

"Lies." Caite's expression switched from perplexed to rage in a matter of a seconds, but Brier did not let up the control of his sword, or of his words.

"He loves me more than anything, which is why he tried to protect me from your villainy. And risked his life to save me again today." The realization swept over Brier and his chest swelled. Roland had always loved him in his own dejected way. And he loved Roland in the most desperate way possible. Hopelessly.

"Do not flatter yourself, Aurelian," Caite huffed. "You are a blight that Rolande could not avoid."

But Brier caught the flash of pain in Caite's eyes, and he head-butted Caite between their swords so firmly he felt his own teeth click. Caite wavered before he fell. He held the place where Brier had sliced him as if he just remembered the open wound.

"Even if that were true, it would not matter!" Brier yelled. He spat out the warm blood that flooded into his mouth from his nose. "Even if Rolande didn't love me, even if he hated me, it wouldn't matter." He dropped his guard slightly before he panted.

"I have a daughter who loves me. *She* is my everything."

"Until she no longer serves your purpose?" Caite let out a strained groan, and Brier watched Caite wobble against the base of the oak tree.

"Do not confuse your fate with my own! Because your father would not have you, did you think I would abandon my own daughter?" Caite's fallen sword teetered in his hands. Even if Roland had betrayed him, even if Quintin hated him for not returning his love, he knew his daughter loved him, and she was the light in his darkness.

"Give up, Caite!" Brier watched the blood drip from the man's ribs. "You're wounded. Let me help you…." He inched near the swordsman, but Caite waved him away.

"Leave me!" Caite screamed. He tried to stand up, but coughed and wheezed dangerously. "Why you of all people? Rolande is a Lord of Thenia! You're nothing—" The man choked. "You're nothing but Aurelian trash."

"Because I love Ronan unconditionally." Brier pointed the tip of his sword toward Caite's heart. "With everything in me. Lord or criminal. His past never mattered to me."

"Gaahhhh!" Caite tried to knock away the sword as he lunged forward and attempted to tackle Brier's legs with brute strength. Brier gnashed his jaw and let out a scream as he sliced through the man's chest.

"Hnnn!" Caite whimpered. Brier mirrored the terrified look on the impaled man's face. He pulled out the sword, and Caite fell with a sickening crunch. Brier could not take his eyes away. Dark blood oozed out of the wound in his chest and commingled with the bright grass.

"C-Caite!" Brier's fingers went numb around the hilt of the bloody sword as he watched the man writhe and suffocate from a punctured lung.

Hooves pounded through the garden as the city's army covered the green, but Brier could only hear Caite's strained breath.

"Brier! Get down!" Roland called out, and Brier turned, but the wayward arrow had already struck him.

Brier cursed as he fell from the impact. He closed his eyes and tensed his wounded leg. Veti's thick body shielded him from the oncoming foes, but pain danced out from the arrowhead embedded in his thigh. Roland ran toward him and pulled his arrow back to make his shots soar. Brier watched in terrified reverence. Roland killed anyone who neared them without a second thought, sure as a huntsman hitting his mark.

"Brier." A strong grip coaxed him to stand. He knew the touch so well that his body burned from the contact.

"I'm fine," he mumbled, trying to keep his voice steady. "You—ngh—shouldn't be here...."

"You can execute me later. Right now I need to get you to safety." Brier groaned as Roland swept him off his feet and carried him toward the entrance of the palace. When he was through the veranda doors, he saw his daughter at the end of the steps with Victoria holding her as if for dear life. Relief exhaled in his chest seeing them safe, albeit shaken. The crowd parted to let Roland through when he placed Brier down tenderly at the end of the grand stairs. Brier tried to sit up, but Roland pinned him to the ground with little strength.

"Don't sit up." His pleading tone made Brier falter. "Please, it's a split spear. Wait for a healer to take the arrow out."

In the next moment, he heard the palace doors bang open with Quintin holding a struggling mercenary. Brier watched as the enraged prince pulled out his dagger and held it to the unknown assailant's throat. Except the assailant wasn't unknown. The long silvery hair swept over his face, but Brier recognized those pale green eyes anywhere. But it couldn't be.... Leighis?

"Move and I will slit your throat!"

Leighis cried out in a foreign tongue, but the guards apprehended him without much effort. Brier watched horror-struck as the guards dragged Leighis away.

"Him too! To the dungeons!" Quintin pointed at Roland. The guards came to apprehend Roland, and Brier watched Roland pull a dagger from his boot. "He is with them!"

Chapter 33
Revelation

ROLAND HELD his blade at the ready. He only wanted to protect Brier, but if he was going to die, he would not go down without a fight.

"He is with them!" Quintin yelled frantically, but Brier's authoritative voice resounded.

"Stop!" Brier commanded, and the guards halted. The hall stilled before Roland heard the whispers of the guests who'd attended the wedding. Most were stunned into silence, but some were still crying from the attack.

"Get the courtiers out of here and call Meade. Let him know we have quite a few wounded," Brier ordered without pause. The guards shifted their attentions to the large crowd while Quintin sent someone for the royal healer. Brier's shoulders drooped and Roland caught the king before his head hit the marble floors.

"*Aida*!" Roland turned his gaze when he heard excited feet stomp. "*Aida*! *Aida*!" Ryanne grabbed the poor nurse's face to drag her attention to him. Roland gave the woman an apologetic glance before he motioned Ryanne toward him.

"*Venur*, Ryanne." His daughter beamed and pointed to the hair on his face.

"*Aida*!"

"Hah… told you someone was… hnh… in Balmur," Brier mumbled in pain. Roland clasped Brier's hand. Brier's resolve must have begun to crumble because he squeezed back for relief.

"Victoria." Quintin turned away from the conjugal scene. "Take Ryanne upstairs. I don't want her to see Brier like this." The toddler squirmed and wailed in Victoria's arms as she took her to the upstairs with a guard.

Time seemed to linger as they waited for Meade. Brier's wide eyes turned to slits, and yet Roland could feel him entwine their bloodstained fingertips.

"Where's the damn doctor?" Quintin demanded. Meade bustled in with three other healers and quickly cleared the space around Brier's wound. He gave Roland a quizzical look before he spoke to Brier.

"This is going to hurt." Meade lifted Brier's leg. He broke off the fletching of the arrow, then pushed the head and shaft through the hole in Brier's leg.

The sound of Brier's torn flesh seemed to echo in the great hall. Brier didn't scream, but Roland's face paled when the hot blood poured from the man's wound.

"Good that you waited. You could have damaged a vein." Meade cast the barbed arrow aside with disgust. He pressed the wound firmly so the blood could clot. Brier let out a muffled cry and leaned in to Roland's chest for strength.

Roland froze.

His heart ached and then pounded. Even the pitiable contact made him stiff with hope.

"I need to get him stitched up," Meade told Roland after the healer instructed him to press the rag on the wound.

"Can he walk?" Quintin's voice cut in.

"He shouldn't move too much. We need to keep pressure on that wound. I don't want him losing even more blood."

"I'll carry him," Roland offered.

"I am his fiancé. I'll carry him!" Quintin spat. "What are you even doing here?"

Roland clenched his jaw. He'd only had one reason to return, and he currently held that reason in his arms.

"I'm here to protect him. And Ryanne."

"It's not your place to protect them."

"You're right!" Roland retorted. "It's yours! And you're doing a shit job!" Meade stood between them and raised his hand for silence.

"Roland." The healer glared. "Pick Brier up and take him to his suite." Quintin clenched his jaw but did not refute the healer's words.

ROLAND HELPED the king up off the ground and took him to his suite. He laid Brier on the silk spread, and the man winced from the pain.

"It hurts almost as bad as labor," Brier whined. Roland let out a light chuckle.

"Something funny?" Brier narrowed his gaze.

"Well, you did make quite a show of it," he teased. Brier growled and turned his gaze.

"Oh, I'm sorry, I think my near death and the birth of our child warranted a little show." Roland did not speak but held Brier's glower. He had grown, but not changed. Matured, but not aged in the months without Roland. Still as beautiful as ever. Roland must have made him uncomfortable because Brier averted his gaze. "How did you know… about today…." Brier fumbled with a piece of silk with red stitching.

"Leighis told me," Roland explained. He told Brier about their meeting days prior. How Lei tried to stop Botcht from raiding the palace. "Apparently he was unsuccessful. I would have informed your guards, but that ran the risk of them capturing me. Then there was the fact that you exiled me from the capital."

"You risked your life and lives of countless men, Roland."

"I needed to make sure you and Ryanne were safe."

"And what if you had been killed? If not by a guard, by one of your own?"

"Then I would have died protecting my king," Roland answered simply. "You are the only thing that matters to me, Brier."

Brier stared at him in silence until they heard the parlor door open and slam shut. Roland walked toward the bedchamber door to inspect the visitors, but he overheard two men arguing.

"He shouldn't be here, Meade," Quintin whispered. "He will do nothing but cause trouble."

"You mean cause trouble for you?" the healer asked calmly.

"Who is it?" Brier hissed in pain.

"It's Meade," Roland uttered softly. "He's preparing things to stitch you up."

"Every time he comes around, there is naught but chaos and heartache for Brier," Quintin challenged.

"That is not for us to decide," Meade retorted.

"I am his lover!" Quintin spat indignantly.

"And yet you sound like a smarmy courtier the way you claim your place about him. Do you think our king so incapable of making his own decisions? He is no fool. He is loyal to the crown!"

"'Tis not his loyalty I question," Quintin replied in a hushed tone, and Roland heard the parlor door open. "Only his heart."

Roland turned toward Brier who held his leg, too distracted from the pain to properly hear the exchange.

"By the gods, where's Meade?"

"Here!" The doctor stepped through the door smiling. Meade padded over and took a seat on the bed before carefully removing Brier's luxurious jacket and trousers. "Hold this," Meade gave Roland the blood-soaked rag and placed the threaded needle on his thigh. "I can give you something to sleep, if you wish," he said to Brier.

"No, just finish it," Brier replied, though he eyed the needle apprehensively. Meade's fingers delved into the bag before he pulled out a bottle of blue liquid. Brier's nose scrunched at the stringent odor, but Roland recognized it as disinfectant from Ryanne's birth.

"This is going to be less than pleasant."

"Has any experience with you ever been pleasant?" Brier questioned. Meade chuckled faintly at the cheek before he cleaned his fingers and the needle.

Brier inhaled before he let out a growling hiss when the needle entered his thigh. Meade pressed his chest down and slid the needle through the skin surrounding the torn flesh.

"Grab his hand, Roland." Roland hesitated before Brier's palm lifted for him to take hold.

"It's the same damned side that bear got me," Brier gritted out and squeezed Roland's hand.

"You'll have another story to tell Ryanne," Roland answered, trying to cheer him up. Brier's fingers held tight.

"I think I've enough stories for her, thank you." The stitching lasted less than an hour, but by the end Brier looked exhausted and deathly pale.

"Done," Meade announced before he dabbed the stitches in alcohol and placed a piece of gauze. The doctor bound the leg and placed a pillow under his knee.

"Haah… I might get sick," Brier muttered before he shoved Roland aside. Meade reached around to grab a tin basin for the king to heave. "Imma get sick…." Roland's face twisted as he listened to deep retching, but he rubbed Brier's back for comfort. When Brier finally emptied his stomach, Roland went to the bureau to pour a glass of water.

"I'm going to give you something for the pain, or you won't sleep a wink," Meade told Brier as he prepared the syringe. "This will put you out for a few hours. Don't fight the sedative, just rest. I'll send someone up to check on you momentarily. Roland." Roland peered up after setting the glass beside Brier. "I'd like to talk to you for a moment."

Roland glanced at Brier's sweaty face. He was in pain, but conscious.

"Call if you need me," he told Brier before he followed Meade out of the bedchamber. He closed the door, but did not shut it all the way lest Brier call for his assistance.

"I trust you know what this is about." Meade placed the items gingerly in his bag.

"I can only assume," Roland answered. "Which in my experience is always a hazardous game."

"I've no time for games, Roland." The doctor's voice grew icy. Roland knew why Meade wanted to speak with him. He'd overheard most of it in the parlor, and his own intuition told him the rest.

"You are worried for Brier in my company."

"Should I be?" The doctor's gray brow raised. "You left the king depressed and withdrawn. The love for his daughter, and the prince's companionship, were the only thing to ground him. Without them he would have been lost—to everyone." Roland hated the thought of Quintin being Brier's only comfort, but he understood the truth of Meade's words. "I've heard many rumors about you, Roland, but I should hope not half of them are true."

"Unfortunately I have no rumors to fabricate." Roland grimaced.

"I only want the truth."

"The truth?" Roland tilted his head. "The truth is I have only ever loved three people in my entire life. Helenas, my late wife, Brier, the light in my darkness, and my daughter, the joy of my existence. They are my everything, the very reason I breathe."

"Yet Brier sent you from his side? Why?"

"Fool that I was, I did not trust Brier," Roland answered solemnly. "I thought that the king would pull away from me if he knew the truth. I thought that he would not—could not—trust me if he thought that I might have had anything to do with a plot on his life. For my part, it is true that I was contracted to kill Brier, but I would never harm either one of them. Even before Ryanne was born when I had many opportunities. Even when I had the anger and motive to do so, I—" He thought of the night he returned to Avenough. "To kill Brier would be to kill myself. I don't even have that courage."

"So you come now with regret in your heart and expect the king's forgiveness?" Meade questioned.

"Regret? No." Roland shook his head. "Had I not taken the contract, I would never have known the man who makes my heart sore when I gaze upon him. I would never see my Ryanne, in her beauty.... Even if I never see her again...." Roland's voice trembled with the thought of losing her once more.

"My only regret is that I did not trust Brier's love. I did not allow my king to protect me... as I have hoped to protect him." The doctor did not speak then. Roland stilled his heart before he stood tall. "I accept my punishment not as a criminal, but as a lover who has betrayed my partner's trust. Brier sent me away because he could not look upon my face without seeing the lies and deceit I cast between us."

"A just king," Meade replied pointedly.

"Indeed, it is not a harsh sentence. Brier has shown me more mercy than I ever deserved."

"Yet you return after he gives you pardon?" Meade sighed wearily. "You may not get a second chance."

"As I have said. My life is his and Ryanne's. If he decides to take it, so be it. I won't let him die when I have the means to protect him."

Meade studied him for a long moment. Roland did not know what the doctor was thinking. About turning him in? Perhaps, but that no longer mattered. He did not come to the palace for Avenough's redemption. There was only one Aurelian he needed to endure.

"I will say nothing more, Roland. I leave the gods to decide your fate." The doctor fixed himself to leave and grabbed the leather bag. "Though I wouldn't wander far from the king while you are here." Meade shuffled toward the parlor door, and Roland exhaled with relief. A stalemate was better than a loss any day.

Roland opened the door fully and stepped inside, glancing to Brier, whose eyes were now dazed and sleepy.

"You should be asleep, Brinan."

"I want to speak with you."

"When you wake up."

"But what if you're not…." Brier's eyes rolled. "What if you're not here when I wake up?"

"I'm not going anywhere." Roland shook his head. He pushed the vanity chair next to the king's bed. "I'll be right here when you wake."

"Promise?" Brier's eyes finally closed.

"I promise," Roland whispered. He stared at the dark circles and pasty skin. The fight had zapped Brier of any vigor he might have had on his wedding day. Now Brier could only sleep.

Roland laid his head on Brier's unwounded thigh, weary from the day's events and tired from the permanent ache in his chest.

"RONAN…." A frail voice called to him and fingers filtered through his hair. Roland stalled to open his eyes. He knew this dream. One he'd had many times. He opened his eyes slowly to postpone the reality.

"Yes, Brinan."

"I want to speak with you," Brier whispered. Roland grabbed his hand before Brier could pull it away.

"Go ahead." He stared into reddened eyes and waited.

"Why?" Brier asked him.

"Why?" Roland frowned.

"Why," Brier repeated before he started a full rant. "Why did you come back? Why did you lie? Why didn't you tell me? Why would you enter a contract to kill—me?

You didn't even know me!" Brier's voice shook before he lowered his head. Roland gazed at him speechless. Brier's eyes were red, he thought from tiredness, but now he wondered if the king had wept.

"I came back because I couldn't stay away from you. I've been to our villa in Balmur several times, but I've seen you only once since you exiled me. I lied for two reasons. One, because I am a coward. I was afraid to lose you. I was afraid to lose Ryanne. It was my own weakness and fear that bound me, not a contract that I signed." Roland paused. "And secondly, because I did not want you to think less of me. To think me… unworthy of your love."

Brier only stared at him blankly, but at least he finally could hear the words Roland so desperately wanted to say.

"I was summoned to Avenough not long after your nineteenth birthday. The queen decided you should train in Aire, and she contracted me to teach you. I accepted her task in exchange for the money to buy out our contracts, but on my way back to Aire, I met someone who had different plans. 'Kill him,' the man said, 'and the Ceve guild's freedom is yours.' I should have expected trickery from an Aurelian."

"Why would Evelyn choose you?" Brier wondered.

"That is exactly what I asked," Roland recalled. "When I met with the queen, she knew about me, Brinan, about my past. Still, she only contracted me to train you."

"But you don't know the person was who hired you to kill me?"

"I don't. He wore a hood to cover his face." Roland shook his head. He could only remember the hazel of the man's eyes, like a crisp autumn leaf. "I was to teach you all that I knew, and then, when you reached your majority, end your life. He signed the contract as AJR, but I never asked him his full name. It's to protect our employers, in case we are caught during the job. We can't turncoat if we don't know who we're working for."

"But then how could you know he was Aurelian?" Brier asked bemused.

"Because of the gold he offered me. More gold than I'd ever seen in my life, Brier, but I didn't give a rat's ass about that. It was the contracts I cared about. He had them in his hand, and he knew me, Brier, he knew the guild before I even introduced us. He promised me our freedom if I did it."

"But the queen said that she would pay you to train me. You bought your freedom."

"I couldn't trust her to keep her word. After what happened in Thenia, my faith in Aurelians is limited. This was a surefire way to know. I could guarantee the guild's freedom," Roland whispered. "I knew what I signed myself to, but I was foolish and reckless. I convinced myself that I could do whatever it took for our freedom. Helenas was gone with our child. What did it matter who I killed in this life? I told myself. But… but the instant I laid eyes on you…." Roland squeezed Brier's hand. "Brinan, I knew I could not harm you. Even as a prince. It was for nothing. I love you. More than I ever thought I could." Roland smiled gently before Brier pulled back.

"It is my wedding day you know…." Roland felt the lost warmth of Brier's hand.

"Sorry for ruining your wedding, but I had to come to protect you. Even if it was the day you were supposed to marry someone else." Roland grimaced. "I know it is not much, Your Majesty, but my life is all I have to offer you."

Brier's jaw tensed. Roland's heart stung from the king's dry icy stare.

"Caite," Brier muttered. "I met him in the battle."

"Aye…." Roland understood the signal to change the subject. "His brother led the charge against the palace."

"Botcht."

Roland nodded once. "After the guild disassembled, he began to mobilize the Thenians to fight against the crown. He used the Aurelian contract to intimidate even the outlanders who live deep in the mountains."

"So it's my fault, because I did not fulfill my promise."

"*Na*," Roland refuted. "Botcht was on the front lines of the Thenian massacre, Brier. Then the situation with Caite's father…. He's held this resentment in his heart for years; all the first generation Thenians have."

"But he convinced those men to fight for him. And die for him… because of my actions."

"They fought for themselves," Roland assured his king. "Our fate is unknown. We only choose the path we take. You are not responsible for their deaths."

"Except one," Brier mumbled. "Caite…." Roland watched Brier's palm smooth over his brow. He'd seen the fight between Brier and his former guild member. Caite came hard at Brier without restraint or remorse, but in the end, Brier bested his once teacher.

"You fought with honor." Roland held Brier's wrist. "That is all anyone could have asked of you."

"I should have done more to help the Thenians."

"The measures you took to secure our territory from crooks and thieves helped more than you know, Brier. You saved countless men who would have joined Botcht's cause had they not seen your efforts."

"But it wasn't enough," Brier whispered.

"Is it ever?" Roland asked him. "Always there will be someone unhappy in everything that you do."

"Aye…," Brier conceded. "Even the Aurelians scorn me for helping the Prolit and Burges. Lord Renli created a coalition to—" Brier paused. Roland stared, blank, hanging for the next word. "Caite said that it was an Aurelian that hired him." Brier hopped from the bed and Roland pushed his shoulder.

"Where are you going?"

"I need to speak to Botcht!" Brier exclaimed. Roland's brow creased. "I need to know who Caite was working for!"

"And what makes you think he'll tell you?" Roland held Brier's shoulders. "His brother is dead, Brinan. I don't think he'll want to talk to the man who killed him!"

"Not even to bring the man to justice who manipulated him?" Brier pulled his shoulder away. Roland gazed into the fierce green eyes and he knew his protests were for nothing. Brier already made up his mind. He would not be swayed.

"All right, but I'm coming with you." Roland released Brier's shoulder. Roland walked, while Brier limped through the chamber door and past the parlor before they met a sour-faced prince in the corridor.

"Where are you going?" Quintin narrowed his gaze on Roland.

"None of your concern." Roland matched Quintin's scowl.

"Where are the men apprehended from the siege?" Brier demanded. Quintin's nostrils flared before he turned to Brier.

"Most are in the dungeons. The injured are under watch in the great hall."

"What about who led the charge?" Brier asked.

"In the dungeons. We picked up an older fellow, around fifty."

"That's Botcht." Roland turned to Brier to affirm.

"Did you ask him who he was working for?" Brier's tone grew hopeful.

"He speaks only Thenian. We cannot understand a word."

"He would die anyway before he told an Aurelian, Brinan."

"Incidentally, Xenothian, you seem to know a lot about these rebels. How did you know they were coming?" Quintin began to interrogate him. "Everyone was caught completely off guard, but you knew they would be there."

"That one you apprehended is my comrade. Botcht Everdane."

"So you admit your allegiance to this revolt?"

"I admit that I know him. I did not lead the charge on Avenough nor do I affiliate with the Ceve guild any longer."

"Then since you know him, find out what he hopes to gain by this raid." Quintin wrapped his arm around Brier's waist.

"And why should I tell you anything?" Roland sneered at Quintin's display of affection.

"Because if you do, we *might* reconsider your punishment for entering Lirend's capital once more."

"*If* my king decides to punish me, so be it," Roland answered coldly. "But I will not do favors for some puffed-up Aurelian prince!"

"You—" Quintin raged, but Brier cut him off.

"Please speak with him, Rolande." Brier pulled away from Quintin's grasp. "I need to know who sent Caite. Tell him his punishment will be lessened if he cooperates."

"That won't sway him." Roland shook his head.

"Then what will sway him?" Brier asked. Roland gazed at the king's pleading eyes. Roland knew he stood no chance of convincing Botcht, but he knew someone who did.

"Come." He hurried past Quintin and down to the great hall.

"Where are we going?" Brier limped after him.

"To find the only person who can sway Botcht Everdane." To find his best friend, Leighis.

Chapter 34
Promise

THEY SHUFFLED through the corridors faster than Brier could keep up. Meade had bound his leg, but walking was still painful, and the bruises and scrapes from his row with Caite did not help. Roland led them to the East Hall where they'd contained the fallen Thenians. Brier did not know Roland's plan, but he ignored Roland's past transgressions and trusted his ex-lover.

"This is a mistake," Quintin whispered when they reached the entrance of the grand hall. "These people hate us. They want to see us dead."

"Once again you presume too much, Quintin." Brier followed Roland. When they entered the room, he could smell the stench of blood and sweat. "These men are wounded. They don't have the will to fight." The sun had set on the backdrop of the glass windowpane, but the summer's air kept the grand hall warm.

They found Leighis quickly, his silvery blond hair recognizable in the sea of black and brown. He knelt beside a wounded Thenian man whose leg had been nearly severed.

"Lei." Roland's commanding voice put eyes on them. Leighis twisted and stood when he saw Roland's weary face.

"Thank goodness." Leighis gave Roland a hug, and Brier heard the bones crunch. "Are you all right?"

"Aye. How are the men?"

"Some worse than others." Leighis gazed down at the injured man beneath him. "Your Doctor Meade has helped a lot. He's sent supplies and medicine for the wounded. Students of the university helped as well."

"Somehow it was worse than I imagined. I didn't think we'd lose so many."

"I tried to stop him. I tried, Ronan—" Leighis paused. He gazed toward Brier and his lips tightened.

"What are they saying?" Quintin whispered.

Brier shook his head slowly. He could not stop to translate. They spoke so fast it took all of his concentration to follow the exchange.

"What is he doing here?" Brier watched as Leighis nudged toward him and Quintin. He waited until Roland turned toward him before he spoke.

"I came for your help, Leighis…." Brier spoke in Thenian. "I'm trying to find out who is behind all of this misery."

"And what makes you think I would help a murderer like you, King Brier Snow?" Leighis's eyes narrowed. "You, like your father, speak of tolerance and coexistence. But you mean to coexist in a world where Aurelians are the ruling class!"

"Lei!" Roland's voice rang out, but Brier raised his hand to silence him.

"*Na*, Rolande. Let him speak."

"You hide behind your castle walls while we suffer! Promises unfulfilled! Contracts to enslave countless generations!' Leighis yelled. "You want to know who did this? Take a look in the mirror! Aurelian!" Brier could see the turmoil in Leighis's pale eyes and the strength he used to hide it.

"You're right," Brier uttered clearly. "I made a promise, and I did not keep it. Like my father, like the queen, like any other Aurelian you know and despise, I gave my word and did not follow through. A part of me was embarrassed that I'd been deceived so easily and a part of me hated Roland and the Thenians. I resented the hope I felt when I was with the guild. I despised myself. I hated everyone, even the gods, because I loved and lost, loved and lost again. I was fed up. I was broken by a man I loved more than myself." Brier paused when he saw Leighis's eyes glaze with tears.

"That I still love… more than anything…. Leighis." Brier's heart ached in his chest as he admitted his love for Roland. "We love fully, wholly, and unconditionally. It is something we both have in common." He walked toward Leighis. "I was wrong for my actions, but I want to make amends. I want to help your people, but I need your help to do that."

Leighis clenched his jaw, and Brier bowed to him.

"*Acai*, Leighis."

"I'll only agree to this if you swear to free him," Leighis whispered in the common tongue. Quintin swore under his breath, but Brier could sense the change in Leighis's disposition.

"I cannot guarantee his freedom, Leighis. He led an army against my palace. I understand, and sympathize, with his cause, but he placed hundreds of men in peril. He threatened my daughter's life." Brier felt Leighis's resolve hardening, and he quickly considered a compromise. "But I swear to you, Leighis. I swear on my honor, on the life of my child, I will do whatever it takes to help him." Leighis gazed at Roland, who wore a numb expression. Brier hadn't considered Roland's reaction to all that he'd confessed to Leighis, but it was the truth. All of it. Every word.

"I'll talk to him," Leighis whispered. "Take me to him."

THE DUNGEONS stank of rust and burnt wood from the furnace. Brier had only ever entered the dungeons once when he got lost as a youngling. As a child he'd trembled in the arched stone dwellings. As a man he still shivered as he limped past men wailing, crying, howling in the darkness. They came to Botcht's cell last. Brier had to raise the torch head to see the man spread on the concrete.

"Botcht!" Leighis's voice echoed as the guard opened the gate. Roland dragged him up and Botcht clutched his rib, crying out in pain. Brier stayed back with Quintin to avoid intruding.

"He's hurt! Lei!"

Leighis's eyes grew wider as the wound began to ooze black blood. Roland tried to lift Botcht up, but the swordsman screamed out. Brier shuddered with his hands balled to fists.

"I assume you're here to kill me?" Botcht's teeth chattered as he spoke to Roland.

"No. I'm here to help you." The sound of Leighis ripping fabric tore through the air. "And hoping for your help."

"My help?" Botcht raised his head with a manic smile.

"Aye." Roland nodded. "There was a man who Caite worked with. We need to know who it was! Where is the contract that he signed! For which Aurelian!"

"Do you think me a fool? Rolande?" Botcht's breath wheezed. "Do you think I don't know who it is who sent you here?"

"Pride has no place in death," Roland answered calmly. "If you help us, we can save you—"

"They slayed my brother! In cold blood! I saw his body!" Botcht gritted through his teeth. Brier squirmed listening to the man rage for Caite. "I would rather die than help the Aurelians who caused Caite's death!"

"Caite tried to kill Brier!" Roland spat back heatedly. "Not for any cause! But for money! He was hired by some conniving Aurelian, and he took the job without a second thought!"

"A lie!"

"It's true, Botcht." Leighis corroborated Roland's account. "Caite came to me before the siege and told me he had an important contract to fulfill. He said after that job, he would never need to work again." Leighis shook his head. "I should have stopped him, but I didn't think he would—" Leighis's high voice quivered. "That he would try to kill Brier." Botcht's gray eyes creased.

"He told me he was going to sail away to Menlor," Botcht croaked as his eyes slid shut. "Caite was going on and on about how he met someone who would pay his weight in gold for one last job. Of course I found it strange. What man had the means to do or promise such a thing for my brother? What Aurelian could earn Caite's trust so effortlessly?"

A man who had the ships and money to get anyone, even a Thenian, anywhere safely. A sailor who had something to lose from Brier's succession. A man whose likeness reminded him of Caite. Empty, cold, hazel eyes.

Botcht's face turned from numb to disgusted. "If I had known it was that man—!"

"What man?" Roland demanded. "What was his name!"

But Brier already knew the answer. A man who despised him as much as the queen in Lirend.

"Caite's father…," Botcht uttered calmly. "Lord Alexander Renli." Brier caught Botcht's haunted gaze before he fainted, and his head drooped into Leighis's arms.

BRIER SAT at the window in the parlor of his suite. For all that had happened, a botched wedding, revelations, and countless confessions, the sun still rose over Lirend's capital.

Brier rested his head against the warm glass and exhaled to release some of the tension in his heart.

Brier twisted when he saw the door open, and Roland stepped in wearily. Roland's beard had grown back full, and his hair reached the start of his shoulder. The olive complexion shimmered bronze from the harsh sun, but Roland's aged eyes shone brilliant blue.

"*Venur*," Brier whispered as Roland walked toward him. "What word is there?" His leg had prevented him from Renli's capture, but Roland and Botcht had to go to confirm the merchant's identity.

"It's him for certain." Roland nodded. "Something about him was familiar to me, but I would have never guessed him as Caite's *aida*."

"Understandably." Brier nodded. "They don't favor each other much save for the hair and the eyes."

"But the instant I heard that smug laugh, I knew it was him."

"He laughed?" Brier frowned.

"Yeah…." Roland grimaced. "He said the Aurelians would never stand for his incarceration. That he would be out in a week's time. Your prince nearly choked him! Told him he'd hang him himself before he saw the vermin walk free."

The guilt pulled at the strings in Brier's heart. Quintin was Lord Renli's friend. Regardless of their differences, he was sure Quintin felt betrayed by Renli's treachery.

"All this for money…," Brier whispered quietly. Renli had lost the most when he took power. His unregulated trades and tax evasions had accumulated the lord a mountain of wealth. So much money he could afford to essentially buy Avenough's Aurelians' loyalty with property, and exclusive dealings. "He enticed the Aurelians with luxury and threatened them with the calamity of the supposed King's Curse. All the while using the son he abandoned to do his dirty work. A true coward."

"True…." Roland mumbled. "Though I have to wonder… was it all just for money?"

"What is it?" Brier leaned forward to catch Roland's eye.

"I was just thinking." Roland rubbed the base of his chin. "Renli risked a lot for just money. It's not as if he was destitute to begin with. Even without your trade lines, he was making more than enough to sustain his way of life."

"Perhaps he thought I would disband his fleet?" Brier replied. "I thought about it after his outburst in the square."

"Yes, but when Renli hired me, he already had our contracts in hand at that time. How does a merchant come across binding contracts to the crown?"

"They don't." Brier shook his head gravely. His mind buzzed with Roland's worries, but he was too tired to think right now. All he wanted was a cup of chamomile tea and a hot bath. Brier yawned as he limped over to the desk and pulled out parchment to write down everything that had happened today for the court records.

"You must be tired," Roland whispered.

"No more than appropriate."

"Then can I ask you…." Roland hesitated. "About what you said to Leighis." Mayhap he'd been too transparent in his true feelings, but he meant every word.

"What I said to Leighis was the truth," Brier whispered. "I should not have taken Ryanne from you. That was my own spite. I was upset. I let my rage blind me from what was best for her."

"And you?" Roland asked boldly. Brier did not raise his head from the parchment, but the pen stopped.

"Of course I missed you," Brier answered. "But…."

I refuse.

"But that doesn't matter anymore." Brier shook his head.

I refuse.

"*A'ma el'*, Brier," Roland whispered. Brier closed his eyes and squeezed the pen till his knuckles whitened.

"And I suppose you think I'm supposed to just forgive you? To just—give up everything, for you?"

"Brier, I—"

"You didn't trust me, Roland," Brier croaked. "You love me, but you couldn't trust my love for you." Roland went silent, and Brier's heart constricted. "I'm sorry, but I'm going to marry Quintin." He continued to write his missive. "I will not keep Ryanne away from you, but I won't let my heart be beaten any longer. Quintin doesn't deserve it, and neither do I." Even if it meant marrying a man he didn't love, he refused to let Roland back into his heart.

"May I say one more thing?"

"If you must," Brier answered.

"I never deserved your love," Roland admitted. "Your affection has always been an unknown to me, Brier. 'Why would he love me when he could have any other man in this world? What do I have to offer him? How can I call myself worthy when I have done nothing to be proud of my entire life'?" Roland swallowed. "I only have one answer to those questions."

"Which is?" Brier breathed. He peered upward and met Roland's tired eyes.

"That I love you." Roland uttered. "Unequivocally. I would die for you tomorrow if you wanted or needed me to, Brinan."

How badly he'd wanted to hear those words in a faraway cabin. How desperately he'd wanted this man's love.

"Aye." And Brier knew Roland loved him, but words were words, promises were promises, and this time, it was not enough.

BRIER HELD the sentencing for Lord Alexander Renli a month after they'd apprehended him. The room fizzled with eager Aurelians, some who wanted to know the truth surrounding Renli's detainment, others who were prematurely convinced of the merchant's innocence. For the second time in Brier's life, the courtroom was full.

"Today I have the task of sentencing a man you all know. Some are friends. Some are associates, some partners in business. I understand this," Brier said confidently. "Some of my advisors have urged me not to bring this matter to the court, but to sentence Lord Renli for treason and be done with it. That is not the way things are done in Lirend." Brier's voice echoed. "That is not the way my father would have done things."

Brier held a plain scroll in his hand and opened the seal while the guards held a bedraggled-looking Renli. Despite the man's insistence he be released to a more comfortable holding, Brier made Renli await his sentence in the dungeons.

"Alexander James Renli, I sentence you to twenty years in a minimum security hold. Your title and lands will be henceforth stripped," Brier uttered coldly. "As for your assets, they will be liquidated. Any monies allocated will go to the late Lord Yaris's wife, Lady Letrish Yaris. Your family will receive a monthly state wage to sustain them."

The room broke out into rumblings, but Brier turned to head out of the court. "Finish up here, Lord Tamil," Brier murmured to his advisor while he gathered Quintin, Roland and several guards who accompanied them.

"Where are we going?" Quintin asked as Brier limped through the corridor.

"To end this properly."

Brier's heeled boots clicked on the stone, but he did not speak until he led them to the west wing.

"I've been thinking about what you said, Rolande."

"What I said?" Roland turned toward him.

"Aye, about when Renli offered you an unbound contract if you killed me," Brier answered.

"What about it?" Roland grimaced.

"Well, it's as you said," Brier replied. "How does a mere merchant come across contracts of the crown? Meade needed my permission just to get into the archives. Think you he would be able to get into the royal vaults?" They reached the queen's gold-lined door, and Brier pushed through without notice. Evelyn wheeled around and her long gown draped the chamber floor. The woman stared at him coldly before she noticed Quintin and smoothed her features.

"Ah, Prince Quintin, King Brier." She ignored Roland's presence. "To what do I owe the pleasure of this visit?"

"This visit is in the way of business." Brier walked toward the queen's desk. "Not pleasure."

"Heh—I see." The queen chuckled at Brier's tone. "However, I am not prepared to entertain your whims at the moment. Even if it is with such a lovely guest." Her eyes landed directly on Roland.

"The company is not a matter of your concern," Quintin said coldly. "The man who threatened our king's life was sentenced today. Have you no cause to make sure he is properly judged?"

"As I have told the king's advisor many times, my day does not revolve around court hearings. As queen mother, I am charged with the reputation of this country."

"Then I'm sure you are working tirelessly to restore my daughter's name in Avenough?"

"Of course," the queen conceded. "Regan's succession is my top priority."

"Ryanne," Roland grunted.

"Are you here to discuss your daughter's name, or her parentage?" The queen grinned wickedly.

"There are several things I would like to discuss, but my daughter, thankfully, is not one of them." Brier matched her simper. "Let us start instead with how Renli acquired secured documentation from the royal vault."

"How would I know that?" Her brow arched. "Isn't that what guards are for?"

"Incidentally, it was your personal guard who gave it to him," Brier answered calmly. "He also gave you that letter regarding Ronan's contract to kill me. Isn't that right, Prince Quintin?"

"Yes." Quintin blinked. "He said that it was given to him by an anonymous source."

"Indeed. I noticed I haven't seen him lately. How is Captain Galer?"

"Unfortunately he sailed to Zhennal just yesterday."

"How convenient for him," Roland seethed.

"Yes. I'm sure Captain Galer would be able to clear all of this up for you. His absence is a true pity." The queen's smile creased her eyes.

"When will he be back?" Brier demanded. "I have a few questions for him regarding his relationship with Lord Renli."

Panic flashed in the queen's eyes, but she quickly smoothed her features. "Captain Galer retired a fortnight ago. He is no longer my responsibility. Nevertheless, it was Renli who contracted Master Roland here to kill you. I only contracted him to teach you, and apparently you learned a bit too much from him. My only error was not collecting you sooner. I should have known I couldn't trust a hound with a whore's son."

Quintin pulled his sword before she could finish her statement.

"I don't doubt Renli's involvement," Brier asserted. "But I also suspect your own."

The queen sucked her teeth and stood tall. At her full height, she was almost as tall as Prince Quintin. "Come now, Brier." Her white teeth shone against her red lips. "If I wanted you dead, I could have done so at any time."

"I thought of that, and then I took your advice for once. I looked into the laws of Lirend," Brier answered, still calm. "Under the law of passage, an Einborn must reach his majority before his title can be rightfully passed to next of kin. If you'd killed me as a child, the monarchy would have simply ended. The republic would have had a free election. So you waited and tried to use my sabbatical against me. When I didn't forfeit my claim to the throne, you bet on Rolande's hatred for Aurelians to get rid of me. Fortunately, that didn't happen, so you chose to besmirch my name instead. You made sure Ryanne's parentage was known before Renli hired Caite for his final contract. Had he succeeded in killing me, the court would have never allowed Ryanne, a bastard and half Thenian, to rule Lirend."

"This is a nice theory, but unfortunately you have no proof," the queen simpered.

"I thought Renli's surplus amount of gold was enough to start at least an investigation. But it seems you two weren't foolish enough to document your transfers of crown gold directly," Brier replied. "Fortunately, I have Renli's full confession." Brier slapped a thick file of papers. "Your name is mentioned several times," Brier lied.

In truth, Renli had not mentioned the queen's name once, but he knew she'd used Renli as her pawn.

"It was a smart plan," Brier remarked. "Your true error was trusting Renli, a man whose loyalty can be bought with gold. He squealed like the rat he is."

The queen folded her arms and glared at him with icy-black eyes. Brier knew that look. He'd conditioned himself against it. He'd hardened his heart against Queen Evelyn's scorn long ago. "What are you expecting to come of all this?"

"Expecting?" Brier gritted through his teeth. "You tried to kill me!"

"And so what if I did?" she whispered. "Your father was too weak to do it! He could not see the detriment in his own house!" Brier's jaw tensed at the woman's cruelty. "I begged him for a child to become the heir, and he would not have me! I warned him that you would be the curse on his line, but he did not believe me! Now look at the consequence of your looseness! A bastard child with a Thenian! It is good that he died before he could see what a disgrace you are!"

"You are the only disgrace," Brier sneered. "Breaking all oaths of fealty to my father with your hunger for power! *You* are the one who sullies my father's memory with lies and malice, not me!" He yelled and pointed his shaking finger. "Would that you look in the mirror and see yourself for the true monster you are!"

"Arhrrgghh!" Silver glinted toward Brier before he could react, and he held up his hand to rebuff the woman as she lunged toward him.

"Brier!" He heard Roland's gruff voice as Roland shoved him to the ground and Brier's head collided with the stone floor. Quintin scuffled for only minutes until he heard the prince shout for the guards to help retain the woman.

"Mghnn…." Brier used his palms to rise from the ground, dazed from his fall.

"Take her away!" Quintin yelled. The guards who'd arrived grabbed the queen and cuffed her. "And call the healer."

The healer?

Brier touched the blood trickling from his temple.

Was he so hurt?

Brier turned toward Quintin to inform him that he was all right when he heard the gagging wheeze beside him. "Rolande!" Brier's choked scream rang out in the closed off chamber. His vision blurred with convulsed tears as he watched the crimson drip from Roland's side. His eyes were closed, but the blood seeped out the crease of his mouth.

"Ronan," Brier whispered as he moved a trembling hand to press against the deep wound.

"Brinan." Brier heard Roland's faint voice call his name. "That bitch got me good."

"Shhh…." Brier covered the whole of Roland's body to protect him. "Don't talk, Ronan, please, just…." The tears dripped as Brier stared into the slate-blue eyes. "It's all right. Meade's coming to help you."

"It hurts." Roland breathed harshly. "My heart hurts."

"I know, just…." Brier clutched Roland's jerkin. "*Acai*… please, Ronan… save your strength."

"*Na*, I have to say this, just in case… just in case I don't make it."

"You're going to make it!" Brier bared his teeth.

"*Acai*, Brinan, listen to me…." Brier sniffed and concentrated to understand the foreign tongue. "No matter what happens to me, I want you to know I love you. More than anything, Brier."

"I know, Ronan… please…." Brier held Roland's face with his bloodied hand. "The healer's coming."

"I'm sorry all I've been able to give you is pain, Brier. Please forgive me. I'm sorry. Forgive me."

"There is nothing to forgive. It's in the past."

"Forgive me… forgive me please…," the huntsman repeated with his voice growing faint.

"Ronan!" Brier screamed Roland's name when his body grew stiff. "Rolande!" Brier leaned in and covered Roland's bloody mouth with his own and breathed desperate air into Roland's lungs. "*Acai*!" He gritted through his teeth as he pumped the man's chest to restart his heart. He tried to pressurize the gash, but the blood flow seemed never ending. Each time Brier pounded Roland's chest, Brier's heart sank. "*Acai*! Ronan! You promised you wouldn't leave me again. *Acai*!" Brier lowered his head against Roland's still chest. "*Acai… A'ma el….*"

"Stand aside!" Meade's voice cut through the sound of Brier's sobbing as he yelled orders to assistants.

"You have to save him!" Brier commanded. He turned when he felt Quintin's heavy hand on his shoulder.

"Brier…," Quintin whispered, gently lifting him away.

"No! He needs me! I can't leave him to die by himself!"

"We have to leave so that Meade can try to save him!" Quintin bellowed. Brier sobered up for a moment when he heard the prince's acerbic tone. He could see the anguish in Quintin's teary eyes. The worry was not only his own.

IN THE first hour Brier managed to find hope. Assistants revolved through the queen's gold-lined door. Meade had not come with good news, but he did not come with bad news either. Marietta tried to sway him to wash and change, but Brier did not move from the corridor outside of the suite.

The second hour Brier tried to numb his restless mind, but the image of Roland's lifeless body flickered through his dreams.

The third hour? Brier began to weep silent tears.

"My King." Brier raised his red eyes toward one of the assistants. "We should bind your leg." The younger man pointed to blood on his thigh. Brier had not noticed his wound had reopened.

"All right…." He answered in a tired voice. Brier removed his pants and the assistant unwrapped the bloody bandage. He watched as the doctor grabbed the needle and medical thread and pierced his pale skin. It'd hurt so much before, and yet, Brier could only feel the pain in his chest right now.

"Meade," Quintin said. Brier raised his head toward the door. "How is he?" Quintin stood up to meet the tired-looking doctor.

"I've done what I can," Meade answered. He cleaned his hands off with a wet cloth. "It's touch and go at the moment."

"Touch and go?" Brier asked.

"Right now he's unconscious." The words rang through Brier's entire body. "His heart isn't in great shape, and he's lost a lot of blood."

I refuse.

"Do whatever it takes," Brier gritted through his teeth and swallowed the ache.

I refuse.

"Whatever it takes—you save him. Okay?"

I refuse to let him die.

"All right." Meade nodded and went back into the room. Brier traced his hand over the stitches in his wounded leg. He paused when he heard Quintin's melancholy tone.

"I just had a horrible thought," Quintin whispered. "When Meade came out here, I hoped that he would say that Roland had died." Brier pressed his lips together at Quintin's dark words, but he did not reply. His heart could not take a quarrel with Quintin right now.

"And then I realized even if he died, it would change nothing. You would mourn him for the rest of your days. You would marry me, and spend your life pining for him, wishing to meet him in the next life." Brier felt the heat under his eyelids as Quintin voice shook.

"I'm sorry, Quintin," Brier muttered, but Quintin shook his head.

"I get it. In the end, no matter what I do, or what I say, I will never have your heart." Quintin paused and met Brier's teary gaze. "Isn't that right, King Brier?"

"Aye."

TWO DAYS passed in a haze for Brier as he sat beside Roland's bed, praying for Roland to stir. Marietta did at least convince him to bathe, but meals were set aside. Brier did not speak to anyone. He spent his time with Roland instead, watching Roland's chest rise and fall.

Meade stepped into the chamber with a stethoscope around his neck and the leather bag he often carried. Brier watched him uneasily as Meade checked Roland's heart and lungs.

"His pressure is stabilized, and I don't see any signs of infection."

"Then why doesn't he wake?" Brier whispered.

"I do not know why he sleeps. The wound is healing, but his body remains passive," Meade answered as he injected Roland with a clear fluid syringe. "Physically he is strong enough to survive, but mentally he's suffered." Meade sighed softly. "I fear he may waste away if he does not wake soon."

"Then…." Brier stared at Roland's peaceful face. "You're just going to let him go?"

"We've done all that we can, Brier. It's up to Roland now."

Meade stepped out of the chamber to speak with Quintin about the arrangements to move Roland out of the queen's suite. Brier hated sleeping here, but since he refused to leave Roland's side, he had no choice. He had not seen Ryanne in days. He did not ever want her to see him like this.

Tired... lonely.... afraid....

He never wanted his daughter to see him broken.

BRIER WOKE to the sound of a child's laughter. He searched for Ryanne in the queen's suite, but found that he was no longer sitting at Roland's bedside. At first he thought he must have been moved to his own suite in the night, but then he heard the water pouring from the wooden beam into a square marble fountain. The white gown he wore covered his arms and draped down to his bare feet.

I'm in Balmur, Brier thought as he gaped across the open plains, glittering with blue ponds. The patio was empty, but he could still hear giggling from the garden adjacent.

"Ryanne?" He called for his mischievous daughter. She must be playing, Brier concluded and he smiled, eager to see the girl's smiling face. He followed the sound until he reached the path toward the garden with flower sprouts and weeds, but when he entered the closed fence, a bang of thunder startled him. Brier gazed up at the graying sky and cursed under his breath. He squinted as the last ray of sun vanished and the first droplets of rain fell on his forehead.

Boom!

Another jolt of thunder, this time with flickering lighting. Now he grew fearful as the rain began to beat more steadily and he still had not found Ryanne.

"Ryanne!" But his voice drowned in another blow of lightning. He finally stepped fully into the garden and searched for the toddler, but he found nothing but a soaked garden bed.

"Ryanne!" His heart pounded now as the water began to spill over the fountain. He did not see her. He could no longer hear giggling, but saw rain pummeling blue slate. "Ryanne! Ryanne! Ryanne!" But the thunder deafened his shouts. He ran through the gardens until he reached the first pond, and his gut knotted. She couldn't have. He stared into the foreboding water that had risen to the bank. Brier squinted to search, but saw nothing and was relieved. When he peered up, he saw his daughter standing at the edge.

"Hehe!" The girl laughed as she jumped in a puddle.

"Ryanne!" he screamed to the child. "Don't move!" He held his hand up to still her. The girl gazed at him curiously before she peered down into the water, equally fascinated by what she saw.

"*Aida*!" Ryanne pointed into the water. "*Aida*! *Aida*!" Brier heard her squeal through the rain. Brier could not help gaping into the water. He knew there was no one there, but his daughter's excited yelps drew his gaze. This time he could see something floating just below the surface. Black hair suspended in the rippling pond water.

"*Aida*!"

"Ronan?" Brier whispered as the fear gripped him. He did not have time to think before Ryanne jumped into the water with her placid, floating father.

"Ryanne!" Brier jumped in, but found that instead of cold, stifling heat absorbed him. He searched through the boiling water to find Roland and his daughter, but he could not see anything below his pale feet.

"Hhm?" He scanned the water above him. A faint orange glow came into view, and he swam to the surface, more afraid than curious. Brier gasped as the smoky air filled his lungs. Somehow the rain had stopped, but Brier could see the flames ignited from the roots of a large sequoia tree.

Where am I now? Brier wondered as he swam to the lake's shore. He could see fire in the distance, but what caught his eye most was the white smoke rising from a house at the foot of the valley. His feet somehow carried him to the bottom of the hill, but he wished they hadn't. A sea of blood and black smoke clouded his vision. Brier tried to cover his mouth, but his eyes burned as he walked through the fog. He stopped when he reached the house with the white smoke. He touched the door handle, but pulled back when the bronze burned his hand red. He turned to walk away, tired of the manic illusion, but then he heard his daughter's laugh from inside of the home.

"Ryanne?" Brier peaked through a crack in the door. He could not see a thing. "Ryanne!" He rammed his shoulder against the door with all his strength, and the door crashed open. "Ryanne, are you—" But Brier's voice trailed when he saw the girl sitting in the lap of a woman dressed in all white. Unlike the bonfires outside, this home was unaffected by the flames. The smooth walls reminded Brier of Roland's cabin in Aire. Brier watched the woman bounce the child on her lap and lean in to rub their noses together.

"Ryanne…." Brier moved closer, prepared to gather Ryanne and flee, but the longer he stared at the child, the more dissimilar she appeared from his daughter. Aye, she did have Ryanne's blithe laugh and olive skin, but this child had dirty blonde hair and full lips like Roland's.

"*Aida*!" The little girl hopped off her mother's lap and ran toward a man Brier most certainly knew. Roland hugged her tight in his burly arms, nuzzling her exposed skin. The woman stood up and kissed Roland's cheek before she turned toward Brier. She walked toward him, and Brier stood stiff. Waiting to hear the woman's voice. However, the woman did not speak. She only stared and smiled at his bemused frown.

"You're Helenas?" Brier whispered. The woman nodded once. Her hair shone gold against the glow of a faint log fire, her lips a pale pink. Brier could tell why Roland had loved her. She had a gentleness in her smile and eyes, even as she just stood watching him.

"Let me guess." Brier continued in Thenian when the woman did not speak. "You want him to stay here with you?" Brier cut his eye toward Roland still playing with the child in his arms. His blue eyes creased into slits as his laugh reverberated in the tiny cabin. His wife, the child he never knew, and the life that was ripped away from him.

Mayhap Roland could find peace….

Happiness….

Love….

Brier gazed at his lover.

But….

"I'm sorry, but… I can't let him go. I still need him," Brier told the woman simply. Even if he could never replace Helenas, he refused to let Roland go.

This man….

Roland, Rolande, Ronan.

Was his everything.

"*Mana el man'*," the woman replied in an ethereal whisper. She grasped Brier's hand in hers. Brier wrapped his arms around the woman's thin back, hugging her tight. Her blonde hair tickled his cheek. She smelled like wildflowers.

"*Diole'*," Brier exhaled as he clutched the woman's shoulders. He buried his head in warm skin and closed his eyes with a gentle smile. He could see why Roland loved her. He wanted to know her. Perhaps in the afterlife he would.

Te'na an'.

"BRINAN…."

Brier felt a warm hand through his enflamed hair and heard the low grumble of a man's voice. Ronan's voice. He raised his head and twisted to see the huntsman, a weak smile on his brittle lips.

"Ronan?" Brier's voice came out hoarse.

"*Venur*." Roland responded gruffly. Brier's lip quivered as he tried to stutter out a reply. "*L'tyva el*?"

"Aye." Brier nodded and stood to touch him, to see the blue of Roland's gaze.

"Why do you look at me with mournful eyes?"

"Forgive me." Brier wiped the tears from his eyes. "I just… I love you, Ronan. I don't want to ever lose you again."

"Is this a dream or am I truly seeing you?" Roland frowned.

"If this is a dream, then I don't want to wake." Brier laughed out through the tears. He slid his hand to Roland's face and placed a kiss on his forehead.

"Correct me if I am wrong, but I do believe the prince kissed the princess's lips to wake her."

"Aye." Brier leaned in again to kiss Roland's lips. A shiver ran up his spine when he felt Roland's hand slide up his back. "I didn't think I would ever see you awake again, Ronan." He tightened his fingers in Roland's hair before their foreheads touched. "I'm never letting you go."

"Then marry me," Roland muttered. Brier pulled back slightly, and Roland held his face. He felt Roland's fingertips brush the frazzled red hair away from his cheek.

"What did you say?"

"You are the father of my daughter and the love of my life, Brinan. I don't intend to be separated from you ever again."

Brier's heart squeezed. "I don't want to be away from you either."

"So then you best marry me, or I'll have to make good on my promise and lock you up."

"That won't be necessary." Brier chuckled and shook his head. "I will marry you, but first you need to get well."

"You promise?" Roland croaked through a sleepy smile.

"Aye, I promise." There was no one else he'd ever wish to love, to marry, to hold. Brier laid his head on Roland's chest and listened to the rumbling breath. He would be here when Roland woke up, and for the rest of their lives.

Chapter 35
Conquest

Roland stood at the ridge between the lake and footpath under the freshly bloomed willows. The sun peeked over the horizon as Roland fidgeted with his stiff collar and straight legged pants. The colur gems in his buttons glimmered against the sunlight and the decorative sword on his waist glared iron. He'd never worn anything so opulent in his life.

Ryanne came first in a blue dress with matching ribbons in her back-length hair. The girl half ran, half walked down the aisle toward him, while her petticoat swished when she bent to pick up the wildflowers she'd just thrown.

"*Aida*!" At near three, her Thenian had improved, but her wayward attention caused the guests to laugh. When she picked up a daffodil pod and blew it successfully, she called to her unseen father to inform Brier of her feat.

"I blew it, Papa!"

"Shh, come," Victoria said and scooped the girl, flowers in tow, off the white runner. Roland snorted. They had no need for resplendent scenery in Balmur. Daffodils, pink knapweeds, and yellow marigolds were in full bloom as a gentle breeze wrapped around the countryside. Roland stood beneath a traditional wooden Thenian arch, bedecked in blue, green, and ox-eyed daisies. He could hear the wild horses neighing in the distance, and the lapwings sang their lullabies along with the melodic violins. Dusk settled over Balmur.

The first vision was white. A glowing light that started at the bottom of the path and rose up on the shallow hill. Then fiery red hair that Brier chose to leave unbraided, straight and adorned with, instead of his colur gem crown, a crown made of elder. Their formal wedding had already long since passed. In the dull stone of Green Hall for protection, with nearly the entire kingdom in attendance. Roland and Brier sat stiff at the minister's feet, praying, reciting their vows without mirth, and never once gazing into each other's eyes. By law and name Roland was considered the king's consort, but only in a true handfasting ceremony could he accept their union fully.

The white silk robe hugged the top of the king's chest, flared out at the hem, with fine metal laced through the stitching of the wide sleeves and a colur-gem-encrusted broach at his neck. They'd embroidered the robe with green thread, stitched into an intricate leaf pattern.

Roland thanked the gods when Brier reached the wooden arch, muttering his silent prayer. He inhaled when Brier stood beside him, but breathed deep when Roland saw his king's exuberant smile. It was official. The sight of Brier made him weak.

"*Aida*! Papa!" their daughter called from the crowd until Marietta scolded her. Brier chuckled softly before Roland watched Brier's head shake.

"I believe that Ryanne will not wait a second longer," Roland whispered.

"Nor will I," Brier murmured back to him.

"I, ROLANDE Liam Archer Snow, take thee Brier Ignacio Archer Snow to be my wedded husband, again, to have and to hold from the days before, and this day, and forever. For better for worse, for richer for poorer, for fairer or fouler, in sickness and in health, to love and to cherish, till death us depart, according to the gods' holy ordinance; and thereunto I plight thee my troth."

"I, Brier Ignacio Archer Snow, take thee Rolande Liam Archer Snow to be my wedded husband once more, to have and to hold forevermore, for better for worse, for richer or poorer, in sickness and in health, to love and to cherish, till death us depart, according to the gods' holy ordinance; and thereunto I plight thee my troth."

"If anyone feel permitted to smite this holy union, speak now, or hold thy peace."

"Heh—" Roland snickered. "They would be a fair year late, eh?"

"Hush." Brier pressed his lips together to stifle a laugh.

"Then—"

"Hold on." Roland raised his hand. The priest stared at him wide eyed as he turned toward Brier. "I'm not smiting this union," Roland joked. "But I would like to say something, if you would permit?" Roland gaped at the man's stupefied expression until the priest nodded.

Roland held Brier's hands and brought the king's fingertips to his lips with a roguish grin. "Brier Ignacio Archer Snow. I did not have a purpose in life for many seasons. I lived with loneliness and heartache for too long. I trudged on simply to exist, but I no longer knew happiness… until I met you." Roland's smile faltered, but he never strayed from the emerald eyes as he spoke. "You are my lover, my friend, and my partner. You are the light in my darkness. I will never have enough penance to the gods for allowing us to cross paths. I will never have the right words to express my undying adoration for you, my king. Thank you, Brinan, for being the beginning of my happiness and the end of my suffering. I promise to love you with everything in me. I promise to connect with you, with all of my mind… and *trust* you with all of my heart. Till the end of our days."

Roland attempted to salvage the ceremony by asking hasty permission for them to kiss, but Brier had slid his arms around the nape of his collar. Roland shivered as Brier's tongue curled fluidly. When they finally broke, the crowd cheered and Brier whispered in his ear so that only Roland could hear.

"*Te'na an*, Rolande."

AN HOUR later when everyone was fed, people began toasting with their wine to his and Brier's handfasting. Brier's smile grew more iridescent as the light paled and the night grew. In fact, it never left Brier's lips, save for when Ryanne decided to topple over a cup of red wine. Brier cursed as the stain seeped through the white robe.

"Do you think anyone will notice?"

"Yes—" Roland started, but a light voice rang out before he could answer.

"In Thenia, it is good luck to spill wine on one's wedding day." Roland gazed at the silver-haired man as Botcht detached from his arm. Roland stood and beamed. Before Lei could even greet him, he yanked his best friend into a hug.

"*Venur*, Rolande, Brinan."

"*Venur*!" Roland squeezed Lei's back. "Where have you been? I searched for you," he said when he'd released Lei.

"We were assigned as diplomats from Lirend to lead the peace terms in Thenia." Lei frowned. "Did Brier not tell you?" Roland whipped his head to the smirking king.

"*Na*, Leighis. I did not want him running off to Thenia behind you before our wedding."

"Ha-ha—" Lei nodded. "You are far more astute than I remember, Brier. It seems you've learned well with me as your teacher after all."

"*Diole'*." Brier laughed out and Roland's brow creased as they fell into a whimsical exchange. As usual his best friend and his husband shared a joke that he was not privy to.

"*L'tyva el*?" Roland spoke to Botcht instead, who nursed a cup of ale.

"Aye, though we should have returned a month ago." The man stared at Brier and Lei. "Either way we missed the formal ceremony in Avenough."

"This is the only ceremony that matters to me and Brier. The one in the capital was a show. Our family and friends mean more to us than our Aurelian constituents."

"Leinan is a diplomat of the republic now. A highly coveted position," Botcht told Roland as if he was unaware.

"You said you two should have returned a month ago. What kept you, then?" Roland inquired.

Roland noticed how Botcht tried to hide the red in his face, but failed miserably. "We stopped to change my registry formally."

"Ahh." Roland raised his brow with a grin. "So Leighis is an Everdane officially."

"Yes." Botcht cleared his throat. "Nevertheless, congratulations on your marriage."

"Thank you." Roland grinned. "And congrats to you, Botcht. I'd heard that you are to head the Thenian soldiers once the provisions are made in Aire."

"That is only a rumor," Botcht replied stiffly.

"Aye." Roland smirked at the man's ever-staunch nature. "But keep in mind who my husband is." Avenough charged Botcht with the crime of an organized revolt on Lirend's capital, but every Thenian refused to mention Botcht's name, and no Aurelian could testify against him. In the end the court sentenced him to time served due to a lack of evidentiary support.

"I see." Botcht sipped his ale. "Then I will look forward to seeing you soon in Avenough."

"Not me." Roland shook his head. "My place is here, in Balmur. With my husband and daughter." Once he might have jumped at the chance to train new recruits, but not anymore. Botcht let out a guttural laugh, and Roland glared at him.

"What's so funny?"

"It's just that I never thought I'd see the day where you would put away your bow and arrow." Botcht laughed again, but gave Roland a smile of approval. "You've changed," Botcht told him.

"For the better?"

"Not for the worse." Botcht shrugged and walked away. Roland saw Botcht interrupt Brier and Lei's animated conversation and lead Lei to the dance floor.

"It seems my companion was stolen from me." Brier chuckled as he continued to sip his wine. Roland's eye twitched when Brier called Lei "companion," but he ignored his petty jealousy and bowed to Brier theatrically.

"May I have this dance, my king?"

Brier laughed at his boorish pomp. "You may, Lord Roland." Brier matched his bow. Roland slid a hand to rest on the dip of Brier's back. Brier's head rested on his shoulder. Roland could feel Brier's warm breath on the now unbuttoned collar of his neck.

"Though I must admit I am biased," Roland said pointedly. "I think this wedding outdoes your others. For one thing, it does not include arrows, and for another there is no Lord Tamil."

Brier snickered. "Aye, and lastly it includes you." Four years later this man still made his heart race. The stars shone bright in the black sky. Dimmed candles now illuminated the gardens and patios, but mostly everyone had departed. They danced in their garden, drenched in darkness.

"Are you happy, Brinan?"

"I have never had a better day in my life." A gentle smile danced over Brier's lips as he peered upward. "This is all I ever wanted, and somehow, it is better than I imagined it would be."

"You imagined this day?" He gazed down to the freckled face, dazed with happiness. "For how long?" He teased his husband's childish nature.

"Since I knew you were the one I wanted to marry."

"Heh." Roland shook his head. "So not very long at all." Brier did not laugh, but clutched Roland's back tighter and Brier's voice trembled as he whispered.

"Longer than you know, Ronan."

ROLAND WAS glad to get out of his dress jacket and grateful that it would be a while before he had to wear it again. He rubbed his shaved face and washed out his mouth, eager for his supposed wedding night.

Their bed, the bed he'd built with his own two hands, remained as sturdy as ever. Sheer drapes hung from the tie poles and tea candles faintly illuminated the room. He could not see the painting of Balmur hanging on the wall adjacent, but he could see Brier's naked marked skin.

"Are you anticipating something this eve, my king?" Roland feigned confusion. Brier leaned back against the silk encased pillows and crooked his knee up. The robe Brier wore in no way hid his skin or desire.

"Mayhap." Brier played Roland's game. "A master to teach me?" Brier's voice ·e with the question. Roland leaned in to kiss supple lips.

"You look pretty well trained," he whispered before he kissed Brier's open stomach. Brier gasped before his back rose up, reflexive. "Where did you get this robe from I wonder. I must remember to send my thanks." The fabric hugged his husband's flushed skin, but revealed Brier's spread thighs, butt, and chest to him. Roland licked down to the cloth that covered Brier's groin, and he mouthed the stiff erection. Roland's heated breath made Brier's member pulse on his chin.

"*Acai*, Ronan." Brier gripped his back. "I can't wait."

"How will you last if you're squirming already?" He tasted the tip of Brier's dripping shaft and savored the orgiastic flavor. "Like this and I've barely touched you."

"That's because—" But Roland sucked the tip of his crown, and Brier's voice died. His breath came out ragged as his hips rolled slightly. Roland slurped Brier's rod like a stalk of sweet sugar cane, the cream buried deep inside.

"Ronan… we can play later." Brier pulled his hair. "Have me now."

Roland lifted up his head and peered at Brier with raised brows. "You are a hungry knave this eve." He chuckled darkly before he gripped Brier's meaty thighs with a slap. He yanked Brier toward the edge of the solid oak bed.

"I think I'll make you wait a little longer. It is our wedding night after all." Roland winked at Brier. He moved off the bed and onto his knees so that he was level to Brier's exposed bottom half. He had to hunch for his height in order to parallel himself with Brier fully.

"Stay just like that, Your Majesty." He spread Brier's legs and lifted them straight up. Brier's ass cheeks squeezed his hairless sac and hole. "I see, so you really *were* expecting something." Roland snorted.

"Mmn… h-hush, Ronan," Brier sputtered, and Roland knew his husband blushed. He grabbed the white jar of creme Brier had near the burning flames.

"You should know there's only one way to hush me up." Before the king had time to ready himself, Roland's tongue massaged deep against the walls of Brier's cleft.

"Aye I know—hnggn—" Brier's head pressed back into the mattress as Roland flicked his tongue to tease the underside of Brier's fleshy sac. Brier's breath paused before he let out a whining moan.

"Ahnnnnnnn! Ronan." Brier inhaled before Roland felt a strong grasp on the back of his head. Brier's thighs and hips wrapped around Roland's face, and Roland let his tongue unwind the shackles on Brier's carnal lust. Roland dipped his index, middle, and ring finger into the white paste before he lathered the man's entrance. He spread Brier's crack and watched the wrinkled skin twitch for more of his tongue. Brier wanted to come already, but not yet. He had to make sure Brier could last through the endless pound. If all went as planned, he'd have Brier through the night.

Roland reached in front of Brier to stroke his strained member. He squeezed the taut skin, then nuzzled his head between Brier's thighs, and dug the king out with his sharp tongue. Brier's scarred stomach quivered and clenched through each ministration, but when the drops of precum beaded at the pink tip, Brier reached out to relieve the ache.

"*Na*." Roland held Brier's wrists to his sides and sucked down the dripping erection.

"Ronan! *Acai*!" Brier pleaded, but Roland only sucked harder as he pulled up from the rhythmic bob. The back of Brier's knees pressed into his shoulders before Roland pulled away, and he heard a painful cry.

"Ahhnn-please!" Brier slurred and writhed to be filled. Roland smirked and shoved his fingers in to split Brier's hole wider, moving his fingertips in wide circles to prick the man like a blunt knife. Brier clenched around his digits, and Roland slapped his plump ass.

"*Acai*!" Brier writhed in defeat.

"You're sucking me in," Roland whispered, slightly amused by Brier's obvious need to be filled. "Tell me, Your Majesty…." Roland licked off a fresh dribble of preejaculate. "Is there something you want?"

"Aye, *acai*!"

Roland thrust his middle finger up, rooted against the spot to make his lover spasm. "Here, right?" Roland kissed the inside of Brier's shaking thighs while he nudged his finger deeper.

"Aye, but please Ronan—not with your fingers." Brier jerked up and clawed his shoulder. "Fuck me." Brier's hungry stare made Roland's stomach flutter before his member tensed. He pulled out all three of his fingers and stood up to show his own erection. He grabbed the white jar and slicked his shaft for good measure before upending Brier to his stomach in a whiplash flip.

Brier inhaled.

"Do not blame me if you cannot move tomorrow."

"Aye." Brier gripped the sheets and bowed his back. "Fuck me until I'm weak."

"I'll plow you till you cannot stand." Roland grunted in Brier's ear before he split the king with his member. "Haah—" The feeling of warmth enveloped him. Brier certainly had sucked in his fingers, but that could not compare to rubbing saturated flesh, twitching, pulsing, clinging to his rod.

Gods, this ass is heavenly.

Roland rutted Brier fast and hard. He wound his hips against Brier's smooth ass, one leg planted firmly on the hardwood, the other leveraged on the bed.

"Hnh… m-more…," Brier whispered faintly. Roland shifted up fully to the bed and yanked Brier's body hard against his pelvis.

"Mpfh!" Brier exhaled with tears in his eyes.

"You feel too good," Roland whispered. He leaned in and licked the symbols on Brier's shoulder, which had begun to glow faintly. Roland trailed his tongue up until it found his husband's appetent mouth. He slammed viciously against Brier's bucking hips. Roland wanted to drill a hole so deep no one could ever fill it: own him, fuck him, hold him, love him.

Gold rippled through the leaves on Brier's peppered skin. "Hgnnnn—"

"Kiss me," Roland whispered before he covered the moan from Brier's gut. Brier tightened around his thick flesh and heat boiled in Roland's groin.

Brier groaned and convulsed uncontrollably. The orgasm pushed through Brier …e, and he released in spurts onto the sheets below them.

"Annh—haah!" Flesh tightened around Roland's penetrative sword, and he felt the blinding pressure. He tried to smother the sudden pleasure, but Brier's hips snapped back against him in a fervent ricochet.

"Brier—!" Roland managed to choke out his husband's name in slight alarm. "I'm about to come…." He panted. He attempted to slide out to avoid spilling inside of his husband, but Brier reached back and pulled him in closer.

"Let go! I can't hold it."

"Hnh…. Don't… haah… don't stop." Brier panted out as his nails embedded into Roland's thighs. "Fill me… *acai*." Roland closed his eyes in surrender. Brier's plea sent a shiver from the bottom of Roland's spine and into the tip of his oozing member.

He grunted and blew out hot air from the rising orgasm. "Ahhh—fuck—" His seed spurted so hard and deep he thought the after-daze would never end.

"Dear gods…." Roland kissed his lips softly. Brier's scarred, albeit flushed skin, gold leaves, and red fiery hair made for a bewitching vision. "You're beautiful."

THEY LAY together in silence against the blue of their bedspread, the draped sheer fabric in disarray. Brier's breath came out in contented huffs while Roland managed to regain his choppy rhythm.

"That was not wise, you know."

"Hmm?" Brier hummed. "What wasn't?"

"Your skin was white gold," Roland mumbled.

"And?"

Roland gripped Brier's chest tight.

Brier gasped at Roland's strength.

"And. What will we do if you conceive?"

"Is there any question?" Brier asked apprehensively. "If I get pregnant, we will have the child."

"While I do love the thought of tasting your milk again…." Roland slid his hands toward Brier's areola and pinched his pink nipple. Brier shivered under his fingertips. "It could be dangerous if we had more." Roland pressed his lips against his husband's ear and traced his hand up the inside of Brier's scarred thigh. "Meade said that at the very least we need to wait several years if we plan to have another."

"Mm…." Brier whimpered from his touch. "We didn't plan for Ryanne. She came and we accepted it."

That was true. By all accounts their daughter might have never been born from a singular coupling had the gods not seen fit to give them the blessing.

"I am happy with Ryanne," Roland whispered.

"I too am happy with our daughter, but… I would also like more."

Roland did not reply, musing over Brier's anxious tone and tensed shoulders.

"It may be foolish, but a part of me, a part of me holds on to this deflated dream."

"It does not sound foolish." Roland sighed out. He understood his husband's wishes, but his desire was to have Brier whole and safe.

"I want more but… I would never force you." Brier curled in his arms. "I want you to desire more as well."

"I do desire more!" Roland twisted Brier to face him. Brier's face flushed, startled from his tone, and Roland frowned. "I *do* want more children with you, Brier." He exhaled to wane his temper. "But what if—" Roland did not want to speak the words aloud. "What if something happens to you? To the child?"

"It's the same risk we took with our daughter," Brier answered simply.

"And she almost did not make it."

"We cannot shed tears for children who have not been realized, Rolande. Everything in life is a risk. Why think you the gods reward us for our courage?"

Roland stared nonplussed. It was just then, when his husband gently scolded him for his cowardice, that Roland realized the truth of Brier's words. He stared at Brier for one long minute before the king finally averted his intense gaze.

"Why do you stare at me as though I've said something deranged?"

Roland closed his mouth and shook his head, smiling. "'Tis only I who had forgotten a lesson. And you just reminded me." He leaned in and felt the familiar tingle of Brier's lips.

"What did I remind you of?" Brier mumbled between another kiss.

"That we save our tears for the outcome and not the possibility. We can only let fate decide."

"Aye, Ronan." Brier flipped Roland to his back and his lover's hand slid down his chest. "So what does fate have in store for me?"

Roland bucked his hips upward and Brier jerked. "Another pounding if you don't behave."

"Promise?" Brier's red brow arched.

"*Mana el man'*, Brinan." Roland thumbed Brier's chin.

They spoke without words, they made love without a care, and for the gods' grace, they found their happiness.

EPILOGUE

BRAEDON WOKE to the sound of birds chirping on his sill, and his sisters squabbling outside his bedroom door.

"Haven't I told you not to wear my shoes? You go gallivanting in them getting them all dirty!" Helenas screeched.

"It wasn't me," Merin replied. "Rosaline had them on!" All three girls congregated in the hallway in front of his door. His sisters, Helenas, at age fifteen, Merin, age twelve, and Rosaline, age eleven, took on an anxious and obnoxious bickering this morning, and Braedon knew why. Today their eldest sister Ryanne was coming back to Lirend.

"Both of you! Stop wearing my shoes!" Helenas stormed off and Braedon heard the loud thud as she slammed the door.

There should be a law against fighting this early...

Braedon sighed and tried to settle himself into a deeper sleep, but before long he heard another booming voice.

"Helenas! Merin! Rose! Braedon! Come, your sister is here!" Thundering footsteps echoed in the hall as the girls clamored toward the parlor. Braedon buried himself under his white cotton duvet and satin pillows.

So it begins.

His older sister Ryanne, rightful heir to Lirend and arguably most loved of his siblings, had decided to grace them with her presence after disappearing to Menlor with her new prince fiancé, Vincent Pascal. It shocked both their fathers when she renounced her title as future queen of Lirend and announced her plans to elope with the crown prince of Menlor. While his Papa took a more practical approach, urging them both to come back to Lirend to wed formally, Braedon's *aida* raged for hours and threatened to drag Ryanne from Menlor himself. For Braedon, it was all very dramatic, very troublesome, and very tiring. Now that Ryanne had shunned her title, the responsibility fell upon him, second oldest and only son of Roland and Brier Archer Snow. His entire life he'd had the world's door open to him, only to have it slammed shut on his hopes and dreams.

"You'll be the king of Lirend," his fathers said.

"And what if I don't want to be a king?"

"This is your fate, Braedon. The gods will it, and they make no mistakes."

Well thank the gods, Braedon thought as he heard a hard knock at his door. He didn't lift his head from the pillow though he heard the door click open.

"Braedon?" Marietta's firm voice called. "Are ya still asleep?" He ignored the nursemaid and steadied his breath. "Your sister is downstairs and we're all waiting for you."

Well, wait, then..., Braedon thought petulantly.

"I'll give ya ten minutes. Up with ya," Marietta said, before she closed the door with a resonating thud.

WHEN HE entered the dining room his family had already plopped down and began eating. Marietta sat at the head with Rosaline to her right. Helenas sat on the gray nursemaid's left, with Merin next to her and Ryanne seated in the middle. Vincent sat next to Ryanne, and across from him sat a cross-looking *Aida*. Braedon clenched his jaw as he walked toward *Aida*. He could feel the tension oozing off his father's broad shoulders, and see the pulsing vein on the side of his head.

"Hello little brother." Unlike Helenas, Merin, and Rosaline who had hazel-blue eyes and auburn hair, Ryanne's lush green gaze and radiant smile lit up the room. Her black breast-length wavy hair fit her like the gown she wore: a trumpet sleeved white dress with a square bosom and silver lining.

"Hello, Ryanne." Braedon smiled and leaned down to kiss her cheek.

"Nice of you to join us. Late," *Aida* said as he sipped from a colur-gem-encrusted goblet.

"I was considering my options, but faking my death didn't seem very practical," Braedon quipped as he sat down next to his father. Both Vincent and Ryanne chuckled, but the others peered up warily. The tension between Braedon and his *aida* had culminated into arguments several times since his papa announced Braedon would succeed as king.

"How are you, Braedon?" Ryanne attempted to divert the conversation her way. "Have you finished that painting you told me about in your letter yet?"

"No, I haven't." Braedon grimaced. "I haven't had much time between training with *Aida* to do much painting, or anything else. Nor have I had the mood. Inspiration comes rarely these days."

"Oh." Ryanne frowned. "Well that's unfortunate. Vincent and I hoped that you would make something for us as a wedding present." She caught her fiancé midchew and nudged his elbow.

"Oh, yes." Vincent nodded before he swallowed his mouthful of food. A piece of egg caught on the crease of his mouth. "Your pieces are exquisite. Ryanne tells me you've been drawing since before you could walk."

"Does she now?" Braedon smirked at the handsome prince. His face was soft, but not feminine, a sweet blue in his eyes. "Have you been bragging on me, big sister?"

"She brags quite a bit on you and showed me several of your paintings in Menlor. You're very talented. Ryanne says it is your dream to become a famous painter."

"Did she also tell you that because you two finally decided to couple in lawfully wedded bliss, that *I* no longer have the option to pursue a career in painting?"

Braedon watched, amused, as the color drained from Vincent's face. "Umm... well." He glanced at *Aida* furtively. "We did discuss what her becoming my wife would mean, not just to you, but to the whole of your family."

"Well," Braedon simpered. "It's nice that you discussed it. Whether it was an afterthought doesn't really matter I suppose." He took a large gulp of tea.

"Do you plan to be this charming the whole meal? Or should I save room in my appetite for your deplorable manners and sour mood?" Helenas asked, raising her brows.

"You should definitely save room." Braedon smiled and she rolled her eyes.

"Come now," Marietta chided him. "Your sister has traveled a long way, and we're all family. Can we have a meal in peace?"

"Oh I forgot, I'm a future king now. I can no longer let my 'deplorable manners' show."

"That's enough, Braedon," *Aida*'s deep voice cut in. "Learn to take a compliment or keep your mouth shut."

Braedon scoffed. Now that Ryanne had opted out of succession everyone expected him to play the gracious prince? He swallowed down the retort and turned toward his food. He despised this place. It wasn't fair. Everything was always his fault. Everyone always blamed him.

Everything.

Braedon scowled as Ryanne reached up and wiped the piece of egg off Vincent's face. *Everyone.*

The table resumed their meal, silverware clinking on gold-lined plates with sausage and poached eggs. The steam wafted out of the leaf-designed teapot as they passed it around to refill their teacups. The blueberries remained untouched in the center of the table. His papa was the only one who had a taste for them.

"Where's Papa?" Rosaline asked, cutting through the silence.

"He'll be here shortly, darling," *Aida* replied with a smile. "He had to finish up in court."

"Everyone's here except Papa." Braedon smiled as he poured himself a second cup of tea. "What a surprise." *Aida* turned toward him with a scowl and Helenas sighed. "But of course, why would he be here? It isn't as if there's a budget to propose, or a war to stop. No one's dying or asking for crown aide. I guess the engagement party of his firstborn just isn't important enough to warrant his full attention. Ryanne." He turned toward his sister with a serious tone. "You might as well have stayed in Menlor until you bore your first child. Maybe *then* Papa would see fit enough to come home."

"I said that's enough, Braedon!" *Aida* stood and the bowls of food shook as he slammed his hand on the table. *Aida* lifted up his finger and pointed it in Braedon's face. "How dare you insult your father." He narrowed his gaze. "How dare you question his devotion to this family after everything he has done for you. You think you're entitled to say whatever you want because you are the crown prince? Learn to think about someone other than yourself for once! Learn some respect for the sacrifices your father has made for all of us!"

"I never asked him to make any sacrifices for me! It was his decision to make us live so far away from the palace in Balmur! I hate this place! I wish I'd never been born into this family!"

Aida's hand raised and Ryanne screeched. "*Aida*!" His father had never struck him, but he'd said too much this time. Braedon covered his head and clenched his eyes preparing for the blow that never came.

"One more word," *Aida* gritted through his teeth as he lifted his shaking finger. Braedon stared at his slate-blue eyes and a chill ran up his spine. "One more word and you'll *really* wish you'd never been born." Braedon tightened his lip before he felt tears prickle his eyes. *Aida* moved gingerly to sit down and Braedon stood up from the table.

"May I be excused?" he whispered.

"No, you may not," *Aida* said coldly. "We're going to *sit* here and eat. In silence if we have to." His father cut his eggs and tore a piece of bread. Braedon seethed as he sat back down in his seat, and refused to say or eat anything for the remainder of the meal.

BRAEDON STOOD in the stables brushing Frieling's silky mane and plush coat. The breeze swept through his long red hair and he used a tie to pull it back from his face. They kept seven horses, no one similar in color or size, and *Aida* predominantly supervised their care. His father had an eye for beasts and often journeyed north to hunt with uncles in Aire. The temperature had dropped, chafing Braedon's pink lips. The grass was still green, though, and the willow by the patio had not yet lost all its vigor. Braedon sighed. They still had some weeks before the worst of winter.

"Braedon!" Ryanne called, breathless from the wind, from behind the stalls. She entered the dank stables when he did not answer. "Are you here?"

"Here!" Braedon called. There was no point in trying to avoid her. His sister had a steadfastness Braedon could never match.

"What are you doing out here?" Ryanne rubbed Frieling's mane, and the horse nudged her gently.

"Nothing." Braedon dropped the brush in the grooming pail.

"Hopefully staying out of trouble," his sister chuckled.

"You're one to talk after your disappearing act."

"I didn't disappear," Ryanne replied taking his place to brush Frieling. "Everyone knew I was with Vincent in Menlor."

"Except, no one gave you permission to travel across the sea to do gods knows what with your intended." Braedon crossed his arms.

"Were you worried for my virtue, little brother?" She raised her dark brows.

"For your virtue?" Braedon scoffed. "You haven't had virtue since you turned sixteen, Ryanne. Who do you think you are fooling?"

"Mayhap *Aida*?" Ryanne smirked wickedly and Braedon stifled his laughter. "You should take a page out of my book and find yourself a lover. I've heard you've become quite an insufferable twat these days. A bother to be around even."

"I never claimed to be sociable."

"Oh but you are the future ruler of Lirend, Your Grace." Ryanne bowed to him. "You will be the epitome of royalty and social decorum when you are king."

"I think not." Braedon turned his back to her and slouched over the stable wall.

"Mm, well… are you at least ready for tonight?" Braedon shrugged. People had traveled from out of the country to come to Princess Ryanne and Prince Vincent's engagement party. The servants had cleaned every crevice of their Balmur estate and cooked all night. People would pander to him, bow to him. Women would fill his head with nonsense and men would go on about hunting, and their wives, and wine, and for the younger lords, sex. He didn't want to be a part of any of that. He didn't want to be king of Lirend.

"Have you seen Papa yet?" Braedon asked.

"Not yet, but he promised he'd be home today in his letter."

"Of course he did," Braedon mumbled. He'd dragged poor Ryanne into his row with his father out of pure spite. "I'm sorry for being a prick at breakfast. You know Papa would skip court for you if you needed him." For Ryanne Papa would walk to Aire in the dead of winter.

"He would skip court for any of us if we needed him," she chided him. "Papa doesn't play favorites."

"Heh—my ass," Braedon scoffed. "If you think he'd let me just decide to sail away to Menlor and renounce the crown, you're fooling yourself."

"He didn't let me just renounce the crown. Not even Papa is that tolerant. But I'm marrying Vincent, and he is the crown prince of Menlor. I will one day be his queen and bear his children."

"So?" Braedon turned to her and crossed his arms.

"So the court would not allow me to rule Lirend and Menlor. Papa knows that."

"The court is as happy that you're marrying Vincent as you apparently are," Braedon replied.

"Only because they see it as a way to purify the bloodline."

Braedon knew that all too well. When he was a child, they would ridicule him for his Thenian father and even now some of the courtiers would make remarks of tainted bloodlines. They would say things of the new "low class" in Lirend. His papa became fierce when anyone tried to belittle citizens of Lirend, and reminded even the highest courtiers that he was happily married to a lord of Thenia. Braedon could not help the pride that swelled in his chest when he recalled his father's fiery possessiveness over *Aida*.

"Some of the courtiers still cling to the days of the law of passage, when 'people knew their place.'"

"Idiots. All of them. What difference does it make? Aurelian, Thenian? In the end we are all still human."

"I agree, but I no longer have the means to refute them. I'll leave it to you to take my place, little brother." She stood and lifted her arm to reach his shoulder. Braedon pursed his lips.

"I'm almost a foot taller than you, you know."

"Aye. I know. But you'll always be my little brother." She stood on her tiptoes to kiss his cheek. "No matter how tall you get."

Braedon shook his head, laughing. "You are a nuisance. You know that right?"

"It is my duty to tease you." Ryanne's smile faltered. "And it is Papa's duty to rule Lirend." King Brier Archer Snow, liberator of Thenians and sovereign of the exalted Lirend. For twenty-one years his father ruled fortuitously. And now they expected him to do what exactly? He wasn't nearly as charming, cunning, or kind.

"I know he has to be in Avenough," Braedon mumbled. "And I shouldn't have said that to *Aida*. I was upset." He shook his head. "He and I… haven't been getting along these days."

"You don't say?" Ryanne's eyes went wide and Braedon tried to mush her face. "Really, Braedon. You act as though you hate everyone!" Ryanne said, laughing as she ducked his hand.

"I don't hate him." He sighed deeply. "I'm not quite sure how to feel at the moment because everything is changing so fast." Ryanne was leaving. His sisters were growing up. *Aida* and Papa wouldn't be around forever. Braedon stared out onto the vast space. The lakes seemed so still, though he knew the waters rippled and swayed from the wind. He wanted to sail away across the sea like Ryanne. But where would he go? What would he do?

"It makes me realize more and more, that one day it will just be me. I'll be alone…with no one beside me," Braedon whispered, and lowered his head.

Braedon felt his sister's fingertips through his hair.

"Did Papa ever tell you the story of how he grew up?" Ryanne asked quietly.

Braedon shook his head. Papa almost never spoke of his past or the life before he and *Aida* married. It was as if they just fell together in perfect harmony, like two connected pieces to a puzzle.

"When grandfather Braedon died, he had no one, save for Marietta," Ryanne explained. "Papa lived in the capital's palace alone. No family. No friends. He could not even leave the property without expressed permission from the then queen. His light was smothered so that he could not outshine her own. Can you imagine Papa isolated in this way?"

Braedon shook his head and frowned deeply. He could not imagine the desolation of the palace without *Aida*, his sisters, Marietta, and of course the King of Lirend, Papa. Honestly he did not like even the thought of it.

"For *Aida*, it was a bit different. After Helenas died he willingly lived in solitude until he met Papa." Helenas, they all knew, was *Aida*'s wife. Before *Aida* lived in Lirend, he lived in a country called Thenia, with a woman Braedon's papa had never met. Still, Papa called Helenas remarkable.

"So you see." Ryanne raised his chin. "It is through *us* that they make up for the years of loneliness they faced. You, me, Helenas, Merin, Rosaline. And, of course, each other."

"Aye." Braedon chuckled. "Papa and *Aida* are meant for each other."

"Mayhap," Ryanne answered. "Though I think a better summation is that they refused to live a life without each other in it. They fought for everything they have."

"Including us?" Braedon asked dubiously.

"Especially us." Ryanne smiled. "Why think you *Aida* is so hard on you? We are the joy of his life, Braedon. They would do anything for us." Braedon felt the guilt weigh on shoulders. He'd spoken too recklessly, and he'd disrespected both *Aida* and Papa.

Braedon huffed as he wrapped his arm around Ryanne's shoulder. "You know, I can see why Vincent is smitten with you."

"Oh?" Ryanne blushed.

"Aye, you are a rare breed of woman." He guided her out of the stables. "You don't bore me with idle gossip and false compliments, unlike the courtier's daughters. They drape themselves on me like an ugly couch they're trying to hide."

"Oh? Too many women? *That* is your concern as a seventeen-year-old prince?"

"Too many women with no substance, dear sister. I'm lucky if they know how to read a book more than ten pages." He chucked mirthlessly. "I think I'll try to escape the party tonight after *Aida* has his third cup of ale."

"Heh—you are terrible, Branan, honestly." Ryanne's laughter died on the wind as they headed back to the villa.

THE FIRST carriage arrived with the sound of beating hooves and crunching gravel. The children, all five of them, leapt up and headed toward the main gate. Braedon fell back to let his younger sisters glomp his uncles.

"Sasta!" Helenas almost bowled him over.

"Helenas, Merin, Rose!" Sasta laughed out. Braedon liked Dur and Sasta the best of his uncles. They were mostly cheerful and always brought presents from their travels. Umhal, the most reserved of the guild, did not often speak, but always gazed at him pensively.

"*Venur*!" The silver-haired man bunched the three youngest girls into a hug.

"*Venur*." Braedon met them at the gates. "You look well, Uncle."

"As do you." Leighis pulled him into a hug. "If it's possible you look more like Brier than you did the last time I saw you, though thankfully taller."

"Thanks," Braedon replied curtly.

"Where are your fathers?" Botcht asked.

"Papa has not yet arrived," he said simply. "*Aida* is on the patio messing with the fire pit."

"Don't the servants usually prepare the food at these things?" Leighis inquired.

"We have servants to do it, but he insists they won't cook the food properly."

Leighis snorted before he walked toward the back patio. His father still had not properly changed and currently cursed under his breath in Thenian about the lack of experience capital cooks had with Thenian cuisine. Braedon watched amused as Ryanne reminded him that their cooks in fact were not Thenian, and threatened to tattle about his cursing to Marietta if he did not go and ready himself for the party.

By the time the Aurelian carriages began to arrive, Ryanne had tangled her nerves sufficiently. Between their father's idle pace, his sisters fussing through the halls, and Papa's delayed arrival, Ryanne was coming close to a meltdown.

"Go and ready yourself," Braedon instructed her. "I'll tend to everything down here." Ryanne nodded between a flustered sigh and headed upstairs to get ready. He caught Vincent looking painfully nervous near the exit that led to the patio. The man seemed be considering whether he should join the banter near the fire pit.

"Eavesdropping are you?" Braedon stood next to him.

"No—I wasn't. I was going to go out and say hello eventually."

"Oh good." Braedon grabbed his arm. "You can come with me, then." He dragged the sputtering man through the veranda doors. His uncles and father had set up a camp fire with goblets of wine and *rotund* cooking over the fire pit. Botcht sat with Leighis in his lap, with Dur and Sasta howling with laughter from a joke one of them had apparently told.

"You are as crude as ever, Ronan." Leighis shook his head. "And here I thought having four daughters would cure your tongue."

"Why would I want to cure my tongue? It's the only way I can keep up with Brnan."

Gross. Braedon twisted his face before he cleared his throat to announce his presence.

"Sorry to interrupt this scholarly discussion, but I wanted to introduce everyone to Ryanne's intended, and my future brother-in-law, Prince Vincent Pascal." Vincent bowed his head and Braedon chuckled.

"You need not bow to us," *Aida* grunted and crossed his arms. "Where's Ryanne?"

"Getting dressed," Braedon answered. "And she's in a right state at the moment since you're taking your time to get ready."

"I'll be dressed by the time your Papa gets here."

"Oh, but he's already here…." Braedon feigned a frown. "Didn't you know? He's tending to Ryanne." Braedon had to fight the smile on his lip at the pace with which his father moved from his seat. He chugged the remainder of his ale and handed the goblet to Sasta before he disappeared into the house.

"Well… that's one way to make a Thenian move his ass!" Sasta exclaimed. Everyone recommenced their raucous laughter.

"When did Brier arrive?" Leighis asked, still giggling.

"He didn't," Braedon answered as he led Vincent over to his father's seat. "But Father idles overlong when Papa isn't here to manage him."

"Aren't you the clever one." Leighis smirked. "Outsmarting your father."

"I try, Uncle." Braedon grinned.

"Mm… just make sure you don't outsmart yourself," Botcht replied coolly. Braedon cut his gaze toward him. Botcht always had a glowering mien. For the life of him, Braedon could not understand what his Uncle Leighis saw in him.

"Come, let's go seat ourselves." Leighis stood and grabbed his husband's hand. They all seven moved toward the tables set up for dining.

The guests arrived in droves, and then slowed to a dignified trickle toward the middle of the evening. They dined in the gardens, sitting at iron tables with heating lamps in the center. The servants tabled rows of food for leftovers after each person received their plated entree. Braedon could tell his father's hand touched many of the Thenian delicacies: salted pork, sweetened potatoes, and boiled brussels sprouts. Merin made a point not to sit near their father as he gobbled down an entire plate of *rotund.*

Braedon donned his new jacket for the party, matching the family's showy garb in a dark green suede, while his father wore a similar style jacket in gold. His sisters wore matching blue to accentuate their eyes, while Ryanne donned Menlor's scarlet in velvet. His sister was long, but not thin, and though the red of the gown made her black hair darker, her curves accentuated the bust and waist. Vincent couldn't take his eyes off her.

Braedon peered out over the guests and noted the change in garb for the weather. The women wore shawls over their square necked gowns, while the men wore capes with hoods. Only *Aida* and his uncles seemed unperturbed by the cool weather.

At almost seven o'clock, Braedon heard the chattering from the front gates and saw Ryanne let out a sigh of relief. His papa had finally arrived. Lords clamored toward the front to greet him while others ogled from their garden tables. King Brier Snow, poised, kind, and comely. Not everyone loved him, and yet no one could refute him. Would he ever match his father's standing? Braedon's eyes followed the king until he settled in his seat next to *Aida. Did Papa ever worry over such trivial things?* Braedon wondered.

"You're late." *Aida* kissed his father's cheek.

"I know, I got caught up in a silly dispute between Bedlorn and Ficodin." Papa peered over the table. "What did I miss?" he asked Ryanne.

"Nothing important." She kissed Papa's cheek. "You remember Vincent, don't you?"

"Oh yes, of course, *venur*, Prince Vincent."

"*V-venur*." The prince stood and bowed low. "Please, Your Majesty, call me Vincent."

"Only if you promise to stop being so formal," Papa answered. "You're my future son-in-law. Call me Brier."

"Or Papa!" Ryanne chimed in. "Since we're all family now!" *Aida* grumbled low.

"Heh." Braedon chuckled. "A little too premature, dear sister." Braedon watched his sister open her mouth to reply when a curly-headed stranger, with a bottle of wine in his hand, bowed before them. They all stood to greet their guest cordially. Braedon could not tell if he imagined *Aida*'s teeth grit at the sight of their guest.

"Uncle!" Vincent grinned. "I hadn't realized you'd arrived already."

"Only just." The man smiled and handed Vincent the bottle. Braedon stared, utterly entranced. Unlike Vincent, who had an air of nervousness and naiveté about him, this man's confidence oozed out from every pore. He stood tall in his blaring orange jacket with a red and white sash. His blond curls did not feminize him, and yet Braedon had never seen a man look so… charming.

"Good evening, Prince Quintin." Papa inclined his head. "Thank you for coming."

"Your Majesty," the man cried happily. "I was hoping we would have a moment together. I must say, I did not expect such attendance so far south of Avenough."

"Balmur isn't so south," Braedon heard *Aida* reply. "Only an hour and a half from the palace by carriage. An hour if you know how to drive."

"Ahh, Lord Roland. How are the years treating you, my friend?"

"I cannot complain." Braedon noted his father's half smile. "My children are healthy and my husband is happy. What more could I ask for?"

"I'm sure I could think of something." Quintin smirked.

"I can think of several things." Braedon smiled at Quintin.

"And who is this?" Quintin asked, turning toward him.

"This is our son, Prince Braedon," *Aida* replied. "Braedon, this is Prince Quintin Pascal of Menlor."

"Hello, Prince Quintin." Braedon inclined his head but kept his eyes locked on Quintin. "It is a pleasure to meet you."

"And hello to you, little prince." Braedon frowned at the address. "By gods, he looks almost identical to you, Brier. How old is he?"

"He is nearly eighteen. He does have my coloring, but he mostly takes after Roland. He hasn't even reached his majority, but he's almost as tall as him." Braedon scowled as they talked about him like he wasn't present. "Not to mention that temper."

Quintin replaced the bottle for a goblet of wine in his hand, and he and Papa unfurled into a full conversation. They spoke without honorifics and there was a familiarity there that Papa never had with other royals or courtiers.

"Five children? Goodness. Though I suppose there isn't much to do in the country." Quintin chuckled at his own joke, ignoring *Aida*'s grimace. Braedon snorted and the sapphire-blue gaze lingered over him. He felt his skin tingle and his heart sped as Quintin smiled at him.

Gods. Braedon's face warmed as he stared down at the food left on his plate and tried to relax. Getting this excited over a smile? Was he a man or a desperate old maid?

"King Brier." A beautiful woman with identical blonde curls walked up to their table and curtsied low. "It has been too long."

"Queen Adeline." Papa bowed. It was his turn to blush now. "It is a pleasure to see you again."

"Since my crass brother has not seen fit to introduce Marie and me, I figured I should make my salutation."

"Although it is not under the circumstances either of us expected, I thank you for coming nonetheless." Papa smiled gently. "And who, may I ask, is your accompanying guest?"

"This is Princess Marie Cotes of Ranolf, engaged to my brother just last year."

"His fiancé?" Papa's eyebrows flew upward. Braedon's eyes widened as he stared at the queen.

"Ah—yes do forgive my rudeness," Quintin said with a brilliant white smile. "This is my fiancé, Marie. We are expected to marry next year." He drained the goblet and refilled it with the bottle of wine he'd gifted.

"I see…." Papa smiled through the hesitance in his voice. "Well, congratulations, Quintin."

"Mm." Quintin took another sip. "Thank you. I figured it was time to stop making my father sick with worry and finally wed."

"And we are happy that he did not shame the line before then," Adeline added sternly. Braedon was sure Queen Adeline was not joking, but Quintin laughed nonetheless.

Engaged? Braedon tried hard not to pout. Of course the prince would have a fiancée. He was at least Papa's age, and he was strikingly handsome, charming, funny and—why did it matter anyway? He didn't even know Quintin.

Papa, Ryanne, Vincent, Adeline, and *Aida* continued to converse until the musicians finally began the ballads. The dance floor cleared of lurkers, and dancers replaced them.

"Ah—" Quintin yelled out as if the thought struck him. "I just got a marvelous idea. Let us all dance the sanpel to get better acquainted. Ryanne, darling, you with

Vincent. Brier and Lord Roland, myself and Marie, and Adeline, you and Braedon will dance together." Braedon turned toward the queen who smiled uncomfortably.

"Uncle—" Braedon cut his gaze toward Vincent. "I don't know if that is a good idea." Vincent could obviously feel the tension from everyone that Quintin ignored.

"Oh but you must. And it has been such a long time since I have seen King Brier, I should like a dance with him afterwards as well." Quintin released his fiancée's arm and stepped over to *Aida*. "You do not mind, right?"

"Right," Roland said pressing his lips together. Braedon watched curiously at the exchange. There was no denying the tension between the two of them.

"I'm not very fond of dancing," Marie spoke for the first time. She was a mousy woman with brown hair and olive green eyes. Her dress was a modest blue and her hair, a dull blonde, had no ringlets or embellished broaches like Ryanne's.

"I hate to be a prig, but I'm also a bit tired, Quintin."

How boring... Braedon thought as Quintin's smile drooped.

"Oh, well. It was just an idea, darling, we don't have to." He kissed Marie's cheek, and Braedon clenched his jaw.

"Excuse me. Prince Quintin, if you wouldn't mind, that is—if you wanted to. I would be glad to dance with you."

"A dance with the Prince of Lirend?" Braedon squirmed under the prince's amused gaze. He could hear the violins singing. The cellos kept the tempo, while the flutes and horns hopped over the Thenian melody. Quintin's silence made him want to curl up and hide. For once he wished he'd taken his father's advice and kept his mouth shut. "I would be delighted."

Braedon stepped toward Quintin and Marie and bowed before he held out his hand and Quintin grasped it. Braedon's fingertips ached as he bent them to lead Quintin to the floor.

"A wonderful idea." Papa nodded as he grabbed *Aida*'s hand to lead him toward the dance floor. Vincent and Ryanne followed.

The sanpel was a simple enough dance. The men stood on the right with the women on the left. The men would bow and present themselves, and then turn to wait for the women to do the same. Then they'd meet in the middle for a series of twirls and two-steps, before they crossed hands to change partners. The dance continued this way, bowing and presenting themselves until they met back with their original partner. At the end of the dance they'd embrace their partners until the song slowed and ended.

"Now," Quintin said as he positioned himself in front of Braedon. "Who will follow in this sanpel?"

"Umm... I don't know how to follow in this dance, Your Grace," Braedon whispered.

"Then I suppose it will be me." Quintin twisted and moved to the left side. "But I expect you to lead me well, little prince." He chuckled.

Braedon kept his face neutral as he nodded and breathed deep. He wanted to lead Quintin in more than just a dance.

The music started and Braedon bowed and outstretched his long arms. He'd danced this dance many times, and yet his heart had never pounded this way before. He was glad when the sanpel's tempo hastened and they could move between the steps without thinking overmuch. By the time he'd relaxed they'd changed partners and Ryanne was in his arms.

"Well this certainly explains a lot," she whispered before he bowed.

"What?" He watched her curtsy. "What are you on about?"

"I wondered why you rebuffed the ladies so vehemently, but now I understand. You have interesting taste, little brother." She twirled and they grasped hands.

"Come now, Ryanne. We're just dancing."

"I can see that you're dancing, but it is the look in your eye while you're dancing that I'm referring to." Ryanne chuckled and Braedon flushed once more. "At least he looked a lot happier in your arms than in *Aida*'s." Braedon's gaze diverted toward Quintin whose expression had turned stiff with *Aida.*

"He's only being polite."

"Mayhap, but you never know." Ryanne winked as she was pulled away by *Aida* and his Papa stood in front of him.

"What a surprise." Papa smiled. "I didn't think I would ever dance with my only son."

"Don't be so dramatic," Braedon replied as he led his father's steps. "We've danced together before." It was his papa who taught him to lead in the first place.

"When you were a child, yes. But now you regard your *aida* and I as your enemy." Papa sighed as he stepped back.

"That's not true, Papa. I just hate the way you two decide everything for me. I am a man, you know."

"Heh—oh yes. I can see that very clearly." His papa glanced at Quintin before he prepared to change partners.

He danced with several others before Quintin was back in his arms. This time Braedon made a show to hold the small of the man's back as he embraced him in the final chords of the song. Quintin did not squirm or stiffen, but moved his feet with Braedon's as though they'd danced with one another many times over. Quintin danced as if he trusted the strength of Braedon's grasp. The music steadied and then slowed before the violins stopped and they stood still. Still, Braedon did not release his hold on the prince's back. Quintin leaned in and Braedon tensed as he felt soft lips graze his ear lobe.

"The song is over. This is the part where you let me go."

Braedon jerked his hand from Quintin's back and stepped away. "Forgive me. I wasn't paying attention."

"No worries." Quintin bowed before he swept off to dance with Braedon's papa.

Braedon watched Quintin and his father dance through several songs before they parted. Quintin leaned in to whisper something, before he bowed and moved away from the dance floor. He refilled his cup of wine and Braedon followed Quintin with his eyes until he lost sight of him in the darkness.

"I'm going for a walk," Braedon told his *aida*. He didn't wait for *Aida* to reply before Braedon headed toward the center of the gardens. He found Quintin sipping a goblet of wine, standing near the shrubs that led to the fountain. The moonlight shimmered on the tops of the dying wildflowers. Braedon paused before he stepped next to him.

"It's been years since I've visited this estate," Quintin whispered. He spoke not to Braedon, but as if he stood alone under the twinkling stars. "It hasn't changed at all. Still dreadfully dull compared to Avenough."

"My father isn't one for exuberance," Braedon replied. "He prefers simplicity."

"Heh—that has not changed either I suppose." Quintin sipped his wine.

"You, however, prefer the finer things in life," Braedon said.

"Oh? How do you figure that?"

"I can tell by the wine you gifted Vincent earlier. A finely aged bottle of wine is invaluable."

"What do you know of aged wine, little prince?"

"I know that bottles of chenin blanc are indigenous to Menlor, so I begged my father to import them."

"You go through quite a lot for a bottle of wine."

"Because it is worth it to me. The scent of a fine uncorked wine makes my mouth water. I like to close my eyes and savor the first sip. For me there is nothing better."

"Nothing?" Quintin raised his brows. "Then you are wasting your youth."

"Mayhap." Braedon grinned. "But like you, Your Grace, I prefer the finer things in life."

"Indeed." Quintin took another sip of his wine. "And you must entertain women quite often."

"What makes you say that?" Braedon frowned.

"You have a way with words, and women appreciate that quality in a man." Quintin smiled knowingly. "In my youth I would… *entertain* women quite often."

"Only women?"

Quintin peered up at Braedon with a smirk before he answered, "Whomever I fancied," and drained the gold goblet.

"How about me, then?" Braedon boldly asked.

"Heh—" Quintin chuckled before he shook his head. "Is that how you entice your partners?"

"I've never…." Braedon paused before he lowered his gaze feeling suddenly sheepish. He'd never slept with a man or woman. His experiences were limited to what Ryanne told him. "I've never had to do anything."

"Hmph—I suppose you wouldn't have to do anything. You are young and handsome, and now you are the future king of Lirend. You probably could get any woman you want."

"I am young, and I'm glad you think I am handsome, but I don't get nor do I want to get any woman."

"Then what do you want?" Quintin raised his brow and Braedon swallowed before he answered.

"To entice a prince of Menlor."

"Oh?" Quintin jeered. He stepped forward and Braedon tensed. "Then here's your chance, Braedon. Entice me."

Braedon's face flushed before his chest tightened at the sound of his name on Quintin's thin lips, in that saccharine accent, with that harmonious voice. Quintin was so close to him Braedon could smell the white wine on his breath. He wanted to taste it too. Braedon held the bottom of the prince's jaw and placed a soft peck on his lips before Quintin peered up at him.

"If you're going to kiss me, little prince…." Quintin dropped the goblet, grabbed the collar of Braedon's jacket and yanked him close. "Then *kiss* me," he whispered with their lips grazed. Quintin plummeted his tongue into Braedon's mouth and wriggled against the inside of his cheek. A tingle trickled down into his gut and fluttered. Quintin's hands raised gradually to Braedon's face, and he grew so warm he thought he might burn from the touch. Braedon huffed as he thrust his tongue against Quintin's and the man's lips trembled against his. The prince felt better than Braedon anticipated, and different than anything he'd ever imagined.

Braedon wrapped his arm around Quintin, clutched the back of his jacket, and pressed their bodies close together as if they were still dancing. He flicked his tongue and Quintin ground against him before he let out a whining moan.

Dear gods…. Braedon hoped Quintin didn't notice his stiff member. It was embarrassing to become fully erect from a mere kiss, but even Braedon could tell the difference with Quintin; the way Quintin's body melted in his arms, the way Braedon's thoughts trailed into nothing, the way his heart thudded. He wanted to make love to this man. The thought struck him like a fist, and Braedon cut their kiss abruptly.

"Why did you stop?" Quintin whispered as he opened his eyes. Braedon closed his eyes to still his heart, but hesitated to speak. He felt as though he might retch or say something dreadfully foolish.

"When do you go back to Menlor?"

"Tomorrow evening."

"Must you go back to Menlor so soon?" Braedon pouted.

"Heh—don't sound so dejected." Quintin tried to release his face, but Braedon grabbed his wrist to keep him there.

"I don't want you to go back." He placed another gentle kiss on Quintin's lips with their foreheads touching. When they parted, Quintin peered up with tears in his eyes. Braedon touched the crease of Quintin's blue eyes and frowned.

"Do I kiss that badly?" Quintin laughed and shook his head.

"You kiss just fine, little prince."

"Then why do you weep?"

"Because you remind me of a young man I once knew, with red hair and pale skin. Your eyes may be gray, but he had the same look in his eyes when he asked me not to go back to Menlor," Quintin whispered as he touched the bottom of Braedon's hard chin. "With the same expression on his face." Braedon's stomach knotted as the image of his papa and Quintin twisted in his mind.

"I'm not my father." Braedon hardened his jaw.

"You're right. You're not." Quintin stepped away from him.

"And I don't want to be," Braedon said. Yes, they looked alike and perhaps one day he would take his papa's place as the king of Lirend, but he was his own man.

"I've something to give you, Prince Braedon." Quintin rummaged through the heavy cloak he wore.

"What is it?" Braedon's heart fluttered anew. He would cherish anything Quintin gave him. "This." Quintin pulled out a carved wooden box. "Please give this to your father, Brier."

"What is this?" He frowned as he grabbed the box from the prince's hand and peered up to find Quintin's face still somber.

"Something that I should have given him long ago. A gift that means a great deal to him."

"Tell me…." Braedon hesitated. He wanted to know, but also didn't. The contradiction made him restless. "What kind of relationship did you have with my father?" Quintin just stared at him, and Braedon squirmed once more under his impassive gaze.

"I was his fia—"

"Quintin?" Adeline's light voice called out. "Are you here?" The prince's lip tightened before he stepped farther away from Braedon.

Braedon shook his head. *Don't answer.*

Quintin smiled sadly and answered, "Here, sister." Braedon listened as the queen's footsteps neared them in the garden.

"What are you doing out here? Getting into trouble?" She surmised accurately.

"I was just talking with Prince Braedon. He was giving me a tour of the grounds," Quintin lied effortlessly.

"Oh." Adeline forced herself to smile. "Thank you for showing my brother such hospitality."

"It was my pleasure," Braedon whispered.

Silence.

He stared at Quintin with a longing in his eyes he didn't want to hide, and Quintin met his desperate gaze.

"Anyway," the queen huffed, flushed by the tense air. "It's time to go, Quintin. Marie is complaining about the weather."

"Right, then." Quintin bowed before he moved to leave, and Braedon clenched his jaw.

Don't leave.

He swallowed the lump forming in his throat.

Don't go.

"Your Grace!" Braedon blurted without thinking. Quintin stopped and turned to face him.

"Is it all right if—" Braedon stammered. "If I visit you, in Menlor?" Adeline blinked before she turned to Quintin with her brows raised. "I'd like to taste more of Menlor's fine wine." Quintin smirked before he inclined his head and Braedon bowed.

"I'll write you till then, Prince Quintin."

"Yes," Quintin said as he walked away with Adeline. "Till then, little prince."

BRAEDON CAME into the house smiling from ear to ear with butterflies still in his stomach. He walked down the hall, seeing his sisters passed out in the same bed. He chuckled lightly, holding tight to the wooden box in his hand, and hurried down the hall to his parents' bedroom.

"Do you believe something happened between me and Quintin?"

Quintin? Braedon halted at the concern in Papa's tone. He stood at the door and listened.

"Goodness. What did he say when you danced to bring such a question on?" Braedon heard *Aida* say. "I have never let myself think about your intimacies with Quintin. He was there when you needed him. When I could not be. When I should have been, but…."

Braedon pursed his lips.

"I have long since accepted my past, and have tried to make up for my mistakes. For the present, you are mine, in every way. You bear my children, and I should say, if twenty-one years are an indication, that I own your heart."

"And I have always been yours, even when you were not here. Yes, Quintin was there, but we never coupled."

"Never?" *Aida*'s dubious voice rang.

"Never," Papa repeated, and Braedon exhaled. "I had no desire to lay with him. You would have made a priest out of me in all but name if you had not come back."

"A priest, huh?" *Aida* snorted. "I can think of several things you do, more than well, I might add, that a priest would not."

"He-he-he-he." Papa giggled and then crooned. "Why don't you ask Quintin if you do not believe me?"

"Nothing to ask," *Aida* remarked. "Priest or not, he would have married you if you'd permitted him."

"Wrong again, Master. Quintin was the one who broke up with me."

"I don't believe it."

"It's true." Papa sighed out. "He knew my heart belonged to you. There is no competition, Ronan," Papa assured him. "Honestly, I've always felt bad about the way our relationship ended, so, will you try to like him?"

"I neither like nor dislike Quintin, Brinan. There is too much bad blood and wounded pride for either of us to truly be friends. But amicable? Cordial even? Yes. Lest why you think I agreed to your dance. I am too old to hold on to malice, my king. Though, I *am* concerned about Braedon's little show tonight. It's obvious he is smitten." Braedon held his breath.

"And why wouldn't he be? Quintin is handsome and charming," Papa replied. "Not even *you* can deny that, Master Rolande."

"Handsome?" *Aida* huffed. "He's at least thirty years older than Braedon. Much too arrogant, and definitely not a match for our son."

"Do I need to remind you that you are old enough to have birthed me yourself?"

"Need I remind you that it was I telling you the very same thing twenty-one years ago? And we see how that ended five children later," he added to press his point.

"Personally I think it's rather cute. It's not as if anything will come of it. Quintin is engaged to the Princess of Ranolf. What does it matter if Braedon has a harmless crush on him?"

"Oh yes, because your crush on me was so harmless."

"Will you behave?" Brier yawned. "Your sour expression is ruining my mood."

"Your son ruined my mood earlier today at breakfast. I almost slapped him when he insulted you."

"Ronan." Papa sighed.

"Don't 'Ronan' me, Brier. He said that he wished he'd never been born into this family!" Papa did not reply right away and Braedon lowered his head, feeling more ashamed than he had with Ryanne.

"I know it hurts to hear him say such a thing, but you shouldn't be so hard on him."

"He disrespected you. And this family."

"And I don't condone his lack of respect."

"Yet you still coddle him."

"Because I understand him. His life in this family has completely changed. Braedon had his own dreams before Lirend decided he would be king, and you of all people know what it is like to have your dreams dissolved in one night." Braedon's heart clenched. He'd insulted Papa, and yet, Papa still defended him. "He is trying to make sense of it all. Be patient with him."

"I will try harder," *Aida* replied quietly.

"Good." Their lips smacked between huffs until *Aida* paused to ask, "Do you think Ryanne and Vincent have had sex yet?"

Papa sucked his teeth. "Stop worrying over Ryanne and tend to your husband."

"Why don't you tend to me?" *Aida* taunted. "Or have you worn yourself dancing with Prince Quintin?"

"Jealous, are you?"

"Absolutely."

"Heh—" Papa snorted. "Your tongue often betrays you when you're drunk, Rolande."

"My tongue requires your attention, King Brier."

"*Mana el man'*."

Braedon heard his father's huffed kisses as Papa coaxed *Aida* to shift in a saccharine voice.

"Hmm.... Wish that you were a priest," *Aida* mumbled and Braedon paled. "Then you could forgive me for what I'm about to do." The bed creaked and *Aida* moaned.

"It has been overlong. I missed your heat, Ronan."

Braedon knocked on the door firmly and cleared his throat to end the lewd pillow talk.

"Did you hear that?" Brier whispered.

"Aye. Go see who it is."

He heard shuffling then light footsteps toward the door.

"Aye?" Brier's impatient voice called.

"Papa...." Braedon tried to steady his tone. "May I speak with you briefly?" He thought for a moment his father would dismiss him, but after several long minutes, Papa opened the door, tying a house robe at his waist.

"What is it, dear?" Papa smiled as he closed the door behind him.

"I…." Braedon squeezed the wooden box in his hand before he dared to peer up at him. "I want to apologize to you, Papa. And *Aida*." He stood tall to harden his resolve. "I said something I didn't mean… something I shouldn't have, and I'm sorry," Braedon said clearly.

"We all say and do things we don't mean, Braedon. It takes a wise man to recognize his mistakes, and a good man to apologize for them."

"Then you accept my apology?"

Papa's lips curved into a smile. "Of course, my son."

"And *Aida*…. He probably hates me, huh?" he asked quietly.

"*Na*. He is only worried for you. You are his only son, and though you may favor me, you are a great deal like him, whether you two want to admit it or not." Papa chuckled as he brushed back a strand of his red hair, and Braedon sighed out. "We could never hate you, Branan. We love you more than anything."

"I know you do." Braedon fumbled the box in his hands and Papa's eyes flickered toward it. "What's that you have? Something you're making?"

"No, Papa. Prince Quintin gave this to me, just before he left for Avenough." Braedon offered his father the box hesitantly. "He said it was something he should have given you long ago. A gift that means something to you."

Papa ran his fingers smoothly over the wood. Braedon inspected the box in his father's hands curiously before Papa's brow arched. "What is it, Papa?"

"Your…." Braedon watched as Papa covered his mouth with a hand before tears started to fall. "Your *Aida* made me this." His father squeezed the box, but his hands still shook. Braedon frowned and held his father's shoulder.

"Papa?" Braedon tilted his head. "Are you all right?"

"Aye." Papa sighed out before Brier turned the box over and Braedon read the words etched in Thenian.

"Forever, my little prince," Braedon read quietly.

"Your father made this for my birthday many years ago," Papa croaked and wiped his eyes. Braedon watched him flip the lid with his finger, and a figurine akin to Papa twirled in the center. "It plays Helenas's love proposal." Braedon finally understood and a smile crept to his lips as he watched the memorizing figurine.

Quintin had given him a love proposal.

"It is beautiful, Papa," Braedon said under the melody of the song. "I didn't know *Aida* was so romantic."

"He tries." Papa sniffed, and he choked out a laugh. "Thank you, for bringing me this. I never thought I'd see it again."

Braedon hugged his father tight. "*Aida* loves you so much. And you love him equally… I hope one day I can find something like that," he whispered.

"You will," he answered in a hushed tone. He pulled away and Braedon saw his father's face red from tears. "But for now, it is time for bed."

"All right, Papa." Papa kissed his cheek. "I'll see you in the morning."

THE NEXT morning Braedon entered the dining room to a table full of hungry men since his uncles decided to stay the week in Balmur. Merin, Helenas, Ryanne,

Vincent, and Rosaline sat at one side, and his uncles sat at the other side of a table added for space.

"Good morning, gentlemen." Braedon bounced into the empty seat next to Leighis.

"Good morning indeed." Leighis turned toward him. "You're beaming from ear to ear."

Braedon nodded and grabbed a piece of toast. "Well, yesterday was marvelous." His sisters jabbered into last night's events. He listened idly and chewed his toast before he heard his fathers arrive.

"Good morning." Papa grinned with a buoyant glow. *Aida*, however, came in after Papa with a frown.

"Good morning," the table called back. *Aida* sat next to him and winced.

"Everything all right, father?" Ryanne asked.

"Fine. Fine. I just feel like a carriage ran over me." The man yawned deep.

"Well that's what you get for drinking so much," Leighis called from the opposite end. "You're not young anymore, Rolande."

"Yeah…." *Aida* sipped out of a mug filled with coffee and Braedon stifled his laughter. If what he'd heard last night continued, he knew the reason his father was sore.

"Overall, though, I'd say everyone enjoyed themselves," Sasta piped.

"Oh yes, we should have another party soon!" Merin said longingly.

"Yes, after the school year ends. Oh, can we, Papa?" Helenas echoed her sister's enthusiasm.

"If your father permits." Brier nodded once. "And only if your grades are sufficient."

"You just want to dance with Lord Delvin's son." Merin chuckled.

"*Who* is Lord Delvin's son?" *Aida* immediately asked.

"His name is Morin, *Aida*. We're just friends."

"What does he look like?" Papa asked.

"Like a troll." Rosaline snorted.

"He does not!" Helenas's face reddened. "He's a bit round in the middle, but he's very handsome."

"Oh I remember him. He's the one with the black hair," Ryanne said grinning. "Tall… dark…."

"Aurelian." Umhal yawned.

"Is he a good kisser?" Sasta blurted.

"Uncle Sasta!" Helenas called. The table broke into laughter.

"How well does he use a sword?" Botcht asked seriously.

"Is he strong?" Dur chimed in.

"Is he kind?" Leighis asked.

Helenas peered up with seven sets of waiting eyes on her. She pressed her lips together and mumbled, "He's very kind, but…." His sister fought the pink in her face. "It's not like that, you know. We're just friends."

"For now." The king chuckled softly. "But he comes from a good family. You should invite him over for dinner."

"Please, don't encourage her, Brinan." *Aida* sighed.

THEY ATE in mostly silence, save for his sisters rambling. Braedon kept glancing up at his *aida*, trying to find the right time to apologize, but kept losing his nerve. Then finally when his father prepared to leave the table Braedon spoke up.

"*Aida*." Braedon stood from the table as every eye settled against him. He straightened his back as he faced *Aida*. "Yesterday, I said that I wished that I wasn't born in this family. It was not only unkind, but it was rude and ungrateful. And I'm sorry." He peered around the room. "You all are my family, and I couldn't ask for a better one."

"Thank you for apologizing, son. And, for once, you and I agree," *Aida* answered before he gazed around the room. "Though we each face our own hardships, the support and love in this family is evident. I owe my life and my happiness to the people sitting in this room and I… I love you all."

"Including me?" Vincent replied. The table went silent for a few terrifying moments. Everyone stared at *Aida*, looking uncertain, but Papa touched *Aida*'s arm and smiled.

"I don't dislike you. I think you two are too young for marriage and think that you're rushing into it," *Aida* replied. "But I also trust my daughter. And my daughter loves you, so you have my blessing." Ryanne squealed before she leaned in and kissed Vincent's cheek.

"However, if you hurt one hair on her head, I will end you." Braedon patted the prince's back and Vincent chuckled nervously. He moved away from the table before *Aida* called to him.

"Where are you going in such a hurry?"

"I have a letter to write," he answered. "And I want it to be there when he arrives home."

They fought for everything they have, Braedon.

Braedon thought of Ryanne's words. He stared at his fathers. *Aida* gripped Brier's hand in secret under the table. Meant for each other? Made from the same mold?

"When who arrives home?" *Aida* asked frowning.

"Prince Quintin of course." Braedon winked. Fate led them together, but love bonded them in the end. His fathers had fought for love and he would fight for his love too.

EAB is an airline steward/stewardess—depending on the day—who loves writing erotic fiction. This translates to serving Wild Turkey bourbon at 38,000 feet and writing smut at 3:00 a.m. EAB spends free-time role-playing and reading. While EAB's true passion is writing, EAB also enjoys reaching high scores in nerdism, spending time with family (cats included), and watching anime. An East Coaster at heart, EAB loves New York's Broadway and greasy, heartburn-inducing pizza. Feel free to drop a line or recommend some good reads! Always looking for a new book to devour!

E-mail: eabemie@gmail.com
Facebook: www.facebook.com/EAB-Author-Page-549015555136236

FOR MORE OF THE BEST GAY ROMANCE

CPSIA information can be obtained
at www.ICGtesting.com
Printed in the USA
FSOW02n0214220117
29877FS